The
Veracruz
Blues

The Veracruz Blues

Mark Winegardner

VIKING

VIKING
Published by the Penguin Group
Penguin Books USA Inc., 375 Hudson Street,
New York, New York 10014, U.S.A.
Penguin Books Ltd, 27 Wrights Lane,
London W8 5TZ, England
Penguin Books Australia Ltd, Ringwood,
Victoria, Australia
Penguin Books Canada Ltd, 10 Alcorn Avenue,
Toronto, Ontario, Canada M4V 3B2
Penguin Books (N.Z.) Ltd, 182–190 Wairau Road,
Auckland 10, New Zealand

Penguin Books Ltd, Registered Offices:
Harmondsworth, Middlesex, England

First published in 1996 by Viking Penguin,
a division of Penguin Books USA Inc.

10   9   8   7   6   5   4   3   2   1

Copyright © Mark Winegardner, 1996
All rights reserved

PUBLISHER'S NOTE
This is a work of fiction. Names, characters, places, and incidents
either are the product of the author's imagination or are used fictitiously.
Where actual persons, living or dead, appear in these pages, the situations,
incidents, and dialogues concerning those persons are entirely fictional.

LIBRARY OF CONGRESS CATALOGING-IN-PUBLICATION DATA
Winegardner, Mark.
  The Veracruz blues: a novel / Mark Winegardner
     p.   cm.
  ISBN 0-670-86636-9
  I. Title.
PS3573.I528V47   1996
813'.54—dc20   95-31804

This book is printed on acid-free paper.

Printed in the United States of America
Set in New Aster
Designed by Virginia Norey

Without limiting the rights under copyright reserved above, no part of this publication
may be reproduced, stored in or introduced into a retrieval system, or transmitted,
in any form or by any means (electronic, mechanical, photocopying, recording or
otherwise), without the prior written permission of both the copyright owner and the
above publisher of this book.

For Sam

Americans have not looked for Mexico in Mexico; they have looked for their obsessions, enthusiasms, phobias, hopes, interests—and these are what they have found.
—Octavio Paz, *The Labyrinth of Solitude*

. . . and its ruins exist saying:
this was the fatherland of a thousand heroes . . .
—Mexican national anthem

Author's Note

Although the events in this novel are based on things that really happened, this book is a work of the imagination.

The on-field baseball stories here are as accurate as I could make them. I read every page of every 1946 issue of several Mexican newspapers, and relied more upon those accounts than I did on anything printed (in 1946 or since) in American newspapers and magazines. *La Enciclopedia del Béisbol Mexicano* (1st ed., 1992) was also a godsend. Still, I stress that my intent here is not documentary. A fiction writer must be, to paraphrase Tim O'Brien, more concerned with the story-truth than the happening-truth.

While many of the characters here are based on actual people, during a time in their lives when they were public figures, I stress that what follows is merely my personal interpretation of who these people were, how they worked, played, thought, and talked. Tolstoy's Napoleon was not Napoleon. Likewise—albeit on a much more modest scale—my "real" characters aren't real. In fact, it is my expressed, written intent that they be seen as no more or less real than the figments of a vivid dream. Any other use of the pictures, accounts, and descriptions contained here is strictly prohibited.

—M.W.

Acknowledgments

For support during the writing of this novel, I am grateful to John Carroll University, the Dorset Colony House, and the Ragdale Foundation.

Thanks to the many people who helped me research this book, particularly Héctor Bencomo of the Monterrey Sultans and Tomás Morales of *La Afición*, whose help while I was in Mexico was invaluable. Thanks to the Baseball Hall of Fame in Cooperstown, New York, and the Mexican Baseball Hall of Fame in Monterrey, Mexico, for indispensable resources. Thanks also to Negro League historians Tweed Webb and James A. Riley, to Father Frank Smith (who provided useful information about the intricacies of Catholic marriage), and to all the players I interviewed, especially Ray Dandridge and Danny Gardella.

Harriet Wasserman, who showed confidence in this book at a crucial time, and Al Silverman, who once placed me in an anthology between Updike and Yeats (a happy accident of the alphabet, but, still . . .), are agent and editor, respectively, from the old school. To work with them is an honor.

I am grateful to Joseph Campbell, whose classic book *The Hero with a Thousand Faces* inspired the structure for the Danny Gardella chapters.

Finally, a warm thank-you to Angela Fasick—smart reader, generous sounding board, and friend.

Contents

Prologue   The Season of Gold
Frank Bullinger, Jr.   1

1.   So Many Boxes of Cigars
Theolic "Fireball" Smith   9

2.   Folie à Deux
Danny Gardella   22

3.   The Original Mexican Standoff
Frank Bullinger, Jr.   37

4.   The Long Home Run
Roberto Ortiz   51

5.   Whenever We Played the Blues
Theolic "Fireball" Smith   59

6.   A Working Reporter
Frank Bullinger, Jr.   76

7.   The Road of the Twelve Trials
Danny Gardella   110

8.   We Been Here
Theolic "Fireball" Smith   138

9.   The Age of Spirits
María Félix   147

10.   El Nudillero
Roberto Ortiz   168

11.   Bullinger *v.* Bullinger
Frank Bullinger, Jr.   182

12.   The Witch's Double
Theolic "Fireball" Smith   200

13.   Los Niños Héroes
Danny Gardella   218

Epilogue   Migratory Birds
Frank Bullinger, Jr.   241

The
Veracruz
Blues

Prologue

❖

The Season of Gold

In the history of baseball and America (the two are of course mirror and lamp), 1946 was a year of transition, in every imaginable way. Tens of thousands of soldiers came home, fiercely eager to resume their lives, make up for lost time, grab what they imagined to be rightfully theirs. Instead they found housing shortages, unfaithful sweethearts, rationed food, and wages that, despite wartime inflation, remained at prewar levels. Postwar optimism blinded us to the serious social problems that peacetime needed to address. As my friend the historian Eric Goldman wrote, "A nation accustomed to the categorical yes and no, to war or peace and prosperity or depression, found itself in the nagging realm of maybe."

Labor unrest was at an all-time high: coal strikes, rail strikes, newspaper strikes, you name it. There were race riots in the North, lynchings in the South; the Ku Klux Klan was formally reestablished. John Hersey's *Hiroshima* filled an entire issue of *The New Yorker*, and—for a nation that months earlier had toasted "Harry's wonderful bomb"—the enormity of the Atomic Age started to sink in. The Cold War loomed on the horizon, though few noticed; weren't the Soviets our allies? Inflation went berserk (it was *nine hundred times* worse in Mexico; one 1946 American dollar is worth about twenty bucks now, while one 1946 peso is worth about 18,000 pesos). The Baby Boom began, too, the very same year Dr. Benjamin Spock published a sane little book that revolutionized the way we would raise those babies. Ground was broken in Levittown. Vietnam rebelled against French occupation. Joseph McCarthy, Richard Nixon, and John F. Kennedy prepared their first runs at elected office. Network TV debuted.

In 1946, for a year, most Americans tried, like all the king's horses and all the king's men, to put 1941 together again. It couldn't happen. Women couldn't go back to being satisfied serving their husbands, even if the 1950s would pretend otherwise. Blacks who'd fought for their country couldn't be asked to endure one more moment of segregation, even if they were in fact asked to endure just that and much more. In time, American life would, in sync with its national pastime, reimagine itself and move forward. But from where I sat—a hard chair at the end of the press box—it was a long time coming.

This is the story of the so-called raid on Major League Baseball by the Mexican League in 1946, in the words of those who were there, of whom I, Frank Bullinger, Jr., was one. We were among the thousands of people whom the late Jorge Pasquel bought for his collection. Whether Pasquel was (a) Mephistopheles, (b) Gatsby, (c) Barnum, (d) an egomaniacal war profiteer, (e) a liberator of oppressed athletes, (f) a civil rights pioneer, (g) a philandering murderer, (h) a visionary who should be in the Baseball Hall of Fame, (i) all of the above, or (j) none of the above—this is a question I have wrestled with for forty-eight years and now, dear reader, leave to you.

Allow me to introduce myself. I have lived life as a liar and an observer, surrounded by strangers, liaisons, and acquaintances. I dreamt of writing the Great American Novel, became the youngest and most lost member of the Lost Generation, and wound up making my adult living as a reporter. For twenty subsequent years I "labored" as a professor of journalism, a job akin, perhaps, to being one of those childbirth-class teachers who show people how to do a self-evident thing. I bought and paid for a house, married and stayed married to a colleague (wife number three), and am now retired and living like a minor king here in Veracruz.

For years I thought of the events recounted in this book as little more than a great baseball story. It was Danny Gardella, of all people, who finally set me straight. Fifteen years ago, when my son died and I returned to my old house in St. Louis to settle his affairs, I received a peculiar phone call. "Us guys who jumped to Mexico, we should have got medals," said a familiar voice. "We should have been called to the White House for improving international relations. And for showing the bloodsuckers who run baseball that it wouldn't kill 'em to have the best ballplayers— black, white, brown, or green—out there on the field."

"Oh. Hi, Danny."

"This is you, isn't it, Frank?"

"Yes. It's me." I spared him the long story about the bizarre coincidence of my being back in the U.S. and, conveniently, at my old phone number in my old house (which I'd given to my son years before). Things concerning Danny Gardella seem, in retrospect, like the kind of flukes upon which fate hangs.

"Listen, did you see the papers this morning, how many millions the Yankees paid this pitcher, what's-his-face? I bet that kid never heard of any of us guys who jumped to Mexico and paved the way for that kind of dough."

"It's good to hear from you, Dan."

"Look," Danny said, "the reason I called is, I know you writer fellows always have people telling you to write this, write that, that such-and-so would make a good book. But I keep waiting to see that Mexican League book you told me about."

I claimed I didn't remember telling him anything of the sort. Back then, all I wanted to be was a novelist, all I wanted to write was my Great American Novel. The idea of doing so was not, in my youth, anything of which to be ashamed. Today that turn of phrase is dead—or, worse, hopelessly ironic.

"Aw, c'mon, Frank. You remember. And now's the time. You have to write that book."

We started swapping stories about Mexico and about 1946. The formation of a players' union, and how it got laughed at in the papers. Brooklyn's signing of Jackie Robinson, and how they covered it up by saying they were starting a new Negro League. The train tracks in the outfield in Tampico, remember that? Plus umpires with guns. Babe Ruth's last at-bat. Et cetera. After we finally hung up, I went to the attic and sorted through boxes until I found the one I wanted. Inside were clips of my stories from that season, a stack of reporter's notebooks, scores of scorecards, my Mexican wedding license, and a baseball signed by Babe Ruth, Jorge Pasquel, and Ernest Hemingway. The next day, I started tracking down other eyewitnesses to what Mexicans still call "la temporada de oro." Nineteen forty-six. The Season of Gold.

Danny Gardella was a muscular, big-eared, five-and-a-half-foot-tall power-hitting Italian outfielder from the Bronx, a combination gym rat and class clown who'd washed out of baseball in 1940, having progressed no further than the Class D Mountain State League. In 1944, he had a job loading supply ships on the docks in Jersey City. An old baseball scout saw him play semi-pro ball and signed him to a contract. A month later, he was the starting left fielder for the New York Giants.

I met Gardella at Sportsman's Park in August, soon after he got called up. It was a fluke I was there. Two days earlier, the fellow who covered the Cardinals for my paper, the *St. Louis Star-Times*, dropped dead in a Chicago hotel room after spending the night with two hookers (one too many, it would seem). I covered the Browns, the other team in town, a ragtag bunch of has-beens, drunks, and one-armed outfielders. My kind of folks. To add to my disinclination to cover the Cards, the Browns (this tells you all there is to know about wartime baseball) were on their way to their first and only American League pennant. But my benefactor at the paper (a chum of Hemingway's, which is how I got the job) was in London covering the war, and the new sports editor—who prized reporting (which bored me) more than writing (which perplexed him)—hated me. So I was stuck. The Browns hit the road and I stayed in St. Louis with the Cardinals, down on the field at Sportsman's Park—which, though not hell, has a similar enough summer climate to provoke confusion.

It was between games of a doubleheader. I'd gone down poking around for quotes, hoping to slap together a story and phone it into the copy desk seconds after game two ended. Then I'd go home to my wife in time for a late dinner, and hear what a bum I was (she was right, by the way).

I was chatting about news from the Pacific with Max Lanier, the Cards' best lefty, when we heard a stir in the Giants dugout. The team gathered around, shouting and laughing. Max shrugged. "Gardella."

"Who?" I said.

"Ace Adams told me about him. Rook outfielder. Life of the party. Can't catch the baseball. Ott hates him." Mel Ott was the Giants' player/manager.

We went toward the crowd. There, clinging to the dugout roof with whitening fingers, was Danny Gardella, in uniform, drenched with sweat, doing chin-ups and belting out *Rigoletto*'s "La donna è mobile," a work with which (I suspect) few of his teammates were familiar, except in the Bugs Bunny version. Gardella, a tenor, sang surprisingly well for a man doing chin-ups. Beaming like a hammy kid in his homeroom talent show, Gardella pumped out chin-up after chin-up. His teammates were counting out each one; they were in the fifties by the time Max and I got there. At about seventy, Gardella's face got as red as Lanier's Cardinals cap and his singing lapsed into arrhythmic shouting. At eighty-five, his biceps started to twitch and buckle. His teammates poked one another and pointed; clearly, money was about to change hands.

At number ninety, Mel Ott emerged from the dugout tunnel. Through the phalanx of ballplayers, sportswriters, and photographers, Ott could not possibly have seen precisely who was at the center of all this attention. Still, he knew. From the far end of the dugout, Ott shouted, "Gardella!"

Rattled, Gardella jerked himself up for chin-up number ninety-eight, slamming his hatless head into the dugout roof and knocking himself stone cold. The players broke out laughing, presuming this was a joke. But Nap Reyes, the big Cuban third baseman who roomed with Gardella, bent down and tried to rouse him. "He's alive," Reyes said. "Ah, sheet."

When Gardella didn't laugh, someone sent for the trainer. As we waited, Ott prodded Gardella's body with the toe of his cleats, as if examining a dead deer beside the road. "Fucking sandlot players," Ott said. "Fucking Hitler, fucking Tojo, fucking war. Fucking fuck fuckitty fuck fuck."

In those days, sadly, this was not a quote I could use.

"That," Max said, pointing to the fallen Gardella, by then coming to with the aid of smelling salts, "is why we're going to the World Series and they're going to the dogs."

After game two, I filed my story (I could write game stories in my sleep, and often did). Looking for an angle, I stopped at St. Louis General Hospital on my way home. When I got there, Danny Gardella was with three nurses and Nap Reyes. A radio blared classical music: Mozart, if memory serves. The nurses took turns rubbing the knot on Gardella's head. At first, no one seemed keen on my interruption.

"I'd like to ask you a few questions, Danny."

"You a cop?"

I told Gardella who I was, what I was doing there. He sat up straight, his tight face opening like a flower. "Siddown, friend," he said. "Make me a star. I'll tell you anything."

"And then some," said Reyes. He added something in Spanish, and both men laughed.

I took out my notebook.

"I was born in the back of a taxicab, smack dab in the middle of the Brooklyn Bridge," Gardella began.

"How's your head?" I said.

But there was no stopping him. The man had the gift. I heard about his father, a failed prizefighter and vaudevillian who, in middle age, went to City College and then became a gym teacher at P.S. 52. I heard about his sainted mother, who ran the household with an iron fist and brought in extra money by making wedding cakes in her own kitchen. I heard about I don't know what all, much of it invented on the spot, the highlights of which I faithfully recorded and duly sensationalized in my feature story in the next day's paper.

"But your head?" I asked.

Finally, he answered. He tapped his skull. "Rock hard."

The headline would read: ROCK-HEAD IS LITTLE GIANT OF WARTIME BASEBALL.

If you'd told me then that Danny Gardella suffered from a rare psychosis—folie à deux—I'd have believed it. But if you'd said that this was also a man destined to become one of the most revolutionary figures in baseball history, I'd have thought you were the one who'd cracked your noggin. Yet it was true. Danny

Gardella was instrumental in bringing about the first fully integrated season in baseball history: 1946, in Mexico, a year before Jackie Robinson debuted for Brooklyn, a decade before the big leagues moved beyond tokenism into true integration. Furthermore, Danny almost revolutionized the business of baseball, too. As a direct result of events of the '46 season, events chronicled in this book, he sued Major League Baseball. A week before the petition was to be heard before the United States Supreme Court, Danny, then penniless, was coerced into settling out of court. Had he persevered, free agency would have come to baseball in 1950.

That first night of our acquaintance, Danny and I sat in his hospital room talking and drinking whiskey well into the wee hours. Eventually Reyes left, one of the nurses in tow. I dragged myself out of there just before dawn. As I left, Danny turned up the radio and, over the strains of Gilbert and Sullivan, called out, "It's G-A-R-D-E-L-L-A. Ninety-eight chin-ups! See you at the ballpark, you ink-stained wretch!" All the way down the corridor, I could hear Danny profess to be the very model of a modern major general.

❖

Just a month ago, I got another call from Danny Gardella, this time here in Mexico. "Did you hear?" he said. "Those rat-bastard owners just called off the World Series."

"Hi, Danny." I hadn't remembered giving him my number down here.

"They wouldn't even negotiate in good faith, can you believe it?"

I don't really follow baseball anymore, but I said, yes, sure I could believe it.

"Me, too," Danny said. "The more things change, huh?"

He wanted to know how work on the book was going.

"It's going," I said.

"The reason I ask is, none of us are getting any younger. Fifteen years you've been writing this thing."

"For me, fifteen years is good." I told Danny about Helen Hooven Santmyer, Harriet Doerr, other writers whose first book came out when they were about my age.

"Okay, Grandma Moses," he said. "Finish it before we all die, okay? Our story makes this strike business look like . . ." He was at a loss for words, a first. We *are* getting old. "Well," he said. "You're the writer. You tell 'em what it looks like."

◆

What follows is derived from the recollections of unrepentant old men like me (plus one old woman, who would not see herself as "like me"). As I am a writer and not a stenographer, the text of these interviews has been modified for the sake of readability. The names of my ex-wives have been changed to protect my ass; however, I can tell you that "Diana James" is someone whose real name any literate person would know. Some passages have been changed at the request of those involved, their lawyers, or their heirs. You will find inconsistencies concerning how much money Jorge Pasquel paid different people. Figures conflict. You can be sure the money was considerable, came with strings attached, didn't always arrive as promised, and may not have been what Americans would call "clean."

Clean money. That's a good one.

As I write this—on a Remington manual typewriter, in the shade of my balcony, a Negra Modelo sweating on the table beside me, Chiclet-bearing children in the street below hurrying to meet the five o'clock tourist train—I am an old man. It is true that we in our quote-unquote golden years can recall episodes from our salad days more vividly than we can things that happened yesterday. For example, I remember a tryst I had in 1939 with a Negro society reporter in a sunny hotel room in Detroit better than I can recall what I had for supper last night.

So, here. Here's a good story, told as straight and true as I am able.

Frank Bullinger, Jr.
Veracruz, Mexico
October 1, 1994

1.

So Many Boxes
of Cigars

THEOLIC "FIREBALL" SMITH

Always been in the right place at the wrong time. Or is it wrong place, right time? Point is, I've lived my life outside lookin in. Like if you was to go stand on the edge of Disneyland, be able to watch everyone ridin them teacups and dancin with Goofy and bein told it's a small world after all. You got money in your pocket to pay your way in, but you walk round and round and somehow you just can't find the damn gate. Some bad dream like that. I'm not bitter, though. I've had myself some kind of life. But that's the kind of life it's been.

Case in point: I started out with the Pittsburgh Crawfords. Flagship of the Negro Leagues. Cool Papa Bell, Josh Gibson, Oscar Charleston, Judy Johnson, Satchel—five Hall of Famers on one team. In '36 they won the championship. But—Theolic's Law—by the time I joined up in '37, things took a bad turn. The owner, Gus Greenlee, fell into money problems, first when the end of Prohibition killed his bootleggin, then when the Pittsburgh police clamped down on his numbers runnin. Half the Crawfords jumped to the Homestead Grays right there in Pittsburgh, which wasn't big enough to support both clubs plus them white Pirates, too. Crawfords teams I played for sold off players just to pay the light bill.

Then, 1938, as I'm comin into my own as a ballplayer, the Negro Leagues vote to cut salaries. The big stars kept gettin the big money. Young men like me, though, we went from $250 a month to somethin like $200. But we didn't complain. No sir. It was the Depression. We were glad to have jobs. But it was still hard to take, watching Satchel make $1,200 a month—year round, what with barnstorming—and know there's no way in hell he's six times the pitcher you are. Some days, not *as* good. I beat Satchel as often as he beat me.

Before the '39 season the Crawfords moved to Toledo. Toledo! Pitiful. Luckily, I got sold to the St. Louis Stars, got to play in my hometown. We started out slow, until me and a couple other of the old Crawfords got hot all at once and made it to the championship. Which we then lost, three games to two, to the Kansas City Monarchs. One game short, close as a man can get without gettin it. Brother, *that's* the Theolic Smith Life Story.

It wasn't just baseball. I got left at the altar. Yes, I did. First year back in St. Louis I courted a young lady name of Doris Blair, a schoolteacher who worked with my mama. She was pretty and buckeye brown, and she knew the names of things: trees, stars in the sky, parts of an automobile, the crowned heads of Europe, what was in my heart, you name it. She could cook, loved jazz, and could bluff the hell out of a poker hand. But see, no woman a ballplayer would want to marry would want to marry a ballplayer. Doris caught wind of my wayward ways on the road and the morning of our wedding decided she needed a man who respected her. She was right, though at the time I saw red. I took a vow while I was still in my wedding suit, alone in a Sunday School room at Holy Redeemer Baptist, that when it came to women I'd just sow my oats. I got married twice, after baseball was through, but it didn't work out. Doris was the love of my life. I came close as a man can to havin that woman in my life all my life.

Mama said I got my out-lookin-in thing from Pop, who was a doorman at the Park Plaza Hotel there in St. Louis, even handled President Warren G. Harding's luggage when he came to town. Here Pop is, day after day, handsome man in a crisp uniform—man who was in the Honor Society at Sumner High School, a deacon at Holy Redeemer Baptist, who read thick history books every night in his armchair—stuck in the doorway of where rich white folks come to be rich white folks, livin off their pocket change. Poor man died when I was ten years old, of pneumonia, from all that standin outside in the cold.

I don't blame Pop for anything I inherited—even if I did grow up to be a handsome man in a crisp uniform standin right on the edge of fame and fortune but never gettin it. It's a theory of Mama's, not mine. Math teachers are big on theories.

◈

In 1940 I come to training camp with the St. Louis Stars, down in New Orleans—where the owner was tryin to save money by sharin facilities there with the Monarchs—and guess what? Half the guys from last season are gone. It's the Crawfords all over again. Where is everyone? Gone to Mexico, someone says. Mexico? I say. Why didn't no one tell me about Mexico?

I was playin dumb, to cover my wounded pride. I knew about those Pasquels that was runnin that league and the big salaries they paid. I also heard about how a black man down there can eat where he wants, drink where he wants, love who he wants, anything. Cool Papa and a few guys from the New York Cubans had jumped down there in '38. And of course Satchel in '39; I'll get to that in a sec. But even though I was one of the best pitchers in the Negro Leagues, those Mexicans hadn't so much as said boo. Another case of me bein outside lookin in.

A week or so into camp, I get into this argument with the owner, who won't give me a raise in spite of the fact that I won eighteen games the year before, including both games we won in that championship series. Forget it, that cheap bastard tells me. It's a business, Theolic. Sorry. Sorry, my ass. I walked out of there determined to make him sorry.

That night a lot of us are on Bourbon Street, whoopin it up, when in some dark little club we happen upon Hilton Smith—the Monarchs' star pitcher. Hilton's in a corner booth with a fancy-lookin Mexican and two redheads. The Mexican is laughin and so are the women, but Hilton's lookin real serious. That was Hilton—serious, with a high-pitched voice that don't match his body. Wore that sour face on the field and off.

I come up to him, just to be polite. We shake hands and he introduces us to the Mexican, who turns out to be Mario Pasquel. That gets my interest. But no one invites me to join them. There's this long awkward moment. These folks want to be left alone. My teammates, they want to head on to another nightclub. But I can be a contrary cuss. I wave my buddies on and sit right down, big smile on my face, like I owned their asses. I call to the waitress, Bring me a bottle of whiskey, put it on Mr. Pasquel's tab. It's a joke, but he just shrugs. Say what you want about the Pasquels, they weren't cheap.

I sit there drinkin, makin eyes at the women, and nobody says a thing about ball. A swing combo comes on, and next thing I know I'm out dancin with the women and havin a time. In the blur of that night, I remember hearin Mario tell Hilton that, if he's interested, be at this bar in Laredo, Texas, by noon Sunday. Place called El Cabrón. Mario writes the name on a matchbook. Someone will meet him, take him down into Mexico. How I could remember that and forget how I got back to my hotel that night, well, that's one of the mysteries of drink. Gave it up long ago. It's a vice only a young man can withstand. Aren't they all?

Next day I work out with the Stars in that muggy New Orleans heat, but all the time I'm thinkin about El Cabrón, big pesos, and my wounded pride. And I get this idea. What if I just show up at El Cabrón and go on down and get me some of that Mexican money? Whether Hilton shows or not, they'd take me. Crazy-from-the-heat kind of plan. Time I get back to the hotel and shower up, I'm thinkin, What the hell you thinkin?

Then up popped fate's pointy little head. I'm cleanin out my pockets from the night before, and I find a matchbook from the Pontchartrain Hotel with "El Cabrón" written on it, along with the address. How it got there, in my smoke-smellin pants from the night before, I don't know. Whether it was the same matchbook Mario slid to Hilton or whether he slipped one to me too, I don't know. To this day I don't know.

I call up that hotel and leave this message: "Tell Mario Pasquel that Mr. Smith called. Tell him I'll be at the appointed place at the appointed time." That's just what I said.

That Saturday night, I jumped camp. Caught me a train for Laredo. Segregated train; that was all they had in the South in those days. Made the whole long-ass ride in some damn uncomfortable hard seat. Like to stiffen up my arm, ruin my big chance, that's what I'm thinkin. By the time I get to Laredo that next morning, I'm tired, sore, and thinkin I must be the craziest Negro in the state of Texas. But I can't see what choice I got but to see it through.

So I'm spendin Sunday morning in this dive called El Cabrón. Everyone is Mexican, all speakin that Spanish. I'm the only black man. I drank coffee at first but then, close to noon, got nervous, wonderin what I'd got myself into, and switched to beer. It was these Pasquels who had Satchel Paige beat up so bad the summer past. Knocked some teeth out, busted some ribs. At the time nobody would have given you a nickel for Satchel's future. You'd have told me then that he'd pitch in the white big leagues and I never would? I'd have said you was crazy.

All of a sudden in walks this Mexican dressed in one of them what-you-call guyabera shirts, all sweated through, burstin through the door like he seen too many cowboy movies.

"Smeet?" he asks me, meanin "Smith."

"That's me." Hilton Smith is a stocky man the color of coffee with cream. I'm skinny and dark. We all look alike to Mexicans too? I'm thinkin maybe Mexicans aren't no different than American white folks. Which of course is wrong.

"I am Ernesto Carmona. Mana-hair of los Diablos Rojos de México." He was a stooge of the Pasquels, bought and paid for.

"Pleased to make your acquaintance, Skip."

"Vaya," he says, pointin at the door.

I drain my beer, grab my grip, and we're off. We walk two blocks to the border, fast as the old man can go. I'm carryin the grip but he's the one huffin and puffin. At the border, the guards see Carmona and me comin and they wave us past. Don't ask for papers or nothin. They knew we was comin to see the Pasquels.

Carmona waves me into a red Cadillac with whitewalls. We drive day and night all the way from Laredo to Mexico City. Two of the longest days of my life, all on twisty roads no smart billy goat would mess with. Me and Carmona don't hardly say a word, which gives me altogether too much time to think about what a dumb-ass thing I did, jumpin camp to play for who knows what sort of people. These folks beat the devil out of *Satchel Paige*, biggest name in black baseball, cause he took $5,000 from them knowin his arm was dead. He'd hurt it that winter in Venezuela. Showed up in Mexico, all he can do is play first and hit, and

Satchel, unlike me, was no hitter. He pitches like ten crappy innings, even pitches underhanded, and then this Jorge Pasquel asks for his money back. If you knew Satchel, you knew he's not givin no money back. Man played for fifteen percent of the gate up in the States, made more money than Feller, DiMaggio, anybody. Satchel just laughed, said they had a deal and Jorge could pound salt. Instead, he pounds Satchel. Or his men do. Wake him up at his hotel, pull a gun on him, take him up in Pasquel's airplane, and, while Pasquel and his woman, that actress María Félix, while they sit there sippin tequila and eatin tortillas off a silver platter, two goons give Satchel the beating of his life, then leave him for dead on the tarmac of the Dallas airport, spittin out teeth, bleedin, can't breathe.

That was the story I heard, from Satchel himself, who was known to stretch things. So I'm tryin not to believe. Man's power to deceive himself knows no limit. Especially when money's involved.

We get into Mexico City and Carmona drops me off at the Hotel Galveston, which is where players stayed until they got a house or apartment. Nice place. Little lobby with round mahogany tables in the window, where we'd gather to play cards and drink and watch those pretty señoritas sashay by. They had a fascination for black men, hadn't seen many of us, and yet there wasn't a taboo against it, like here. But that first night, I went up to my room alone, thanked Jesus for delivering me, and was asleep before my tired bones hit the bed.

Next morning there's a knock at the door. I call out to wait a sec. I sleep naked, and I needed to grab some clothes. But I hear a key in the door and, *pow,* there's Jorge Pasquel.

He introduces himself, but I knew it was him. He's dressed to the nines: white double-breasted suit with shoulder pads and navy pinstripes, patent-leather shoes, diamond rings, diamond cufflinks in the shape of little dragons, hair slicked back, mustache trimmed just so. Best posture ever. Then he looks at me funny. "You are not Hilton Smith," he says.

Perfect English, hardly no accent.

I sit up in my bed, squinting up at him. "I'm not?" It was all I could think to say.

He stands, he frowns, then he pulls back his jacket, and I can see he's got a holster on, with these pearl-and-diamond-studded revolvers on each hip. For a second, I'm about to make a run for it, out into the street, stark naked.

"You're right," I finally say. "I'm not Hilton Smith. I'm *better* than Hilton Smith. I'm—"

"Theolic Smith," he finishes. "I didn't recognize you at first without your uniform."

Now it's my turn to frown. "You know me?"

Jorge Pasquel's face just opens up into this big dazzling smile. "You were the starting pitcher for the West team in the East-West Negro All-Star game, at Comiskey Park in Chicago."

Back then that was the biggest draw in baseball. Sellouts every year, 45,000-plus, even in the Depression. The white All-Star games and World Series can't say that. "Were you there?"

He shakes his head. "My brother Alfonso was, recruiting. I saw your picture in the program." Pasquel had trouble with *s*'s and *p*'s; he sprayed you. "Half the East team," he says, tappin himself on the chest, "now plays for me." He comes over to the side of the bed, his hand stuck out for me to shake. "Welcome to Mexico."

"Much obliged."

"My driver will bring you to the ballpark at noon," he says, sprayin some more. He takes out a wad of bills the size of my mitt, peels off a thousand pesos—two hundred bucks, a month's pay back home. "After practice he will take you to the finest tailor in Mexico, for a new suit."

"Thanks," I say. "That's great, Mr. Pasquel."

"Women?" he says.

"Excuse me?" I say.

"Women. Would you like women for this evening?"

"I can fend for myself," I say. "But thanks."

He looks all disappointed, and he shrugs with his palms toward the ceiling the way Mexicans do. "I look forward to seeing you play baseball," he says, "Mister Fireball."

Never did get to know Jorge Pasquel too well. Never figured him out. I can't tell you one way or the other about those rumors. Like for instance they say he killed a man. Duel over a woman. Sounds true. Whether it happened I can't say.

What can I tell you about him that's fact? Well, he was commissioner of the league, plus the owner of the Veracruz Blues plus, every so often, when he wanted to put on a uniform and show off for a woman, the first-base coach of the team. Only thing like it was when Rube Foster ran the Negro American League, owned a club, managed a club—*and* played for it. Difference was, Foster started as a player and worked up. Pasquel, it was the other way round. Baseball was a big toy for him to play with. Me, I was just another black checker on his checkerboard.

Where his money came from, you hear different stories about that too. Jorge's granddad had a sleepy cigar factory in Veracruz. Jorge and his brothers inherited it, built it up into an empire. They ran all the import/exports, the oil-drilling business, sold all the General Motors cars that come into Mexico, God knows what all. The national lottery, some said. Them Pasquels made Gus Greenlee look like a busher.

The 1940 Veracruz Blues was the best ball club that ever was. Player-manager was Martín Dihigo. That cat could play all nine positions as well as anyone. Batted .400, stole bases, won twenty games a year with ERAs you'd need a microscope to see. Good-lookin cuss, too. Never been a white player like him. Don't give me Babe Ruth. When he pitched, he wasn't a full-time hitter, and when he hit, he'd quit pitching. Plus he was ugly.

At catcher they got Josh Gibson, best slugger ever. Drink hadn't caught up to him, yet. First base was a Mexican, Castro, what a sweet swing. Shortstop was bowlegged Willie Wells, an immortal. Third was my buddy Ray Dandridge, who was more bowlegged than Wells. Best third baseman ever. Right field was Santos Amaro, the Kangaroo. His boy Rubén and grandbaby Rubén Junior played in the big leagues, but Grandpa was the player. Center was Cool Papa, fastest man alive. Even Jesse Owens wouldn't race him. Cool went from first to third on bunts, not once in a while, like a stunt thing, but *all the goddamn time*.

And the pitching! After Dihigo was Leon Day, who ought to be in the Hall of Fame [*Ed.: Day was elected to Cooperstown in 1995*], and Ramón Bragaña, this tough-ass black Cuban with a diamond for a front tooth. Then came Double Duty Radcliffe, who was a star, and Barney Brown, who was no slouch—won sixteen games that year, and all we played was ninety!

Me, though, Jorge Pasquel assigned me to play for Carmona

and the Mexico City Red Devils. There were pluses to bein with them. Like playin with Burnis "Wild Bill" Wright, who used to be with the Newark Eagles. What a player. What a man. Nickname "Wild Bill" was sort of a joke, like callin a fat man "Tiny." Burnis was quiet. Though he could be wild, too, after a fashion.

We had a good team in 1940, and I had my best year, 19–9, with a good ERA for them sky-high parks. Hit over .300 playin left on days I didn't pitch. But we ran a poor second to Veracruz. To make it worse, we shared a field with the Blues, Delta Park in Mexico City. When Jorge Pasquel bought the team he moved it from Veracruz, his hometown, to Mexico City, which was where his business was. He kept the name for sentimental reasons. Mexicans are a sentimental bunch. Certain songs, like that "La Bamba" wedding song, will make them cry like babies.

I bring all this up, this great Blues team, our Reds club, not to tell you about how poor Theolic again got so close to the brass ring his finger like to turn green. My point is, we had big-league ball in Mexico *six years* before the white boys got there, before newspaper fellas like yourself made a fuss. It's like jazz. We had jazz for forty years before white big bands came along. Then, Glenn Miller, he made more money than Louis Armstrong! See what I mean? You want to talk about 1946, fine. Some wild shit went on in '46. But first I need you to understand, Frank: The Mexican League didn't begin and end when the white folks came down.

I was playin ball in Puerto Rico when the war started. Me and Burnis were out shaggin flies. "We're under attack," says Roy Campanella. He was on our team, too. "Japan attacked Pearl Harbor, in Hawaii."

I never heard of Pearl Harbor, didn't know much about the Japanese. Was the whole country under attack? Were we in danger there in Puerto Rico? Nobody knew. We found a radio and stayed glued to it till game time. We played that game, won it off of a homer by Burnis, that cool customer. All the Americans showered up and went to buy plane tickets home, but the airplanes been commandeered to fight the war, so we went down to the docks and got tickets on the only ship going to the States, into Newport News, Virginia.

The seas were so rough everybody set to drinkin, wanted to be drunk when we drowned. Only food was cold cuts and stale peanuts, and that was all we had for five days. Five days of gettin sick and moanin and makin things square with Jesus. At one point Campy said we all should put our money in a bottle and throw it overboard, said somebody ought to get it. The hell with that! I always been close to my money. Not cheap. Just lookin out for what I got.

Turned out we made it to Newport News in one piece, got out, kissed the ground, and you know what? Things were just fine on the home front. But we had choices to make, whether to volunteer to fight or whether to stay home, play ball, make a living.

I never had no hesitation. I did not want to go to war. At *all*. I was twenty-eight years old when the war started. Even if I didn't get my ass shot off in some forest or on some beach, goin off to war could be the end of the line for me. A teacher, a lawyer, someone like that, they could go, fight, and come back to what they was doin. Me, I'd have nothin to come back to. That was only part of it, though. I knew what they'd have the black man do in a war: clean pissers, bury bodies. "Nigger work." Later on, they did let us serve. You know the Tuskegee Airmen? Men like that, trailblazers, I take my hat off to 'em. But a lot of us didn't believe the military would give us a fair shake. If we saw combat duty, I figured we'd be cannon fodder.

Two years in Latin America changed my attitudes about the U.S.A. We were heroes to those fans. They treated us just like they did their own. America was no democracy for a black man. Everything in America was limited by my color. They accepted foreigners in the big leagues, long as they was white, but redblooded American black men? Get your own league, nigger. In Mexico I was a *man*. I could go as far as my talent took me. I could live where I wanted, go where I pleased. That's freedom. That's democracy. Mexico went to war, maybe I'd have fought for them. America? Not unless my mama's little house, there in the Ville in St. Louis, not unless that was what was under attack.

After the '42 season, though, the Pasquels said the war had crushed their import/export business, and they'd have to cut everyone's pay in half. Whether this was true, I don't know, but I wasn't in no position to bargain. I had an off year in '42. Trouble with home runs, which worked against me hard in those high-elevation bandboxes down there. Out of nowhere I got an offer from a new Negro club, the Cleveland Buckeyes. Negro Leagues thrived during the war, for the simple reason that our big draws—Satch, Josh, Cool Papa—was all too old to be drafted. Offer from Cleveland wasn't much more than I made in Mexico, but I took it. Spite of what I said, it still made you feel guilty bein away from home in time of war.

That spring I started gettin telegrams from my draft board in St. Louis. Inform us of your whereabouts, they said, or we'll send you to jail. All they had to do to find my whereabouts was check the ball-game schedule in the *St. Louis Argus*, the Negro paper. But the telegrams kept comin. Amidst of all this, I had a fine season for a so-so club, and was the only Buckeye chosen for the East-West game. Struck out Josh on four pitches. Last time I ever played against that troubled soul, may he rest in peace.

Week after the season, I got two letters, on the same day. One was my draft notice. The other's from Jorge Pasquel, sayin that despite the efforts of Burnis Wright, who won the triple crown, los Diablos Rojos de México finished last, causing loyal fans to demand the return of their beloved Fireball. The offer was good. But the way I saw it, letter one ruled out letter two.

I sent word to Pasquel, sayin I'd like to come but I can't on account of the draft notice. I settled things up in Cleveland, cleaned out my room, and drove home. I wasn't sure how to tell Mama her boy been drafted. Then I got there and there was this homecoming, big family barbecue. I sat beside her on her front porch and tried to tell her, but I couldn't find the words.

Monday morning I go to the draft board for my physical, hopin in the back of my mind I can get out of this somehow, when who do I see but old Quincy Trouppe. Quincy was one of the finest athletes ever come out of St. Louis. Started in the Negro Leagues a couple years before me. Winters he boxed amateur and backroom, won the city Golden Gloves title in '36. Later, made it past the gate to the white big leagues at the autumn of his career. "Quincy!" I says. "They got you, too?"

"Theolic," he says, "you don't know the half of it."

Which I sometimes think should be carved on my gravestone. "What you mean?" I say.

"Pasquel," he says. "He's tryin to work out a deal."

I nod, but I don't see how that can be.

We stand in a line marked "Colored," and me and Quincy get felt up by a Negro doctor who classifies us both 1-A. Our gooses are cooked. But believe it or not, before we even get our shoes back on, an old white man in a uniform comes up to us.

"You boys must be some fine kind of nigger ballplayers."

I look up at him, starin a hole right through the man. "Yessir," I say. "We surely are."

Quincy, a cool head, shoots me a look like, *steady now.* He knows, reason I'm called Fireball is two-thirds fastball, one-third temper.

Old man hands us each an envelope. "Never heard such shit, niggers and Mexicans calling the shots for the United States Army."

I start to talk, but Quincy slaps me in the chest, backhand.

Inside those envelopes is our deferments.

Quincy grins. "Told you," he says to me. Then, to the white man, he puts on a fake smile and, as a dig, this Tom accent, and says, "Bawss, we gots usselves frens in ha-a-ah places. Whyn't you go awn back tuh fahtin them Nazis by pushin s'mo *pay-puhs?*" He clears his throat. "Boy."

Now it's the old man's turn to boil. For a second, looks like he wants to punch old Quincy, which would've been a nice quick way to choose death. But he thinks better of it and walks away. Me and Quincy have ourselves a good laugh.

Till we found out just what happened.

Jorge Pasquel struck a deal with the U.S. government, lending eighty thousand Mexican workers to fill the wartime manpower shortage just so Quincy and me could play ball for Mexico City! Think of it: eighty thousand people I'd never meet left their homes to go pick cotton or work in hot factories for two years. Made me guilty till Quincy pointed out that most of those folks probably be glad to have the work. So I got past the guilt, even started to feel pride in the fact that because of me all those folks came to the aid of the war effort. But I never quite got over the fact that I was playin ball for a man who didn't have no military rank, no government office, nothin, and yet he bargained the lives of eighty thousand strangers like they was just so many boxes of cigars. And the American government, shit. They only too happy to go along with it.

That's the world we live in, Frank. Things haven't changed. Things like that go on in back rooms every day of our lives.

I spent the rest of the war down in Latin America, Mexico summers, Cuba winters. There kept bein rumors they was gonna let blacks in the big leagues, and every few months there'd be wind of some trumped-up tryout. Big news came when that Judge Landis—the commissioner of baseball?—when he died. I spit on that bastard's grave. He was a big part of what kept us out, and in '45, soon as the next man took over, Chandler, he made noises like it might happen.

Meanwhile, put yourself in my shoes. Imagine how it felt to have the major leagues trot out broken-down old white men when you're shut out. Imagine how it felt to see a fifteen-year-old white kid playin in the big leagues when you're shut out. Lord have mercy, Frank, they was so strapped for ballplayers they let a one-armed outfielder into the big leagues, right in my hometown! Can you *imagine* how that made me feel?

Right after the war, when they finally do sign one of us, is it Josh, Satchel, Dandy, Hilton, Quincy—one of us who paid his dues? Hell, no. Is it one of our young stars like Irvin, Miñoso, or Jethroe? Hell, no. It's a college boy, Jackie Robinson, rookie with the Monarchs. Brooklyn said at the time they was gonna start their own Negro League, but that was just another lie we got fed.

I'm not bitter. I'm only askin you to imagine how it made us feel, specially we who never did get a chance to find out how good we really were, who'd get sent to our cold graves wonderin.

Folie à Deux

DANNY GARDELLA

I

My meeting with Jorge Pasquel happened by the merest chance. It was my day off from Al Roon's Midtown Manhattan Gym. And Pasquel caught me at just the right time. Not only had I caught manic depression from Rocco Coniglio, this mixed-up genius from my old neighborhood in the Bronx, but also I was all ticked off about my contract problems with the New York Giants, those cheap war-profiteering bastards. Plus, I'd fallen in love.

It was January of 1946. A heavy snow was falling, giving New York that magical feel it has when winter shakes things up. People who didn't have to go out in it, didn't. But spring training was opening in a month, and I was so nervous over my problems I decided to take the subway into the city on my day off and lift weights. That was why I had so much bat power for a little man. Weights. There was a lot of stupid ideas around then that if you lifted too much you'd get muscle-bound. Today they all lift. That's one reason today's ballplayer is better. Most men my age say otherwise, but that's nostalgia talking. The good old days, my hairy heinie.

Al Roon's had a swimming pool, basketball court, weights, steam baths, and rows of tables for calisthenics and rubdowns. It was the leading gym in Manhattan, and it attracted all kinds of celebrities—Fredric March, Cary Grant, Frank Sinatra, all them. And, oh, the showgirls, all the pretty showgirls, worried about their thighs. I'd been hired for my name. My picture was hung in the lobby, and Mr. Roon was always having me sign autographs for some guy's kid. In those days, see, ballplayers didn't make the money they do now, with the free agency I helped bring about. Today a guy coming off a year like I had in '45—.272 average, eighteen homers, seventy-one RBIs—imagine the millions he'd get! But we needed jobs in the winter, just to pay our bills.

So I was going through a rough workout, trying to forget my problems, and Bob Janis was spotting for me. You find young men like Bob in every gym in America, muscular kids who want to be professional athletes but don't quite have it. Bob was a sweet dumb ox with big dreams.

Suddenly, in walked six Mexicans in drab overcoats, stomping their feet to get the snow off. In the middle of this crowd was a man in a long mink coat that came down to his ankles. On his feet: beautiful Russian-army fur boots. He had an energy that just rose off him. Rocco Coniglio had charm, but this man had a magnetic aura.

The bodyguards helped him off with his coat. Underneath, he was dressed like a prizefighter, in a long white robe with a dragon sewn on the back. He caught my eye and smiled. His teeth was whiter than the robe, than snow, than anything. I nodded. I meant to go back to work, but I couldn't. Bob and I stared like boys who'd just seen their first naked lady.

Mr. Roon came charging out of his office, his hand stretched out for a shake fifty feet before he got there. "Bonus días!" he said. "Welcome back to New York!" He could be surly around us, but to the customers he was like a low-grade Toots Shor.

The man took Mr. Roon's hand, pulling him into an embrace. Much backslapping went on. As they separated, Mr. Roon waved me over. Bob followed, which was what Bob did best.

"Señor Paskwel," he said, "this is none other than Danny Gardella, the great left fielder for the New York Giants."

What a crock. Even I wouldn't have called me great.

"Dan," said Mr. Roon, "this is my very good friend George Paskwel. He's also involved in baseball. He's behind the Mexican League and owns one of the teams, too, right, George?"

"Los Azules de Veracruz," said Mr. Pasquel. "The Veracruz Blues."

As we shook hands, he had me locked into eye contact. I was terrifically aware of all the rings he had on, big ones on every finger. Finally he let go. Bob cut in and introduced himself. Pasquel shook his hand, too, but he kept looking at me, all smiles. "Danny Gardella," he said, bowing in a courtly way, "if ever the Giants of New York do not treat you well, or pay you well, you must come play baseball for me in Mexico."

It was like he could read my mind, just like Rocco Coniglio. Not that Mr. Pasquel's offer appealed to me right away. What I knew of Mexico you could have fit in a thimble. But the Giants not treating me well, how could he know about that?

Then Mr. Pasquel broke out into a booming laugh, and Al Roon and Bob Janis led him into the calisthenics room. Mr. Pasquel's bodyguards just hovered around on the edge of things.

Jorge Pasquel kept himself in decent shape. His broad shoulders and barrel chest helped him carry off a little extra weight. Also, there was that air about him, that helped.

Mr. Roon had Bob take Mr. Pasquel through a brisk workout: sit-ups, push-ups, leg lifts, toe touches, dumbbells. Mr. Pasquel and I talked baseball, about this team and that, about the players coming back from the war and whether their skills had gotten rusty. This was a subject too close to home, but I didn't let on. Then he asked why I didn't play ball in Cuba that winter.

"I got responsibilities," I said. "A friend I'm tryin to help out. My job here. Also I got a sweetheart—"

"Ah!" He winked. "That's what keeps you here, eh? Love."

That was part of it, so I agreed. "I know some of the guys who played down there, though. My roommate with the Giants last year, Nap Reyes, he's Cuban and he—"

"Plays for me now."

I frowned. "For you?"

"Napoleón Reyes signed a contract with me two days ago to come play this summer in Mexico. He is one of many players from the Cuban League who have chosen to join us."

Later, when I thought about how the Cubans got ridiculed by the writers for not speaking the King's English, how guys resented them for taking jobs away from Americans and just for being different, Nap's decision to go play in Mexico made perfect sense. But at first I was shocked. "I can't believe a man would turn his back on big-league baseball to go play—"

Mr. Pasquel had fire in his eyes all of a sudden, and I stopped before I had my foot all the way down my throat.

"We are bettering our league." Mr. Pasquel's voice was quiet, even, angry. Sweat was rolling off his face. "I have purchased one hundred seventy-five thousand square meters of land in Mexico City, on which I will build a stadium, a cathedral of baseball." He started walking around me, pacing like a cross between a preacher and a tiger. "My brothers and I plan to build new parks in Torreón, Monterrey, and San Luis Potosí. Ours will be baseball of first-class caliber, open to men of all races, with our concern being only how well a man plays the game."

I nodded. "I didn't mean nothing by it."

"Of course not," Mr. Pasquel said. "Permit me to ask a question, Danny. How is it that a major-leaguer like you needs to work in a stinking gymnasium, eh?"

He had me there, of course. "Some clubs pay better than others, I guess. The Yankees paid their batboy more than some of the fellas on my team made last year."

Now it was Mr. Pasquel's turn to be shocked. "Surely you exaggerate."

"That's what I heard." Which was true; though to be honest, I didn't believe it, either. "The owners made as much money during wartime as before, only they paid us less, on account of they said we was just fill-ins. But with the war over, we should all get a fair wage now."

"Those of you who make the club. What about everyone else?" He motioned to his flunkies, and one got him his silk robe. "Do you mind me asking," said Mr. Pasquel, "how much the Giants paid you last year?"

A lousy four grand, but I didn't figure it was his business. "As a matter of fact," I said, "I do mind."

"Fair enough." He pursed his lips. "This year, your contract includes a big raise, no?"

In fact, they was trying to give me a pay cut. But pride made me lie to Mr. Pasquel. "Yes," I said. "A nice raise. I'll be making five thousand dollars."

He grinned. "Mr. Gardella," he said, "I spent that much on lunch." Then he whispered something to one of his bodyguards, who handed me Mr. Pasquel's card. "If for any reason you change your mind, I will pay you ten thousand dollars, American cash, half for signing, the other half for the season. My offer will remain open all spring. If you call, please reverse the charges."

Then he turned to Bob Janis. "And you, you are a good trainer and a big man. How much does Mr. Roon pay you?"

Bob told him, exaggerating by half.

"I will pay you twice that much money to be my trainer and American bodyguard."

Bob's eyes got real big. He looked at me. I shrugged. "Starting when?"

"This moment."

"But Mr. Roon—"

"I shall compensate Mr. Roon."

A smile spread over Bob's face. "You got yourself a deal!"

Mr. Pasquel put his hand on my shoulder. "Your friend," he said, "stands on the threshold of grand adventure. I hope you will lose no sleep over your own choice, Danny Gardella. I wish you luck. Here." He reached in the pocket of his robe and peeled off ten crisp C-notes. "Please give this to Mr. Roon, in consideration of the loss of Mr. Janis from his employ."

And then he and his people headed for the door. On my way up to Mr. Roon's office, I had the money in one hand and that business card in the other, holding them out like some altar boy with a tray full of Hosts.

II

Talking like this makes me remember what a crazy little so-and-so I used to be. Crashing a high-school prom in a hotel in

Pittsburgh and singing "Indian Love Call" while those teenage
girls swooned. Goose-stepping around on V-E Day through the
lobby of a hotel in Philly, with my hair combed over one eye and
a fake mustache pasted on, pretending I was Hitler and shouting,
"*Nein*, I am not dead!" Scared the pants off a bunch of maids. All
the crazy things I did on the field—like hitting a game-winning
pinch-hit homer with my shoes untied and then falling down
three times as I circled the bases—that all pales compared to
what I did in those hotels.

Back then I didn't know I'd caught a mental illness from Rocco
Coniglio, or even that such a thing was possible. Did you? It's
called folie à deux, insanity for two.

The way I got involved with Rocco was this. I was raised in a
working-class, Catholic, Italian-American immigrant family. After high school, I played minor-league ball a couple years and
quit. Something was missing from my life, but I didn't know
what. I returned home the winter of 1940, after I quit baseball the
first time, and got a job as an elevator operator at the Hotel New
Yorker. In the spring, I happened to be passing by Carnegie Hall,
where the great Ezio Pinza was performing, and I saw all those
dressed-up people, and I knew I needed to broaden myself: to
learn about opera, literature, all the arts. But I had no idea where
to begin.

Several weeks later I was playing handball with a school pal
named Joey Coniglio, who had become a cop, and we got to talking about Joey's brother Rocco. Rocco, who was ten years older
than us, was this great violinist and poet who had won all these
scholarships, to Columbia, Harvard, Oxford—it was amazing.
Pride of the neighborhood. Rocco Coniglio had more degrees
than a thermometer. Turns out he's back in town, teaching English at both Fordham and Sarah Lawrence as well as playing in
two orchestras. And it hits me: This man can teach me things.

Little did I know.

I called him up, and to my surprise he agreed to help me. When
I got to his apartment, he had his windows open and he's playing
his violin—that sad, gorgeous part right before the cellos take
over at the end of Tchaikovsky's "Pathétique." You know that? At
the time I didn't, and I came bounding up the stairs all excited to
ask him. First he looked at me like I was a bug, then he sized me

up and said, "You're small, but you're not little anymore." What that meant, I hate to think about.

He started lending me books and records and getting me free tickets to the orchestra. Sometimes I'd get to his apartment and he'd be flying around full of energy, planning elaborate practical jokes or else doing impressions of celebrities like he was his own radio variety show, and we'd sing together and laugh about hotel-room doors I glued shut or phony draft notices we wrote out and mailed to people we didn't like—and to friends, too, come to think about it. Who knows what all we laughed about. But then, other times, I'd come over and Rocco would be hunched over his kitchen table, hardly moving a muscle, and I'd sit and talk to him about great music and the weather and try to cheer him up. I was so hungry for what he could teach me.

Then war broke out. Joey Coniglio volunteered and got killed about five seconds after he shipped out. Where, I can't remember. Europe. Losing Joey, it destroyed Rocco. After a while he hardly got out of bed. He lost his all his jobs and started talking about all the different ways a man could kill himself. He had lists with the pros and the cons for hanging, gunshot, gas, jumping off a ledge, off a bridge, drowning, pills, all kinds of ways, and he'd leave the lists out where I could find them, like for instance in the middle of a big stack of 78's that he knew full well I'd put away the next time I came over. A couple months of this and Rocco looked like a man sixty years old. Sometimes I'd catch him carrying on conversations with Joey. Rocco had done so much to enrich my life, I wanted to help. But I was working at a naval yard, which exempted me from the draft but which didn't pay enough for me to have extra money. Finally, I felt so bad I asked Rocco to move into my tiny apartment. I gave him my bed, and I slept on the couch.

This goes on for two years. The killing-himself thing never got real far past the lists, though I would every once in a while find a rope just sitting out. For a while, Rocco gave violin and French-horn lessons to neighborhood boys, until one of them called him a fairy—actually, a "chicken hawk," you know what that is? Which at the time I didn't believe. Rocco stopped playing his own violin and in fact packed it up and mailed it to Franklin Delano Roosevelt, don't ask me why. Rocco's poetry got so strange and filthy I can't give you specifics. I'd read it and feel dirty, like I was the one who wrote it. After months and months of trying to help Rocco through these hard times, I found myself having wild highs and lows, just like Rocco. Sometimes I'd be sitting on the docks and catch myself talking to Joey Coniglio. I'd always been kind of a clown, but I began to go on stretches where all I could think about was my next practical joke. I even thought about suicide.

Then in 1944 a miracle happened. I was playing ball for the shipyard team against a bunch of Navy guys, including a few big-leaguers. I hit three home runs and a Giants scout happens to see me do it, and the next thing I know I'm playing for Jersey City, the only farm club the Giants had during the war.

Getting away from Rocco and back to baseball, I saw what a trap I'd fallen into, and I began to feel better. I tried not to even think about him, alone in my apartment, staring at the walls and refusing to exhibit any of his gifts.

Then the Giants called me up. In six weeks I'd gone from a dockworker to a big-league ballplayer, playing for my hometown fans. The pressure was enormous, but I pretended it was all a big joke. The worst part was going home after games in Ebbets Field or the Polo Grounds and having Rocco there, waiting. Sometimes he was on fire, and we'd stay up all night listening to Verdi. Mostly, though, he was a zombie.

On the road I was the life of the party, but it wore on me. I went in a slump. Suddenly my depression hit. So did suicide feelings. I confided this to Nap Reyes, who was made my roommate when nobody else would room with a Cuban. What a grand guy Reyes was. But I felt embarrassed, unmanly, for talking like that, so one road trip to St. Louis, on the tenth floor of the Chase Hotel, I woke up early, opened the window, crawled out, and hung from the ledge by my fingertips. Then I yelled, "Goodbye, cruel world!" Reyes leapt out of bed and ran screaming to the window. Almost gave him a heart attack. I busted out laughing, and he wouldn't help me back in. I can't blame him now, but at the time I thought he was being a sorehead.

The press is always looking for colorful angles, so when that story made the rounds I got famous. This didn't sit well with my manager, Mel Ott, the great home-run hitter. Him and I was oil and water. He's the one Durocher said "Nice guys finish last" about. When Mel Ott sent me back to Jersey City, he said I'd come back over his dead body. Funny thing, I made the team the next spring and Ott was still alive. But Kate had everything to do with that.

She was the girl next door, for real. We met in November of '44, when she and her pop moved into the brownstone across the street, as I helped him carry in a secondhand Norge. She had long auburn hair, legs like Betty Grable's, and smart, too—dean's list at City College. Hoped to be a schoolteacher. The first time I saw her, I was sure I knew her from someplace; then I realized she was the spitting image of that goddess on the clamshell, which Rocco used to have a print of on the wall of his W.C.

Kate was the first to point out the effect Rocco Coniglio had on me. She had a cousin I asked her to fix up with Rocco, and we double-dated. (I tried to find women for Rocco now and then because I felt sorry for him and maybe because I knew in my subconscious that Rocco liked to frig around with boys.) What a disaster that date was! Rocco didn't talk to the cousin and he grilled me about Kate, right in front of her. To make it worse, I answered like she wasn't there. "You're another person around that man," Kate said afterward. "It's like you're hypnotized." Of course, she was right. More and more, I kept my distance from Rocco, sleeping at my brother's place, things like that. And when time came to report to the Rockefeller estate in Lakewood, New Jersey, for spring training, I was ready. Of course, some of it was undone when the season started and I was in New York all the time, which you can see from that Hitler stunt I pulled in Philly.

Kate was also the first person to tell me I should take Mr. Pasquel up on his offer to go play in Mexico, although when I first told her about it, that same night, her face fell. "Heck, no, I'm not going," I said. "I'm a Giant." Though I didn't have a contract, which she knew.

We was eating dinner at a great little Italian place on Willis Avenue, I forget the name. We sat in the front window, and you could hardly see the street for the snow.

She frowned. "It might be for the best, Mexico."

"How do you figure?" But I knew what she was getting at: Rocco. "I'd miss you something fierce, doll."

"Cut it out. That's not what I mean."

"Mexico, it's a region I don't know nothing about."

"That's not what I mean, either."

It's a lucky man who finds a woman like Kate. "I'm gonna go down to Miami and win that left-field job and the Giants will pay me what I'm worth, and everything will be great."

"That won't solve things." She had those pretty brown eyes focused on me, and I knew that if I lost this woman, I'd kick myself for all eternity.

"I go to Mexico," I said, "I don't just lose Rocco." And what I'm thinking is, the only way I can hang on to her is to propose, which I'm nowhere near ready for. Marriage was another unknown region I feared.

So what do you think she says next? "I'm not looking for a proposal, Danny."

Was this was my day to have people read my mind or what?

"I know," I said. What else *could* I say? This: "I love you."

"I love you, too." She reached into her purse and pulled out a subway token, the old kind that people kept for luck. "Take this," she said. "Whatever you choose is up to you. Just promise that when you make a decision, you'll take a moment, rub this token, and think of me."

"I promise."

She smiled. It was also a day for great smiles.

❖

Later I kissed Kate good night, crossed the street, and went up to my apartment. Rocco was sitting in the dark beside the radio, listening to static, staring out at the falling snow. I turned on the lights, turned off the radio, and told him about the offer.

"Not all who hesitate are lost," he said when I finished. "In fact, willed introversion is one of the classic implements of creative genius and can be employed as a deliberate device."

I got up to get us a couple beers. "Is that from a book?"

"No," he said, but it was. Years later I heard the line quoted on that PBS show, the one about myths.

"Anyway," I said, "I'm still property of the Giants."

"Like a mule," he said. He had a point. I laughed and put on a Puccini record. We sat and listened and all that beauty washed over us as the snow drifted past the streetlights. You see, Rocco

Coniglio was not all good or all bad. My original motive for being with him was good. I wanted to extricate him, free him, so he could be the person he could be. He always had a side of him tuned into beauty and the other tuned into the lowest side of life. I was attracted to the beauty but instead got a blast of the other. That's usually how it is, with people.

I'd had wine at dinner and drunk beer with Rocco as we listened to the music, but still, that night I couldn't sleep. When finally I did, I had a dream I was lost in a maze, with my pop and sainted mother guarding the gates. They both had their own heads but dragon bodies. They didn't know me. It was unclear whether they was keeping people in or out. Haunts me to this day.

III

The Giants had bought up every room in the Venetian Hotel, the biggest place in Miami, a huge place, and yet I got stuck across town in some dump. Even the writers got to stay in the Venetian. That should have clued me in where I stood, but I just figured they was punishing me for refusing take a pay cut.

They'd invited over a hundred guys to camp. Infield drills, we stood ten deep at the positions. In the outfield shagging flies, you felt more like a punt returner on a football field. And it seemed like you never got a chance to swing the bat. As for the locker room, forget about it. My most vivid memory of that place was standing in the shower, feeling something warm on my leg, and looking over to see big Van Lingle Mungo peeing on me, grinning ear to ear.

I arrived in Miami in tip-top shape, with a picture of my girl that I put on the bureau and kissed each night. In these regards I was an oddball. I don't blame the soldier boys for still celebrating V-J Day, but not ten men out of that hundred were in condition, or cared. And the girls they chased! Morning, noon, and night. Again, I don't blame 'em. I was a black pot once.

The real reason we was there so early wasn't that guys was fat but that the clubs wanted to make their own wallets fatter. In '46 they called us down early, then split the team into a bunch of

squads and barnstormed through Cuba, Puerto Rico, all over
Florida. The Yankees even went to Panama. Made a fortune.

The fans turned out like every game was the World Series. In
1946, every attendance record was shattered to pieces. But
while on the surface everything was skittles and beer, for the
players it was a time of terrible nervousness. The men who'd
been gone didn't know if they'd be able to get their skills back.
We who hadn't was afraid we'd just be pushed aside, like strike-
breakers, which in my case is what happened. I'll grant you I
wasn't the most graceful fielder [*Ed.: One Gotham scribe once
wrote about Gardella having caught a long fly ball "unassisted"*],
and I'll grant you I hit a lot of those eighteen homers in the Polo
Grounds [*Ed.: where the right-field fence was 11 feet high and a
mere 279 feet away from home*], but what else did the Giants
have in the outfield? Willard Marshall was back from the
Marines, I'll give you him. But Mel Ott was washed up, and the
best of the rest was Johnny Rucker, the Crabapple Comet, who
got replaced later that year by a rookie greenfly you never
heard of.

I tried to do my job, but it was tough. The squad I was assigned
to didn't have no established big-leaguers on it. The only guy
you'd have heard of was Sal Maglie, the pitcher, and he was just a
spare part then. On top of that, the men in my hotel got less expense money, don't ask me why. The worst part was, even with
that group of bushers I hardly played in any games. The only time
I started was when the owner of the Milwaukee club—which back
then was Triple A—came to see me. The rumor was I was going to
get sold there, as a gate attraction. The Giants could sell me to another club, even though I didn't have a signed contract. What allowed that was the reserve clause.

Think I was screwy, how about that cockamamie reserve
clause? It bound you to a club forever, even after your contract
ran out. The owners of baseball had control of you like in no
other business. Even in the service you finished your tour of duty
and then went to work where you pleased. I'll go to my judgment
happy I helped kill off that reserve clause.

So one day I showed up for morning practice and there's no
uniform in my locker. Right away I went into Mel Ott's office, figuring I'd been sold to Milwaukee. No, Ott said, it's just a new

club policy: no contract, no uniform. For years the Giants had dickered with players during training camp, and I knew for a fact at least two other guys hadn't agreed on terms. [*Ed.: Twenty-one of the fifty-five players in the Giants camp did not have contracts.*] On my way out, I checked their lockers: uniforms, clean and pressed.

I sat around all day in my crummy hotel, wondering whether to give up the ghost and take their lousy $3,500. I tried to call Kate; no answer. I took out Jorge Pasquel's business card, which I had hidden in the lining of my suitcase. I got all set to call, even had the operator at work on placing it, when I chickened out. There was just too much I didn't know about Mexico. The safe thing was to sign with the Giants and compete for a job right here in the U.S.A.

But the more I thought, the madder I got. What really stuck in my craw was the expense money. It was maybe the smallest piece of my puzzle, but that's how it goes sometimes. My anger built up all day. I tried to stay calm, think things through. Finally I made a decision: I'd go down to the Venetian Hotel, swallow my pride, sign my contract, and get on with life.

When I got there, the first club official I see is the team secretary, Ed Brannick, handing out expense money at a table outside the dining room, like some gnarled old troll guarding a bridge. "I'm here to sign my contract," I said. "So pay me all those back expenses you owe me."

"Where's your coat and tie?"

I forgot, to be honest. I was in shirtsleeves, with a nice new sweater-vest over the top. "Give me a uniform, I'll follow your dress code," I said. "Now, where's my money?"

"You'll have to talk to Mr. Stoneham." Mr. Stoneham was the owner.

I started to go in the dining room to do just that, but Brannick stood up, blocking my way. He was a shrimp, and I could easily have pushed past. But I decided to be a nice guy.

"Fine," I said. "Why don't you go in there and get him?"

Brannick shook his head. "You'll have to wait."

Sometimes it amazes you how *few* murders there are. At that moment I was capable.

Brannick and I locked eyes, a war of nerves, standing there on the threshold of the Venetian Hotel dining room. By then some of the players had noticed what was going on, and I could hear them rumbling. There was no turning back now. I was going to push by that old man and go give Stoneham a piece of my mind, tell him my price was five grand or forget it.

But then I thought of that subway token. Still staring down Ed Brannick, I reached into my pocket and I rubbed the token for luck, and I told Ed Brannick he was a little prick, and then turned in the general direction of the entire New York Giants organization and, at the very top of my lungs, yelled, "You buttholes haven't seen the last of Danny Gardella!"

IV

Valentine's Day, 1946, in the middle of the night, during a raging thunderstorm, I boarded a propeller plane at the Miami airport with big dumb Bob Janis right behind me. The Pasquels had sent Bob to retrieve me from the Giants camp, to protect me. But no one bothered us.

I had never flown in a private plane before, and even though they had it all upholstered and carpeted and nice, it was a lot smaller than I'd thought. I felt like I'd been swallowed up by some terrible beast. We took off amid all that wind and rain and thunder and lightning, and the airplane is bucking and shaking, and I'm rubbing that subway token for dear life and thinking, *This is it, dummy. Now you've done it. End of the line for you.*

Then a funny thing happens. We get up in the air, up over the Gulf of Mexico, climbing, climbing, climbing, up into the heavens, up above that storm, and the most incredible feeling of peace comes over me. Far away to the east I can see the sunrise. And the sun keeps shining bright, and time just flies—if you'll pardon the expression—and the next thing I know, my ears are popping and we're starting our descent into Mexico City. Below me, for the first time, I can see the strange and wonderful landscape of Mexico, a blur of mountains, cactus, dirt, and brush.

The plane lands, smooth as glass, and we taxi down a long runway to where a big group of people are standing. The door opens, filling that dark belly of an airplane full of brilliant white light. Bob Janis elbows me, like a kid about to pull a stunt, then me and him put on sunglasses and walk down those stairs toward this cheering mass of a crowd. In the very front are all five Pasquel brothers and a husky old gent who turns out to be the president of Mexico. I stand as tall as I am able, put on a serious face, and try to keep from cracking up.

3.

The Original
Mexican Standoff

On February 1, 1946, my own season of gold began as I, Frank Bullinger, Jr., arrived at the front door of La Finca Vigía, expecting to be Hemingway's only guest, clutching in both hands the manuscript of my novel. Suddenly, several charming famous men with guns plus two wary-looking women, also with guns, came bounding down the front steps, drunk and dressed in peacoats and flannel, leather patches in all the right places. Me, I wasn't drunk, struggled to be charming, and never would become famous. I was a slight man, drenched from the storm that hit the Cuba Line on my way from Miami, dressed in a blue sport coat and a tie I'd gotten for Father's Day. Gene Tunney brushed past me, portrait of the working-class hero turned patrician millionaire. Babe Ruth patted me on the head and said, "Hiya, kid."

Although I knew them, the surreal sight of Hemingway, Ruth, and Tunney—those icons from the twenties, together in one hunting party—rocked me back on my heels. I'd met Ruth once—when he came to St. Louis begging Bill DeWitt to hire him to manage the Browns. Tunney, the gentleman rags-to-riches heavyweight champ, had been my boyhood hero; I'd managed to stammer through an interview with him during the war, when the Fighting Marine headed the armed-services athletic program. I'd known Hemingway for fifteen years, and had benefited from his acquaintance, but in truth I did not know him well.

"The late Mr. Bullinger," said Hemingway. "You know everyone, right?" The gun he held was big. It was a big gun. It was good (I suppose he felt) to have a big gun and to hold it.

"Most," I said. "I haven't been introduced to this lovely creature. Mary, I presume?"

Hemingway's new, blond wife winced. She was wife number four, younger than Hemingway, and clearly not one for flattery. Neither was I, but I was tired. I shook her hand. She smiled then. She was the kind of woman who liked it when a man shook her hand.

As for the others, three were Cubans I'd never seen before. The woman was Polly Tunney. I knew Lou Klein and Fred Martin (my job was to cover the St. Louis Cardinals), but not as friends. For years I'd covered the Browns and had friends among them (Jakucki, Kreevich—the drunks). But the Cards writer died, as I've told you, and the Browns writer came home from the war and I got given the Cards. Theoretically it was a promotion, and if I'd thought of myself as a sportswriter I might have seen it that way. It's a curse to be good at a job you hate; what's worse is to need that job.

Before I got a chance to ask about the Cubans, or how journeyman ballplayers like Klein and Martin got invited to join this bunch, Hemingway thrust a rifle toward me. He had a shotgun slung across his back. "C'mon," he said. "We're hiking to the gun club."

I held up my manuscript. I had been working on the novel for ten years. "What should I do with this?"

Hemingway frowned. "Shove it up your arse!" He pressed the rifle firm against my chest. He smelled of whiskey. Then he roared with laughter. "Aw, just kidding, kid. Go set it inside the house, fix yourself a drink, and let's get going."

I did as I was told. I was thirty-six years old and had just been called "kid" twice. I had never been to Cuba, didn't speak Spanish, and had never hunted—never fished, either, which is what I'd been invited to come do. Whichever it was we were doing, it was a new one on me.

I made myself a Tom Collins and ran through grassy fields and scrub woods to catch up to the group, far ahead of me by now.

◈

At the Club de Cazadores we were followed around by a man with a portable bar. We shot both clay and real pigeons and at targets. Klein and the big Okie Martin took beer and went out to shoot grouse, which were raised for the sport of club members. The best shots were (1) Jorge Pasquel, the most dashing of the men I thought were Cubans, (2) Tunney, the only one not drinking, and (3) Mary, who was a crack shot. I don't know exactly what it means to be a crack shot, but Mary was one, and I called her that. She smiled at me again. I was on good footing with her, and she was the one who finally introduced me to the Pasquels.

Only one of the Cubans was really Cuban. The other two were Mexican businessmen, Jorge and Alfonso Pasquel. Jorge was a man about my age with a pencil-thin mustache, a diamond stick-pin in the lapel of his field jacket, and a habit of spraying his hard or sibilant consonants. The diamond must have been two carats. Alfonso was thinner, younger, and bald, with the same mustache as his brother but no jewelry and no presence. The lone actual Cuban, a man as squat and bellicose as Hemingway, turned out to be the great Dolf Luque, who'd pitched in the World Series for the 1919 Reds and the 1933 Giants and who, Hemingway said, raised excellent fighting cocks. I had not recognized him. He had started out shooting better than anyone but soon got too drunk to hit anything and his face got redder and redder until he grabbed hold of the barrel of his rifle and shattered the stock against the cement walls of the gun club.

"Old Luke never could hit worth a shit," said Ruth. "Gotta keep the trademark up, Luke!" He laughed his horse laugh, gone raspy from years of smoking, then looped a big arm around the sputtering Luque. The two headed off to the clubhouse in search of a few big steaks. Polly Tunney, who looked as uncomfortable as I felt, got Gene to go for a walk with her.

As for Hemingway, he was having a bad day with his guns, and so he was talking. The novel he was writing was about two sets of lovers and the loss of identity within each pair's lovemaking. "It's filled with great fucking," he said, and could be the book people would think of centuries from now when someone said "Hemingway." He'd written four hundred pages since Christmas. Throughout his long explanation, Hemingway did not once ask me about *my* writing.

My shoulder was sore from shooting skeet. I wanted to go join Ruth in the clubhouse, but he was, after all, *Babe Ruth*, and I just couldn't figure out how to relax and bullshit with *Babe Ruth*. Same with Tunney. A younger writer might have felt the same about Hemingway. But I had known him in Paris, in '31, right after I graduated from Oberlin and right before he left.

More than my shoulder, what got to me was how badly I missed my son, who was back in St. Louis with his mother, my putative wife, who'd found out about Frances, and about the poet in New York, too, and who had already filed for divorce. Given the circumstances under which I'd left—my belongings strewn on the treelawn, Harriet screaming on the other side of the front door with its new lock—I was unclear when or how I might see Jerome again. He was seven years old and a pistol. Maybe that's why I missed him so much, all this shooting and the fact I called him a pistol, and when I did he would laugh and make his hand into a gun and say, "Pow."

After dark at La Finca Vigía, Hemingway's Chinese cook made mariscos veracruzanos in honor of the Pasquels, who were from Veracruz. They were joined by a dark and striking woman whom Mary introduced as "María Félix the famous actress." She had just finished a film and had been sleeping all day in the guest room. She kissed Jorge Pasquel full on the mouth and sat down beside him.

Throughout dinner no one spoke to me. Babe Ruth and Ernest Hemingway, both drunk, at a single dinner table, swapping suspiciously exciting tales of manly prowess (here a dead beast, there a pair of friendly twin redheads, everywhere a sweaty triumph), provided little chance for others to talk. And Lou Klein, a loud-mouth's loudmouth, grabbed most of what chance remained. The

Tunneys couldn't get a word in. Even Jorge Pasquel said little, which I did not, at the time, know to be odd. What was normal was my feeling of being alone in the midst of a loud group, which was how I'd spent most of my life.

Above the sideboard were framed photos of Hemingway with famous men and dead animals. I was in none of them. I had taken one of the ones from Paris, a blurry shot of Hemingway and Scott Fitzgerald (in for a brief visit), each in a brand-new beret. In another, Hemingway and Jorge Pasquel sat side by side, Indian-style, atop a fallen rhinoceros.

After dinner everyone, even the women, lit Mexican cigars— coals to Newcastle, brought by the Pasquels from their factory. The boozing grew serious and the conversation sank to the level of baseball talk. What did I expect? That Hemingway and I would go fishing alone and reminisce about Paris, and then go back to the house and eat like kings and Hemingway would sit in a good chair and read my novel straight through, chuckling approvingly as I watched and was redeemed, and Hemingway would finish and say, What a damn fine book, Frank, what say I cable Perkins and tell him to publish it? Is that what I expected? Yes, that.

But it was baseball. First the Cuban League season, which is how Martin and Klein came to know Luque, who managed their Cienfuegos club, and the Pasquels, who were in Cuba to recruit players for the summer Mexican League, which they ran. At least this is what I gathered from the conversation, much of which was conducted in Spanish. Polly Tunney said she had a headache from the cigars and went to lie down.

Then it was on to American baseball, especially the Cards and the Dodgers, the favorites for the '46 pennant. Hemingway knew many of the Dodgers from the years up until '43 when they trained in Havana, and favored them, though he allowed that St. Louis, with Max Lanier and Stan Musial back from the war, would be damn tough. Dolf Luque, a pitching coach for the New York Giants, did not in any way defend that team. He sat in a corner, in a red wing chair that seemed to swallow him up, drinking wine from a bottle. He was stone quiet.

"What about you, Frank?" said Hemingway. It was the first time all day anyone had made an attempt to draw me into the conversation. "How do you see it coming out this year?"

"Whoever wins, wins," I said. "Whoever loses, loses. I just go to the park and write about whatever happens."

Everybody laughed. They thought I was joking.

"Okay," I said. I did not want to talk baseball, but I wanted to talk. And so I talked baseball. "I'll tell you what the biggest baseball story is this year," I said. I paused for effect, and it worked, and I felt powerful. "It's the rumors about a players' union forming."

This brought about even more laughter.

I frowned. "Why is that funny?"

"Bawl-playahs," said Lou Klein, taking a long pull from a beer bottle, "don't cotton to unions." Fred Martin drank beer, too, and nodded in agreement.

And I thought: *You dumb-ass hayseeds.* "You've got no pension, you've got no minimum wage," I said. "They have you coming to training camp this year a month earlier than usual, and you don't get paid five cents extra for it. Attendance could double this year, but the owners won't give you guys any of that money if they don't have to."

"Son," said Klein, who was seven years younger than me, "your American bawl-playah is an individualist." Klein was from Louisiana and drunk. He milked that word: *ian-dihv-ID-you-a-lisst.* "If we wanted to be a bunch of damn Wobblies," he said, "we'd go back to the shit towns we came from."

Everyone laughed at this, too. Except Jorge Pasquel. Jorge Pasquel did not laugh, and he was looking at me. His eyes shone. I couldn't help but look back at him.

Everyone was done talking about unions. Then Hemingway opened a bottle of Cutty, which he drank from and passed to me.

"Boy, it must be great to write about these men and baseball," Hemingway said. "I'll tell you, Frank, after all that nasty business in the war, writing baseball sounds pretty damn good. Even back in Paris, when you were just a pup and I helped you get this job, I thought, Jesus, why am I getting Desmond to give this job to young Frank when I'd like to have it myself? I don't for the life of me know why you want to write fiction. Fiction tears your soul end to end if you let it, and sometimes even if you don't. By God, Frank, if I could, I wouldn't mind chucking everything to go write about baseball."

I meant to stop drinking, but that made me take a long swig. "Do it," I said. "Chuck everything."

More laughs. People thought I was a comedian.

❖

I went for a walk to clear my head and to pee, and when I returned, the Babe, Mary Hemingway, María Félix, and a revived Polly Tunney had moved to the kitchen table to play gin. I would have given anything to join that game. I stopped to watch. I wondered if the Babe would try to steal the lovely María, but there were no eyes being made. Unless you count Mary, who was sexy in an aging-tomboy way, and who kept looking at me. I did not count this.

Back in the living room it was still baseball. I was sure it was some kind of record. Jorge Pasquel, whose English was perfect, had the floor, that beautiful terrazzo floor, and was holding forth on how it was *true*, Mexico *could* support a third major league—all this while Gene Tunney was lacing boxing gloves onto Pasquel's hands. Klein and Martin were nodding and grinning, as if they half-believed what Pasquel said, but mostly didn't. Alfonso Pasquel looked worshipfully at his brother. Hemingway went to pee. By now everyone was spectacularly drunk in that big raw way that lived and died in the 1940s.

"The major leagues will not give one of the best baseball minds alive today," Pasquel said, pointing a gloved fist at Luque, "an opportunity to be a manager." Now he pointed the glove at himself. "I will. Adolfo Luque will manage for me in the Mexican League." Tunney was getting annoyed with Jorge Pasquel's gesturing and slapped his glove, hard. "The major leagues will not give the great Bambino, the game's greatest player, an opportunity to manage. I will."

"Thanks, George," Ruth called from the other room. "You're a sport."

From down a darkened hallway came Hemingway. He was stripped to the waist. He already had his gloves on. Somehow he must have pissed with his gloves on. He had a mean look in his eyes but was also smiling. He was getting fat.

"If," said Pasquel, "with all the competition on the Cardinals of

St. Louis, you gentlemen should have dissatisfaction, please consider joining us in Mexico."

"Right," Klein said. He rolled his eyes.

"Yeah, thanks," said Martin. "Thanks a lot."

Alfonso Pasquel cleared his throat, loudly, for attention, then looked eagerly around the room, smiled like a happy child and, apropos of nothing, blurted, "My brother once killed a man in a duel."

It was the non sequitur of all time. I broke out laughing. I was the only one.

"Up on your feet," said Hemingway.

I stood. But Hemingway was talking to Jorge Pasquel.

Pasquel had taken off his holster. His pearl-handled pistols lay on a coffee table, on top of a copy of *Look*. He also had taken his shirt off. He was not fat, but neither was he thin. Hemingway was more muscular.

"You know, I sparred with Heeney in '35," said Hemingway, referring to an Australian meatbag Gene Tunney had carved up in the Polo Grounds in '28. "Gave him all he could handle."

"Right," said Tunney. "I know. We all know."

"This is not 1935," said Jorge Pasquel. "In 1935 you were as young as I am now."

Hemingway laughed at this. It was a mirthless laugh.

Tunney agreed to serve as referee. Everyone came in from the kitchen. "Hey!" said Ruth. "Watch how long Tunney counts!"

"Good Christ." It was Mary Hemingway. "This again."

"It's all in fun," Hemingway called.

"Your head," she said, pointing at her own. Hemingway called her a hateful name. She did not say anything. She stood her ground.

"I bet on the Mexican," said Ruth. "One hundred dollars American on George."

Alfonso took the trouble to correct the Babe. "Jorge."

María Félix laughed. "I will take that bet. I bet on the great Hemingway."

Jorge Pasquel shouted something at her in Spanish, and it was hard to tell if it was angry or teasing.

At last, Pasquel and Hemingway came out, from a corner by a bookcase and a corner by a floor lamp, and began to box. Pasquel had a longer reach, Hemingway had a better punch, but they were both awfully drunk, and Tunney began to laugh at them.

They went dancing around in circles and knocked over the floor lamp. End of round one.

Dolf Luque slumped down in his chair. I figured he was passed out.

At it again, Pasquel and Hemingway kept circling, circling. It was not a good fight, but it took a long time, and things kept getting broken—ashtrays, highball glasses, another lamp. Little things. For me this made the fight worthwhile.

Mary Hemingway watched with her arms folded across her chest. She did not move to pick up any of the broken things.

The fighters got into a clinch, fell together over the back of a sofa, and popped back up, still together in that clinch.

Gene Tunney separated them.

Hemingway feinted with his left, then, just as it looked like he was going to throw the right with all his power, and just as it looked like he had an opening to do it, he swung his right leg forward and narrowly missed kicking Jorge Pasquel in the balls.

At that, Dolf Luque sprang to life, leaping to his feet, drawing a long-barreled revolver and firing a shot into the ceiling. Plaster rained down upon him. We all dropped to the floor. Then Luque leveled the gun at Hemingway, and fired. He missed. "Fight fair," he said, and sat heavily down.

For a long time, no one knew what to do.

"Fight fair," said Luque. "No tengo intención de matarlo." His voice was deep. He was a bantam of a man. "If I want to kill you, you die. Get up. Fight fair. I no try to kill anyone."

There was another long pause. Finally, from the floor, Alfonso piped up, "My brother once killed a man. In a duel." And this time everybody laughed like hell.

While everyone was still laughing, I caught sight of what Luque's second bullet had ripped into: the manuscript of my novel, sitting atop a small desk in the vestibule. A dead hit. Papers flew everywhere.

Hemingway stood. "I'm sorry as hell, Jorge. I don't know what got into me."

Pasquel said something in Spanish—some kind of quip, obviously, because Hemingway laughed. "True," Hemingway said. "At *least* a fifth."

Alfonso frowned. "So is my brother the winner?"

Hemingway smiled. "Let's call it the original Mexican stand-off," he said, which fortunately Jorge Pasquel found funny. It was that part of the cycle of drink where everyone found everything funny.

Near dawn, Hemingway stood in his moonlit yard, bleeding from a cut to his eye, seeing everybody off. He handed each male guest an autographed copy of one of his books. Tunney said he had already read, and greatly admired, *For Whom the Bell Tolls*, so Hemingway gave him *Winner Take Nothing*, too. Everyone else accepted whatever he was given.

Mary Hemingway had gone to bed before things completely wound down. As she'd said good night, I thought I caught a look from her. I did not know what kind of look it was. No, that wasn't it. I knew. I would have liked to fuck her, for all sorts of reasons, all of them the wrong reasons for fucking a woman. Also, I *was* drunk, and maybe wrong about that look.

Klein and Martin had both vomited on the front lawn of La Finca Vigía and passed out. I liked those boys better already. "You men have a game in eight hours," I said, shaking them. The Cardinals were playing an exhibition in Havana against the New York Giants, the first of the spring. I had to be there, too. Luque, of course, was now employed elsewhere. "Plus Hemingway's giving out books. You fellows can read, can't you?"

Luque and the Babe sat on a stone bench talking about the old days. They were drinking Cuban beer. They were the oldest men there, and the only ones still drinking. I heard them making plans to go to a casino.

That was when I noticed a strange thing. Ruth had come here not with the Tunneys, as I'd presumed, but with the Pasquels' entourage, of which Klein and Martin were not a part. Alfonso was calling to Luque and Ruth to get in the car.

"How'd you guys get here?" I asked the two Cardinals.

"Cab," Martin said.

"Cuban cabbie," said Klein. "Fuckin '35 Chevy."

By then, the Pasquels had loaded Ruth, Luque, and María Félix into their car.

Hemingway's chauffeur had the car idling, the Tunneys sitting in the back. Hemingway handed Klein and Martin copies of *The Torrents of Spring* and showed them into the front seat.

Hemingway was out of books, having given two to Tunney, and he insisted I wait while he went to get one. I thought I had all of Hemingway's books, but I relented.

The Pasquels' car pulled away, turned out onto the road, and then came to a stop. Jorge Pasquel emerged from the car and called my name. "Come quickly!" he said. "I have a proposition for you. I think you'll find it amusing."

I was dog tired, and sick of being bossed around by the likes of these people. Still, I found my legs obeying. I hated my legs for obeying.

Pasquel handed me a stack of business cards. His lip was puffy, but he was not as bad off as Hemingway. "I believe what you said about the union," Pasquel whispered. "I have lately learned a great deal about the enslavement of the American baseball player by the magnates of the major leagues. If you know of men who would be interested in playing in Mexico—where our players earn more, work less, and receive better treatment—please, will you pass along my card?"

I nodded, automatically, without real commitment.

Pasquel pulled a wad of bills from the game pouch of his field jacket. He peeled off a C-note and stuffed it into the breast pocket of my sport coat. "An advance," he said. "For your troubles. I will pay you twice this amount for any men you help my brothers and me to sign."

In my head I heard myself refusing the money, but my heart said *Take it.* "I don't know . . ."

"I am not asking for your soul," said Pasquel. "Just your assistance. No strings attached. If you can help, splendid. If you cannot, buy yourself some clothes and a woman." He laughed. "I am giving you the scoop of the year, Mr. Bullinger. Perhaps the scoop of your career."

"That's all I need."

We stood together on the side of the road. Hemingway's car pulled past us. Pasquel hugged me. I am an American midwesterner. I stiffened. Nonplussed, I forgot to ask for a ride to my hotel in Havana. Pasquel got back in the car, which spit pea gravel as it roared away. I was alone in the dark.

I sank to my knees and threw up. This was what I had come to: I was a smelly, retching drunk beside a dark gravel road in rural Cuba. I had not served my country in time of war. I had just accepted $100 from a stranger. I was deeply in debt. I was without a home. My belongings were stored in the corner of my neighbor's garage. I was going through a divorce. My son might never see me again. My mistress, a classics professor at Washington U. named Frances Kingston, whose husband was still overseas, was pregnant with my child. The woman I believed myself to be in love with was a tiny redheaded twenty-three-year-old raw talent of a poet in Greenwich Village, Diana James, who was the best lover I had ever had but who did not love me. I had published seventeen short stories in little magazines, including one, "A Dream of Cincinnati," that had been reprinted in *The Best Short Stories of 1940*. Since then I had published nothing but journalism. For a decade I wrote and rewrote a novel that now lay shot up and haphazardly reassembled in the house of a famous writer who would probably hate it and whose wife I had considered fucking. It could happen to anybody.

"There you are, Frank," said Hemingway. "Thought you left without your book." I looked up expecting to see my own manuscript being handed to me. Instead it was *Three Stories and Ten Poems*, Hemingway's slim first book.

In a daze, I stood.

"This one's kind of rare," said Hemingway. "I only have two other copies myself. Worth some money, probably."

We began to walk back toward the house.

"Damn sorry about your novel. That crazy Luque."

"Yes. Jesus. What a day."

"I looked at the manuscript, Frank. Most of it's readable. I'll read what's there. You made a carbon copy, didn't you?"

"No."

"Damn shame. You must have notes. Longhand."

"Yes. Some."

"That's good. Say, Frank. You want to go for a swim? A swim can get the blood going so the hangover isn't too bad."

"I didn't bring my suit."

Hemingway laughed. "Aw, go without."

"That's fine," I said. "A swim sounds good."

We went around to the back of La Finca Vigía. We took off our clothes, dove into the pool, and began to swim laps. I was a much better swimmer than Hemingway. He did not seem to need to compete. Our unerect penises were, for the record, both on the small side of perfectly normal.

Hemingway pulled on his pants, then made coffee and brought me a steaming mug of it. We sat on chairs beside the pool and watched the sun begin to rise. "I'm going to need to start writing in about an hour," he said.

I nodded. I could hear the chauffeur, on the other side of the house, returning with the car. "I have to go, anyway. I have a god-damned baseball game to cover."

"You want to be in my shoes, don't you?"

"What do you mean?"

"You know exactly what I mean."

I did not want to give him the satisfaction. "You don't even have shoes on, Hem."

Hemingway shook his head sadly. "I have to go to work," he said. "This book could be the one. And I have to get it finished. I must. Lately I've been getting a big impending sense I might die within a year. So, Frank, you want to be in my shoes, I've got one piece of advice."

I could think of no way to keep from hearing it.

He gave me an avuncular slap on the back. "I look forward to reading your novel, Frank, and I'm sure it's fine work. But you're a good baseball writer. I have ex-wives from St. Louis, and I see your columns sometimes. You're good. Problem is, you're the kind of man who only wants what doesn't come easily."

"That's true of everybody."

"The opposite's true of everybody. My advice is, go cover that goddamned baseball game. Go cover thousands more god-damned baseball games, Frank, and write about those games and the men who played them. Write true sentences about that great game."

And then we rose and shook hands, and I caught the chauffeur before he went to bed, and Hemingway trudged to his study to go write more of that book he thought would be his masterpiece, a novel which would grow to fifteen hundred manuscript pages but which he never quite managed to finish. A portion of that manuscript was published, twenty-five years after its author shot himself, as *The Garden of Eden*. The critics, alas, were not kind.

The Long Home Run

ROBERTO ORTIZ

> [*Ed.: In 1971, long before I began to work on this book, I sold a freelance piece on "the militant black in baseball," which necessitated a trip to spring training. While in Miami, I looked up Cuban home-run legend Roberto Ortiz, gentle giant (6'4", 200 pounds, huge for that era) of los Diablos Rojos de México. And a good thing I did. He was killed in a hit-and-run accident seven months later. We sat for hours in the back yard of Ortiz's small house abutting a shunt of the Intercoastal Waterway, sifting through a box of memorabilia and drinking Coca-Cola. We talked about 1946, and much else.*
>
> *Interview conducted in Spanish; translation by the author.*]

At the urging of my baby brother Oliverio, I declined a generous offer from Mr. Jorge Pasquel to return for another season in the Mexican League and agreed to rejoin the Senators of Washington for the 1946 season. I did this against my better judgment. I had been signed to the Senators in 1941 by Joe Cambria, and my experiences in America had not been agreeable.

It speaks volumes about those times that the only man signing Latin players to come to the U.S. was one who did not bother to learn Spanish. Yet Americans expected you to speak perfect English; otherwise they thought you were an imbecile.

About Joe Cambria I have mixed feelings. On one side, he was the only man giving Cubans a chance to play in the major leagues. On the other, he exploited us. He drove around Cuba in a limousine, dressed in a white linen suit and smoking big cigars. He would hire a lackey as a translator. He signed dozens of Cubans per year to fill up minor-league rosters. It was not a just competition. We had to be twice as good as an American to get to play. Even if Fidel Castro *had* signed the Senators contract that Cambria once offered, he would not have prospered in American baseball. (Actually, it's probable he wouldn't have prospered even under ideal circumstances. I played against Fidel. He was a knuckleballer who did not throw hard enough to break a window.)

In 1941, my first season in America, I was twenty-five years old and established as a pitcher and outfielder in the Cuban League. Cambria brought me to the training camp of the Senators in Orlando. He introduced me to the manager, Bucky Harris. I didn't understand what they were saying, although I did hear the names "Walter Johnson" and "Jimmie Foxx," and I learned later that Cambria had compared me to those two immortals. I was a scared young man trying to make a good impression, and I stood there, smiling as they talked gibberish. They were both trying to ask me a question. Harris was pretending to swing a bat and Cambria was pretending to pitch. I shrugged; what were these crazy Americans trying to ask? Then they became more crazy, as Cambria started asking the same question again and again, each time louder than the last. At the time I thought they were furious at me. Americans believe you will magically understand English if they shout it in your face.

Luckily, Alejandro Carrasquel, that cunning Venezuelan, came into the locker room. He translated for them. They wanted to know if I was a pitcher or an outfielder. I understood the question, but again I shrugged, because in Cuba I had always played both positions. This made Bucky Harris even angrier.

What an aversion that man had for me! He made me ride the bench, even though I hit .329 in what action I saw. I was not called upon to pitch. And for the first time in my career, I did not hit with power. This I attribute to the trouble I had adjusting to life in America. The tasteless food. The loneliness. How the Americans shunned us! We stayed at separate hotels from them. One day at breakfast, Carrasquel translated an article from *The Washington Post* in which Bucky Harris said of the Cubans, "They're trash. They're doing no good and they aren't in place here. If I have to put up with incompetents, they better at least speak English." If you want to see incompetence, examine the record of Bucky Harris as a manager! Carrasquel considered killing him, many times. But I was different. As much as my pride was wounded by that man, I kept it to myself. Unlike many Latins, I do not show much emotion, on the field or off.

That winter I returned to Cuba, where I had another good season, and I reported to spring training in 1942 determined to prove Bucky Harris wrong about me and all the Cubans. But I did not get the chance. I was exiled to Albany, New York, in the minor leagues. Joe Cambria was part owner of that team, and he supported me. He insisted that I get called up to Washington, but when I did I was given no chance to play.

Harris was fired at the end of the season, and Ossie Bluege took over. He was better to the Latin players. He made Carrasquel the official team translator, and gave Roberto Estalella the third-base job. I got injured in spring training and spent the whole year in Albany, but in 1944 I was the starting center fielder for the Senators. Only because of the war did they give Cubans a chance to play. It was good to play in the major leagues, but by then I was so disgusted with life in America that I found the achievement of my goal to be something I no longer cared about.

What bothered me most about the U.S. was the racism. Sportswriters cut us to ribbons for not speaking English, spelling the words wrong so our accents were exaggerated, making us sound like stupid children. One writer made fun of Carrasquel, who was the first Venezuelan in the major leagues, for claiming that not only were there other Venezuelans capable of playing in the U.S. but also that one of them was his brother-in-law, who would have signed with the Senators but couldn't bear to be so far away from his family. All that was true, by the way. But the reporter made very bad-taste jokes about this man having a "bevy of barefoot bambinos." Then Alejandro said that his little nephew—the brother-in-law's kid, who was ten years old at the time—might end up being better than anybody. The reporter had a big laugh about that. Well, the joke's on him. The nephew turned out to be Luis Aparicio, Jr., one of the greatest shortstops of all time!

Carrasquel pulled many jokes on the Americans. When he joined the Senators in 1939, he was thirty-three, but he told them he was twenty-seven and they believed him. But here is the best joke of all: He was a Negro! He was a Negro, and he pitched regularly in the major leagues eight years before the arrival of Jackie Robinson. It's true! I met Carrasquel's father once, and he was as brown as my shoe here. Alejandro was lighter, but still dark enough that when he first met Joe Cambria he gave his name as "Alex Alexandra," so no one would connect him with his Negro family.

It is said a major-league scout was ready to offer a contract to my boyhood idol Cristóbal Torriente, the Baby Ruth of Cuba, until Torriente removed his cap to reveal kinky hair. Imagine! Torriente was a haircut away from being a major-league star. I began to feel like a traitor to my country, accepting American money just because I had light skin, while great Cuban Negroes like Martín Dihigo, Silvio García, Ramón Bragaña, and Claro Duany were shunned. In frustration, I left the Senators in 1945 and came to play for Mexico City.

Baseball was fun again. I married Elena, my tall, beautiful blond sweetheart. I won the home-run crown with twenty-six in a season of but ninety games. Only Josh Gibson ever hit more. The fans cheered me and the press treated me with dignity. And my team: What a congenial group! Terrific American Negroes like Burnis Wright, Raymond Dandridge, and that other one, the wild pitcher, the one they called Fireball. Also Tomás de la Cruz, a Cuban, who was our best pitcher. He'd been with the Reds of Cincinnati the year before. He had a good year for a team with bad pitching, yet they released him. Do you know why? They found out that he had a Negro grandmother! It's true!

That winter, I again played in Cuba, but I could feel the winds of change blowing. For one thing, my friend Silvio García told me he was interviewed by Mr. Rickey of the Brooklyn Dodgers, who was considering signing a Negro to play in the major leagues. Mr. Rickey asked how García would act if a white man slapped him.

"I would kill him," Silvio said.

What a question! I played four years in America and never once saw anyone get slapped. Of course that was the end of Silvio's chances.

Another precursor of change came in the form of Bernardo Pasquel, the oldest of the five brothers, who was encamped in the Sevilla-Biltmore Hotel, in a luxurious suite where any player was welcome to stop by. For all Jorge's charm, charisma, and tempestuousness, it was in actuality the quiet and bald Bernardo who ran the family business.

Bernardo was indeed there to sign ballplayers for the Mexican League, but for the record, let me dispel one of the myths of the 1946 season. The Pasquels did not start out with any intention whatsoever of "raiding" the major leagues. I remember Bernardo explaining it to me like this: "Roberto," he said, "almost fifty of your countrymen played in the major leagues during the war, but now that the war is over?" He shrugged. He did not have to finish the sentence. We would be consigned to the minor leagues. The Pasquels were doing us a favor, matching the money we would be making in the U.S.—*if* we remained in the major leagues, which was doubtful—while also giving us a chance to play ball in a Spanish-speaking country.

Elena and I spent many happy hours with Bernardo, partaking of his hospitality and telling others, especially those who had not played in Mexico before, about how much we had enjoyed our stay there. Napoleón Reyes, Adrián Zabala, René Monteagudo, and my teammate from the Senators Tarzán Estalella all signed up. Also present was the veteran pitcher, Lázaro Salazar, who recruited many other Negro ballplayers and who was made manager of the Monterrey club. Bernardo's big coup, in my opinion, was signing Cuban legend Adolfo Luque, who had been the first great Latin star in the major leagues and was then pitching coach of the Giants of New York—the first Latin pitching coach. Luque was given a share of the Puebla team and made its manager. Reyes and Zabala, who had also been with the Giants, both signed up just to remain with great and fiery Luque.

I spent all winter intending to join them. Elena very much wished to return that summer to Mexico. We believed we had washed our hands forever of the strange, violent United States.

But I was persuaded to return there by my impetuous baby brother Oliverio, who had been signed to an American contract by guess who? That's right, Joe Cambria, who was also trying to get me to re-sign. Oliverio was my opposite: left-handed, a drinker, very hotheaded, very political, and very small also. He was not much of a player, I'm sorry to say: a wild curveballer who did not throw hard. He signed with Cambria on an impulse, without asking me, then wept and begged—at the dinner table of our mother and father!—that I not abandon him to the unknown fates of America. It was a display that engendered disgust from the fair Elena, who thought Oliverio a childish bum. But the plea had come before my parents; what could I do? I reached an uneasy accord with Elena, then apologized to Bernardo Pasquel. Mr. Pasquel was quite understanding about a man upholding his family obligations.

Oliverio and I traveled to training camp in Orlando along with Carrasquel, who had also been in Cuba that winter. When we arrived, Alejandro could not find his room and locker assignments. He thought it was but an oversight. But he learned from the clubhouse boy that he had been released from the team. We were all shocked. Alejandro was among their best pitchers in '45 [*Ed.: 7–5 with a 2.71 ERA in 123 innings*]. You do not simply release a man like that. Of course it's clear to me now that it was done for reasons of race.

Carrasquel went on a rampage in the dressing room, kicking lockers, throwing trash cans, socks, tape, and uniforms, getting out of there before the police came. Oliverio and I and a few other players just watched in disbelief, and after Alejandro was gone Oliverio still kept staring off into space. Forget it, I told him. That's baseball.

The White Sox of Chicago put in a claim for Alejandro, but he signed with the Pasquels instead. Amazing, isn't it, that Carrasquel, who was released, would be banned from organized baseball along with the rest of us?

Well, camp started up and things got down to business for a week or two. Oliverio seemed destined for the minor leagues, but I had hit three home runs in games and began to wonder if I might get fair treatment after all. Although quite a few good players had defected to Mexico, nobody seemed particularly alarmed.

No, I don't even remember when Gardella jumped. In our camp, it made no impression. What infuriated the magnates of the major leagues was when Luis Olmo jumped from the Dodgers of Brooklyn.

What a great player he was! The best of anyone who jumped, including the white stars like Max Lanier and Arnold "Mickey" Owen, who came later. Olmo was the first great Puerto Rican in the major leagues, a swift outfielder who had batted in more than 100 runs the year before. Only twenty-six years old at the time. Poised to become an immortal. And it was the loss of Luis Olmo from the major leagues which prompted the commissioner of baseball, Happy Chandler, to ban anyone who played in Mexico from ever again playing in the major leagues. A lifetime ban.

According to the papers (which by then I could read), Olmo made only $6,000 for that big year he had in '45, and Brooklyn was only offering a $500 raise. Luis had asked for $10,000. Even that would have left him underpaid. Into this controversy came Mr. Jorge Pasquel, who offered Luis $20,000. Later Luis told me he would have gladly stayed in Brooklyn for $10,000, but Mr. Rickey wouldn't budge one dollar over $6,500. In those times, you see, you had nothing to bargain with. That is, until the Pasquels came along.

I never played baseball for the money, though. I played baseball for the love of the game, the cheers of the crowd, the glory of the long home run. And for the women, although by that time I had my fair Elena. It wasn't money that made me jump camp from the Senators. It was that insensitive imperialist Calvin Griffith, the owner of the team, and his big mouth.

The Senators owned a monopoly on Cuban ballplayers for years, signing us but then never treating us like equals. Suddenly, a few Cubans go play in Mexico, and he worked out a back-room deal with the Cuban Winter League, getting them to go along with that five-year ban. In the process, he said many hurtful things about Cubans. I cannot remember just what. I am a man who tries to forget insults.

I am slow to anger, but when a rich white American who won't give equal chances to anyone other than other white Americans manages to turn one Latin American country against another, to turn brother against brother . . . Well, that was all I could take.

That night I told Oliverio I was leaving and that I would be calling Mr. Jorge Pasquel to make arrangements. Did he want to accompany me?

He said no.

The stubbornness of youth! This marked the advent of our estrangement. We would reconcile, of course, several times, but looking back, I see that the seeds of our woes were sown that night. He is now in Cuba and I am now in Florida and I am forced to accept that we might never see each other again.

I said goodbye to him outside the rear door of our hotel. There was a full moon, but it was otherwise long after dark. Oliverio told me he did not understand how I could bear being banned from the major leagues. I embraced him, and told him it was no loss to be excluded from a place you do not wish to be.

Oliverio spent his season in the bowels of the American minor leagues. I embarked on one of the great adventures in baseball history.

Whenever We Played
the Blues

THEOLIC "FIREBALL" SMITH

How'd we know Jackie Robinson would be the one? The Pasquels made him a six-grand offer, same day they signed Luis Olmo, and he turned 'em down. That spilled the beans right there.

Six thousand was amazing money for a Negro ballplayer. I made three hundred a month, and that was considered good. Burnis made the same. Highest-paid on the Reds was Dandridge at three-fifty. Other than Satchel, who got a share of the gate and made about $40,000, no Negro ballplayer ever made more than six. And Jackie, shit, he couldn't crack the Monarchs' lineup until Bonnie Serrell left for Mexico. Jackie wouldn't turn down no six thousand to play minor-league ball, or to play for some new Negro League. College boy like Jackie, only way he'd turn down so many dead presidents would be if he was gonna be the one.

Luis Olmo himself told me about the offer to Jackie, the day he arrived at our big training camp in Mexico City. Would have been the end of February. The Pasquels had all the teams train together for two weeks there at El Parque Delta, not to save money but for publicity. Every day, we had five thousand screaming Mexicans watchin us. Even cheered us bendin over to touch our toes.

What a circus: two hundred men sweatin our asses off in those flannel uniforms, runnin in circles and waitin our turn to hit. Wild part was the new guys. First day of camp we're told to go stand in the field, and out comes Jorge Pasquel with a megaphone, dressed in one of his wide-shouldered suits, waving to the crowd. He sashays to home plate and introduces his pal Alemán, who's runnin for president. Big cheers. "Just as Licenciado Alemán will make Mexico a major-league country," Pasquel says in Spanish, "so will my brothers and I create a new major league!"

Man, the crowd goes berserk.

When the noise dies down some, Pasquel introduces four guys he's signed up. First is Booker T. McDaniel of the Monarchs. Then Jesse Williams, Kansas City's All-Star shortstop.

Dandridge starts frownin. Somethin's eatin him.

Burnis says, "Looks like K.C.'s gonna have a down year."

Bonnie Serrell smiles. "They want to keep us, they can pay us better." The Monarchs didn't pay so bad, but everybody resented how damn much more money Satchel made.

Pasquel milks the moment, then brings out Martín Dihigo. Lord, you should have heard 'em. Dihigo strolls out in street clothes, with that jangly walk he had, wavin and smilin. Pasquel says Dihigo's going to manage the new Torreón club, and pitch and play outfield for it, too.

"Man's forty years old," Dandridge says. "What are we, man?"

"Younger," I says.

"Shit, that's not what I mean. When do *we* get introduced?"

I didn't say nothin. Dihigo deserved respect, he was an all-time great. Course, so was Ray. Ray's mood didn't get no better when Pasquel introduces that roly-poly Cuban hothead Dolf Luque, like he's the best that got saved for last. Loudest applause of all. Luque was near sixty, just down there to manage, but he was the first Latin fella to be a star in the U.S., and that counted for a lot with those people. Same as it'd be years later with black folks and Jackie.

Pasquel ends his little dog-and-pony show by showin who's the dogs and who's the ponies. He points to us behind him. "Y finalmente, el resto de los hombres de la Liga Mexicana de Béisbol! Una liga grande! Una liga mayor!"

All of us together don't get the hand Dihigo, Luque, or even Alemán got. "Hey, Dandy," I says. "You got your introduction." As you might guess, that don't put him in no better mood.

◈

In the U.S., the only ones who called Burnis "Burnis" were his mama, his wife Peggy and me. Everyone else called him "Wild Bill." But in Mexico they all called him "Burnis" because "Wild Bill" made no sense and "Wright" is unpronounceable to a Mexican. Shoot, they had trouble with "Smith."

Like Dihigo, Burnis been gone from Mexico a year. Anyone had cause to be mad over those introductions, it was Burnis. He spent 1945 with the Baltimore Elite Giants, made the All-Star team, but he and Peggy, they'd been in Mexico five years, and they had a bad time with America. That fall, way before the big money started gettin tossed around, the Wrights signed back up with Pasquel and used a nest egg they'd built up to buy a little house near Chapultepec Park. Nice part of Mexico City: doctors, lawyers, what-have-you, and, again, nobody paid a mind to what color you were. "All I miss about America," Peggy would say, "is family, old friends, and jazz music." In the States, the Duke, the Count, Hampton, Armstrong, everyone, they came to our games, and we'd go see them at night. We were all black folks in the entertainment business. Peggy, she loved that Lena Horne. She was fair like Lena, and she had a picture on their mantel there in Mexico, a framed picture of her, Burnis, and Lena at a club in Kansas City. Lena signed it "Two wrongs don't make a right, but two Wrights make for a lovely evening."

Burnis and Peggy invited me to stay in a back room they wasn't usin, and after years of lonely hotels and boarding houses, I jumped at the offer. Peggy was a fine cook and the Wrights had the best collection of jazz records in all Mexico. Also, they kept their bar real well stocked.

◈

The players kept comin and Dandy kept simmerin. Sometimes it was a different Pasquel with the megaphone, and Alemán was only there if Jorge was, but other than that it was the same drill. Personally, I could accept the red carpet for men like McDaniel and Dihigo, but some of them others? One day Bernardo Pasquel introduces Bob Estalella and Nap Reyes; well, those boys been in the big leagues, I can maybe see why they get the treatment. But it don't sit well with Ray. Then comes Alex Carrasquel, who played for the Senators. Carrasquel was passing and we knew it. Some said, Good for him, pullin the wool over on white folks. Anybody'd do it if he could. But an American fair-skinned black would've never got away with it. You had to be a foreigner to get the benefit of the doubt. People said the same of Tommy de la Cruz, who pitched for us, but he was white, I think. Look, Alex rubbed me wrong, I'll leave it at that.

Couple days later, Alfonso Pasquel, the baby brother, introduces two Canadians from out of the Brooklyn system, Gladu and Roy. I knew 'em from Cuba; they played for Cienfuegos, for Luque, which is why they got signed.

Bushers. Burnis nudged Ray. "Wonder how much those boys gonna make?"

Ray gave Burnis a look that'd peel paint.

"I'll ask 'em," Burnis said. And he did. But they didn't speak English, just French. Later, we found out they weren't making as much as we feared. They were just men squeezed out back home, lookin for work. But that wasn't how we saw it at first.

The next day out walked Ray Brown and Ed Stone, stars in their day, both now about a hundred years old. Brown was Homestead's best pitcher in the early 1940s, and Ed played with Dandy's in Newark. Right off, Ray asked about money. "Three-fifty a month," Brown said.

"We asked Jorge Pasquel how much *you* made, Ray," Ed said. "And asked for the same."

We laughed, though I couldn't help but think we deserved more money than these old-timers. And then we were limbering up, alongside the third-base dugout, and Ed Stone dropped the bomb. "Plus our signing bonuses," he said.

Dandy froze. "How much was that?"

"Two G's." Stone looked over at Brown. "How 'bout you?"

Dandy pounded a ball in his glove.

"Thirty-five hundred, cash," Brown said. "Jorge Pasquel gave it to me in a little brown bag, like you pack a lunch in."

I thought Ray might have a heart attack. He stood there thinkin about those bonuses, then hauled off and screamed and threw that ball all the way over the roof of the ballpark.

Crowd goes wild. Thought it was part of the show.

Couple days later came Danny Gardella. Ten grand for that crazy little motherfucker! He gets the royal intro, with Jorge and Alemán and Jorge's movie-star gal. Nothin against Gardella. Boy would have been at home in the Negro Leagues, where we played tough, acted the fool at times, and *always* put on a good show. His first day he blasted five home runs in practice, did a lap of the field walkin on his hands, and sang some damn opera through Jorge's megaphone. Guarantee you the Pasquels didn't know what they'd gotten themselves into with Dan Gardella.

Right after our workout, me, Burnis, and Ray went to see Jorge Pasquel at the family offices on Insurgentes. We'd played in Mexico for years and never until then had any complaint about our treatment. But the only Pasquel there was Gerardo. Kid about twenty-five, already bald. Turned out Jorge's on his way back to the U.S., with a big surprise scheduled for tomorrow.

That night, we got drunk as skunks and bad-mouthed the bejesus out of the Pasquels. I can't recall the specifics, other than the drunk-as-skunks part—recall, in fact, sayin, "We drunk as skunks, fellas." After a long night, Burnis and Ray, they was family men and went home to their families, but I had two women that night, two at once. Art students, both named Inés, one short and one tall. In Mexico, good-lookin black men can get girls as easy as rich men get friends. I needed an escape from baseball, and, brother, I got one.

The big surprise? Luis Olmo, who got the full treatment, plus a mariachi band and confetti rainin down from the upper deck. Bigger surprise was his $10,000 salary. Biggest was that offer to Jackie. Olmo stood right in the smelly Delta Park clubhouse and swore upon the honor of his Catholic mother that he saw the Pasquels make it, with his own sleepy-lidded eyes.

And at that point, money took a back seat, at least for me. *Why?* Frank, I'll clue you in on something. I thought it could have been me. Even after Jackie signed with Brooklyn, I thought I had a chance. I wasn't the only one; you couldn't go out there year after year and play like we did *without* thinkin that. We didn't talk about it, but we thought it all the time. We'd play in big-league parks sometimes, with their full cakes of Lifebuoy soap and hot water in the showers comin out with good pressure, and big thirsty clean white towels, and a box of new sanitary socks, which the big-leaguers wore once and threw away, and a fresh coat of paint on everything, and by God, any man who says he didn't think about bein the first is a liar.

I remember Burnis and Ray pumpin Luis for details and me just walkin away, standin alone in the open doorway of that dark, stinky locker room, dressed in just a towel, and lookin out across that empty Mexican ballpark at the big Sambo-face billboard on the center-field fence—it was an advertisement for Chiclets, with a tiny hole in the mouth and a sign sayin that any batter who hits a ball through it wins five hundred pesos—and thinkin, *Damn, Theolic, it ain't gonna be you, kid.*

We didn't catch Jorge Pasquel that day either, and that night, over a steak dinner at Ray and Henrietta Dandridge's apartment, with their two little babies squawkin, Burnis and Ray and me all faced up to what that offer to Jackie meant.

Burnis was the only one that had played against Jackie, and he took it better than anybody. "Jackie's fast." Burnis shrugged. He was good at makin peace with what he ain't gonna change. "He's smart. Got a good glove, ought to be a solid everyday player in the big leagues."

"But no star," I says. I couldn't get past it. From where I sat, he was a man who hadn't paid his dues.

Peggy Wright took up for Jackie, too. "He's what they were lookin for, Theo. He's got a college degree from out in California, where whites and Negroes play together from the time they're kids. Plus, Jackie's a war veteran." Like that's supposed to make us feel better, none of us bein veterans ourselves. "Well," she says. "He's what they were looking for, is all I'm saying."

"It's over," I said. "Men our age"—we were all thirty-two— "never gonna get through that gate. Only men Jackie's age and younger."

"In case you ain't noticed, Theo, we got it pretty good," Burnis says, wavin his arm at that nice apartment the Dandridges had. "Compared to folks back home." Henrietta and Ray even had a maid. Back home, closest we got to havin maids was bein maids. So Burnis was right in a way. You knew he was one of the black ballplayers who lived out the rest of his life down in Mexico, right? Sometimes I think he made up his mind that night to do just that.

"*Let* Jackie be the first," Ray says. "He won't be the last. We'll all get there." He raised his beer bottle to toast our bright futures. I raised mine, too. We believed.

Ray, of course, bein Ray, was still stuck on money matters, though he'd calmed down some, the way a man will when he's mad in a serious way. Me, I just blow and let the chips fall, but Ray, in spite of that ball he whipped out of Delta Park, wasn't generally one for outbursts.

"You know, the Pasquels have always been square with me," he says. "The way I see it, it's just a matter of sittin down with Jorge Pasquel and ironin things out."

Burnis agreed, but he was in an agreeable mood. I had to get my mind off things, so I finished my beer and called up the Tall Inés. She took me to a party down on the Coyoacán, at the blue house of those Communist painters, Rivera and Kahlo. Great painters. Jesus, you think *ballplayers* drink and sleep around, you should see artists.

Diego Rivera looked like Gomez Addams, you know, from the Addams Family? Actually made passes at girls while his wife was right there in the room. He got drunker and drunker on that milky what-you-call pulque, that crazy cactus liquor, and so did we all. Once all the tongues got loose, those Mexicans started talking history and politics. Like how Atlantis used to connect Mexico with the Euphrates. Did you know that? A lot got said about their revolution, about Villa and Zapata and them, and how America had made a bad situation worse. America, they called it "the colossus to the North." And that Mexican War back in the 1840s, which we spent maybe a day on back at Sumner High in St. Louis, they talked about it like it ended that morning. I didn't like them bad-mouthin America, despite the fact of how I felt. You can chide your own kids but just let the neighbor start, right? But I kept my mouth shut. I was a guest.

What stuck with me from that night—other than the love me and the Tall Inés made later on—was that weird speech Diego Rivera made.

Rivera, he climbed up on an iron patio chair and hollered for everyone's attention. When he got it he thanked us for comin and assured us that more beer was on the way. Then he just up and launched into a speech. "What is a Mexican," he said, all puffed up like he's used to bein listened to, "but a compromise between the great cultures of the Aztecs, the Mayas, and the Toltecs and that of the Spanish oppressors?"

That got him a big hand, right out of the chute. I'd been about to laugh, but the crowd was with him, and I kept still. Rivera was a talker, rhythms like Pop used when he read from the Gospel at Holy Redeemer Baptist. The party guests were Rivera's congregation. Except Frida, his wife. He got rolling, she went to bed. That was what I wanted to do, too, with the Tall Inés. But Rivera won me over, and—against my will and inclination, believe me—I found myself hangin on every word.

"The Mexican," Rivera finished up, "is trapped by a past that belongs to everyone and no one, least of all himself. A past of unhappy compromise. A past where he contents himself with symbolic victories in actual wars, a present where he believes nothing can change, and a future he hasn't bothered to imagine."

Hoots, shouts, and another big, big hand. Diego Rivera got helped down off the patio chair, and the beer plus also more tequila and pulque arrived. I grabbed two beers and a bottle each of the others and me and the Tall Inés made our exit.

Later, in her apartment, I sat up the rest of the night, there in the flickering glow of these wild religious candles she painted for her daddy to sell in the market, lettin a half-empty beer grow warm against my hip and thinkin about what Rivera said about Mexico, about how you could say that same thing about the American Negro. In spite of the beer and pulque I'd drunk and the fantastic love I'd had, I never got a wink of sleep. Kept staring at pictures of saints and Jesus on those candles. Long night, brother.

Next day, the other clubs shipped out to the four corners of Mexico, and all it was in Delta Park was the Mexico City Red Devils and the Veracruz Blues. I get there hungover and late, glad to miss whatever new meat they was throwin out, and who's in the outfield givin the fans a show but big, gentle Roberto Ortiz. He'd been with us the year before, and personally I was glad to see him back. That fella could pound the baseball. Good arm, too, but not always real accurate.

Ernesto Carmona, our manager, is standin behind first base, bangin fungoes to Ortiz in right field, and Roberto's grabbin 'em and gunnin the ball into Sunset Colás, who used to be with the New York Cubans. Strike after strike he's throwin, and that Mexican crowd goes bananas.

This is too much for Danny Gardella. He couldn't stand it when someone else had the stage. He runs out, elbows Ortiz aside, circles around under the next fungo like a man usin sea legs, then dives to make the catch. Gardella made everything he did look hard, but the fans loved it. Gardella's throw didn't remind nobody of Roberto Ortiz, but he makes a big grunt and his hat falls off, which makes him look impressive to them Mexicans.

Next up comes Luis Olmo. By now, other players have stopped to watch. Carmona bangs out a long, long fly ball, and it's clear he's messed up and the ball's gonna carry out of the park. Mexico City's two miles above sea level, and after a while you know how the ball's gonna carry. Olmo's new to Mexico, though, and he gets a late jump. But, Lord, then he's on his horse, breakin for the fence, runnin all out but lookin silky-smooth. Just as the ball is leavin the ballpark, Luis Olmo leaps and soars up and over that seven-foot fence. Next thing we see is just his glove, which he's holdin up over the top of the fence with the ball in it.

Crowd like to tear that rickety wood park *down*!

That's too much for me. I sprint out there for my turn. Carmona gives me a stare, mad 'cause I'm late, then he hits me a screamin line drive, tryin to show me up, but I charge in, spear the ball on a dead run in short right, and without breakin stride I fire a fastball right at Carmona's head, and he drops to the ground like a man in a gunfight and the ball whistles right in there to Sunset Colás, who catches it and then takes off his glove and shakes his hand like it stung so bad. Playin to the crowd, you know, and they eat it up.

Roberto Ortiz, that gentle soul, he finds himself standin there wonderin what he started. Carmona dusts himself off and, all pissed off, takes a big whack at the ball and misses it. Brother, the laughter rings out all round that ballpark. Next swing he connects and sends a towering fly to far right. Ortiz settles under it, takes it with his back to the wall, sets, throws, and heaves this wild thunderbolt in the general direction of Sunset Colás. Ball keeps risin, risin, up the third-base line and over Sunset's head, into the stands.

Who do you think spears that baseball, bare-handed and clean, but Jorge Pasquel, there in his private box! He pulls Alemán to his feet and both them fancy scoundrels stand there grinnin, wavin to the faithful, takin credit for everything.

Opening day, 1946. March something. It was a Saturday morning. Weekend games began at eleven, cause of the heat and so as to allow folks to catch the charreadas and bullfights later in the day.

I was supposed to start—it was even in the papers, me for the Reds, Bragaña for the Blues. By rights I should have, I was staff ace. But after that stunt where I about took his head off, I was in Carmona's doghouse. He'd founded the Mexican League back in the thirties, but he sold out to Jorge Pasquel, and I always got the feeling Carmona didn't come out of the deal with much, and that's what made him a sorehead.

Burnis and me took a cab to Delta Park. Even though we was hours early, the crowd was so thick our driver couldn't get no closer than that cemetery beyond left field, beyond that hill where the fans had to go to pee. Burnis and me are in uniform, so we wouldn't have to dress in that dark clubhouse, and when we get out of the cab, folks mob us. Not in a bad way. They just shook our hands and patted our backs and wished us muy buena suerte. Then one of Jorge Pasquel's soldiers—he had his own militia— one of them guys came ridin up on horseback and parted the way through the crowd so we could pass. God, those people were lovely to us.

Wasn't till then I learned I wasn't startin. Carmona sat in the dugout smilin, glad as hell to tell me he picked Tuza Ramírez instead. "Esta es la temporada de oro en México," he says, "y mi lanzador será una pelotero mexicano."

Those Mexicans can be a pridefully patriotic bunch. Fine, I say. I'll be in the outfield.

"No," he says. "Mis jardineros serán Olmo en el centro, Ortiz en la derecha, y Burnis en la izquierda."

Good outfield, I grant you, but I figure my bat ought to be in the lineup somehow. So I ask, "¿Y en la primera base?"

"Chorejas."

Jesus. Chorejas Bravo played in the league for years, never hit better than .220. But one thing I learned from playin all those years for Carmona, it's never dig in your heels against a Mexican. "Y mañana, ¿quién será el lanzador? ¿Yo?"

"Acaso." Maybe. Which means yes, long as Theolic's a good boy and takes his medicine.

Once I thought about it, I was just as happy to start the second game, since Ramón Bragaña's the manager of the Blues and he's gonna start himself in game one. Tough pitcher, Bragaña, remember that diamond he had for a front tooth? Man won thirty games in '43, in a ninety-game season! Also, I was glad for the chance to square off against Carrasquel in game two.

Delta Park sat fifteen thousand—biggest in Mexico—but there was that many there before we was done takin infield. They packed folks in the aisles, then they opened up gates onto the field. Pasquel's militia filled up foul territory with people and roped 'em off. The militiamen stood there the whole game holdin ropes. Come game time, there were thirty-thousand baseball-crazy Mexicans stuffed in that ballpark, plus a few thousand more up on the pee hill.

Of course, this was the grand moment for Jorge Pasquel. After we finished b.p., the players and coaches were ordered into the dugout. There was a terrible emptiness out on the field, for the longest time. The crowd got louder, and all we had to look at was each other and that grassy diamond, shiny and perfect under the Mexican sun. More inviting than a cool lake.

Then, pow, Jorge Pasquel steps out that secret door he'd had built behind home plate and strides to the mound. As he waves to the crowd, two brass bands set up, one on top of each dugout. And then out of the secret passageway comes the other Pasquels: Bernardo, Mario, Gerardo, and Alfonso. Then all the players are motioned out, and we line up behind the Pasquels. The yells and screams could make you deaf.

Jorge Pasquel asks Sunset Colás for his catcher's mitt.

Then that door behind home opens one last time, and from behind it comes none other than Manuel Avila Camacho, the president of Mexico. He gets to the mound, which is the cue for them brass bands to break into the Mexican national anthem.

We all turn to face the flag. Even *I* got my heart in my throat, mumblin words I don't know for somebody else's national anthem.

The song finishes and there's Jorge Pasquel, squatted down behind home plate. Beside him, Chile Gómez, second baseman for the Blues, is holdin on to the man's suit coat. The long gold chain to Jorge's pocket watch like to drag in the dirt.

Little Alfonso Pasquel has the megaphone, and he's squawkin that for the first time in the history of Mexico the president will be throwin out the first ball of the baseball season. Like anyone but us can hear him, the noise is so great.

Avila Camacho's a broad, proud-lookin little guy, dressed in the darkest suit. It's clear as he's gettin ready that he ain't played much baseball. He steps to the mound and manges to lob the ball halfway to Jorge.

On top of the dugouts, the men in those brass bands each pull out a megaphone, all with VERACRUZ painted across the sides, and all together, they holler, "Pla-a-a-a-ay bo-o-o-o-o-ll!"

And we did.

We batted first even though we were the Mexico City team. It was the Pasquels' league, the Pasquels' park. Whenever we played the Blues, the Pasquels' team, we were visitors in our own yard.

Ramón Bragaña was unhittable at first—set down Olmo, Colás, and Dandridge, strikeout, strikeout, strikeout.

Bottom of the first, Tuza Ramírez gave up two walks and a three-run shot to Danny Gardella, and it was pretty much over. By the time Carmona pulled Ramírez in the fifth, we were down 8–0, and a couple late homers by Olmo and Ortiz didn't change nothin. We lost 12–5.

After the game, a bunch of us showered up in that dark locker room and headed off to a charreada. That's a Mexican rodeo, which is where the idea for American rodeos came from. No offense, Frank, but name me one thing American white men contributed to world culture that didn't come from somewhere else, usually ripped off from people darker than them. Baseball? So folks say. Me, I'm skeptical.

We got to the charreada and Dandy, who was oh-for-four but had some amazing plays in the field, said he'd talked to Jorge Pasquel before the game, in his private box behind the Blues dugout. "Told him, 'Look, you're payin these new players more money than you're payin us.' "

Down in the ring, three sombrero-wearin charros on horseback chased an unbroken pony.

"What'd he say?" I asked, wavin to the man carryin a big tin bucket full of ice and beer, gonna buy a round for the fellas.

"He looked offended," Ray said. "You know how he gets. Then he pointed at the president and said that today wasn't the time, that I ought to come talk tomorrow."

The charros twirled their lariats in long arcs, and finally they roped that pony. The crowd loved it.

"What you gonna do," I asked.

Ray shrugged. "Go back tomorrow, I guess."

"Hey, Ray!" shouted Wild Bill Wright. "You more bowlegged than these charros!"

"Might be a better selling point," I said to Ray, "if you go better than oh-for-four the day you go talk money with Jorge."

Course, Ray didn't need no incentive to have a good day at the plate. But it *was* my day to pitch. Couldn't hurt none.

◈

Carrasquel and I both got through the first clean, but in the second, Dandy doubled and Ortiz hit a homer all the way to the pee hill. Then Colás walked, and I came up. Carrasquel sails the first pitch up under my chin, which I expected. I got up, dusted myself off, and roped the next pitch into left-center for a triple. Would have only been a double but Carrasquel must have cut the ball and it sailed through the air weird-like and Gardella misplayed it, bad. I stood on third and called out to Alejandro, "Nice pitch, white boy."

He gave me a look, then went back to face the music. But he had nothin at all, anyone could see it. What was strange, Bragaña started to the mound to take Carrasquel out, and then stopped, turned around, trotted over to Jorge Pasquel's box, said a couple of words, and sat down.

Never in twenty years playin ball had I seen that. And Ramón Bragaña's nobody's company man. But they left Carrasquel out there to rot. Which tickled me. Also gave me a chance to collect another single off that white nigger before Bragaña couldn't take a bit more of it and took him out, trailin 7–0.

No lead's safe when you play ball two miles above sea level, where even the laws of gravity got nobody to enforce 'em, but I did okay, and we won 10–6.

After that game we went to the bullfights. Sunday was bullfight day, and March was when the best matadors came to fight the best bulls. The Pasquels gave us tickets, seats in the shade, which cost twice as much. In spite of that small generosity, Dandridge was steamed but good at Jorge Pasquel. Ray'd had five hits, including a homer, and, like always, made a couple plays in the field that saved my ass. "What'd he say?" I asked him.

"Said he couldn't give me no more money. Said he needed it to sign up more men."

Down in the dusty ring, a fast black bull with long horns gored the horse of one of the picadors. The crowd gasped. The picador ran like hell. This bull was going to be trouble.

"More white men, you mean," I said.

Ray shook his head. "White and black both, I think."

I bought Ray a beer. "What you gonna do?"

Just then the crowd broke into applause. Out came the matador, a Spaniard named Nicanor somebody. He had on a pale blue suit with rubies sewn on it in the shape of crowns.

"I'm thinkin maybe I'll go back to Newark," Ray said.

Nicanor what's-his-face swept his red cape in circles, and the crowd fell in love with him. Mexicans love the grand gesture.

"More bullshit in you than in that bull," Burnis said. "You won't make ten cents more playin for Effa Manley than you will down here. Unless you Terris McDuffie."

We had a good laugh. Manley owned the Newark Eagles. She was a sharp businesswoman, I'll give her that. The crack about McDuffie, who used to be with the Eagles but who played for Torreón now—well, he used to do Effa Manley. Don't be shocked, Frank: Owners doin it to players for years, only not so literal.

"It's not the money," Dandy said, pullin back on a beer. "You can't bring in men who ain't proven nothin and pay 'em more than the best players you already have."

We all thought Ray had a good point there. Course, it's a point these owners nowadays in baseball ain't learned yet.

Nicanor got his bull that day. Never before or since seen a bull bleed so much.

Tommy de la Cruz starts the third game for us and guess who starts for the Blues? Carrasquel! They're bound and determined to get their money's worth out of them new guys. A lot of money's worth they got out of Alex that day! Man couldn't make it out of the first, gave up five singles and three doubles—one by me, I was playin right field, with Ortiz at first—before Bragaña took mercy and brought in Schoolboy Johnny Taylor, who if anything pitched worse. We had twenty-some hits that day—including five from Dandy, who was on fire—and we won 19–8.

In the middle of that game, I see Dandy sulkin at the end of the bench. "So," I said, in high spirits from the plasterin we gave Carrasquel, "you all packed for Newark?" I was kiddin.

Dandy looked up at me, angry and sad like a man whose dog been stolen. "You see the papers this morning?"

I hadn't.

"Says in *La Afición* that Jorge Pasquel offered Hank Greenberg a hundred thousand dollars to come down here. Said he even gave Ted Williams a blank check to come down here!"

Even if I had read that stuff, Frank, I'd've figured it was just you newspaper boys playin fast and loose. But I found out later those were true offers.

Then it was our time to take the field, and I was out there before I realized Dandy hadn't answered me, and I realized that he really might bolt the team for Newark.

After the inning, I ran up to Ray. "It's too late to change my mind, Theo," he said. "I already told Jorge. I'm gone."

Maybe you know the rest, Frank, but here's how I heard it: After the game, Ray takes a cab home, still in his uniform. Everything's packed and ready. Ray tells the cabbie to wait, runs in, showers up, gets dressed, and helps load up all their stuff and their kids and everything. He's in a hurry, 'cause despite his good relations with Pasquel, he's heard the stories.

They had their tickets for the 4 P.M. coach train to Laredo. They get all their bags and boxes stored and they're all settled in, ready to return to America. The train even starts to move. Then all of a sudden here comes this American, Bob Janis, who was one of

Pasquel's bodyguards, along with like a dozen Mexican soldiers. Not Pasquel's militia, mind, but the actual Mexican army, and they get that rollin train to stop.

Janis boards the train, the soldiers right behind him, and they come up to Ray. "Jorge Pasquel wants to see you."

"Him and me got nothin to talk about," Ray says.

"This train's goin nowhere until you talk to Mr. Pasquel."

Finally, Ray and Henrietta don't see what choice they have. Plus, the soldiers are scaring the children. So they get off the train. The soldiers see to their bags. There's a white Cadillac, motor runnin. Pasquel's chauffeur drives the Dandridges back to Jorge's offices.

Jorge is alone, sittin behind his desk in a big dark office. "What have I done," he says, "to inspire such disloyalty in one of my most beloved players?"

Ray tells Jorge to cut the shit. "You're a businessman, Mr. Pasquel," Ray says. "You've had business deals where you had to put money and fair treatment over personal loyalty."

Pasquel frowns. There's a long pause, and then he reaches a hand slowly into a desk drawer. Ray thinks *Oh, man, he's gettin a gun.* This is a guy who has the power to set the Mexican army after some underpaid ballplayer. Who'd care if he killed that same ballplayer?

But instead, Jorge Pasquel pulls out two crystal glasses and a new bottle of the finest bourbon, cracks the seal, and pours Ray a drink. "Sit down," he says, "and share with me your demands."

They drink and haggle, haggle and drink. After a while they invite Henrietta and the kids to come in, and they announce that Ray will receive $10,000 for this season and next season he'll take over from Carmona as manager and make $12,000. Plus a four-bedroom luxury home and two full-time servants, all at the Pasquels' expense. At news of this, Henrietta faints dead away.

The next few days, the better black ballplayers got raises and bonuses. I got six grand, same as they offered Jackie.

◆

What neither Dandy nor Jorge knew was that Dandy wouldn't have been welcome with the Eagles, or with any Negro League club. Our first road trip, we're up in Monterrey, and we see Nate Moreland, who'd just jumped from the Monarchs to the Sultans.

Nate was real bitter about baseball, and he had reason. In '43 he got a contract with the Los Angeles Stars, a white Triple A club, and then they reneged. Then in '45 he and Jackie had a tryout with the Chicago White Sox, and nothin came of it. Then Jackie gets signed to the Dodgers. But the thing that made Nate wash his hands of American baseball came when the white big leagues got the Negro Leagues to go along with banning everybody who jumped to the "outlaw" Mexican League.

"Hell with 'em," Nate said. "I'm tired of sayin how high when they say jump. I'll control my own damn jumpin."

I was in shock. I was banned from my own country. I don't care what gripes you have against your country, it's still yours, and it's still a blow to be barred from makin a living there.

I spit on all them white owners' graves. I *piss* on their graves. Brooklyn steals Jackie Robinson from the Monarchs, and it's nothin. I'd been playin in Mexico for years, where I don't have to be no particular color, where all I gotta do is play good ball. Where we don't have to play but five games a week, not like the Negro Leagues, where you played that many league games plus just as many exhibitions on top of that. All of a sudden a few white guys come down and the shit hits, it's war between the major leagues and Mexico. From where I sat, the Negro Leagues came in on the wrong goddamned side of that war. Well, fuck 'em. And fuck you, too, Frank. Shut off your damn tape player and get the fuck out of my house.

A Working Reporter

Frances Kingston, nude and only just beginning to show, threw open the French doors to the balcony of our tenth-floor room at the Floridian Hotel. The breeze from the gulf tossed back her short brown hair. In one hand she held a cigarette. With the other she traced the new curves of her stomach and breasts. She was a married professor on Easter break, old to be pregnant, in a messy hotel room with a man who was not her husband. Our room smelled of sex and cigarettes.

"Frank," she said, "I don't think I love you."

She'd never said she did. I sat on the bed, fully clothed except for the wing tips I was putting on. I looked in the mirror. I looked like I felt. "So what is it you're saying?"

"I don't know," she said. "I don't think I love you. I don't think I love Ted either, but I don't know if I want to leave him. Not that I want you to marry me. I just like fucking you. That's good, isn't it? That's enough for now, I think."

"Yes." I was content. "Fucking is good."

"Depends," she said absently, "on the fuckers in question."

She was a woman who said *fuck*. In 1946, you had to do some looking to find a woman like this. "Have you told Ted?"

"That I don't think I love you?"

"No. The other." The pregnancy.

Ted was a captain in the Air Force. He'd been stationed in the Pacific and would be home next month.

"No," she said.

"We're bad people, Frances. We belong together. Why don't we fix Harriet up with Ted?" I was like a kid with too many prom dates, except that I was thirty-six years old, one of my dates was my wife, another was somebody else's, and the third—Diana James, the one I was increasingly tempted to bestow with a corsage—had been, in the year of my real prom, two years old. "I bet Ted and Harriet would hit it off. Then everyone would be happy."

Frances faced me. "Do you think that's funny?"

"No. I hadn't said it to be funny."

"Then why did you say it?"

I closed my eyes. Who knew why I said what I said? "I have to get to the ballpark," I said. "I have to go to work."

"Nice work if you can get it." As I got my things together, she lay on the bed, spread her legs, pulled up her knees, kept eye contact with me, and masturbated. It was a pet tactic. It unnerved me. I went, she came.

When I got to the park in St. Pete, there were two telegrams waiting. One was from a law firm, notifying me of my court date with Harriet and asking if I still planned to proceed without an attorney. The other was from Harold Desmond. Dez, who drove ambulances with Hemingway in World War I, was back in St. Louis from London, resuming his post as managing editor. He'd cabled to ask why I kept writing about that kooky players' union, which even if the *Star-Times* weren't a conservative paper still wouldn't warrant the coverage because of what a crackpot idea it was. ESP GIVEN LABOR STRIFE IN REAL PROFESSIONS, THIS IS POWDERKEG. NO ORDER, JUST FRIENDLY ADVICE. BUT I HEAR THINGS. WHY NOT LOOK INTO MEX LG STORY NY PAPERS SO KEEN ON?

I sat in the pressbox rereading the telegram. Down on the field, Stan Musial was putting on a show in batting practice. Slats Marion, the leader of the players' union, stood beside the dugout, giving another speech to a few teammates. Warming up in the bullpen were Max Lanier and Freddie Martin. Beside me in the pressbox, the cigar-chomping shill for the *St. Louis Post-Dispatch* had just committed his lead to paper:

> Under sunny Florida skies, the sleek new '46 model of the Redbird diamondmen has been rolled onto the showroom floor, and if their first seven exhibition games are any indication, these boys can do everything but bake shortenin' bread and fill teeth. With all their true-blue soldier boys back aboard the U.S.S. *Sam Breadon* [Breadon was the Cardinals' owner], this reporter foresees smooth sailing ahead.

I reread my telegrams, then reread my colleague's hackery. I rose, tossed the telegrams into a trash can, went to the pressbox telephone, and placed a collect call to Jorge Pasquel.

SALVATORE ANTHONY "SAL THE BARBER" MAGLIE
[Interview conducted November 1956, in the kitchen of Maglie's small frame house on Pierce Avenue, in Niagara Falls, New York. He had bought the house ten years earlier for $10,000 cash. It was the day after Eisenhower was elected to his second term, four weeks after Maglie was the losing pitcher in Don Larsen's World Series perfect game. I was doing a story for *Look* about Maglie's '56 season, when at age thirty-nine, given up for dead by my hometown Cleveland Indians, he was traded to Brooklyn and led them to the National League pennant. It was his last hurrah.]

I played minor-league ball before the war, but I lost twice as many games as I won, and in 1942, once the minors were cut to the bone, I quit to take a job in a defense plant here in town. Kathleen and I'd just got married, and I needed something stable. Why I wasn't in the war was on account of my sinus condition.

I played sandlot ball over in Canada, but I thought my future was in basketball. I once scored sixty-one points in a muny-league game and I played on a team in Welland that was the 1944 Canadian amateur champs. In 1945, I had an offer from the Rochester Rens to go play in the NBA. Would have taken it, too, if it hadn't been for Dolf Luque.

Why? You didn't even meet Luque until late that summer.

Yeah, but it was because of him. That spring, I also had an of-fer from the Giants' Jersey City club. Teams were so desperate then that any healthy man left on the home front who'd played even way down in the bushes got an offer. I understood that, but Kathleen knew that baseball was my first love—other than her, that is—and she encouraged me to give it another shot.

Well, I got to Jersey City and stunk up the joint. My record was 3–7. And lo and behold what happened but the Giants called me to New York! They had to be desperate. At first Mel Ott didn't want to use me. I didn't blame him. I got a few relief appearances and managed not to embarrass myself, but I couldn't figure out what I was doing in the majors, a twenty-eight-year-old rookie with no record of success in the minors. And then I started work-ing with Dolf Luque.

Some guys didn't like him, especially because his English wasn't good but also because of his temper. Ott was generally such a nice guy that maybe Luque was hired just to balance him out. But I tell you what, that man could teach pitching. My only good pitch was my curve, but it was nothing great. Luque told me he could help me put a sharper break in it, to make it as good as the one he him-self learned from "Mar-tee."

"Marty who?" I says.

"Mar-tee. Bestest pitcher in all the world. S'motter, you no know Creesty Mattison?"

Well, that hit me. The man who was giving me curveball lessons learned it himself from the great Christy Mathewson.

Late in August, Luque convinced Mel Ott to put me in the rota-tion. I won five games, three of 'em shutouts. I was as surprised as anybody.

How did the Giants treat you then?

Good, I thought. They gave me a seventy-five-hundred-dollar contract for 1946, which was a huge raise, and I figured they be-lieved I was for real. The only one who seemed to have any doubts was me.

But I couldn't get any of that money until the next season, and I had bills. So when Luque asked if I'd pitch for Cienfuegos in the Cuban League, I was glad for the chance to pick up a little dough. Kathleen and I treated it like a second honeymoon.

How'd you do down there?

Unbelievable. Even better than in New York. The powerhouse club in Cuba was the Havana Reds, and I beat 'em all seven times I faced 'em, including a shutout in the championship game. Back home I was just another wartime ballplayer. In Cuba I was a national hero.

The people treated us great. Kathleen and I loved the spicy food and the great dance music. We felt like a magic spell had been cast over us, and I kept waiting for the spell to break.

Did it?

Yeah. Sure. Well, yes and no. The first sign of trouble was I reported to Giants camp and Luque was gone. I wasn't surprised. I met with the Pasquels in Cuba, too, but I turned 'em down. They offered to match my contract with the Giants plus give me a signing bonus of three grand. Kathleen and I talked it over and politely said no. The Giants wouldn't have given me such a big contract if I didn't figure in their plans.

At first it seemed like I did the right thing. When I reported to camp in Miami, Mel Ott came up and slapped me on the back and said, "We're depending on you, boy!" Things kind of went downhill from there.

Were you nervous about pitching without Luque around?

I felt he had more to teach me, but that alone wouldn't have made me leave the Giants. What burned me up was Ott pitched me six innings in the second exhibition, against the Boston Braves, and then nothing. The guys coming back from the war got most of the work. I got stuck at the bushers' hotel, not the main one, and it came clear I'd have to go back to Jersey City and prove myself. There goes my seventy-five-hundred-dollar contract. In those days, nobody's contract was guaranteed.

Right about then, Danny Gardella jumped ship. He was in the hotel room right across the hall. He ransacked the place before he left. To be honest, I hadn't thought of Mexico until then.

The next day at practice, I was approached by tiny Georgie Hausmann, the second baseman, and Roy Zimmerman, a backup first baseman. Both those guys were losing their jobs. They knew I had an offer from the Pasquels and they wanted to know how to reach them. I said I'd have to call Kathleen to get the number and that they ought to come by my hotel that night.

Kathleen wasn't home, and that's when I thought of you,

Frank, from that interview you did with me in Havana, and that's where we got the number. From you.

I was just looking for a scoop, Sal. So what happened next?

Georgie wanted to call Mexico immediately, and since he was reversing the charges I said okay. He and Zim reached Bernardo Pasquel and discussed their terms. I got on at the end and asked for ten grand for two years, guaranteed. Bernardo said he'd have to get back to me.

The so-called raid on the major leagues began the next day. February something. First we see in the morning papers that Luis Olmo jumped the Dodgers camp. Also, having big-leaguers like Hausmann and Zimmerman contact the Pasquels directly, that's what made them start going from camp to camp, throwing cash around in brown paper bags. That was the trigger, that phone call. It was then they saw what was possible. And it was also then, that same day, that the commissioner announced that anyone who went to play in Mexico would be banned for five years.

On our ball club—well, you know how word gets around a locker room. Like a grammar school. Ace Adams, Harry Feldman, Van Mungo, lots of guys asked me what I knew about the Pasquels.

And you told them?

I didn't do anything you didn't do, Frank.

I'm not accusing you of anything.

I've caught a lot of heat for this over the years, but I didn't do anything wrong. I want to be clear on that.

We're clear, Sal.

All right. Just so we're clear.

Well, a couple weeks passed, and spring training was winding down and I still didn't know for sure what I'd do. What probably ruined me with the Giants, the switchboard operator must have clued them in about that call from my room. The day before we're supposed to break camp and go north, I get to the clubhouse, and I knew something was up. There was deathly quiet. Ott comes out of his office and tells everyone to sit down and then goes from locker to locker asking every guy to swear out a loyalty oath. As he goes down the line, I wonder what I'm going to say. I'm a twenty-nine-year-old glorified rookie with just a few months of professional success who obviously isn't held in high esteem by his manager. I wonder if Kathleen and me will ever have enough money to buy a decent house. I'd talked to her about Mexico, and she thought we should chance it. Maybe it'd be like Cuba. We'd had such a grand time in Cuba.

And so when Ott came to me, I stood up. I'm much taller than he was. "Are you an agent of the Mexican League?" he asked.

"No," I said.

"Have you ever been contacted by the Mexicans?"

"Yessir."

He got amazingly red in the face, but he didn't raise his voice. "Is that right? And are you going to jump, Maglie?"

I nodded. "Yessir, I sure am."

Calmly, he reached into my locker and threw all my stuff out onto the floor. "Then get the hell out."

He did the same thing to Georgie and Zim. We walked out of there, and none of us even had our final terms with the Pasquels ironed out. We all figured that was the last time we'd ever darken the door of a major-league clubhouse.

When I called Bernardo to tell him we were coming, he acted surprised. I wasn't exactly one of their prime targets, which you can tell by the fact that I didn't get put on the Veracruz or Mexico City clubs, or even Torreón, which the Pasquels also owned. I got assigned to the Pericos of Puebla. The Puebla Parrots, a team of mongrels nobody wanted to play for.

Except me. I got off my plane in Mexico City, and a Cadillac was waiting, right on the landing strip. Behind the wheel was the manager of the Parrots. It was Dolf Luque. "Geet in, Mahglie," he says. "Today you pitch. Today you show May-hico the curve of the Great Mar-tee."

My scoop on the Maglie-Zimmerman-Hausmann story—beating the New York papers to the punch—engendered from Desmond this telegram: YOU SAY YOU'RE A WRITER, NOT A REPORTER. "GIANT JUMPERS"—ONE SWELL JOB OF REPORTING. CONGRATS. Often the worst things people say about you are supposed to be compliments.

Once Frances left Florida to return to her classes in St. Louis, I had a lot of time to think, which is another way of saying I had too much time to think. One way I filled my time was by writing a letter each day to Jerome, who could read awfully well for a kid his age. I had no way of knowing if Harriet saw the Florida post-marks and threw the letters away unopened. To fool her, I tried different typewriters and stationery, but I couldn't do much about the postmarks.

In the letters, composed in diners, pressboxes, and hotel bars, I tried to tell Jerome wise, true, and loving things. But it's hard to think up things like that, and even when you do you say the same things over and over and it sounds like you're talking down to the kid. Kids have a built-in alarm that goes off when someone talks down to them. So I started telling Jerome about myself. I tried to tell the truth about myself.

Maybe you can't tell a seven-year-old boy that you would al-ways be a failure to your taciturn parents in their huge paid-for house on Fairmount Boulevard in Cleveland Heights because you did not go into medicine or law or follow in your father's foot-steps at Standard Oil but instead tried to become a writer, which is the kind of a story that would sound better if you grew up to be somebody like Hemingway, or somebody period, instead of some nobody like Frank Bullinger, Jr. But I told Jerome the story anyway.

Maybe you can't tell a seven-year-old boy that you married his mother—your college sweetheart at Oberlin—for all the wrong reasons, which seemed like all the right reasons at the time. I told him. Maybe you can't tell a seven-year-old boy that you have a bad habit of falling into the arms of strange women in faraway hotels, or smart literate women anywhere, and that maybe all that's wrong with you is you have a job that puts you on the road and keeps you up late and thereby gives free rein to your biggest character flaw, and that in your experience most people wind up with just such jobs, whatever the flaw. Maybe you can't tell that to a seven-year-old boy. But I did.

Maybe you can't tell a seven-year-old boy that those strange women in those faraway hotels and crosstown apartments have a way of becoming familiar, and the loneliness, sleeplessness, cu-riosity, and desperation that brought you to those women has a way of turning into love. Not the kind of love you have for that lit-tle boy, a constant ache of caring, where you'd give your life away if it meant delivering him from evil, but the kind of love men and women blunder in and out of. Maybe you can't tell that to a seven-year-old boy, either. But I did.

I vowed to be honest with this boy. Adults are so phony with kids, maybe that's why there's so many troubled adults. I vowed to err on the side of genuineness and honesty. Even if it meant to err grotesquely. That was my plan.

❖

That spring training, everywhere I traveled with the Cardinals I saw the Pasquels or their men, and they saw me, and everyone tried to be discreet. In every locker room, players were whispering. Once in a while the whispers were about the union. But mostly it was Mexico. It was the all-time record for naked men whispering in locker rooms, and it stands to this day.

Even in the umpires' dressing rooms there was whispering. There would be a labor surplus among big-league umpires, too. Signing up a few of those guys would help with credibility, I thought. I got no bonus for umps. It was just my good deed.

I scooped the Washington papers when René Monteagudo left the Senators for Torreón. I scooped the New York papers on Dodgers wall-banger Pete Reiser's $100,000 offer. And I scooped the Boston papers when Ted Williams met with Jorge Pasquel in a smoky Sarasota hotel suite and, though put off by Jorge's spitting problem, seemed to weigh seriously Jorge's offer, carrying away a blank check, a box of cigars, and a promise of six shotguns.

The telegrams from Desmond kept coming. 1946 PULITZER IN SPORTSWRITING SHOULD GO TO FB, said one. WHY IS THERE NO PULITZER FOR SPORTSWRITING?

I cabled back: WHY IS THERE NO OSCAR FOR BEST VD TRAINING FILM?

The telegrams from Harriet's lawyers kept coming too. One thing you can count on in life is that telegrams from lawyers will keep coming.

When Tigers shortstop Moe Franklin signed with Tampico, I filed my story—scooping the Detroit papers, of course—and used my commission to buy and ship to Jerome a Lionel train set and to wire Diana James a plane ticket from New York to Florida. Most of the rest I sent to creditors in St. Louis, holders of notes on chifforobes and davenports, the family car, the new carport and the mortgage on the house I was locked out of. The last $30 I kept inside a balled blue sock in my typewriter case. My nest egg. About four hundred bucks now.

Diana's first book of poems was coming out from a chichi little New York house. She was nervous about how it would be received and was glad for an excuse to leave town. I knew the publisher (from Paris in the thirties) and had put in a good word for her. I imagined that this had helped get the book published. The same man would, in 1947, and again in 1950, and again in 1962, reject my novel.

Diana and I spent a happy few days rolling around on the bed and the floor of our tenth-floor room in the Floridian Hotel in St. Pete, ordering room service, drinking Jameson's, and smoking marijuana cigarettes Diana had brought with her from New York. I stopped doing after-game interviews. I wrote during the games and filed my stories from the hotel an hour later.

How to describe Diana! She was 4'10", built like a taut miniature of a voluptuous farm girl. She had, in fact, grown up on a North Carolina tobacco farm. She'd gone to Barnard, graduated in three years, moved to the Village, and become a bohemian. She and I had met in the lobby of the Algonquin Hotel; late that night she professed to hate only four things: earrings, sestinas, made beds, and abstractions. She could come with me inside her, whether on top or on the bottom, the only lover I had ever had or would have (out of ninety-two) who could do this routinely. She delighted in giving and receiving oral sex, which in those days, in my experience, was uncommon in a woman. After lovemaking, she and I would read poetry aloud. It was the kind of love affair you'd design for yourself if the gods were mean enough to let you.

"You know what I really want?" she asked one day, apropos of nothing. We were having coffee on the balcony and had been laughing over her father's quixotic efforts to buy a new Frazier. It was the day before the Meat Stephens business conspired to shunt us off to Mexico.

"No one knows what anyone wants," I answered. "People don't even know what they want themselves, and if—"

"Shut up." She held a marijuana cigarette to her lips. "You think too much. Not too deeply, just too much. Too often."

"So what *do* you want?"

She laughed. "Other than to fuck you again in a few minutes? If you can, old man?"

My wife did not say *fuck* and had protested whenever I had. I was going through a stage. I was in love with the word *fuck*. All bookish men in their thirties go through this stage.

"Yes," I said. "Other than that."

"I want to travel. I want to see the world, like you have. America, Europe, you name it, I want to go there. Zanzibar."

"I've never been to Zanzibar. Where *is* Zanzibar?"

She ignored this. "I don't want to keep writing poems about my own little life," she said.

"So whose life do you want to write about?"

"Mine. I just want to make it bigger."

I kissed her hand, then massaged it, proceeding up her arm, across her shoulders and neck, down the other arm, to the other hand. "So," I whispered, kissing her cannabis-scented fingertips, "what are you saying?"

Diana rolled her head back and opened her eyes. "Maybe I'm saying I love you. There. I said it."

I was stunned. In 1946, women did not say this first, though this only made me love her more. "Love you, too," I chimed. I should have said it first, but I'd been afraid. She was fearless. "I thought you hated abstractions."

"Being in love doesn't mean you like it," she said. "Besides, what makes you think love is an abstraction?"

❖

VERN "MEAT" STEPHENS

[Interview conducted July 29, 1956, in the dugout of the Pacific Coast League Seattle Rainiers, for whom a washed-up Stephens was a player-coach. The starting pitcher that day for the opposing San Diego Padres was Theolic Smith. I was doing a where-are-they-now piece on Stephens for *Sport*, in which I made him—a six-time All-Star, one of the best-hitting, best-looking, best-dressed shortstops ever, and a nice-enough guy—look pathetic. Jealousy. Sorry, Meat. Twelve years later, Stephens died of a heart attack. He was forty-eight.]

The DeWitt brothers, who ran the Browns—ran 'em right out of St. Louis, eventually—they had no business owning a big-league team. Those clowns never had the money to do things right. And it made you sick to share a ballpark with the Cardinals. Back then, the Cards were the *class organization. In '44, when we played 'em in the World Series, I had visions of David and Goliath. I was twenty-three. What romantic horseshit. Today I root for Goliath. Goliath winning is like the sun comin up in the east. Who wants it to come up in the west, or not at all, just so it'd be an upset, huh? People say they want upsets, but that's romantic horseshit. Viva Goliath, I say. The trick to life isn't figuring out how to beat Goliath. It's figuring out how to* be *Goliath.*

In 1944 I won the RBI title, and in '45 I led the league in homers. It was against wartime competition, but you can't be better than best. DiMaggio, Feller, Williams—they made forty G's. I only wanted seventeen-five, but the DeWitts and me went round and round, and the best they'd offer was thirteen. That same spring they got in a salary dispute with our catcher, Walker Cooper, and they sold him like a stick of furniture to the Giants for a hundred and seventy-five thousand, not a cent of which got into Coop's pocket. I figured something like that would happen to me. I was steamed, but what choice did I have? I read in the papers about the Pasquels and their Taco League, but they were in Florida. The Browns, White Sox, Cubs, and Pirates trained in California, and as far as I could see the Mexicans forgot about us. But then I thought of you, Frank. I know I told you that Sig Jakucki told me to call, but I lied. I knew you and Sig were bottle buddies, and that you'd bend over more for me if you thought Sig was behind it.

How did you know I could put you in touch with the Pasquels?

I told you I read the papers, Frank. There for a while, it looked like the Pasquels were your beat.

Oh. So, um, what were your first impressions of the Pasquels?

We had a game against the Cubs on Catalina Island. I showered up, ducked out of the clubhouse, and instead of catching the ferry back to L.A. I met Jorge Pasquel on some big yacht. More than the yacht, what impressed me about him was his clothes. All that jewelry was a bit much, but his suit—a suit, on a boat!—was a terrifically made white double-breasted job, which you could see from a mile was tailor-made. This was right after the war. It was impossible to get top-grade tropical-weight wools. That was my first clue about those people. You couldn't get material like that if you weren't up to your ass in the black market. I was so ticked off at the Browns, I didn't care, at first, but it sent up a red flag.

I told Jorge Pasquel I wanted seventeen-five from the Browns but that it'd take more than that to get me to jump to Mexico. Pasquel laughed. He spit at you, remember? He said he'd double what I wanted. He offered me a five-year deal for a hundred and seventy-five thousand. Nothing on paper. Jorge said he'd iron out the details when we got to Mexico City. I was just a kid, but I had sense enough not to agree to anything unless it was spelled out and my dad could see it. Dad ran a milk company in Long Beach, which is where you land from Catalina, and he helped me with all my business. I asked if he could come talk to them. They said there wasn't time, the Mexican season had already started and they needed me in Mexico City by the weekend or the deal was off. That hard sell should have been another red flag. They had other reasons for getting me down there so fast. They'd heard Hap Chandler, the commissioner, they'd heard he was talking to the owners and trying to figure out if there was a way, other than that ban, not only to keep guys from jumping but also to get some of the guys who jumped to jump back.

I'm not sure that's right.

That's what I heard, later on.

Pasquel said to go check out of my hotel and that he'd have an airplane waiting for me at the Palm Springs airport, and that he was leaving at midnight, with or without me. Then Pasquel saw me eyein his threads. "You admire my suit?" he says. Hell, yes, I say. I got eyes, don't I? He waves to his bodyguards, and the next thing I know one guy whips out a measuring tape and starts takin down my sizes, barking out numbers to another guy, who writes it all down. Pasquel says if I arrive at the airport as sched-uled, he'll call ahead and have his personal tailor work all night to make me five custom suits just as nice as the one he has on. [Laughs.] Jorge Pasquel was like a prizefighter who knew how to open up your cuts.

They dropped me off on shore, and I caught a ride with Red Hayworth. You remember how Red loved cars. He had a cherry '39 Chevy convertible, canary yellow with whitewalls, which he'd kept in a garage while he was overseas. Poor Red. He was at Toledo with me in '41 and got drafted the very day he got called

*up. He got back in '44, and he started for us in the World Series,
but by then he was too old for much of a career. I get Red to
swing by my dad's milk plant. Dad knew I was contacting
Pasquel. He told me to, so I'd have a bargaining chip with the
DeWitts. "I gotta make a decision now, Dad," I said. Told him the
whole story. "Make 'em put everything in writing, in English,"
he said. If they'd do that, he'd show it to the company lawyer.
That wasn't what I wanted to hear. I was already imagining what
color those suits would be. I wanted Dad to say, "Junior, one
hundred seventy-five thousand dollars is too much money to pass
up. You have my blessing." Instead I got "Look before you leap."*

*Of course I ignored him. Red took me back to San Bernardino,
and I ate with the club and then went upstairs, called my wife in
St. Louis and gave her the news, then I packed up. Red was glad
to take me to Palm Springs, said he wanted to see these Mexicans
for himself, like he thought they'd all be dressed like Pancho Villa
or Zorro. But I needed the ride.*

*There was the hottest Santa Ana wind I've ever felt, and I'd
lived most of my life in California. Red's seats were covered with
that nubby, scratchy fabric they used to use. I was sweating from
the wind and from nerves, and just completely uncomfortable.
Red found Mexican music on the radio, which he thought was a
hoot, and he wouldn't change the station.*

*Then we got to the airstrip and the first familiar face I saw was
yours, Frank. I hadn't agreed to anything yet, and there's this freeloading reporter chasing after me with his notebook.*

The Pasquels tipped me off.

*You weren't looking for a story, you were looking for a free trip
to Mexico. You even had some little redheaded tomato along.*

That "redheaded tomato" . . .

*Forget it, huh, sport? Hey, is that all you need? I'm supposed to
pitch b.p. in a minute here.*

I need it in your words. What do you remember from that flight?

*Not much! I don't know which of us was more drunk, you or
me. Let's see. I remember Pasquel calling in my suit order from a
pay phone. I remember taking off and seeing Red Hayworth beside his car, shaking his head. I remember Pasquel's woman, I
guess she was some fancy actress, nice rack on her. I remember
waking up the next morning in some hotel, still in my clothes,*

and not knowing where the hell I was. I remember going to the window and looking down at a filthy street, with beggars, hookers, chickens, and goats runnin around and beat-up old cars honking and trying to get by. What an awful place, Mexico. I wanted to call my wife and my dad, except that there was no phone in the room. Even from the lobby phone I couldn't call home because I couldn't get an operator who spoke English. You believe that?

It is a Spanish-speaking country, Vern.

You can have it. The only good thing was those suits. Pasquel was good on that promise. Later that morning, there's a knock at the door. I answer it. In walks Pasquel's tailor with five double-breasted suits: white, cream, royal blue, navy with yellow pin-stripes, brown with white, all with the latest lapels, made of the best-quality cloth I'd owned since before the war. Plus ten pressed white shirts, Egyptian cotton. But before I could try everything on, Pasquel's henchmen threw me in a car and took me to that concentration-camp firetrap of a ballpark. They stopped the game to introduce me. I had a hangover, and there I was, sweating my ass off in a brand-new suit, wavin like a funny-farmer while those Mexicans made the biggest racket you ever heard. Pasquel followed around behind me, takin credit. We shook everybody's hand, and then we watched the rest of the game from Pasquel's box. I asked him when I was going to see my contract, and he kept sayin, Mañana, mañana. That's how Mexicans are, everything mañana.

It wasn't a big-league-caliber game. I recognized maybe four guys. Bob Estalella won it on a homer in the ninth, and Alex Carrasquel was the winning pitcher. There were a couple bushers whose faces rang bells, and some colored guys I'd played against in barnstorming games.

My fondest memory of Mexico was when we all went to that fancy nightclub with all those celebrities there because of it being the last big bullfighting week of the year. Remember? Errol Flynn, John Wayne, Gloria Swanson, all the stars. The Pasquels bought I would say fifty beautiful English-speaking women for us, and we were told to take our pick, either for there or to take 'em with us on our way out like a party favor! Hey, don't put that in your story, Frank.

I won't.

Danny Gardella, remember that lunatic? Remember when he took off the tablecloth and grabbed a long candlestick and pretended to be a matador? Singin some Spike Jones song. Let's see, who else? Babe Ruth, and of course all the Pasquels. And that one guy, the famous writer.

Hemingway.

Yeah, him. The highlight of the night was when you yelled at him and he hauled off and knocked you cold.

I wasn't knocked cold. I just wouldn't fight anymore. I didn't want to make an ass of myself.

Too late for that! Then, when your girlfriend slapped him back! That was great!

Let's stay focused on baseball, or at least on you. Tell me about your debut.

Not much to tell. I won the game with a two-run single in the bottom of the ninth.

I know that. I mean, tell me what it was like, your impressions.

I remember being struck by all the American brands on the out-field billboards: Coca-Cola, Valvoline, Seagram's, Calvert, Bacardi, like that. The stands were full of bookies, and money changed hands on every pitch. Instead of organ music they played that Mexican stuff. Actually, that game was kind of fun, and not just 'cause I won it and the Mexicans cheered their heads off. You know how sometimes you're on vacation and it's not like it looked like in the brochure and you're miserable, but then it sinks in and you relax and start to think maybe it'll be fun after all? That's what that first game was like.

What queered me on Mexico was what happened after that.

You mean the game in Monterrey.

Before that. My first game was Sunday, and the next one wasn't until Thursday, in Monterrey. Monday and Tuesday, other than practice, I had nothing to do except shit. I was one sick dog. I spent my time in Mexico perched on a toilet. Who knows how Mexicans stand to eat that food.

I moved out of the hotel and into a furnished apartment Pasquel got me, which I guess was plush by Mexican standards. Back home, it would've been the kind of place a mechanic lived. They gave me a housekeeper, an old Mexican woman who got in

my way and didn't speak English. I had a phone, but placing a
call back to America—Christ, you'd have thought I wanted to
move heaven and earth when all I wanted was to hear my wife's
voice. On top of it all, I didn't know anybody on the Veracruz
club—the only white guy was Danny Gardella, for chrissakes—
and a lot of 'em resented me because some busher got sent to an-
other team to make room for me. But, yeah, Monterrey was the
last straw.

◈

I used the Mexican League story in general and the Stephens
story in particular as an excuse to leave Florida, the Cardinals
beat, and the U.S.A., and to go to Mexico on the *Star-Times's*
nickel, in search of a few sports stories and a new place to fuck.
Though I didn't sober up in time for my first Mexican League
game, I did manage to check into my hotel, make passable love to
Diana, and catch a taxi to the park by game time. All day, the image of Diana splayed diagonally across the bed, covered only by
the shirt I'd worn the day before, shimmered in my mind's eye.

There was no press gate. Defying every fiber of my freeloading
being, I bought a ticket. When I finally found the pressbox, past a
flank of Mexican soldiers and up a ladder to the wooden roof of
Delta Park, it was empty. I tried to ask the soldiers where the
other reporters were. I didn't know the word for "reporter." It
took two innings for them to express to me that the pressbox contained much heat and that the other, less loco writers watched
the game from the lower deck, in the shade.

Finally the soldiers ushered me to Jorge Pasquel's private box,
behind the Veracruz dugout. Stephens was with Pasquel, shaved
and sobered up and poured into a new suit. After the game a
chauffeur drove me to Pasquel's office, and I called in my story.

Back at the Hotel Galveston, Diana was gone. There was a message at the desk: "I am with Hemingway." It gave directions to a
nightclub, the same club where Jorge Pasquel had invited me. I
would need to know somebody to get in, Pasquel had said.

I clutched the note and sank into a sofa in the lobby. Hemingway? How the hell did she know Hemingway? What the hell was
Hemingway, of all people, doing in Mexico City?

I went up to my room, showered, changed clothes, and took the time to write one letter to Jerome and one, also on the stationery of the Hotel Galveston, to Frances Kingston, which I posted to her office at the university. Both letters were drenched with bewilderment and apology. When I finished, I sat at the desk in the window, a whiskey glass in one hand and a cup of coffee in the other, listening to traffic and watching darkness fall.

It was the eve of the last day of bullfighting season. Hemingway sat at a table with the great matadors Procuña and Manolete. The club was dark. I couldn't see Diana. The place was filled with Pasquels, movie stars, ballplayers, stray wives, lackeys, and whores. On stage the guitars and trumpets and steel drums of a música tropical combo blared bright melodies.

I approached the table of Hemingway. He was talking to Procuña and did not look up. Jorge Pasquel, at a round table, motioned for me to join him. Onstage, Danny Gardella, a blue sombrero askew on his head, joined the band and gamely tried to play the accordion.

I was drunk enough to be straight with Hemingway. I had two questions. The first was not about Diana.

He looked up, frowning. Finally he said, "Did I read what?"

"My novel!" Two months. I had given it to him two months ago!

Hemingway said something in Spanish, and Procuña and Manolete laughed. Just then, Diana returned to the table. She kissed me on the cheek, like a schoolgirl.

"Oh," Hemingway said. "I lost it before I could finish it."

I started screaming. I called him every name in the book, shouted out every small-minded thing I'd ever thought about him and his writing. "The sun also *sets*, asshole."

I stole the line from Gertrude Stein, except for the "asshole" part, but Hemingway must by then have heard it once too often, because he never coldcocked Gertrude Stein, but he landed a right cross on my jaw. The last thing I remember was looking up at the bottom of the table to see that it was made from old doors sawed in half and then hearing Diana slap Hemingway and the combo singing "Se busca, se busca, mi amor linda."

The next day, Hemingway came by the hotel to apologize. He offered to buy me breakfast at a place he knew. He and Diana had worked this out the night before, carrying me back to the hotel. At breakfast, we talked about the Nuremberg trials, the weather, the movie *The Lost Weekend*, what sort of halfwit still reads Dreiser, and about how Truman had seized the coal mines. Finally the food came and Hemingway said, "I was damn drunk, Frank."

"We were all pretty well in our cups."

"How's the jaw?"

"Fine. How does it look?"

"Like the devil."

"Well," I said. "You'd know."

Hemingway had with him a copy of Diana's book of poems, which he claimed he had been sent. He said he would say good things about it in *Look* magazine.

"That's nice of you," she said. "But don't feel obligated."

"My only obligation," said Hemingway, "is to the truth."

Diana wasn't the sort of person to make a lot out of a thing like this. I was. I had been trawling in Hemingway's wake for ten years, fishing for compliments. "I'm glad you liked the book," Diana said. "But I think my new poems are better."

"New ones always are," said Hemingway. He was peeling mangoes with a knife. It was a big knife. Was it good, Hem, to have a big knife and to peel mangoes with it? Huh? Me, I was using my bitten-down thumbnail to do battle with an orange.

"You have talent," Hemingway said, to Diana. His mouth was full of mango. "No substitute for talent, kid."

Diana ate pan dulce and guzzled coffee. She wore no makeup, nor any kind of look on her face, particularly not the kind of look you might have if you had sport-fucked the wrong man. But I could not believe Hemingway would be good to a woman writer unless he'd fucked her. Even then. Mary, Hemingway's wife, had been a writer, and somebody else's wife, when Hem—who had been somebody else's husband—first had her. Not long after that she quit writing.

"I'm sorry as hell about your novel, Frank," he said. "What I read had things going for it."

"You didn't really lose it, did you?"

"Afraid so. It was in a car that got stolen. I'd look on the bright side if I was you."

"If I *were* you," I blurted.

Hemingway stroked his beard. Then softly said, "You're not."

I looked at Diana. I took a breath. "The bright side?"

He adjusted himself in his chair. "In 1922 Hadley was coming from Paris to spend Christmas with me in Lausanne. I was there covering a peace conference for the *Toronto Star.*"

Sweet Jesus. *This* warhorse.

"She packed a valise," Hemingway said, "full of all the stuff I'd written—stories, poems, even the carbons. But at the train station she gave her bags to a porter, and that was the last she saw of the valise and the last the world saw of those stories."

Diana looked like someone who'd just heard news of the violent death of a baby. She must have been the only person in the world who hadn't yet heard that story. "Were you able to rewrite any of it?" she said, taking the bait.

Hemingway shook his head. "Never even tried," he said. "At first I was in a bloody state, but Hadley felt so bad I couldn't take it out on her. Then I thought about how lucky I was, how my apprentice stuff got lost forever and wouldn't be around to embarrass me later." He laughed. "That's the bright side, Frank."

"I have my longhand pages," I said.

Hemingway shook his head.

Diana's eyes were still big. "You lost *all* your writings? They were never found?"

"Nearly all. Never found." The check came and Hemingway paid it. "That was the night I became a true writer."

In Gertrude Stein's version, which I heard from the horse's mouth, Hemingway returns to Paris in a futile search for lost carbons, then shows up at her and Alice's doorstep on Christmas Eve with two whores, no overcoat, a belly full of Pernod, and tears streaming down his cheeks.

Hemingway made a showy goodbye and was off to the bullring. Diana and I were alone. "I wonder whatever became of those stories," she said. In profile she looked like a woman on a coin.

Moments later Diana came down with what Mexicans call la turista and what Americans romanticize as Montezuma's Revenge. When I left for the ballpark she was in the bathroom, and when I got back four hours later she was still there. Nothing in the room looked different.

◆

The biggest volley yet in what American newspapers called "the Mexican War" came on April Fool's Day, when Mickey Owen, the Dodgers' All-Star catcher, agreed to come to Mexico. (Most American newspapermen couldn't have told you a thing about the real Mexican War, a hundred years earlier, when the U.S. stole Texas, Arizona, New Mexico, Nevada, and California.)

I didn't hear about Owen until Wednesday the third, on a train from Mexico City to Monterrey. Sunday, I'd dutifully witnessed and reported upon Meat Stephens's debut and game-winning hit. Monday, April Fool's Day, while the Pasquels were in Florida signing Owen, I filed a piece about the Mexican League's high caliber of play, which was better than U.S. wartime ball. Tuesday was also a day off; the Mexican League played only four games a week. I filled a slow day with a column:

MEXICO CITY, MEXICO—One visiting gringo's opinion . . .

Ironic, isn't it, that so many ballplayers fought as soldiers for world freedom, for the overthrow of tyrannical dictators, only to come home and have the magnates of baseball behave the same way?

Baseball owners' response to the nascent players' union and to the healthy competition of the Mexican League would, in any other business, be illegal. Union-busting. Violations of right-to-work laws. Fascist monopolies. We fought Mussolini for this?

America, a country which so deplored the racism of Nazi Germany that it sent thousands of its sons there to die, is itself a country which, on every front, endorses the idea of a master race. As long as Negroes are excluded from the Major Leagues, maybe those leagues should more properly be called the Master Race Leagues.

While we're at it, isn't it time to change the name of the World Series, which features only white players and includes teams only in the northeastern quadrant of the United States? How about "The Eastern White Folks Baseball Championship"? Or "A Day at the Master Races"?

During the war, baseball owners were war profiteers of the most shameless kind. Attendance was down, but salaries were down even more. The owners used the war as an excuse to pay the players insultingly low wages. This is an abomination.

The fine people of St. Louis do not take the trolley to Sportsman's Park and fork over their hard-earned dollars to see the Cardinals and Browns because Sam Breadon and the DeWitts own the teams. Cards fans pay their money to see Musial, Lanier, and Marion. Browns fans pay to see Galehouse, Lucadello, and, until last week, Vern Stephens.

Is it radical to suggest that the players are the ones who deserve the biggest share of that money, especially now, with the war over and attendance likely to go through the roof?

Baseball owners might call ideas like this Communistic, but last I checked America was a capitalist country under the free-enterprise system. Perhaps the least-free enterprise in the country is baseball, the so-called National Pastime. This is a disgrace, a bigger scandal to the game even than the nefarious doings of the Black Sox.

Here in sunny Mexico, free enterprise lives. A business-man and baseball maven named Jorge Pasquel—a Mexi-can Horatio Alger—has tried to upgrade the caliber of play in his baseball league. To do this, he signed several American players, both whites and Negroes. He never wanted to fight with the Master Race . . . er, I mean the Major Leagues. If they had truly wanted to keep the play-ers who've come to Mexico, they would have paid them a fair wage.

In this scribe's opinion, when it comes to the game of baseball, Mexico, not America, is the land of supply and de-mand. America, not Mexico, is the land of outlaw baseball.

As often happened, I started writing my column not caring about anything and finished it bitter and angry about everything.

In between all this Diana and I squeezed in some sightseeing, a feat because of how sick Diana was. We managed to make it to the Monumento a los Niños Héroes, in Chapultepec Park. The Boy Heroes were six cadets who during the real Mexican War stood on the ramparts of the national military academy and, facing certain slaughter at the hands of the U.S. Army, wrapped themselves in the flag and leapt to their deaths. Every town in Mexico has a street named after them.

"We have Audie Murphy," said Diana, quietly moved. "All they have are these poor boys."

I started to quibble with her analogy, but a wave of nausea overcame her, and we hurried away to find a bathroom.

We both had taken precautions: avoiding the water, rinsing out toothbrushes with beer, et cetera. But I had not gotten sick. If one lover gets sick and the other seems immune, the sick lover will feel betrayed. It is not logical, but neither are lovers, and neither is love. I didn't truly accept this until I was much older. By then Diana was just a talented, red-haired memory.

It is 952 kilometers from Mexico City to Monterrey. Diana spent the trip in our berth writing poems or in the bathroom. I stayed away, avoiding Diana and the sore subject of Hemingway and drinking scotch along with the Blues. The players who'd been in Mexico the year before were used to drinking on these long trips, to make the time pass but equally to keep from looking out the window and wondering why the train didn't jump its bumpy tracks and fly off the side of the mountain and into that brown, brown valley below.

I took out the latest telegram from Desmond. COULD NOT SAVE YOU FROM APRIL FOOL'S STORY. LUCKILY COLUMN OF 4/2 DID NOT RUN. CHANDLER HAS ACCUSED YOU OF BEING AGENT OF MEX LG! WANTS US TO FIRE YOU! HAVE TOLD COMMISH YOUR INVOLVEMENT WITH PASQUELS CAME IN PURSUIT OF SCOOPS. WIRE NO-NONSENSE STATEMENT TO THAT EFFECT TO CHANDLER'S OFFICE. Dez gave the address of the baseball commissioner. CAN DO NO MORE TO PROTECT BULLINGER FROM BULLINGER. CONCERNED, DEZ.

I felt someone looking over my shoulder. It was Chile Gómez, the Blues second baseman. "Forgive me." He was a serious man who didn't drink. "Curiosidad." He smiled. "Dispénseme."

"It's okay." I slipped the telegram into the pocket of my sport coat. "It's from my boss."

"From the newspaper in San Luis?" Gómez wore round wire-rimmed glasses. If you saw him on the street you would have guessed he was a doctor which is what he wished to be until he got a baseball contract and became the second Mexican ever to play in the big leagues, back in '35. He was now thirty-six, the same age as me. "You are in trouble, yes?"

I shrugged. "The newspaper game," I said.

Gómez nodded, as if that made sense. "Focking newspapers." He patted me on the shoulder, as an affectionate uncle might do on his way to bed.

Diana sat cross-legged on her bunk. In front of her, in my Remington, was half a poem. I did not read it. I did not want her to see me as I saw Gómez. "When would I have fucked him?"

"After I was out. After you brought me back to the hotel."

"I slapped him," she said. "For being a mean S.O.B., and for treating you like something that got stuck to his shoe. How could I go from hating his guts to fucking him?"

I was finally getting tired of her saying *fuck*. "That's not such a leap and you know it."

"You're just threatened to have a woman defend you."

"That's not it."

"Do you really think I fucked him?"

I looked out the window at the brown valley. "No. Of course I don't." I laughed a little. "No."

It just looked bad.

"I love you," I said.

"Love you, too," she said, too quickly.

"You don't have to say it just because I say it."

"I'm not," she said. "But you say it a lot."

"Do I say it too much?" I felt like I was sixteen years old.

She shrugged. "You say it a lot," she said.

"I say it too much."

"Jesus," she said. "You say everything too much."

Things had been different since Diana and I left Florida. Not bad, not good either, but different. Traveling tests a couple as much as, and to the same degree as, marriage. With travel you cling to the belief you will soon go home. Married people are always traveling. And so our little threadbare berth—on an old train riding to Monterrey on rough rails—was a smaller place than it might have been for another couple, and for any couple it would have been small.

"So what do you think of the signing of Mickey Owen," asked Chile Gómez. That was how I heard, from Gómez, most of the way to Monterrey.

"He'll never live down being the goat of the '41 Series, but he's a good catcher." I knew Owen from when he broke in with the Cardinals. "Seems like a good signing for the Pasquels."

"I do not think is good," said Gómez. "I hear that Mickey Owen will be the player/mana-hair of Torreón. Pero Torreón ya tiene un pelotero/manager: El Maestro, Martín Dihigo."

My Spanish was still weak. So was my knowledge of great Latin ballplayers. I did not know of Martín Dihigo, an appalling ignorance. "No entiendo," I said. "No comprendo."

Gómez explained, half in English, half in Spanish. After Roy Campanella returned to Newark, Torreón needed a catcher. Owen was it, but the great Dihigo will be mortally offended to be removed as manager in favor of the American. Gómez managed to tell a story critical of the Pasquels without in any way criticizing the Pasquels. He did it astride two languages and with the same slick grace he used to field his position, where he was among the best I ever saw.

Monterrey is Mexico's Pittsburgh, and also its Milwaukee: a smoke-belching city of factories. El Parque Cuauhtémoc—named for the country's biggest brewery, which itself was named for a great Aztec emperor—was an old wooden grandstand that seated about ten thousand (and strained under a crowd twice that), with tiny dugouts, no locker rooms, a pressbox no one used, and concessionaires who sold nuts and seeds and tacos and enchiladas and tamales and whole roasted chickens and cold bottled beer from huge tin ice buckets.

The Monterrey Sultans were mostly Negroes. The crowd had no Negroes. Yet the fans cheered their heads off. I thought of Bill Veeck's scuttled plan to buy the sad-sack Philadelphia Phillies and stock the team with Negro League stars; hard to imagine white Philadelphians backing such a club, even today. But Monterrey is not Philadelphia.

When Veracruz took the field, the crowd broke into a deafening whistle, like a tornado.

"Why are they whistling?" Diana was feeling better. She had been asking questions ever since we arrived. I knew this would wind up in a poem. I didn't want to be a character in her poems. "What's the whistling for?" she persisted.

I shrugged.

"This," volunteered a young reporter from the Monterrey paper *El Norte*, "is how Mexicans boo." He sat beside Diana. The seats were small and their elbows were touching.

"Why are they booing before the game even starts?" I said. "In Mexico City they didn't whistle at the visiting club."

"Of course not," said the reporter. He was a recent graduate of the University of Arizona and spoke excellent English. "They don't whistle because it is the visiting team. They whistle because they resent the Pasquels for stocking the Mexico City teams with all the imported talent, trying to buy a championship for the capital. It is no different in your country."

I nodded. "I suppose."

"What do you mean?" Diana said.

The reporter was dark and doe-eyed, with high cheekbones and a bright white smile, if you find that kind of thing attractive. "Americans hate the Yankees of New York," he said. "And why? Because they have all the money."

"I live in New York," she said. "I know lots of people who love the Yankees."

"True," the young man said. "And do you know why?"

"Because they're the home team."

The young man shook his head. "The Giants and the Dodgers are also the home teams, and yet they are not as loved in New York as the Yankees, correct?"

Diana tipped her beer at him in a gesture of touché. This boy was her age exactly. "That's because the Yankees always win."

"And why do they always win?" The young man smiled. "Because they have all the money." He was pleased with himself. He had been a philosophy major.

Diana laughed and bought herself another cold beer and joined in the whistling of the capitalist running dogs.

Alex Carrasquel, the Veracruz pitcher, gave up a three-run homer in the first to Claro Duany, a big Cuban. That was all the support the Monterrey pitcher needed. He was a knuckleballer called the Coyote. He had the Blues swinging at anything. Meat Stephens looked worse than anyone; like most sluggers, he did not hit knuckleballs well. Each time he came to bat, the whistling grew louder. The sections of the stands where the bookies sat were a frenzy of waving pesos.

Diana took more notes during the game than I did. I drank more beer than Diana. The young reporter kept a neat scorecard, cheered shamelessly for the home team, and drank Coca-Cola. I would have cited the American rule about no cheering in the pressbox, but we weren't in a pressbox or in America, and also I didn't give a shit, not about quote-unquote objectivity, not about sportswriting, not about my ridiculous job for the *Star-Times*, not about much.

In the eighth, I made a list on the back of my scorecard of what I did give a shit about: Number one, Jerome Tristram Bullinger, age seven. Number two, Frances Kingston (written as "King of France"; Diana was right there), the sensible choice. She was smart, my age, and—oh, yeah—pregnant with my baby. In base-ball terms, she was, as a lover, a canny veteran who knew how to pitch, a Coyote. Diana was a wild, smoke-throwing phenom. Number three, Diana. The only reason the gods ever let you de-sign the perfect love affair, I then realized, is as punishment. But I *did* want her. Things were just new. New things need time. Number four? A place to pee.

When Stephens struck out to end the game, I was in line for the park's lone urinal trough. The fans stormed the field, pelting the vanquished Stephens with fruit, nuts, and wadded scorecards. He fled like a man chased by a bear. The fans bore the tri-umphant Sultans on their shoulders, as riotous as a World Series crowd. It was game eight of a ninety-eight-game season.

By the time I realized Stephens had disappeared, and along with him the St. Louis angle on the Mexican League story, and therefore any reason I could expect the *Star-Times* to foot the bill for my trip, it was Saturday, game two of the series. I'd spent two days drunk and smoking marijuana, with Diana and without her. Amid my bouts of unconsciousness and into my role as a male escort—without which, we had been told, a woman would be presumed to be a hooker—stepped the kid from *El Norte*, who showed her the city in his father's green '37 Dodge.

Saturday's game was two innings gone when I realized the runt at shortstop wasn't Meat. I found the kid reporter in the shade of the pressbox and asked if he knew where Stephens was.

"Gómez said he returned to the United States, under the cover of darkness, like a rat."

"Did Gómez see him?"

The kid shook his head. He was enjoying this.

"So maybe Stephens is just late."

"No. He left a note." He handed me that day's *El Norte*. A headline read ¡VERNON STEPHENS SALTÓ A LOS CAFÉS DE SAN LUIS! Underneath was the kid's byline.

"*Saltó* is . . . ?"

"Jumped."

"So you scooped me, huh, kid?"

"Our readers," he said, "are hardly the same people." He reached into his pocket and pulled out a telegram. "This came for you, to the team offices over at the brewery."

It was, of course, from Desmond. STEPHENS BACK IN U.S. WHERE IS BULLINGER? WHERE IS HIS DENIAL OF CHARGES? COMMISH HAS BANNED YOU FROM BASEBALL, AS OF TODAY. It had been sent that morning. GAVE CARDS BEAT TO GILLESPIE. RETURN HOME NOW.

"Not bad news, I hope?" said the young reporter.

"All news is bad news, kid."

"I'll remember that," he said. "Sir."

I stayed for the rest of the game, which Monterrey won. Afterward I didn't interview anyone, didn't write a story, just filed out of the park along with the jubilant Monterrey faithful. In the lobby of the Hotel Colonial, an old woman sold me two wilted roses. Upstairs, Diana was waiting. We looked at each other. I gave her the flowers. We embraced. "I'm sorry," I said. "I can't even remember—"

"Forget it," she said. "Let's start over, okay?"

I handed her Desmond's telegram. "Gotta go home," I said. "We'll start over there, I guess."

"Now?" she said. "We've hardly been anywhere. I'm just start-ing to feel better. I've hardly seen any of Mexico."

I explained about Stephens and about the hysteria over the threat posed by the Mexican League. "I may already be sacked."

She considered this. "Why go back if you don't have a job?"

Of course I had reasons to go back—namely, Frances and Jerome—that I didn't want to mention. But I wouldn't necessarily be able to see either of them. "I can maybe save my job."

"Why not stay here? Can't we just stay here?"

"All I really need to do is say I was looking for a scoop. That'll get me off the hook."

Diana frowned.

"What?"

"You hate your job," she said.

"I don't. People gripe about their jobs in inverse proportion to how hard they are."

She grasped me by the shoulders. "Stop making everything a joke. Stop living your life wriggling off of hooks."

We were quiet for a long time. We stared at each other for a long time. Then I said, " 'Wriggling off of hooks'?" and we both broke out laughing, and soon our clothes began to fly.

I did not respond to Dez's telegram. I made no plans to return home. I stayed at the hotel, hoping my problems would take care of themselves. You'd be surprised how often they do.

"I didn't fuck that boy," said Diana. It was Sunday. We were coming from Mass. Diana was Catholic. The church had been built in 1879, and smelled of sweat, ammonia, and cheese.

"That *boy*," I said, "is your age."

"He's still a boy."

"A good-looking boy. You'd have to say he's good-looking."

"What do you want me to say?" she said.

A good question. "Just tell me the truth."

"I did. I am." She laughed. "Can I tell you a secret?"

"Yes."

"Something I just learned that I didn't know about myself."

"Yes."

"It sounds ridiculous, now that I say it."

"It doesn't sound ridiculous. You're not saying anything."

She laughed again. "Jealousy," she said.

"Jealousy?"

"Jealousy excites me," she said.

When we returned to the Hotel Colonial, Chile Gómez was waiting in the lobby along with a muscle-bound ox from the Bronx named Bob Janis. "George Paskwel wantsa see ya," Janis grunted.

"What for?" I said.

"Wantsa see whatcha know about dis mess wid Stephens."

"I don't know anything. Gómez here knows more than I do."

Janis shrugged. "Also, Mr. Paskwel told me to tell you he's got a job offer for you."

"Doing what?" I looked at Diana. She smiled.

"Fuck do I know?" said Janis. "He wants you in Mexico City by the time Mickey Owen gets there. We got a plane waiting."

"Jorge Pasquel's in Mexico City? I can't go. We're supposed to go back to—"

Diana leaned toward my ear and whispered, *Do it.*

"Press secretary of the Mexican League," blurted Gómez. "Señor Pasquel has heard of your job difficulties with your newspaper in San Luis. He fears he was the cause of your troubles, and he wishes to make you our press secretary."

Diana laughed. "I don't know the cause of Bullinger's troubles," she said, "but it's not Jorge Pasquel."

I was stunned. "How on earth does Jorge Pasquel know about my 'job difficulties'?"

"I have learned never to be surprised," said Gómez, "about what Jorge Pasquel knows. I am also not a fool large enough to ask how he has come to know it."

Janis asked me how much I made from the *Star-Times*.

"Three thousand a year," I said, which was $500 high.

"He'll pay six," Janis said. Back then you could buy a house for that, if you could find a house to buy, which, with the shortage, you couldn't. "Plus a case of booze a week."

I asked if Diana and I could talk it over. We went upstairs to pack. Actually, there was nothing to talk over, no chance I had the nerve to refuse. Right then, all I had to hold on to was Diana, a pampered little thrill-seeking bohemian, and my new job, which had "Faustian bargain" written all over it.

Things were definitely looking up.

❖

MYRON "RED" HAYWORTH
[Interview conducted July 4, 1975, on the showroom floor of
Hayworth Buick-Pontiac, on the Winston-Salem (N.C.) Auto
Mile.]

*I grew up over in High Point, North Carolina, where most
everyone is connected directly or indirectly to either tobacco or
furniture. We lived right in town there. My daddy owned a two-
bay Sinclair service station on Tobacco Road. When I was a boy,
I'd spend my days either playin ball or sittin in Daddy's garage
watchin him fix cars. It was a working-class town, Fords and
Chevys, but the furniture bigwigs and the tobacco-mill owners
tooled around in Cadillacs, Lincolns, Duesenbergs, Packards.
When the fancy cars came in for work, I'd grab a cold grape soda,
sit on a stool, and just look at 'em like you do a movie star on the
silver screen. The hood would go up and I couldn't have been
happier if I was seein Jane Russell's big bare titties.*

*My brother Ray—he was a catcher, too—he got a cup of coffee
with the Detroit Tigers in 1926. What a fuss that raised in town:
Local boy makes good. I was only a kid, and you can imagine
how puffed up I got about Ray's success.*

*Ray finally established himself in the big leagues in 1930. That
winter was the greatest time of my life, even to this day. I was fifteen years old. Ray came home driving a shiny black 1931 Cadillac and proposed marriage to his high-school sweetheart. Daddy
was best man in the wedding and I was an usher, and also the
chauffeur. Ray let me drive that Cadillac away from the High
Point Reformed Baptist Church, and, brother, was I in heaven! I
swore three things that day: I'd make it to the big leagues, just like
Ray; I'd marry my high-school sweetheart, just like Ray; and
when I did, I'd drive away from the church in a long black Cadillac, shiny and new, the envy of every living soul in High Point,
North Carolina. Just like Ray.*

*Things didn't work out the way I planned. I did have a high-
school sweetheart, a beautiful girl named Jeannette, whose family
was in tobacco, like your wife's people.*
Ex-wife.
Really? Jesus, I'm sorry to hear that.

It's been years, Red.

Well, that's women for you. They'll take your heart and—

Forget it. Let's talk about you. Tell me more about your plans.

Well, I got signed by the St. Louis Browns, but I had a devil of a time makin it through the minors. I was bigger than Ray, taller than Ray, and the same kind of player as Ray—a good defensive catcher but only fair at bat. But I kept getting hurt, like catchers will, broken fingers, bum knees, and whatnot. Then right when I was on the brink of making it, in the pink of health, the war breaks out. I was one of the first ballplayers drafted.

While I was overseas in Italy refueling planes, Jeannette met Roger Hassett, of Hassett Furniture, and I got a "Dear Red" letter, and those horny rascals went and got married. That was the end of that dream.

I served until '44, lost the heart of my baseball career. The only break I caught was coming back in time to play that season. With the war still going, I went right to the big leagues for the Browns. Even started in the World Series that fall.

But as for my dream of tooling down Main Street in a long black Cadillac, I was s.o.l. They didn't even make new cars until the war was over, and even then, it was impossible to get ahold of one. People waited for years. Winter of '45, I stop into Bilgere Cadillac, there by Sportman's Park in St. Louis. I show 'em my car, a canary-yellow '39 Chevy, mint condition, which I offer in trade. I want to order a Caddy. The salesman smiles and says, No problem—so long as I'll accept ten bucks for my Chevy!

It was the same everywhere. I had my name on waiting lists at every dealership from St. Louis to High Point. Spring training of '46, I went in a showroom in Los Angeles, to see if it was different out west. I saw a fella with another salesman. He pointed to a picture of Harry Truman on a wall fifty feet away. "Hey," he says to the salesman, "betcha five hundred clams I can hit Harry with my hat." The fella tosses the hat maybe a foot, forks over the dough, and an hour later he drives off the lot in a new blue two-tone Caddy. That's how it was sliced.

I remember, Red. Look, I know the parade starts pretty soon, so before you go, I need to know about how you came to Mexico. Stephens didn't speak highly of it when he rejoined the team.

Well, when the Pasquels first contacted me, I was shocked. I'd had a bad year in '45, I was thirty-one, and I was havin a poor spring—though the other catchers in camp, Mancuso and Helf, they weren't no better. Two days before the season opened, I met with Bernardo Pasquel in the penthouse of the Chase Hotel in St. Louis. He'd ordered up a feast, and all kinds of beer and liquor, and he asked how much I was making from the Browns. I told him. He offered me twice that. I said, Thanks but no thanks.

What was I thinking? I was a broken-down thirty-one-year-old journeyman who'd hit .195 the year before. I guess maybe what Stephens said about Mexico did get to me a little. But the real reason he left Mexico was that the commissioner said anyone who rejoined his team before opening day would get amnesty. Meat just used Mexico as a bargaining chip; he went down there knowin he'd stiff 'em. He figured the Browns would trade him to a contender, and that club would give him the money he wanted, and then he'd come home. It just didn't work out the way he figured. Welcome to the club, Meat.

Bernardo, though, kept pushin me, sayin I came highly recommended. I thought he must be mistakin me for Walker Cooper or Mickey Owen or somebody. But I stuck to my guns. As uncertain as my career was, I didn't want to be banned from playin ball in my own country.

Bernardo was polite, even amidst his high-pressure pitch. Twenty-six years sellin cars, I never seen anyone walk that line better. We shook hands, and he saw me out. As we rode down in the elevator, he didn't say a word. Genius: no oversell. It made me think I made a mistake.

Outside the hotel, what was idling at the curb but a brand-new black Cadillac. They were so scarce, I'd never seen one in person. I stopped dead in my tracks. The back door opened, and out came Bernardo's brother Jorge, all smiles. The seats were cream-colored leather. It had been five years since you could get a car with leather seats.

Jorge Pasquel walked up to me, introduced himself, then pointed at the Cadillac."This is to your liking, yes?" he said.

I couldn't talk. I tried, but I still couldn't.

He reached into his pocket and he tossed me the keys. "Congratulations," he said. "You are now the starting catcher for Torreón. Welcome to Mexico!"

And that's the same car you're driving in the parade?

One and the same.

How did they know that was the kind of car you wanted? Or that you were such a car buff?

[*Frowns.*] *I always figured you told 'em, Frank.*

No. I didn't. I never said word one.

7.

The Road of
the Twelve Trials

DANNY GARDELLA

I

The first crisis was when Vern Stephens got me thinking about all that was wrong with Mexico in general and Mr. Pasquel in particular. The second one was when Kate had Rocco Coniglio put in jail. Babe Ruth's last at-bat: also a crisis. Actually, it was more like the beginning of the end, the point the great Mexican League experiment went haywire.

By the time Stephens came down, I'd already survived things that could have been crises. For instance, Kate and I kept things going, writing letters and feeling more in love every day. Also there was Spanish. From rooming with Nap Reyes I knew enough to be dangerous, but I got there and—ba-*bing*—I could speak it. Maybe I got a gift or something. Another example was when Ramón Bragaña, who started out as our manager, tried me at positions other than left field: right and then first. To my surprise, first was my natural position. I was left-handed and flexible, so I could stretch for throws. I'd never played it before. Back home they always wanted a tall guy.

Like everyone, I got sick when I first got to Mexico, but you learn to take precautions. Also, you build up a tolerance to those microbe things in the water. Mexico gets a bad shake for that. Americans hate to go any place they need to adjust to. That's how it was with Stephens.

On the one hand, Stephens was a whale of a hitter. He gave credibility to the Mexican League and to us already there. He could have helped our club, but that's the other hand. When he joined us our hitting was going great but we was 2–3. What we needed was pitching. At shortstop we had Frank Rizzuti, a glove man who couldn't hit, but by the same token Stephens wasn't no prize in the field. When he arrived, Mr. Pasquel sent Rizzuti to the Red Devils, just like that. No trade, nothing. Then he paraded Stephens around Delta Park, these two conceited sharps.

In Stephens's first game he got the winning hit. Big hero. The next game, in Monterrey, he was green around the gills and went oh-for-four. In the fifth inning he crapped his drawers, right on the field. We gave him the business for that. But grant him this, he had moxie. He cleaned himself off between innings and finished the game in those soiled flannels.

After the game I tried to make it up to him. I paid for our cab, even offered to buy dinner. "Dinner in this blankety-blank country?" he said. We was in the lobby of the Hotel Colonial, waiting for an elevator, still in uniform. Stephens stood there in his soiled pants, bad-mouthing Mexico. Any Mexican who knew English would have come over and cut off our balls. Stephens said, "I've had the last meal I'm going to have in this blankety-blank hellhole."

"Suit yourself," I said. I was back in my room, showered and changed, before I realized what Stephens meant by that. I ran down to his room. "You can't leave," I told him.

He had on a long silk robe with a dragon on it, just like the one Mr. Pasquel wore when I first saw him back at Al Roon's Gym. He didn't invite me in. "Who said I'm leaving?"

"You don't know who you're dealing with," I said. I'd heard the story of Ray Dandridge trying to leave, from the horse's mouth. "I'm Italian," I said, "so I can tell you."

"Tell me what?"

I lowered my voice to a whisper. "You're dealing with this country's version of the Mafia."

Stephens laughed. I got him to let me in, and we ordered some steaks. I told about Mr. Pasquel's private army. I told how Mr. Pasquel was like a brother with Alemán, who was going to be the next president. I told how Mr. Pasquel had killed a man in a duel. Stephens wasn't laughing no more, so I told him a rumor I'd heard about how the Pasquels really made their money.

"Refueling Nazi U-boats?" Stephens said. "Come off it."

"That's what I hear," I said.

"I already called my dad," Stephens said. "He and a scout from the Browns are flying down tomorrow to bring me home." He looked scared. No more big hero.

I've always loved a challenge. That's how I got to Mexico in the first place. Plus I was on a roll when it came to dealing with things. So I offered my assistance. "It's the least I can do," I said, "after how I razzed you about crappin yourself."

In a strange land when you don't know nobody, you trust any friendly face.

The next night, Stephens and I went out drinking with the guys, so as not to arouse suspicion. I had to convince him to leave his clothes back at the hotel. All I heard was about these new tailor-made suits that he wanted to take with him. "You think you can walk away with two wardrobe cases and nobody's gonna see you? What are you, nuts? Forget about it."

He agreed, but that didn't keep him from bellyaching. Like a girl he was, with clothes. He insisted on wearing one of the suits. I said it made him a marked man—nobody in Monterrey had threads that fancy. He said he had an image to uphold.

Finally it came time for our rendezvous. We took two different cabs, zigzagging across Monterrey so we wouldn't be followed. I got the idea from a movie. It was midnight before we hooked up with Stephens's people, in a cab outside the beer garden at the big brewery where during the day you could get all the free beer you want. They was as nervous as subway rats.

I was already this far on the adventure, so I rode along. Also, I was drunk. I'm lucky I lived to tell about it. Not because of what Mr. Pasquel might have done, but because of that cabbie—a lead-foot kid who was maybe fourteen—and those roads. Over and over I thought we was going to crash into a burro cart or a cactus or a goat. Nobody said much but the kid. We told him we was in-surance men, figuring it was the dullest thing to say. Turned out, the kid's uncle sold insurance, and he thought it was the glamorous life. All the way to the border it's actuarials this, annuities that. I was thinking I could use some insurance, seeing as how I was about to die.

We had the kid drop us off at a hotel, then we waited in the lobby until he drove off. "I got an idea," I said to Stephens. "Change clothes with your dad."

They was about the same size. His dad had on a snap-brim hat, sport shirt, and chinos.

"You think we been followed?" Stephens said.

"No. But I wouldn't be surprised if the border guards was connected to the Pasquels somehow. You can't be too careful."

The fat stooge from the Browns agreed with me. Vern and his dad found a men's room and traded clothes. Then we hailed another cab and drove to the border.

Stephens got out. "Wish me luck, men," he said. Then he turned to me and said a thing that changed my whole summer: "Why in God's name do you want to play ball for a man like George Paskwel?" He didn't wait for an answer, he just turned around and walked toward America.

We hid behind a house trailer and watched Stephens, cool as a cuke, duck his head and keep walking. The guards waved him past. He got to the middle of the bridge, took off his dad's hat and threw it into the sky. As it sailed down into the Rio Grande, he yelled for joy and ran toward the streets of Laredo. A little later his dad and the Browns scout followed. The guards saw the dad, in that suit, saw how old he was, and waved him and the fat man home too.

There I was, alone in Nuevo Laredo, with no idea how to get back to Monterrey. Listening to Stephens bad-mouth Mexico had got to me. You know how you can date a girl and think she's great but then your buddies dog her and she never looks the same? That's how it was with me and Mexico. The border was right there. I rubbed Kate's subway token, for luck, thinking what to do. I came *this* close.

Just then the kid cabbie came by. "Mr. Insurance!" He tooted his horn. "Need a ride?"

"Only if you let me drive," I said. "I'll pay you double if you give me directions back to Monterrey and let me drive."

A Mexican cabbie will set you up with his sis if you offer to pay double. But I had no driver's license, hadn't driven a car since before the war. Forty miles out of town, on a gravel road the kid called El Camino de las Doce Pruebas, I pulled over and gave up the wheel.

We got to Monterrey an hour before I needed to be at the park. I paid the kid, went up to Stephens's room and took his suits. Then I called Mr. Pasquel's office to tell him his new fancy-dan shortstop was missing. That was the first game all season where I didn't get a hit.

II

Meanwhile, back home, Rocco Coniglio, this mixed-up genius from the old neighborhood . . . oh, right, I told you. Well, Rocco bought an expensive pistol at the Sears Roebuck in Peekskill—he bought it on time, in *my* name—and went home, to *my* apartment, and called Kate and told her to come over right away, it was an emergency.

Kate wanted to know what kind of emergency.

"I don't know," Rocco said. "Let's say a fire. Would that get you over here? A fire?"

"Is there a fire?"

"No," he said. "Worse than a fire. Come quickly, please."

Kate's pop was a fireman, and she brought him with her. They rang the bell, but there was no answer. They could hear movement inside. They rang the bell again, and this time Rocco called out, in a sweet voice, for them to come in, it was open.

When they did, he was sitting in a ladderback chair in the middle of the room, stark naked. "Good evening," he said. Then he showed them the gun. "Stand back, please," he said. He stuck the barrel in his mouth and pulled the trigger.

Nothing happened.

He tried again. Nothing.

He hadn't bought bullets; he thought guns came loaded. Geniuses can be the dumbest people you'd ever want to meet.

"Drat," he said—or that's what Kate said he said. He held the gun out toward Kate's pop. "Do you happen to know how to work one of these?"

Kate's pop was a take-charge guy, like firemen are. "I sure do," he said. He strode across the room to help Rocco finish the job. Kate screamed for him not to, but, like I said, no bullets. Kate had the presence of mind to call the cops. They arrested Rocco. It was clear to everyone Rocco had committed a crime, but no one could figure out what. For a day they left him in the lockup with drunks, pimps, and thieves, to shake him up, then they set him loose.

Both Kate and Rocco wrote me about this. "See what you made me do?" Rocco wrote. "But prison, God, Danny, how alive! I'm writing music again, a minor-key symphony for thieves."

Kate's account was the one I relied on. "Pop says you must evict Rocco right away," she wrote, "or I'll be forbidden to see you anymore."

How was I supposed to do that, being in Mexico? And so my troubles began, in earnest.

III

With the Pasquels everything was done excitedly. Everything was done with flash, gusto, machismo. It was a bad influence on a man recuperating from a mental illness he'd caught.

Take women. One time, Mr. Pasquel had me and Ramón Bragaña in his limo, driving out to his private country estate. He asked if we wanted some pretty girls. I pretended to have trouble understanding his Spanish. The car screeched to a halt. The chauffeur got out and opened the door. In crawled three blondes. I tried to say no thanks as graciously as I could, but the chauffeur got back in and started driving, and I was stuck.

Next thing you know the girls take off their clothes. Two of them sat in the far backseat, side by side, with their legs spread. Bragaña and Mr. Pasquel dropped their pants, climbed onto the women, and started thrusting with furious speed. They was both awful noisy. Both their shiny rumps was framed by the outstretched naked legs of the girls, and, to tell you the truth, for a minute it struck me as comical, like an image from some crazy surrealistic painting.

But then the other girl began to rub her hands over me. I was tempted. Who wouldn't have been? "Tengo una novia," I said. At first she looked hurt, but I kept saying I had a sweetheart. Finally she smiled and put her dress back on, and we pretended nothing unusual was going on.

Bragaña and Mr. Pasquel changed partners. Both those poor girls had their wigs falling off. Bragaña finished before Mr. Pasquel. The split second Mr. Pasquel finished, the car stopped. The women got out, and the car roared away. The only money that changed hands was from Mr. Pasquel to Bragaña, who won fifty American dollars for finishing first.

Later I found out these women weren't whores, just secretaries for one of the Pasquels' companies. Mexico at the time did not offer many opportunities for working women. They was just ambitious Mexican girls who knew what side their bread was buttered on.

IV

Mickey Owen didn't know what he got himself into. He was serious, rational, methodical. Mexico is a place full of bold colors and wild impulses. Mickey and Mexico was opposites.

Days after Stephens left, Owen showed up in Nuevo Laredo, where we was getting swept. Mickey brought his wife. Not many of the fellas brought their wives down, for just the reasons you'd think. Mickey Owen wasn't like that.

The Nuevo Laredo crowd whistled at Owen louder than the Monterrey fans did Stephens. That was a rough place, Nuevo Laredo. Border town. The fans *arrived* drunk. Every park in Mexico had gambling going on in the stands, but in that place I even saw ballplayers place bets.

For some reason, Owen didn't play in Nuevo Laredo, didn't even travel with the club but in Mr. Pasquel's plane. At our next game, in Mexico City, Owen finally got introduced. Here he was, an All-Star, and he got weak applause with some whistles! Chico Hernández, our catcher, a Cuban who played for the Chicago Cubs during wartime, told me the Mexican people was sick of all the Americans. "The Pasquels have overdone it. We play good baseball here already. We do not need all these Americans to prove that."

That's when I realized the whistles was about Chico, who won the Mexican League home-run crown in '44 and was a fan favorite. Owen's arrival meant that Chico—who was just as good—

would get moved to another club, like a pawn on a chessboard, the way it happened with Rizzuti.

Owen himself had a lousy attitude, which didn't help things. He claimed Mr. Pasquel promised him he could manage at Tor-reón—which I doubt, seeing as they had Martín Dihigo—and now, instead, here he was joining up with Veracruz.

"Welcome to Mexico, Mick," I said. He was sitting in Mr. Pasquel's box, in street clothes. "That's the way they boo, you know. That whistling."

He frowned at me. "Who the hell are you?"

"Dangerous Dan Gardella," I said, using the name the newspaper sharps called me. "Late of the Giants." I couldn't believe he didn't know me. Maybe he wanted to yank my chain.

"So," he said, looking around Delta Park. "This is where wartime ballplayers go to die."

"Right," I said. "You're here, aren't you?"

Owen and his wife moved into a nice apartment off of Reforma—that wide boulevard with the statues—but for a week he just took b.p. and rode the bench. It got to him, and to Chico, too, who'd been hot until Owen got there and then, with Mickey looking over his shoulder, right away went in a slump.

One day I told Mickey I'd ask Bragaña why he wasn't playing.

"How are you gonna do that," Owen asked. Bragaña didn't speak English.

"If you're gonna take their money, Mick, maybe you might trouble yourself to learn Spanish. Broaden your horizons." My conversational Spanish had clicked, plus I'd bought books to try and be fluent. I've lost most of that knowledge now. It's criminal what we forget in life.

Bragaña, when I asked him about Owen, just said, "No es mi decisión," and nodded toward Mr. Pasquel's box.

"He wants you to get used to your new surroundings," I told Owen. The man was already sullen enough without me telling him Mr. Pasquel was up to something.

Finally it came clear what. Back in the U.S. the season started. That same day, we lost at home to Monterrey when Chico Hernández got tagged at the plate to end the game. Chico broke his leg. I guess Mr. Pasquel couldn't have controlled that, but it sure solved his Chico problem.

The next day the papers said Owen would make his debut with

Veracruz. Way down in the story, Happy Chandler, the commissioner of baseball, said that amnesty for players who jumped to Mexico ended as of opening day. That's why they didn't play Owen. They was baby-sitting him. They wasn't going to let him play until he had nowhere else to go.

V

It was about then I decided to ask Kate to marry me. I was crazy from loneliness. I began to notice myself losing control. On the field, I was the hottest hitter in the league. But we had too many off days, and I started acting up again. I'd rather not go into specifics. Let's just say it was like Rocco Coniglio's spirit was possessing me. I was hundreds of miles separated from him, but I felt his presence. Night and day I worried how to get him out of my apartment so Kate's father would allow her to keep seeing me. Then it occurred to me that if I left Rocco there and brought Kate to Mexico and married her, all would be solved. Kate was a grown woman, twenty-two, and didn't absolutely need her father's permission.

I started hinting around about this in my letters, and I felt she was hinting she might accept. She was about to graduate from City College, so I wrote that as a graduation present I'd like to give her an expense-paid luxury trip to Mexico—that is, unless she was previously engaged. How much more a hint can you give than that? She wrote back that she'd be delighted to accept my gift. I was on cloud nine. What did I know? I was a kid in love, and my girl loved me back. Nobody tells you this, but that's the easy part.

VI

The Pasquels had us around to add to their luster—no different from Al Roon putting my picture in his lobby, except Al Roon was small potatoes in comparison. Movie stars, ballplayers, politicians: all props in a big show. Jorge Pasquel was the star and Bernardo was the director.

When we was in Mexico City we'd be summoned to Mr. Pasquel's estate. You drove past miles of people in shacks until you came to a big white mansion on a hill. It had a bowling alley, tennis court, swimming pool. A hundred-foot-long game room lined with guns and mounted animal heads and filled with tables for billiards, Ping-Pong, and cards. There'd be girls, booze, and music, and always some kind of competition. Eight ball. Poker. Tennis. Swimming races. Peeing for distance. Archery. Boxing. The color of the next car to come down the road. Everything was a contest, and every contest had money wagered on it.

Early in the season, Babe Ruth was always there, slathered in suntan oil and tanked up on highballs. He wasn't well, which I attributed to the drinking and cigars and to age. Still, he was *Babe Ruth.* Big. You know? *Big,* in every way. The only thing I'd say against him was that he kept his distance from the black guys, but in that respect he was a product of his times. Also, there was a rumor he had black blood, which he was touchy about. At any rate, he was the only fellow around who could overshadow Jorge Pasquel.

One off day, most of us was there relaxing and doing the mambo by the pool when Mr. Pasquel's plane landed in the airstrip next door. He and his girl, María Félix, the actress, they entered and the mood changed, like a speeded-up movie. Mr. Pasquel went around his swimming pool, greeting the guys, slapping us on the back, asking us if we needed anything. Our needs was already well seen to. Then Mr. Pasquel and Miss Félix slipped into the bathhouse to change. You could hear them making love in there. Everything Mr. Pasquel did was loud.

Mr. Pasquel and Miss Félix emerged from the bathhouse, by which time the air was charged with energy. Mr. Pasquel noticed Babe Ruth and some American starlet he was playing Ping-Pong with. A big western was being filmed nearby, which I'm sure Mr. Pasquel had something to do with. "A tournament of table tennis!" Mr. Pasquel exclaimed. "I challenge every man here!" The ladies was expected to stand back and watch.

He called over his little brother Alfonso and had him draw up a tournament bracket, right on the adobe wall of the game room, in between a rhino head and a case of fancy shotguns.

We all signed up. We knew to humor our host. The fellas that got paired with Mr. Pasquel had the good sense to let him win. The one who gave him the closest game was Cantinflas—you know, the famous comedian? That fella was a rotten Ping-Ponger, but he did these hilarious mime antics—the man in the box, the man walking against the wind, the man pulling a bird out of his nose—and it cracked Mr. Pasquel up. But Mr. Pasquel still won.

I was good at Ping-Pong, but Babe Ruth beat me in the first round. I thought it was me, nervous about competing with a hero of my youth. I could hardly look at him, I was so nervous. But the Babe could have beat me even if I'd had more poise. He looked bad doing it, but he played Ping-Pong better than anyone. Even the Chinese on TV, who stand back from the table thirty feet, even they'd have been mincemeat against Ruth. He was lighter on his feet than he looked. His reaction time was amazing. When he reached back to slam a ball, you knew you was about to hear a deafening whack. He broke five or six balls a game.

The final game paired him against Mr. Pasquel. Ruth wasn't taking things too serious, but he also wasn't a guy who let somebody win something. Mr. Pasquel was stripped down to his bathing suit, sweating heavily. You could tell he thought he could win. Ruth didn't *look* like he could beat anybody, but really there wasn't anybody he couldn't beat.

As the game progressed and the score got lopsided, you could see Mr. Pasquel about to blow. Twice, he lost a point, hauled off, and threw his paddle. Once, it hit the trumpet player from the mambo band. He needed stitches. The game just went right on like nothing happened.

"Game point, George," the Babe called out. He had a big grin on his face. This was just another opponent to toy with, another man who didn't belong in the same game with him. His whole life was a chain of moments like this.

Mr. Pasquel had the serve. He stood there concentrating on how he was going to hit that little ball. The wait went on and on, and finally the Babe broke out laughing. "C'mon, Hannibal Harry," he said. "Drop the bomb."

Mr. Pasquel tossed the ball up and tried to put a fancy spin on it, but he slammed it into the net. The Babe laughed, harder now, and had just started around the table to collect his money when Mr. Pasquel went over to the wall with the tournament bracket on it and punched a hole in it with his fist. Then he threw open the door of that gun cabinet, grabbed a shotgun, and fired two blasts right at the wall. There must have been fifty shotguns in that case, all double-barreled, all loaded. He fired every last one at that tournament bracket until you couldn't see it no more. What you could see was daylight. The man had blasted away the side of his house.

When he finished, the Babe, who'd gone for a drink in the middle of all this, walked calmly up to Mr. Pasquel. "Missed me, missed me," he said. "Now you gotta kiss me." He planted a big smooch on Mr. Pasquel's cheek. And Mr. Pasquel had to laugh, because, like I said, nobody overshadowed Babe Ruth.

Seconds later, a squadron of cop cars roared up to the house. They'd heard the shooting and automatically figured someone had assassinated Mr. Pasquel.

Later that night I remember sitting on a lounge chair next to you, Frank, watching your fiancée compete in a diving contest against Chile Gómez, our second sacker. I never figured out what you did as press secretary. All I saw you do was sit around and hit the bottle. Mr. Pasquel already had a crew at work repairing that wall.

"Poor Babe," you said. "For years he's had this crazy dream of becoming a manager. Nobody in American would ever give him a chance."

That confused me. We had Bragaña, plus Mickey Owen, who thought he was supposed to be somebody's manager somewhere. Now Ruth?

"Plus Gómez," you said. Just then Gómez did a real nice jackknife. "Gómez has got Pasquel's ear. Believe me."

"So is Ruth going to manage us or not?"

You shrugged. "I doubt it. He has it hard enough managing himself." Right then, the Babe was over at the poker table with a pair of ladies' undies on his head. "Also," you said, "I think he got a look at the operation down here and thought better of committing himself to it."

Wrong. Ruth refused the offer because he knew he was dying of cancer. But nobody else knew it, then. Probably not even Mr. Pasquel.

"The Pasquels are good at exploiting a guy's crazy dreams, aren't they, Frank?"

"The rich usually are," you said. Boy, were you drunk.

By the way, your fiancée sure could dive. I don't know what

kind of dives she did, but it was pretty to see, out there in the Mexican desert. She twirled around like some wild, angry bird. Beat the tar out of Gómez.

VII

Mickey Owen, in his first game with the Blues, hit a sac fly to win the game. In spite of this we remained in last. That was a thorn in Mr. Pasquel's side. Bragaña, old diamond-tooth, caught the flack for it. He got it in one ear for his own performance as a pitcher and in the other for managing a pitching staff that gave away homers like they was tickets to a bad play. Bragaña didn't like getting it in either ear. Our pitchers was graybeards or babies, like in the States during the war, so I don't know what Bragaña was supposed to do. He'd been player-manager since Rogers Hornsby quit in '44 [*Ed.: the* Rogers Hornsby; *he also batted twice: a walk and a three-run double*], and Bragaña had got the job as a bonus for having a thirty-win season. A year and a half was a long time to manage for Mr. Pasquel.

Playing just four games a week, all you needed was three good starters, a rubber-armed reliever, and a couple warm bodies. For us, everyone pitched like warm bodies. Lukewarm. Bragaña's problem was that he was a ground-ball pitcher—which is what it took to win in those tiny parks—who was having a hard time keeping the ball down. Also he was forty and probably not what he once was. Carrasquel, the number two starter, was good with the Senators, but with us he started out like crap. A month into the season, though, he settled down and was our best pitcher for a while. Our third guy was a nineteen-year-old Mexican greenhorn named Tito Herrera [*Ed.: Herrera pitched 2.1 wretched innings for the St. Louis Browns in 1951; my son caught one of the home runs he gave up, which I got Herrera to sign and which Jerome still had among his effects when he died*]. And our reliever was Schoolboy Johnny Taylor, who was a long time removed from his school days. All in all, a sorry sight. We'd score six, eight runs and lose. Biggest payroll in the league and we was in the cellar.

You know what? I couldn't have cared less. Baseball wasn't fun no more. I was never a guy who concentrated on the fine points of the game, staying late to practice bunting or hitting the cutoff man. I didn't kick water coolers or wreck lockers when my team lost. But baseball had always been fun. With all I went through in '46—worrying about remaining a Giant and about my troubles at home, thinking about who made how much money—the game stopped being fun. Baseball seemed like a cross between a second-rate circus and going to meet the tax man.

I spent my free time working on my Spanish as I went sightseeing. I went alone, climbing around on that famous pyramid south of the city and buying cheap Chac Mools. One place I loved was the Zócalo, an open-air market where you could buy anything and the price was always negotiable, which gave me a chance to work on the conditional tense, where you say you'll take something on the condition the price drops. I'd gotten Kate some turquoise earrings there, and another time I got her pop an onyx chess set. He was a big checkers man at the firehouse, and I thought he'd want to broaden himself. One amazing find was a set of Mahler records by the Berlin Philharmonic. German orchestra recordings was still impossible to find in the States. I felt sorry for poor Rocco Coniglio, so I mailed him those records. I thought they'd cheer him up. What was I thinking? Who gets cheered up by Mahler?

One day I was in the Zócalo and I came upon a booth of votive candles, hundreds of hand-painted glass cylinders with images of the sacraments. You name it, there was a candle for it, as well as ones with different saints and for different emotions: love and grief are two I remember. Many of them had dancing skeletons wearing masks of human faces, oftentimes of laughing children. Mexican people have a different view of death. They're not so conceited, thinking their lives are so important the world can't go on without them. They know they're goners, and they accept it. They celebrate death as a part of life. Once a year everyone goes to the cemetery dressed in feathers and masks and throws a party on the graves of their loved ones. I learned more about Mexico in that candle booth than most American guys learned all season.

There was a wrinkled fellow there, tall, especially for an old Mexican, and I asked if he was the one who did the painting.

"No," he said in Spanish. "The artist is my sick daughter Inés. You should buy her works now because she is very sick and not destined to produce much artwork. After her death, what will become of us, I don't know."

In those days a good sales pitch could've got me to buy one chance at Russian roulette, get five free.

Just then I happened upon the most beautiful of all the candles. Ringed around the top was a canon of saints, of which I recognized Sebastian and the Virgin Mary. Lower was an altar, with gold and rubies and trays overflowing with Hosts. Facing it was a priest, viewed from behind, a hood over his head. Then there was a long red path circling the glass cylinder like the threads of a screw. Beside it was all the beasts of the kingdom, lions and lambs, jackrabbits and bears, cheek to jowl, in peace. At the bottom was a man and a woman in silhouette. The man kneeled, with his hand held out to the woman. Her hands was over her heart.

"¿Cuánto cuesta?" I said. I forget how much it was. I took out my wallet and paid him the asking price. It threw him off to have me not bargain, which ordinarily I liked to do. As he wrapped up the candle, he kept looking at me out of the corner of his eye like he expected me to do something even crazier. He didn't understand, and I'm not sure I can explain it, except to say that for this candle I wasn't going to haggle.

VIII

Here's how bad our pitching got. One night most of us was at a nightclub when Mickey Owen and his missus introduced me to friends who'd come to Mexico for a second honeymoon. It was the year of second honeymoons, people was so glad to be alive and reunited after the war. Roy Kniklebine Henshaw was the fellow's name, I can't recall the wife's. Mickey called him Knik. Knik and Mick. They went way back. He was a guy my size, pudgy and bald.

The whole night had just about played itself out when Jorge Pasquel showed up. He made his way over to our table, and when Mickey introduced him to his buddy, Mr. Pasquel recognized the name. "The same Roy Henshaw who pitched for the Cubs in the 1935 World Series, against the Tigers of Detroit?"

Knik nodded. "Unfortunately, yes, that's me."

I guess he didn't pitch so well.

Mr. Pasquel was pleased with himself for remembering. He had movies of every World Series from the time newsreels started, he said.

They got to reminiscing about when Mickey Owen was a rookie with the Cardinals, which was when he and Knik got to be friends. Knik was a minor-league pitching coach when the war broke out, and when players got scarce he came out of retirement. I had never heard of him, but he claimed he pitched some for the Tigers in '42 and '43. He felt guilty about it, he said, and in '44 he volunteered for the service.

"Are you planning to reenter baseball?" Mr. Pasquel asked.

Henshaw laughed. "Those days are gone, friend. I haven't so much as picked up a baseball in two years." When him and his wife's vacation ended, he was going to go into business with his father, building houses on the North Side of Chicago.

I left those guys to their boring stories of the good ol' days and went back to my hotel to finish my daily letter to Kate.

The next day, when I got to the park, guess who's loosening up in the bullpen, in a uniform that's tight across his middle and too long in the arms and the legs? Yep. Knik Henshaw.

Bragaña went the first six innings. The game was 3–3 when, on orders from Mr. Pasquel, Bragaña put Henshaw in. I believe the Spanish verb for what Torreón did to Knik is *aplastar*. To crush. He gave up a run in the seventh, four in the ninth. I homered twice but it wasn't enough. We lost 8–7. That was Knik Henshaw's one and only game in Mexico, and the last game of his career.

What stays with me, though, is what happened after. Knik showered up and got dressed in that dark clubhouse at Delta Park. We was the only ones there. The only reason I stayed around, instead of going home where I could shower up in more comfort, was that I was waiting for Mr. Pasquel's cobbler. Anytime you hit two homers in a game you got a new pair of shoes.

Knik Henshaw shaved, got dressed, then neatly folded up his sweaty uniform and his borrowed hat, glove, and spikes. He walked past me and nodded hello. He went onto the field and set his gear right on home plate of that deserted ball diamond, then he looked for his wife in the stands. She was sitting in Mr. Pasquel's box, alone. He waved at her. She waved back. He shrugged. She shrugged back. He rolled his eyes and laughed.

She laughed, too. He limped over to her, held out his hand, and she helped pull him up over the railing. The last I ever saw of those two old married people was them walking out of the ball-park, arm in arm.

IX

April 27, 1946

Dearest Danny,

Thank you so much for the beautiful candle! It got here just fine. When I opened it up I thought perhaps it was a box filled w/newspapers & then I saw it. It's gorgeous. I have it on our mantel, beside the snapshot of us at Coney Island & one of your bubble-gum cards Pop gave me. I am in love w/a man on a bubble-gum card! Swell! Do they have those in Mexico?

Time to be serious for 1 moment. I think I know what you're trying to say by sending me that candle along w/an airplane ticket, but, sweetie, you're going to have to say it. Do you see? You are right in thinking that I do not have *to have Pop's consent, but, inside, I do. Since Mother died, he's all the family I have. Also, I am not, as you know, the kind of girl who is going to "shack up" in the tropics w/her beau—no matter how funny & handsome he may be! Please understand that I am absolutely* not *asking you to do or say anything. Take your time. Look in your heart. Don't rush into anything. I will wait for you.*

Congratulate me! As of today, I have finished student teaching & am certified to teach elementary school any-where in the State of N.Y. I have not started to look for jobs, but I hear they are plentiful. There is a shortage of teachers. These days, there is a shortage of everything.

I saw your brother yesterday. Al said to say hello & to tell you your belongings are O.K. & stored in his attic, except of course for the sofa Rocco set on fire, which has been thrown out. Nothing else was damaged, apparently. I have not seen that horrible Rocco since Al got you out of your lease. Al said they only kept him at Bellevue for 5 days. The apartment was rented to a nice Negro couple, by the way. The Moores. He is a Navy veteran & she is a nurse & they are expecting in

November. Some people on the block have Said Things, but Pop & I have tried to make friends & be good neighbors. I brought them lasagna. It was strange to be in that apartment w/new people in it.

I have checked w/Eastern Airlines & they say you can get your money back for the ticket if you contact their Mexico City office by May 15. All you need is your reservation number, which I have enclosed.

Congratulations on the new 2-tone wing-tip shoes & on your excellent hitting so far. I am so proud of you. Go Blues!

All my love,

K.

X

In Tampico, in May, Mr. Pasquel got us some pitching help: Ace Adams and Harry Feldman, who'd been teammates of mine with the Giants. Ace was an old wine-drinking reliever, and Harry was a quiet, skinny Jew from Arkansas. They was off to slow starts [*Ed.: Adams's ERA was 16.88, Feldman's 18.00*] and figured they better take Mr. Pasquel up on his offer before it was too late. They left a game at Crosley Field in Cincinnati, snuck out of the bullpen, and kept running until they met up with us in Tampico. What a first impression: Tampico was a hot, smelly port town, a big outdoors version of Al Roon's steam bath.

The Alijadores of Tampico—literally, cotton ginners, but we called 'em cotton pickers—had been in first from the start of the season, and I was eager to get a look at them. Johnny Taylor and I caught an early cab to the ballpark together, and, boy, was we in for an eyeful.

First of all was that ballpark, a gray wooden grandstand that looked like it was built in a day and then been expected to stand for a generation. The bleachers extended to the foul poles, where they abruptly ended for one simple reason: A set of railroad tracks there ran right through the outfield grass. The outfield fence was on the other side of the tracks.

"Well, that's that," Johnny said. "Now I seen everything."

"Remind me to thank my lucky stars Bragaña made me into a first sacker."

About then the Tampico club came on the field to loosen up, and I thought, *These* are the guys in first place? I didn't recognize none of them. I asked John if he knew any guys from the Negro Leagues. Only three: Bonnie Serrell, at second; Ray Brown, that day's pitcher; and an outfielder named Kangaroo Amaro, who John played against in Venezuela. The shortstop, Franklin, we found out he had a cup of coffee with Detroit before the war. Other than him, Tampico didn't have no one with big-league experience. No Negro stars. They was in first, we was in last, and their whole club made less money than Mickey Owen.

If people in America would have paid more attention to the Mexican League that year, they wouldn't have been so afraid of losing that cockamamie reserve clause. They'd have seen that free agency wouldn't kill baseball. They'd have learned what these big-league owners today still don't get, that you can't buy a pennant. Players don't win pennants, teams do. Tampico was a *team:* good pitching, good fielding, good baserunning, good at the little things like moving men along on grounders and bunts. Steinbrenner, that penny-ante version of Mr. Pasquel we have here in New York running the Yankees now, he should have seen those Tampico Cottonpickers mop the floor with us in 1946.

In the first game, Harry Feldman started and got lit up like a Christmas tree. Ace—that was his given name—he came in and threw gas on the fire. Our outfielders was always looking down to avoid those train tracks, and it seemed like every ball fell in for a hit. Their fielders knew just how to play it, and their starter, Brown, pitched a shutout. That set the tone for the series. Their next three starting pitchers was Mexicans nicknamed Cocaína, Cochihuila, and El Loco: Cocaine, Little Pig, and The Crazyman. Who knows what that was supposed to mean, but they all pitched great, and we got swept. Me, I went oh-for-Tampico.

XI

When we got home, the front page of the papers was covered with Alemán, who looked like a shoo-in for president. Every time you saw a picture of Alemán, you'd look close and see a Pasquel in the background. On the sports page it said that four men from the St. Louis Cardinals—Stan Musial, Max Lanier, Fred Martin, and Lou Klein—had jumped to the Veracruz Blues. Lanier we could use, he was the toughest lefty in the league, but if a star like Musial came down, it'd be curtains for yours truly. I'd become a Parrot or a Cactus Fruit, a city boy in one of those little towns full of big churches. I tried not to worry; there'd been rumors about Ted Williams and DiMaggio too, and they'd proved false. But the biggest news—written up both on the front page and in sports— was about a hitting exhibition at Delta Park by "El Gran Bambino, El Sultán de 'Swat,' Baby Ruth." Mexicans called him "Baby" because "Babe" is hard to say in Spanish, which doesn't have no silent vowels. I remember the word for home-run hitter now: *jonronero*. They called him the maximum jonronero of all time. It's coming back to me, the Spanish.

Why Mr. Pasquel kept Babe Ruth in the wings so long was that he wanted to unveil him during a series between Mexico City and Veracruz. He wanted those games to be a showcase for the world, with the stands full and the clubs with the best-known players on display. American reporters would come, and the maximum jonronero would lend the circus its crowning glory.

At the Thursday game, Mr. Pasquel contented himself with introducing the Babe to the crowd. We knew the drill, but with Ruth it was different. Next to Mr. Pasquel he looked sloppy, dressed in a cheap baggy suit with his shirt open, no tie. Didn't matter. He was Babe Ruth. I can't begin to describe the cheers that old man got. For those fans, who'd never seen him play, it was like some mythological creature had come down from the sky. After that, the game itself was a bonus. We won; Carrasquel beat Fireball Smith in a pitchers' duel. I homered off Smith, my ninth, which put me third in the league behind Ortiz of the Reds and Estalella of the Blues. The home-run champ was supposed to win a free house. We was all aware of where we stood.

Saturday was the day of Babe Ruth's show. Again there was a full crowd. They had a few thousand fans down on the field, roped off, more than on opening day. That hill beyond the outfield where people went to pee, it was packed with Mexicans wanting to catch a glimpse of a baseball god.

The Babe loosened up with us before the game. Remember, I'm a New Yorker born and raised, a Bronx kid to boot. My dad took me to one ball game before he died: my very first one, two subway stops away at Yankee Stadium. It was 1927, the year Babe hit sixty homers. He hit one that day, to left center, right where that monument to him now stands. My pop, who didn't know ball from bupkiss, was jumping up and down, shouting Ruth's praises in Italian. I was seven years old. You don't forget a day like that. A year later, my old man was dead of consumption.

So imagine the thrill it was for me to stand on the same ball diamond as Babe Ruth, out in right field, shagging fungoes. The Babe stood there in an undershirt, slacks, and street shoes. He wasn't catching nothing. He just waved to the crowd and did some stretching. According to the papers, he hadn't swung a bat since he played in an exhibition in Washington, D.C., three years earlier, to help sell war bonds. Maybe he was nervous. Probably he was nervous. I didn't notice, because of how nervous *I* was.

Then came the biggest thrill in all my baseball days, the only time I exchanged words with the great Babe Ruth. "Hey, kid," he growled at me. "Gimme a chew."

"I don't have a chew," I said. Then I remembered I had a Cuban cigar in my back pocket. Tarzán Estalella's wife just had a baby, and he'd been passing out cigars all day. "All I got," I said, "is this. It's yours if you want it."

The Babe grabbed the cigar, screwed open the tin tube, stuck the stogie in his mouth, and bit off half. He put the rest in the tube and handed it to me. "Thanks, kid," he said, chewing on the cigar tobacco. "You're a lifesaver."

That was it, my conversation with Babe Ruth.

The Babe's hitting show was a letdown. Right after the Mexican national anthem, he dragged his bat to the plate. It was a fifty-two ouncer, like he'd always used, but he was old, and it was too much. Mr. Pasquel had gotten the bat made out of special Cuban tropical wood. It had commemorative things carved onto it. The Babe stood there with that log, flailing at batting-practice pitches that a coach from the Red Devils floated in there, an old black guy they called the Witch. All the Babe managed was a line drive, a Texas Leaguer, and one long foul ball. When he quit, the fans gave him a standing ovation. That impressed me, that respect they showed. I don't mind telling you, there was tears in my eyes.

❖

The next morning I read a rumor Babe Ruth was going to play that day, in the *game*, for Veracruz. Even though a league spokesman denied it—you, Frank?—still, the papers went nutso, saying Mr. Pasquel had packed his team with too much imported talent. They talked about Lanier, who was supposedly coming, and Musial, who, thank God, denied signing anything. But allowing the Babe to play for the Blues was more than the newspaper jackals could stomach. What their problem was I don't know. Maybe they hadn't looked at the standings for a while.

We got to the park and there's no sign of Ruth—that is, except for that scary overflow crowd. People sat on each other's laps and on the armrests. By game time there was a fog of tobacco smoke under the overhang and no foul territory left, just the area behind home plate. The ropes that kept the fans away ran right next to the foul lines. Narrow paths was roped off so we could get from the dugout to the on-deck circle. Mr. Pasquel's private militia, twenty armed horsemen, was positioned inside and outside Delta Park.

I asked Bragaña what he knew about the Babe Ruth rumor, but he was in a surly mood and wouldn't talk. At the time I just chalked it up to him being the starting pitcher that day.

The game began, and still no sign of Ruth. Mr. Pasquel was in his box, along with his brother Bernardo, Miguel Alemán, and two of the little bald brothers. But no Bambino.

Ramón Bragaña was the sharpest he was all season, painting the corners and throwing nasty breaking balls. The Red Devils could murder the baseball: Ray Dandridge, Luis Olmo, Wild Bill Wright, Roberto Ortiz. Yet Bragaña mowed 'em down, inning after inning. It gave me a glimpse of the Bragaña I never got a chance to see, who once won thirty games and was a Negro League star. Every old player, it seems like, gets that one last shot, when everything returns to him, all his powers, one last time. In the third inning, we had a big rally, including a homer by Estalella that he dedicated to his baby daughter, and we chased Tommy de la Cruz, the Reds pitcher. Bragaña only needed one run that day, and we got him seven.

Going into the ninth inning, Bragaña had given up only three scratch singles and an error I made that luckily hadn't hurt him. That mammoth crowd got on its feet. Bragaña got the first batter,

Roberto Ortiz, to strike out on three pitches. He turned his back on the plate and looked out at the center-field sky, and he smiled. The sun glinted off that front diamond tooth.

Next up was Dandridge. Bragaña and him got locked in a cat-and-mouse, with Bragaña throwing knee-buckling curves and Dandridge fouling off pitch after pitch until he saw one he liked. Mickey Owen called for a fastball; that was the one. Dandridge sent a smash screaming through the box. Chile Gómez raced over from second and, in short center field, dove for the ball. He speared it an inch from the ground. The crowd couldn't believe it, and to tell you the truth neither could I. Gómez was their boy, the second-ever Mexican big-leaguer, and they gave him a hand I thought would tear the roof off that old park.

Gómez flipped the ball in to Bragaña. Two down. One batter to go for the shutout. On deck, Fireball Smith.

Just then, the hatch behind home plate popped open. Out came none other than Jorge Pasquel, all fitted up in a Veracruz Blues uniform. He doffed his cap to the crowd and jogged to the pitching mound. The umpire didn't do nothing, but Bragaña, he had fire in his eyes. I couldn't hear what they was saying, but it was clear they was having words.

Mr. Pasquel signaled to Ernie Carmona, the Mexico City manager, who then went out to have Fireball sit down for a pinch hitter. Fireball wasn't much happier than Bragaña.

The roar of the crowd went up before I even saw Babe Ruth. Where he came from I don't know. Out of that hatch, I guess, but I didn't see him. All I know is I looked up and there stood the Babe, with that black Cuban club on his shoulder, dressed the same as yesterday, undershirt and slacks. The only difference was today he had on a Red Devils ball cap.

So you see? Mr. Pasquel didn't stack the deck for us. He had Ruth bat for Mexico City. You just knew it made Mr. Pasquel heartsick to have the Babe not play for his beloved Blues, with Mr. Pasquel's hometown spelled out across his famous chest. That's maybe why the Babe didn't have a uniform on.

Gómez and Owen jogged out to the mound, but I didn't have to. I knew Mr. Pasquel was telling Bragaña to groove a pitch. Boy, did he pick the wrong man to do that. If anybody was going to put on an exhibition that day, it was Bragaña.

Mr. Pasquel took a seat in our dugout, and everybody got back to their positions. Bragaña looked in to Owen for the sign, shook him off a few times, then smiled his meanest-looking smile and reared back and fired what must have been the fastest pitch he'd thrown all game. Babe Ruth took it for a strike, then stepped out of the box and frowned at Mr. Pasquel.

The crowd didn't know who to root for. It's a damp, creepy feeling when a crowd that size grows silent and confused. I looked over my shoulder at the people on the pee hill, and in my mind's eyes I saw Comanches riding over the crest of a butte in some western movie.

Owen called for a change-up, and set up right in the strike zone. Bragaña didn't even bother shaking him off, he just hauled off and threw a roundhouse curve, a major-league yakker. It looked outside, but Ruth lunged at it. The pitch broke so sharply it about hit him. It was in Mickey Owen's glove before the Babe got his bat through the strike zone.

Strike two.

Now the crowd erupted. They'd chosen a favorite: Bragaña, this Cuban Negro who'd played in their country for years and who was working on a shutout and who was about to strike out the biggest Yankee of us all. There was also the matter of brown versus white. I glanced at the fans piled together down the first-base line, not six feet away. They looked like a pot of boiling water, all smoke and movement and heat.

Mr. Pasquel ran to the mound and he and Bragaña screamed at each other, nose to nose. What a shower Bragaña must have got! I ran to the mound, too, mostly because a part of my Spanish that needed work was swearing. But by the time I got there, the decision was made. Mr. Pasquel was sending to the showers a proud man who had a three-hitter going, two outs, bottom of the ninth, ahead in the count to a fifty-one-year-old dying drunk. "Give me the ball, you son of a whore," Mr. Pasquel said in Spanish.

"Go to the devil," said Bragaña. He was holding the ball behind his back, and Mr. Pasquel was trying to grab it from him. Then Bragaña said the only thing I ever heard him say in English: "F—— you and the whores you rode in on."

Bragaña wasn't going to give up that baseball, and he wasn't going down without a fight. He spun around and heaved the ball out to center field. There was a big Chiclets billboard there, with a

Negro face on it and tiny-size hole in the mouth. The ball rattled in and out before it fell to the warning track.

Then Bragaña stormed off the mound and headed straight for Babe Ruth. He pulled back his fist and, before the Babe even saw it coming, coldcocked the Sultan of Swat.

That tore it.

The crowd stormed the field. Thousands of fanatic Mexicans, whipped into a frenzy. The home-plate umpire pulled out a long-barreled pistol and shot it in the air six times. Right beside me, the first-base ump did the same, only his gun was smaller. Umpires with guns! We'd been playing ball for half a season in a place where the umps carried guns! I hit the dirt. I honest to God thought I was going to die.

The gunshots stopped a lot of the Mexicans in their tracks. Mr. Pasquel's militiamen took over from there, galloping down the foul lines in formation, rifles drawn. Two of them scooped up Ramón Bragaña, handcuffed him, and carried him away.

Throughout all this, there was two little islands of calm.

One was behind home plate, where the Babe had recovered from the sucker punch and was leaning against the backstop with Mickey Owen, the two of them shaking their heads and watching the riot unfold. They was *laughing*. That's what it is to be cool-headed, to laugh at the craziness of a riot as you're right in the middle of it. Me, I hightailed it into the dugout and had my back against that cement wall, like in a tornado drill.

The other pocket of calm was in the Reds' dugout, where Mr. Pasquel was talking to this Mexican named Alberto Romo Chávez. Romo Chávez pitched for Mexico City in the '30s, and he'd been mooning around all season, trying to get assigned to a club. All he'd been given up to that point was a job driving the team bus. Now he was changing into a Blues uniform.

When the crowd got herded from the field and order was restored, Mr. Pasquel marched Romo Chávez past his soldiers and out to the mound. He stood beside him as Romo Chávez warmed up. So did we. I don't think he threw a single ball over the plate; Owen was jumping all over the place to knock down those throws.

When the home-plate ump signaled it was time to play ball, Mr. Pasquel put his arm around Alberto Romo Chávez. "Throw right down the middle. If you do not, not only will you never pitch in my baseball league," he said, "but I will have you shot."

He pointed a thumb at those militiamen on horseback, with their bullet-belts crisscrossed across their chests. Then he grinned, patted Romo on the butt, and trotted over to our dugout.

Babe Ruth resumed his place in the batter's box. He didn't look one bit more comfortable there than before. I was surprised Mr. Pasquel hadn't made him use a lighter bat. Still, I was afraid the Babe might hit the ball, more afraid he might hit it to me. Was I supposed to let it go? That was my plan. I wasn't going to risk getting shot for catching a baseball.

Old Romo was drenched in sweat, just like that. Mickey Owen set up his target. Romo took a deep breath and fired the ball in— much faster than he probably intended.

The pitch was in the Babe's wheelhouse. He cocked the bat and, with furious speed, swung from his heels and connected. The ball shot off his bat. I never saw it leave the park, never saw it at all. It simply disappeared, and the people on the pee hill ran toward where they thought it might have landed.

The Babe circled the bases. As he passed me, I dropped to my knees and salaamed the Sultan. He winked at me. The crowd noise rang in my ears for a week.

Afterward, Pasquel sent in Ace Adams to face our old shortstop, Frank Rizzuti. Ace got him to ground out to me. I made the play clean, and we won the game, 7–0.

The next day, Ramón Bragaña got suspended from the Mexican League for six weeks. Mr. Pasquel named Mickey Owen the new manager of the Veracruz Blues. Alberto Romo Chávez didn't get a contract after all and finished the year with an ERA of infinity. Babe Ruth never again swung a bat. Eighteen months later he died. That ball he hit was never found. As for his bat, that last bat he ever swung . . . well, that's another story.

XII

My proposal to Kate was written on a big black typewriter in Santo Domingo Plaza, near the Zócalo, where professional scribes write letters for you for a fee. My scribe looked like a Mexican version of Robert Frost, the poet. He banged out the letter with amazing speed, declaring my passionate love and undying commitment. Before I mailed it I showed it to Johnny Taylor's wife, who was Mexican. It brought her to tears with its beauty.

I knew Kate was expecting me to try to talk her into using that airplane ticket to come down, so I didn't. Instead, I mailed her a second ticket, this one in her pop's name.

Then I mailed her the scribe's proposal, knowing she didn't read Spanish but just to get her curiosity up.

Then I bought a diamond ring from the Pasquels' jeweler, took a snapshot of it, and mailed it to Kate, just the snapshot.

The next day I laid myself out bare. I wrote her a simple letter asking her to marry me, and I wrote a separate one to her pop, inviting him to come to Mexico to stand up for us.

The church was that famous old yellow one in the Coyoacán, the Iglesia Santa Catarina. Perfect, eh? The priest owed the Pasquels a favor from when the government was hard on Catholics. I never figured that out; Mexico's mostly Catholic, yet there's laws against wearing habits or collars on the streets. The laws wasn't enforced, but they used to be, which was when the Pasquels somehow helped our priest out, which explained why he helped Kate and me get our plans together so quick.

I covered all the bases, getting ready, every good-luck charm I could think of. Kate's subway token was in the front pocket of the pants of my suit, which I'd gotten tailored from when it was Vern Stephens's. My shoes was the two-tone wing tips I won for hitting two homers against Torreón. In my vest pocket was the cigar Babe Ruth ate half of. In my head I had a picture of Knik Henshaw and his wife, in love, walking away from the boy's game of baseball.

Finally I heard organ music and opened the door of the nave. The church was empty except for the organist, the priest, and my brother, Al. I'd flown Al down, too, to be best man. Three angels from New York—Al, Kate's pop, and Kate—flying down to grace me.

Rocco Coniglio, who I'd promised could be my best man a year ago, was a world away.

I took my place at the altar.

At the back of the church, out came Kate's pop in his navy-blue dress uniform from the N.Y.F.D. On his arm, in her mother's long white wedding dress, was my Kate. I guarantee you there has never been a lovelier bride, anywhere.

I reached in my pocket, rubbed the subway token, whispered the Hail Mary, then a quick prayer asking for the blessings of my father and sainted mother, may they rest in peace.

That's when I noticed that in Kate's free hand, like a wand, was the wedding candle I'd mailed her. Her father passed her to me. She passed the candle to the priest, who passed it to the altar boy, who lit it and placed it on the altar before us.

We Been Here

After my falling-out with Theolic Smith, and his subsequent refusal to speak with me even over the phone, I approached Ray Dandridge in hopes of interviewing him for this book. As I waited for him at the tiny neighborhood bar he owned in Newark, New Jersey, on TV Baltimore was beating Pittsburgh in game one of the 1979 World Series—no thanks to Orioles third baseman Doug DeCinces, who made two errors in the game. The bar patrons were hard on DeCinces, all convinced that Brooks Robinson—who had retired two years earlier—would have made those plays. "Brooksie was the best third baseman of all time, bar fucking none," said a white Newark policeman, just off duty. Everyone among the mostly white clientele seemed to agree. Three young black men in a booth near the bar started talking about Robinson's brilliant play in the 1970 World Series, so they must have agreed, too. The lone dissenter was an old white man at the end of the bar who was wearing one of those ugly mustard-yellow stovepipe Pirates caps. He argued for Pie Traynor, whom he'd seen play in the 1930s. Typical fan talk, but I was aghast. "What about Ray?" I said, pointing to Dandridge, who was in the kitchen rolling a fresh keg *of Miller High Life out of the cooler. How could they have this argument, in this bar, and not have the decency to mention Ray Dandridge? Yet people looked at me like I'd just dropped in from Uranus. "Ray played major-league ball?" said the cop. Another patron, white, shook his head. "Just in the minors," he said. The cop asked me if I needed him to call me a cab. I got up and looked around the bar. Baseball memorabilia everywhere, and none from the Negro Leagues, nothing at all from Dandridge's own august playing career, except for two things: a tarnished plaque commemorating his 1952 batting title for the Class AAA Minneapolis Millers and a signed baseball, atop a dusty shelf in a corner that read, ironically enough,*

> *To Ray, the greatest third baseman who ever lived*
> *Thanks for your help,*
> *Willie Mays*

Ray connected the tap and set up his customers with fresh beers. He greeted me warmly and gave me a drink on the house. We caught up, talking about whatever became of certain people. When the game ended and the bar thinned out, I opened my notebook. "I'm pleased to see you again, Frank," Ray said. "But I talked to Theolic, and him and me agree on one thing, which is why should you make money off a book that's mostly about us? Why shouldn't we make that money? Lots of folks seem to find ways to make money off the Negro Leagues, but none of it ever gets back into the players' pockets. We got no pension, no medical, nothin. My pelvis needs operated on, how you think I'm gonna pay for that, Frank? Huh?" He held up a quarter. "Off of the cheap bastards who come in here, drink beer all night, and leave me a two-bit tip?"

"I can't pay you for an interview, Ray," I said. "In my profession, it's considered unethical. It taints the interview. A journalist paying for an interview would be like a ballplayer throwing a game."

"I'm not a little boy, Frank. I can understand things without you relating them to baseball. Look, you gonna pay me for this or not?"

"I can't, Ray."

"Then looks like we got nothin to talk about. Last call, Francis. Boy, you're still a drinking man's drinking man, I'll give you that."

On the plane home from Newark, I decided that if I were going to have to pay for an interview anyway, it might as well be with a man who'd already given me so much.

Therefore, I hereby disclose that the following interview was conducted in 1981, two years after the interviews that were the basis for Chapters 1 and 5, not in Mr. Smith's house but rather in a Big Boy restaurant in South Central Los Angeles. It was a lovely day. We each drank a spectacular amount of coffee. Our waitress was Mr. Smith's daughter Octavia, who was then a student at USC but who later, along with her husband, Marvin, would own that and six other Big Boy franchises in greater Los Angeles. For the record, this and all subsequent utterances from Mr. Smith are examples of checkbook journalism. The amount paid was modest. The results of said practice were not, in this writer's opinion, unduly biased.

—F.B., Jr.

THEOLIC "FIREBALL" SMITH

You want me to talk about Babe Ruth, fine, I'll talk about Babe Ruth. Man was the Satchel Paige of white baseball. Understand? Full of bad behavior people wouldn't put up with from nobody else, bigger than the game, with one eye always on that greenback dollar bill. Know how much money he made for that lame-ass staged exhibition of his? Ten thousand dollars. Not pesos. Dollars. Price of a two-story home in a white neighborhood, for a man we didn't have a uniform big enough for, to come to Mexico and screw around on his wife with hookers Pasquel paid for and to take batting practice. Ten grand for *that*. Jesus. I rest my case.

What skinned my ass wasn't Babe Ruth, wasn't having the bat taken out of my hands so that chain-smoking white fat-ass could put on his little show. It was what happened the next day.

We'd got off to a slow start as a team, but things started to click. Halfway through the season I realized this could be the year old Theolic gets his championship. Mexico City, all their years in the league, they never won a pennant, either. But the way we shot up through the standings, it just felt like it was our year. Me, I led the league in wins and was right up there in batting average. I'd always been deviled by control problems, but not that year, least not at first.

Day after the riot, I got to the park early like I always did on days I pitched. An army of groundskeepers were fixing up the place. The only players were Luis Olmo and Roberto Ortiz, loosening up in the outfield. And then I noticed a strange thing, which was that Olmo had on a Veracruz uniform.

"I been traded, I guess," he told me.

"For who?" I said.

He said he didn't know.

"Not traded," said Ortiz. "In this league, players are reassigned."

"Yeah, but for who?" I said. "Who got assigned to our club?" Louie Olmo was our leadoff hitter and center fielder. I couldn't imagine what we'd get that was better than him.

"For Alejandro Carrasquel," Ortiz said.

That passin-for-white sonofabitch! But Carrasquel and Ortiz were buddies, both Cubans, so I didn't say nothin. "Do you fellas know why?"

Together, they said, "Mickey Owen."

"What's it got to do with Mickey Owen?"

They looked at each other, gettin up the nerve to tell me. Finally, Olmo said, "Now that Owen is the manager of los Azules, he told Jorge Pasquel he didn't want to catch any Negroes."

"Carrasquel is not a Negro," said Ortiz, and they started bickering in Spanish.

Of course, he *was* a Negro, Frank, I told you that. But I didn't want to get between those fellas. Looking back, I should have taken more offense, but at the time what upset me was how this all affected our ball club, losing Louie Olmo and gaining a rag-arm forty-year-old Venezuelan.

Turned out that swap was only the beginning.

Just before game time, I'm finishin up my warm-ups when Ray Dandridge asks me if I heard about Schoolboy Johnny Taylor and I say, No, what about him? Shipped to the Monterrey Sultans, Ray says. Caught an airplane early that morning to meet up with 'em in Torreón.

"Who'd Veracruz get in return?" I ask.

Ray points to the dugout, at three white guys, two in Veracruz uniforms, the other one in one of ours.

"Who the hell are they?" I say.

"Jesus," Ray says, "don't you read the papers?"

"Sometimes." Actually, I didn't usually. I got so tired readin the papers all throughout the war years, worryin about Tojo this and Hitler that, that I kind of took a vacation from what you newspaper fellas had left over to poison our days with. "So who the hell are they?"

"Max Lanier and two scrubs from the St. Louis Cardinals. The tall one"—he pointed at the one in the Reds uniform—"is some Okie named Fred Martin, a pitcher. The squatty dude's a southerner named Klein, third white boy Pasquel's brought in to play short for the Blues."

"Only one I ever heard of is Max Lanier."

Jorge Pasquel climbed out of the owner's box and he's talkin to the new fellas.

"This thing's gettin bigger than the both of us, Theo," Ray says, and we take our places for the introduction of the white guys and the playing of the Mexican national anthem.

The starter that day for Veracruz was some cat who used to be with the New York Giants. They should've changed the name of that club to Los Blancos de Veracruz. This was the same club, Veracruz, which in 1940 had the best Negro talent ever assembled; I told you about that club, right? After all those years Jorge Pasquel was a friend to the black ballplayer, seein his own team take the field without a black face on it—well, Frank, it was hard to think what to think. We heard rumors about the Blues gettin invited to Pasquel's hacienda to party and whatnot, but did I ever get invited to one of those fancy parties? Hell, no. My hunch is Pasquel didn't want the black man around his Mexican women, see. Didn't want no competition. Whatever his reasons, seein him start to favor the white player, it sure went down sideways.

That day, as I recall, I didn't have my best stuff. First time all season. Walked a bunch of guys and fell behind five-zip. Would've been worse except for a couple great plays Ray made at shortstop. Only strikeouts I got were on Owen, twice. Mickey Owen was another fella who hit like a sandlotter. If that man could've made three All-Star teams, then ninety percent of the Negro Leaguers were big-league ballplayers.

Right after Carmona lifted me, Feldman, who wasn't half-bad, gave up a grand slam to Burnis Wright, and we were back in it. The game turned into one of those seesaw things we had so often, especially in Mexico City, San Luis, and Puebla, where the air was so thin pop-ups carried four hundred feet. Score was tied 7–7 in the sixth inning when Jorge Pasquel orders Mickey Owen to throw Max Lanier right into the game, not even warmed up or nothin. First batter Lanier faced was Dandridge, who smacked a homer that must still be in orbit. Lanier stood there on the mound, shakin his head, and I thought, *Welcome to Mexico, Lefty.*

Well, Lanier settled down. He was a hell of a player, not like most of the sorry-assed big-leaguers I'd seen down there. Anybody who can snap off a curveball, for a strike, in that thin air two miles above sea level, that man's a baseball pitcher.

Come the ninth inning, though, Lanier walked one guy and gave up a dink single and up came Dandy. Same result—only this time for three runs, and we led, I believe it was 11–10. No shame hangin a curveball in Mexico City, and no shame in givin up a shot to Ray Dandridge, but it got to old Max Lanier.

Bottom of the ninth, Carmona sends Carrasquel in to pitch for us. Sure enough he gives up a triple to the first batter. Second batter sends a screamin liner up the middle, and the runner breaks for home. But up and behold what did my tired eyes see but Ray Dandridge racin for the ball, divin for the ball, spearin it as it kissed grass and, in the same motion, poppin up, plantin his feet and firin that horsehide to third. Double play. Best defensive play I ever saw.

Not that it mattered. Carrasquel walks the next guy and then gives up a homer to—guess who?—Luis Olmo, and they win the ball game 12–11.

We file onto the field to shake hands after the game, like you did in those days. It's hard to lose a game like that, but baseball's a long season, and as a veteran you learn to shake off your frustrations and come at the sonsabitches harder tomorrow.

I'm in line behind Ray and in front of Burnis when we come to Max Lanier in the other line. He stops and shakes Ray's hand, for real, not good game, good game bullshit, and he compliments Ray on that magnificent double play. Still shakin hands, he introduces himself. Ray don't say nothin back. "No disrespect," Lanier says, "but who the hell are you?"

Ray frowns. He's tryin to decide how to take that. Finally he says, "Name's Dandridge. Ray Dandridge. This here's my teammate Theolic Smith, and this here's Wild Bill Wright."

"Never heard of you," says Max Lanier. "I never heard of any of these guys from the States down here. Where in the hell did you fellas come from?"

Now Ray smiles. "Man, we been here," he says. "Been here a while now, just waitin for *you*." He puts his arm around Lanier, then whispers: "Waitin, so's we could do some rasslin."

◈

Mexicans are even crazier about sports than Americans, but their ideas about winning and losing, it's real complicated. Americans expect to win, at least sometimes. Most Americans expect to win most of the time. You know the saying, win some, lose some? Mexicans don't see it like that. Mexicans aren't surprised if they lose 'em all. Havin the capital-city team, our club, never win a championship, it wasn't like in the States, where everybody made fun of those piss-poor Washington Senators. Or in the Negro Leagues, how everybody made fun of the sorry-ass Black Yankees, which despite bein in the biggest city in the world didn't never win a damn thing. Mexicans accepted that we'd never won it all, accepted that we might never. A Mexican wears his defeats like a badge of honor. Kind of like a country full of Chicago Cubs fans.

But, you know, same token, Mexicans are a prideful bunch. They win and they swell up like Macy's Parade balloons. Day we moved into a first-place tie with the Tampico Cottonpickers, all over the city, overjoyed Mexicans drank doubles to our health.

Best way I can explain Mexicans' feelings about winning and losing is those crazy old ball courts they have at all the pyramid ruins. Ever see those?

I'd been to the pyramids outside Mexico City before, the first year I played there, quick tourist trip on an off day. Didn't go back until '46, escorted by the Short Inés, who was an authority on the Aztecs and Mayans and Toltecs, all of them. Things were going great with the Ineses, by the way. They knew about each other, obviously, since the first time I met 'em we all made love with each other. I told you that story, too, didn't I? Well, that was the only time I was ever with both Ineses together. Sometimes I'd be with one and we'd run into the other at a party or some such, and the odd Inés out would act like she didn't know us. I was surprised they never talked about each other or put up a fuss that I kept seein 'em both. They were real cool about things. I guess it was that they were artists. My experience with artists is, they don't think the rules apply to them. They're worse than ballplayers in that respect.

When I'd gone to the pyramids before, with the fellas, I don't remember even seein that ball court, but the Short Inés, who wasn't no particular sports fan but was just the sweetest thing, she pointed it out special, for my benefit.

"This," she said, pointing at this huge H-shaped pit, "was an ancient form of basketball."

Supposedly, basketball was invented by a white man in Massachusetts. Like most things, when you learn the truth about history, you find out it really came from brown people.

The Short Inés said that the teams on these ball courts knocked a rubber ball around the court with their hips and legs and elbows, tryin to get it through a stone hoop on one wall. Court used to be surrounded by huge stone bleachers, enough for thousands of people. The refs were priests, and the games had some kind of mystical religious significance. Afterward, one team got their heads chopped off.

"You're pullin old Theolic's leg," I said. 'They killed the losing team after every game?"

The Short Inés shrugged. "It is not known."

"What, they just killed the losers sometimes?"

"No," she said. "Someone was always killed." She said that the walls of the court were decorated with mosaics of beheadings, with blood spurtin from guys' necks, and that those bloody mosaics were a real big influence on her own painting. "What archaeologists disagree about," she said, "is whether the priests beheaded the losers or the winners."

I laughed. "C'mon," I said. "Take it from a ballplayer, sweetheart. If the winners got beheaded, they'd still be down there playin the first game, tied zero–zero, in one billionth period of overtime."

She frowned. "You do not understand Mexico, Fireballs." She always called me that, "Fireballs," which tickled me. "To the ancient indigenous people, participating in death was a creative act. Even to the modern Mexican, especially men, violent death has a kind of nobility, even a kind of poetry."

I looked down at that crumbling old stone pit, trying to imagine those Aztec boys playin ball like their lives depended on it, cause they did. It wasn't the priests who risked their lives down there, it was a bunch of doomed young men, playin for glory. But the priests used that glory to keep things in control, keep their hold over the people.

No different from my day, no different from today, with the players playin for money, stickin our necks out, so to speak, while the fans watch and someone else gets the lasting benefits. But it was crazier in olden-days Mexico: those poor ballplayers, who by my standards lose if they win and win if they lose.

Brought me to near tears. I looked up, and there was this pack of American white folks walkin by me and the Short Inés like that ball court wasn't no more interesting than a ditch. "You're right," I said. "I sure as hell don't understand Mexico."

But I believe maybe I was startin to understand it all too god-damned well.

The Age of
Spirits

*[Interview conducted at Cannes, on the eve of the 1989
Film Festival, in Ms. Félix's hotel room, with the drapes
drawn and a dubbed episode of* Dynasty *on the TV.
Wearing a lizard-skin vest, cowboy boots, and emerald
earrings, the seventy-four-year-old Ms. Félix, a longtime
resident of Paris, was in Cannes to promote her return to
the screen—after a twenty-year hiatus—in a film called*
Eterno Esplendor. *For the record, I have discussed with
Ms. Félix the possibility of ghostwriting her memoirs; this
may account for her remarkable candor.]*

MARÍA FÉLIX

The pearl-handled revolvers my Jorge carried were the
same he used the day I saw him kill a man. It happened
the summer of 1938, in Veracruz, ancestral home of the
Pasquels. It was eight years before Jorge Pasquel, that great
big boy, was undone by his Season of Gold (and I by my Season of Shit). The year of the duel I was but twenty-three
years old, making ten pictures a year and already, if I may
say so, a star. The man—an American—fell dead at my feet.
His spilled blood ruined a pair of silk stockings. Had I any

sense, I would have quit Jorge then and there. I had no desire to be the lover of a macho, the passive instrument of masculine control. For this, my Jorge had a wife. But I did not quit Jorge. I had no sense. When it comes to love, who does?

I met my Jorge a year earlier, on the set of a picture called *La Mala Mujer*, which was filmed on location in Veracruz. The brothers Bernardo and Jorge Pasquel, though only in their thirties, had become the political dons of the region, and it was with their patronage that the financing of the filming had been secured. Jorge at first struck me as a costumed, puffed-up dandy, strutting around the set repeatedly shaking the hand of everyone from the director to the carpenter's apprentice, handing out cigars like a man whose wife had just delivered twin sons. Soon the set, despite the gulf breeze, reeked of cigar smoke.

From the first, he had his eye on me. He circled and circled, summoning the nerve to speak. When we finally made eye contact, he smiled nervously and left. I heard from another actress, an equine but bosomy woman playing the doomed sister of the hero, that Jorge had been asking about me. She said this with an edge to her voice, though it had been some time since she and I had been briefly involved, almost chastely so.

I waited and waited for Jorge's advance. As the filming wound down, I lost patience and sent a message summoning him to my dressing room at the Hotel Pacífico. He arrived minutes later. "I wish to buy property on the beach," I said. "Could you recommend a good location?"

He believed me. It was so sweet! He drove me around in a black sedan, showing me parcels, introducing me to builders. All human relationships are about manipulation, but when you are the lover of a great big boy, it becomes a benign game, irresistible for its ease. The film wrapped before Jorge managed even to kiss me. I returned to Mexico City. The next week, he came to the capital on business. After dinner, we stumbled back to my villa in the Coyoacán. We kissed in the darkness of the vestibule. I could hear music, a lone strumming guitar from someone in the street. I grabbed Jorge Pasquel by his stiffened manhood and held him fast. "Before we become lovers," I whispered, "you must understand that I am neither prostitute, goddess, grande dame, or mistress. I am no little doll for men to cuddle."

Jorge looked like a perplexed child in mathematics. "So who *are* you?"

"I am María Félix," I said. "Do you understand?"

He nodded. Of course he did not understand. But by then, I was as aroused as he. Outside, it began to rain. "Okay," I said, tugging him toward the floor. "Let us make love."

I already had my diaphragm in.

He made love like a boy, too, at first, all velocity and no technique. The second time, as such hammering ceased to be amusing, I showed him some things. That he was receptive in such matters gives you a measure of the man. Despite the extravagant mask he wore in public, in private, stripped bare, he was a good person.

Afterward, he told me the saddest story I had ever heard.

We lay in my bed, our commingled sweat drying on our bodies, sipping cold beer and listening to a spring rain on the cobblestone streets of the Coyoacán. Our talk moved from this to that, as it will after love. We talked about our childhoods, mine as the daughter of artists and diplomats, his as the son of a small-time patriarch. I told him about my best birthday—still my happiest, so many years later: my seventeenth, when my father, an obscure muralist and onetime vice-ambassador to Greece, took me into the country and taught me to drive his beloved red Dodge. When we got home to take the rest of the family out to eat, there, at my parents' doorstep, was the great director Emilio Fernández, who had decided to cast me, an unknown, as the lead in his next picture—and had come to deliver the news himself. Wine flowed, spirits soared. I ate enchiladas with mole poblana, which, if I concentrate, I can still taste to this day.

As I told my story, Jorge lay quiet and still. "Tell me about your happiest birthday," I said.

"I do not celebrate birthdays."

At first he would not tell me why. But we were so happy and relaxed that I coaxed the story out of him. He began in a whisper:

"My seventh birthday party was to be the best day of my life. My parents, who lived apart and rarely spoke to each other, worked side by side in planning my party. For weeks they planned. Our cook was assisted by a staff of twenty, baking cakes, grinding ingredients for sweet sauces, filling pastries with gooey creams. The house was ablaze with the aromas of baking treats.

"The morning of my birthday, a carnival troupe set up on the grounds of our home. A zoo appeared near the carriage house. Ten ponies were hitched to a pole. Best of all, on the polo field, a cadre of gardeners carved out a baseball diamond, complete with bleachers and a food stand, from which the smell of hot dogs and roasted peanuts drifted across our estate.

"The first of my friends to arrive was my school chum Miguel Alemán. He and I ran out to the ball diamond. But before we got there, the bombing started. We thought, despite the blue sky, that it was thunder. No. It was the United States Navy, acting on direct orders from President Woodrow Wilson.

"The zookeepers rushed Miguel and me into the cellar of the house, and along with our parents and all the servants, we huddled there in terror for two days, watching the smoke and fire from the city. Only once did a bomb land on our estate—a direct hit on the carriage house. All my father's horses were killed. The fence around the zoo was destroyed, and lambs, zebras, and monkeys escaped into the hills. Shrapnel from the bomb killed two of the Shetland ponies. As Miguel and I watched through a crack in the cellar door, the other ponies, still yoked to the pole, panicked. They ran in furious circles, dragging their fallen brothers until, one by one, their hearts gave out. By the time the shelling stopped, all ten ponies were dead.

"Although my brothers, my parents, the carnival workers, zookeepers, and servants all cried during the invasion, Miguelito and I did not cry. We stayed in that cellar, shoulder to shoulder, and we did not cry."

At this, my Jorge cried. He did not do it well, or for long, and in all our years together, I saw him do so but one other time. I held him until he resumed his story.

"The next few days, as my four hundred slaughtered countrymen were mourned and buried, as the Americans declared martial law and illegally occupied my hometown, we were confined to the estate. My birthday was never observed. After Miguel and his parents left, I tried to get my father or my brother Bernardo to go play baseball with me. My younger brothers were only babies then. No one would play with me. I went alone. On my head was

my New York Yankees baseball cap. The forgotten hot dogs at the
ball diamond had turned rancid. The peanut roaster had caught
fire and burned down the bleachers. I stood at home plate alone
and tossed a new white baseball into the air. I wanted to hit it so
hard it would go sailing out of our estate, over the city, and onto
the deck of an American gunship, killing the captain. But I was a
boy. I swung and missed. Only then did I see the irony of my Yankees cap. But I did not take off the cap and burn it. I did not
switch my allegiance to another team. At that moment I became
a man—a seven-year-old man, but a man nonetheless—who
learned to despise American authority without forfeiting his love
for American culture."

And then I wept, too. It is a sad story, no? Sadder for my having
heard it in the dark, after love with a new lover, accompanied by
the sound of rain and my own beating heart. If all life were like
the time after love, there would be no misunderstandings between men and women. And it was after love, as I heard the story
of those ten dead ponies and that frightened little boy playing
baseball amid the rubble and the stench of death, that I fell in
love with Jorge Pasquel.

He was my first great love—though, as everyone knows, not my
last. As the song says, I fall in love too easily. I loved them all in
his or her way, did I not? Or did I, in loving so many, cheapen my
idea of love? Maybe I truly loved no one. These, these are the
thoughts that darken an old lady's days.

The dead man was a red-haired American expatriate named
Hartman. He ran a small fleet of fishing boats that sold their
catch to American restaurants. He did no fishing, spending his
days instead in the Café La Parroquía, banging his spoon on his
cup and laughing as a waiter with a vat of hot milk scurried over
and, in a torrent of white, filled his café lechera, never spilling a
drop. To Veracruzanos these legendary milkmen are a source of
pride. Hartman, like most Americans, saw them as especially well
trained monkeys.

Hartman met plain, bookish Ernestina Pasquel at a fiesta for
one of the city's patron saints, found that she shared his European tastes in art, music, and literature, and set himself to the

task of squiring her. They attended plays and concerts together. They were seen on park benches in the Zócalo, reading Balzac aloud, in French. By all accounts they never so much as kissed, yet Hartman fell in love with Ernestina—a thing my Jorge could never do.

Ernestina was the daughter of Plutarco Calles, the exiled Catholic-hating ex-president of Mexico. Jorge, a Catholic, married her so he could be anything to anyone. The motto of Mexico should be "However you see us, that is we." Americans can be hypocrites, but we *are* our contradictions. In this way, Mexico, home of the first revolution of this century, is the perfect postwar culture: rich with masks, poses, irony, and paradox. Hartman, no doubt, knew little of this. Few Americans do.

Ernestina had for years remained quietly in Veracruz as Jorge went about his business and his amours in Mexico City, making love to her only on their wedding night and in attempts to sire children. (Even this made me jealous. The only other lover I had in my first year with Jorge was Frida Kahlo, who was more a mentor.) Yet when Jorge finally heard of Hartman's courtship, the thought of being a cuckold galvanized him. He flew home immediately, dragging me along. I did not know why we were going; I went only for a chance to make love on his airplane.

It was March, the festival of the birth of Benito Juárez. Bernardo Pasquel, who had inherited the family estate, was hosting a gathering of local políticos—a group that to this day carries the oxymoronic name "Party of the Institutionalized Revolution." Hartman was of course not party elite. Some say he gate-crashed, some say Ernestina brought him. I believe he was invited so that he might be shot.

We arrived at midnight. Jorge made a triumphant entrance, handing out gifts, embracing Bernardo, Ernestina, everyone— even Hartman, even me. Only in the retelling does my presence seem odd. For the señor to have a lover was expected. For the señora to have even a chaste suitor? Scandalous. Today I identify more with plain, love-starved Ernestina than with the selfish girl who was me. Ah, time.

As to what happened next, accounts conflict.

Some say that Hartman demanded that my Jorge allow Ernestina to renounce her Catholicism and become divorced. An argument ensued, culminating in Hartman's challenge to duel.

Others say that Jorge, during his embrace of Hartman, challenged the fish exporter to a duel—two hours hence, the better to make the American's fear simmer.

Still others say that the men met in Bernardo's study, smoking cigars and discussing the matter with civility until it became clear to both reluctant men that a duel was unavoidable.

I do not know exactly how the duel came to be. I was exhausted from my filming schedule, drunk on sangría, and caught up in telling tales of the famous to my Jorge's starstruck little brother Alfonso, who was home for the summer from his fancy American prep school. My recollection is that Jorge and Hartman sized each other up during their initial embrace and then kept their distance for some time, like prizefighters in opposite corners. I have no doubt, however, that it was my Jorge who somehow initiated the duel. The world is made up of actors and reactors. Jorge Pasquel lived and died as one of mankind's great actors.

Very late in the hot, raucous party—so typical of the port town of Veracruz—I enlisted Alfonso to help me find Jorge. Find him we did, on the well-lighted patio. He and Hartman were choosing pistols from among many matched sets spread across a billiard table. Ernestina stood against a far wall, sobbing, restrained by Gerardo and Mario Pasquel. Jorge's second was Bernardo. Hartman's was a squatty cook with glasses. When I entered, heads turned. I was young and did not know this condition was temporary. I saw it as my birthright. That people stared at me because it was indiscreet for me to be there, rather than because I was the most beautiful woman at the fiesta, this did not occur to me.

"Trust me," I whispered to Alfonso. "My Jorge only means to give the American a scare."

The eyes of Alfonso were wide. "Perhaps," he said.

"Those guns will be loaded with blanks," I said.

"Blanks," said Alfonso. "Perhaps."

The guns chosen, Jorge and Hartman stood back to back. Jorge caught my eye and winked. It was then I knew the guns were loaded. His wink was a cover-up for fear.

A different sort of young woman might have feared for her beloved, but I had never been more angry. The least of it was that he was fighting a duel over another woman.

A drummer from the mariachi band was summoned to play the cadence, just the sort of touch you expected from the Pasquels.

A half-step from their tenth, the duelists whirled around in unison and fired. Both men had cheated, and justice was served: Both missed. Other party guests rushed onto the patio.

Hartman looked at his gun, as if he could not figure out what it was doing in his hand, and in badly accented Spanish said, "I suppose this settles nothing, my friend."

Jorge laughed. "True," he said. He lowered his pistol.

Ernestina Calles Pasquel removed her hands from her eyes. She had stopped crying.

Hartman shrugged. "What now?" he said.

"You cheated," said Jorge. "My *friend*," he said in English.

"More a false start than cheating," said Hartman, in English, too, now. His face shone with sweat.

"You cheated," Jorge said again.

"Yeah, well," Hartman said, "so did you, my friend."

"So I did," said Jorge. He started toward Hartman, hand extended. The red face of Hartman spread into a grin. Suddenly Jorge stopped, raised his pistol, and fired. The bullet caught Hartman in the eye. It made a hole in the back of his skull the size of, well, a baseball.

The crowd was silent, stunned.

Jorge bent over the corpse of Hartman, picked up the other pistol and cracked it open to reveal a second bullet. "He could have fired at any time himself," said Jorge, "but he was just a stupid, philandering American who did not know his weaponry."

I caught the glance of Ernestina. If anyone should have been fighting a duel, it was she and I. But she would not give me the satisfaction of looking wronged, and I would not give her the satisfaction of looking guilty. We eyed each other through impassive masks. Then she pointed at my ankles and smiled.

I looked down. Small pieces of gore covered my shoes. My white silk stockings were spattered with blood. Jorge sat on the edge of the billiard table, disconcerted but putting up a false front that could have fooled only another man. Bernardo Pasquel and the fat cook saw to the details of removing the body. The Veracruz chief of police offered congratulations to Jorge.

"Boys!" I shouted, stomping my foot, then turning around to leave. "You violent, impossible boys!"

On my way out, I flung trays of tortillas and bowls of salsas to the floor. I pulled down a string of lights, I slammed the patio door behind me, and I swore like a man. I was Mexico's greatest actress. I knew how to make an exit.

The years passed in a haze of liquor, lovers, rolling cameras, lavish gifts, naked ambition, and artificial lights. Jorge and I had our ups and downs, our stormy separations and hungry reunions. When we were together, our love was always magnificent. Always. He grew to be afraid of me, which is what I thought I wanted. He dragged me to baseball games, I dragged him to operas and symphonies, and we both grew to admire, if not enjoy, the other's odd passions. During that time, I became an even bigger star and made so many pictures I cannot now recall a fraction of their titles, while that group of Veracruzanos, of whom the Pasquels were the moneymen, ascended to political power. Miguel Alemán, their slick figurehead, became minister of the interior, a training ground for presidents. Unlike the warhorses who had run the country since the revolution, the Veracruzanos were young, brash, and cosmopolitan. They represented hope for a new Mexico, one not disengaged from the world.

In Mexican Spanish there is a word, *malinchismo*, which means a preference for foreign things, particularly American things. The word comes from Malinche, the name of the Aztec princess who willingly married and bore the sons of the conquistador Cortés. It is a profound insult to call a Mexican a malinchist, as bad as saying his mother pays well-hung sailors to sodomize her and then fellates goats to orgasm—and swallows. That bad! At first the Veracruzanos, with their worldly ways, were called malinchists. After all, the source of their wealth was the import/export business. Yet it was the Veracruzanos who made our country see the benefits of enlightened malinchism. It was they who lobbied for Mexico to enter the war on the side of the Allies, placing us for the first time in the disconcerting position of fighting with, not against, the Giant to the North. It was also they who kicked out foreign oil companies, nationalized the petroleum and mining businesses, and made Mexico such an important supplier to the war effort.

How Mexican that the anti-Nazi efforts in my native land were spearheaded by a man named Alemán, no? [*Ed.*: Alemán *is Spanish for "German."*] And that his best friends and financial backers, the Pasquels, had gone from affluence to colossal wealth by supplying petroleum to Franco, Mussolini, and Hitler? The Pasquels will deny this, but I know. The *Lusitania* was sunk by a U-boat propelled by Mexican gasoline. For years there were as many ass-pinching Nazi businessmen orbiting around my Jorge as there were ballplayers. And there were endless numbers of those tiresome ballplayers.

Baseball! It was, you see, the tragic flaw of poor Jorge. Had it not been for the way that silly pursuit invaded his life as surely as the bottle did mine, my Jorge, despite his somewhat crude bearing, could have been anything: senator, general, president. He could have died a national hero rather than an embittered playboy. And yet it is the Mexican League for which he is now remembered. It was baseball, that artful boys' game, which kept the boy alive in him, which humanized him. It was what set him apart from the bloodless Bernardo and the ambitious, callow Alemán. When my Jorge donned a team uniform and consorted with the members of his beloved Blues, my heart melted. When you see your lover at his happiest, you melt. If what makes him happiest is frivolous, it matters not. If it matters, is it love? No. Unless, of course, what makes your lover happiest is another lover. In this, too, sadly, I speak from altogether too much experience.

During the winter of 1946, as my life was disintegrating right along with the Mexican film business, my Jorge took me with him on a business trip to New York so I could see a doctor about my drinking. Had I done so in Mexico, it would have been in the newspapers, and I would have been ruined. In those days, it could ruin you. I was the most famous actress in Latin America, but in New York I could disappear. This is the allure of New York, no?

The 1940s were the age of spirits. People drank more then, and harder. In this way, I was perhaps only a product of my times. I am proud, looking back, that I recognized I had a problem. This, as we all know these days, is the first step.

I tried to quit drinking often, but I would eventually be faced with a trying film role or, as often, a trying life role, I would reach

for a bottle. I had been acting so long that there was no line between my performances on and off camera. I was thirty-one, no
longer an ingenue. In sober moments I knew that if the drinking
continued to take its toll on my looks, I would soon be playing
matrons, whores, and jolly best friends.

About my brief stay in the clinic, I prefer to retain my privacy. I
will say that it involved a sadistic Freudian and that it was, for a
time, successful.

After my discharge, Jorge and I went to exquisite restaurants
and a Broadway show every night for a week. He bought me a
cello and paid for me to take lessons from a Fordham professor of
music. It was a time to fall in love again after years of taking each
other for granted. Our hotel suite smelled of the huge bouquets
delivered every morning. When Jorge was out, I wrapped myself
in blankets, stood on the snowy balcony, and dropped red roses,
one at a time, into the white abyss. Even today snow reminds me
of Jorge.

Our last day in New York, inspired by a sober night of love,
Jorge told me his quixotic dream. We were breakfasting at the
table in our suite. The room was dark. We were wrapped in silk
robes. "You realize, no, that Miguelito"—meaning Alemán—"will
be the next president?"

"Of course," I said. "He is the candidate of the PRI."

"And do you realize what this means?"

"My lover will be the best friend of the president."

"And what that means?"

He had exhausted me. I did not.

"Nor do I," he said. "Miguelito may not need his old friends as
much. He will give us positions, money, patronage, of that I have
no doubt. But we, the Pasquels, could disappear from the public
eye, usurped by our friend Miguelito. The same thing happened
to the cronies of the outgoing Avila Camacho. It could happen to
me, too." He grinned. "Unless . . ."

I realized he was waiting for my reply. "Unless what?"

He tapped himself on the breastbone. "Unless I create the impression that he cannot do without me. Unless I overshadow his
election. Unless I become a more beloved figure in Mexico than
he." My Jorge leaned across the table, his eyes blazing. We kissed.
"And now I know how to do this."

I fed him a grape. "How?" I said.

"Baseball," he said.

Baseball was his own alcoholism. "Baseball?"

"I will make our baseball as good as anyone's. I will employ men of all races—including American whites—and show the world a true mestizo baseball, never before seen anywhere."

I smiled. He had utopian ideals in one fist, big plans in the other.

"I will parcel out the players so that each team is of equal talent. My league will be an egalitarian symbol of the new Mexico," he said, pounding his fists on the table, spilling our coffees, "a symbol that will ring throughout the world when we defeat the American baseball champion in a true World Series!"

I laughed for joy. "I believe you will," I said, though I had no idea what he was proposing.

"Imagine," he said, "if the Mexican movie business were to rival Hollywood."

"I cannot," I said. "It is impossible."

He rose from the table, walked to the balcony door, and threw open the curtains. The sun shone. His robe went translucent. I could see his taut body. Beyond him, the ice in the East River glistened like a meadow of diamonds. "Imagine it," he said.

"And what does this all have to do with Alemán?"

"Very little," he said.

"So what *does* it have to do with?"

He pointed at me with a sweet roll. "Imagine," he said. That was his answer. *Imagine.*

In 1946, Jorge Pasquel and I were the toast (and also the scourge) of Mexico. Our smiling faces were plastered on newspapers and magazines throughout the land, and yet you would have had to scour the hottest, poorest, dustiest villages to find any two people as miserable as we. We became the kind of couple who grope each other in public, putting on a show they wish themselves to believe.

I was receiving the best notices of my career for *Enamorada*, Emilio Fernández's film adaptation of *The Taming of the Shrew*. Six films of mine came out that year, all of which made money. And yet the Mexican film business was doomed. Mexico's military allegiance with the United States had whetted the country's appetite for American things, and the theaters were overrun by such great films as *Cuéntame Su Vida* [*Spellbound*] and *Días Sin Huella* [*The Lost Weekend*]. The studio that made *Enamorada* went broke even as the film filled theaters from Mérida to Tijuana. Cantinflas and I were the only Mexican stars whom people still wanted to see, and even we knew our time was short. Though the European movie industry was bouncing back, Frida had returned from Paris with such horrible impressions that I was loath to make such a move regardless.

In April, my mother died. Jorge, in America courting baseballers and headlines, left me to cope with my grief alone. A difficult breach to forgive. Had he been there, much might have changed, starting with the funeral itself, at which his militia would have been useful. The location of the funeral appeared in the newspapers, and the church was mobbed by thousands of my fans—as if they had not already seen my tear-streaked face in every movie I made!

Frida and Diego both came to the funeral, but as they knew by then that I had been intimate with them both, they did not stay long afterward.

My poor, dignified father! He was broken by the loss and disoriented by the unruly if well-meaning crowd. After police escorted us home from the cemetery and we managed to dispatch the cousins, aunts, uncles, and jealous costars, we stayed up all night weeping and talking and, finally, drinking Cuba Libres. It was my first drink since before New York. Nothing had ever tasted better. I drank to drown not only my grief for my blessed mother but also the sorrowful revelation that I would probably never have a marriage as long and sturdy as that of my parents.

Of course, once I started I no longer needed an excuse.

As for Jorge, I am the only person who knew how unhappy that great big boy was, even at the zenith of his fame and glory.

He was happy at first, of course. Baseball always gave that big ham a stage. His grandiose efforts in 1946 gave him a bigger stage. The bigger the stage, the happier the ham. The travel, the huge press conferences, the throngs of fans, the fierce fight against American authority—all of it made my Jorge as vibrant and alive as he had ever been.

But Jorge, like most ambitious Mexicans, tried to reinvent the world in an afternoon. What began as a great drama on behalf of his country dissolved into a farce of riots, lost money, and defecting Americans. What cut deepest for my Jorge was the failure of his beloved Veracruz Blues. Try as he might to infuse his own club with the best talent, it lost game after game. Perhaps, I said, his team was like a movie so bloated with big stars that no one can keep track of the story. He did not accept my comparison. The result was that he was pilloried in the press for violating the spirit of fair play and stacking the Blues with too much foreign talent. One reporter even, in print, called my Jorge a malinchist. All this in spite of the fact that his Blues lost many more games than they won!

Jorge held up well under the strain. I first saw it get to him in the matter of Mickey Owen. Famous American, the worst hitter on the Blues, and yet making the most money. And how does he handle it? With grace? Gratitude? No. He becomes a trouble-maker, complaining, complaining. His only skill is to play a boy's game—poorly—and for this he makes more money than I! He and his absurd shrew of a wife are given a luxury apartment on the same street as my father. And he has the nerve to lie to the American press about finding insects in his kitchen!

One night, Jorge and I were at dinner, in our dark private booth in the back of La Fonda del Sueño, when this Owen came belligerently to our table. "I got a bone to pick, George," he said. "It's the coloreds."

My Jorge forced a smile. I never once saw him correct those vulgar Americans when they mispronounced his name. "Sit," he said. "Join us."

"I already ate."

"Join us," Jorge snarled. Owen sat. Jorge introduced me to Owen as "the finest actress and the greatest beauty in all the world" and ordered us some drinks. For me, Coca-Cola; I was hiding my drinking from Jorge. Owen refused his tequila and asked for Coca-Cola, too.

"You never told me about playing with coloreds," Owen said.

"Surely you are not a bigot, Mr. Owen," said Jorge.

"No sir, I'm not," said Owen. "I'm talking about breach of contract. You said I'd be player/manager for Torreón, yet I haven't set foot in Torreón. You also told me this would be a major-league operation. In the major leagues, sir, there are no coloreds. If conditions don't improve, I'm going to talk to a lawyer about rejoining the Brooklyn Dodgers."

"Bien." Jorge set one of his pearl-handled revolvers on the table. "Take it. Pick it up."

Owen looked like a little boy who had been challenged on the playground. "Why?"

"Shoot me," said Jorge. "Shoot me dead, Mickey Owen."

Now Owen looked even more confused. "Why?"

"This league is my child," said Jorge. "You, with your demands, are killing my child. So I ask you, as a gentleman, please, do the more direct thing and put a bullet through my heart."

Owen looked at me. "Is he kidding?"

I arched one eyebrow and gave Owen my most devastating mysterious smile. Inside, I was furious at my Jorge for his pathetic machismo.

"It is loaded," said Jorge. "Pick it up and see."

Mickey Owen sat there, quietly, for a long time. As with most men, you could see the gears turn when he was thinking. At last he said, "I'm going to assume this is a joke." He got up from our table. "See what you can do about the coloreds, okay?"

After Mickey Owen left, my Jorge and I had words. He felt that with the election only days away and with the bad publicity from the Babe Ruth riot, he had no choice but to appease the American. That was what he thought I was angry about! Men. Jorge and I slept in our own beds that night, alone.

My final night of love with Jorge was interrupted. It was July of 1946, days before the election. In the wee small hours, as the song says, Alfonso Pasquel banged on the door of my villa in the Coyoacán with the news that Mickey Owen and his wife had packed up and snuck away under the cover of darkness. The Owens had been intercepted at the border; officials there were awaiting Jorge's instructions.

Alfonso was old enough not to be surprised that his brother answered the door naked, heard the news, told him to wait in the vestibule, and returned to the bedroom to finish making love to me. And I took my time. I stole time. I detained my Jorge in the throes of love for hours. I even, as afterplay, played the cello for him—badly played bits of sad concertos, nude. It was dawn before my Jorge showered, dressed, and left with his brother.

Jorge had acceded to Owen's demands, appointing him manager, ridding the Blues of Negro talent, and for what? Nothing. In my experience, this is what to expect from Americans. Time and again, big-talking Americans expressed interest in bringing me to Hollywood and making me a star there. It never happened. My English has always been much better than Carmen Miranda's or Dolores Del Río's. But, for me, nothing an American promised me ever came to anything.

Later that morning, a car came to bring me to the ballpark. That day's game was one of the last campaign rallies for Alemán. My Jorge's box was to be filled with dignitaries, lending influence to the next president, as if the election weren't already a fait accompli. The chauffeur opened the door. To my shock, already sitting in the backseat was Ernestina Pasquel.

"Hello, María." She was a cool one, Ernestina.

"Hello, Señora Pasquel," I said, twisting the knife. I was a cool one myself. I immediately set to the limousine's well-stocked bar.

As we drove, Ernestina sat in silence, an unnerving technique made more maddening by being a favorite one of my own. "You do know," she finally said, "what you have cost Jorge?"

"No." I tried to look haughty. "Tell me, Señora Pasquel."

"He will receive no post in the new Alemán government. The openness of his immorality with the likes of you has made him a laughingstock throughout Mexico."

"Just how do you know this?" It was a foolish question. If she knew she would not tell me, and if she did not know she would not tell me. I could have guessed she would have responded by not responding, which is what she did. "No one in Mexico," I said, "cares about the amours of a man of Jorge's stature." Even to this bait, Ernestina did not rise.

Finally, near Delta Park, she said, "That we are riding here together, it was my idea, and Jorge accepted it. If the public sees us arrive together, they will be duped into believing the rumors about you and him are false."

I shrugged; I would not give her the satisfaction. "The real reason he isn't getting a political post," I said, "is that everyone knows he murdered your American paramour in a duel."

Her eyes betrayed her. She tried not to react, but I saw enough to know I'd guessed right. "You are a whore," she whispered, emerging from the car and waving to the gathering crowd.

"And you," I whispered, "are a frigid cow who could not distinguish her clitoris from a pimple." As I stepped into the sun and the crowd saw me, they roared. They would not have noticed Ernestina Pasquel if she had disrobed, swallowed nitroglycerin, and exploded into flame. I did not need to smile or wave. I was María Félix. And the crowd, *they* knew what that meant.

Of the historic game played that day, I regret, for the reasons you would imagine (the passage of time; lack of baseball acumen; Carta Blanca), that I cannot give you a detailed account. I can give you only the snapshots that remain in this old gray head of mine. I remember that before the game speeches were made about liberty and progress—the usual everything and nothing. I remember staring down Ernestina. I remember that during the game I sat beside Miguel Alemán, which became the genesis of our very brief affair later that year.

What I most remember is the absence of Jorge. It was not like him to miss a chance to don one of his wide-shouldered suits and a drawerful of jewelry and stand before an adoring crowd and take credit for everything. I kept asking where he was, but the men ignored me. Finally, as the speeches wound down and the players took the field, I cornered Bernardo Pasquel in the dugout of the visiting San Luis Potosí Cactus Fruit. You did not see Bernardo often, but I had learned by then that he was the master puppeteer.

"Do not bother your pretty head," said Bernardo, "with politics." He laughed.

Men did not laugh at María Félix. "Where is he?"

"Where he can do no further harm," said Bernardo.

I smiled, picked up a bat, and sweetly rammed it into Bernardo's crotch. It was not a direct hit, but I made my point. I stepped onto the field. He could not strike the most famous actress in Mexico in front of a sellout crowd at Delta Park. "Where is he?" I repeated.

"He will be out shortly," said Bernardo. He had the bat in his hand, impotently. "He is in the locker room with his team."

At that I headed straight for the dugout of the Blues. As I crossed the diamond the crowd roared, and I waved gaily. Never, even at your lowest ebb, spurn your public; this is the secret of my long popularity.

When I flung open the door to that dank shithole of a dressing room, men cried out in surprise. Their hairy nakedness was nothing to me. What I was looking for, I found: clothed in the uniform of the Veracruz Blues, sitting in the corner of the room on a stool, hanging his head.

"María," he said, looking up.

I kissed him on the forehead. Behind me, ballplayers wolf-whistled.

"What is happening?" I said softly.

Jorge shook his head. In other circumstances, I am sure, he would have banished me, this *woman*, from the baseball players' locker room. "Everything is happening," he said.

"Why are you in uniform?"

"I have appointed myself the manager of the team."

He's mad, I thought. Commissioner, owner of one team, de facto owner of two others, and now manager? What next, pitching? It was a farcical squandering of a great man's time.

"What happened with Mickey Owen?" I said.

"He is rejoining us," said Jorge. "He has no choice. He is banned from American baseball. But I will no longer have him in charge of my ball club."

"What is happening with you, querido?"

Again he shook his head. "I have tried to give the people what they wanted," he said. "I have brought excellent baseball to Mexico, and yet everything is going wrong. In the newspapers, I am criticized for violating the spirit of fair play!"

To my amazement, tears of wounded pride rolled down Jorge's cheek. To my further amazement, he did not wipe them away.

It shames me to admit what happened next. I stepped back from my Jorge and assessed him. I was flooded with contempt for what I saw as weakness. I did not wish to be associated with a weak man. "I will see you after the game, I suppose," I said, knowing I would not.

"Yes," said Jorge. He rose, pulled on his silly baseball cap, and embraced me at arm's length, hands on my biceps, as he would a man. "After the game."

I took my place in Jorge's box. When he emerged from the dugout to stand for the national anthem, the crowd whistled and jeered. We in the dignitaries' box pretended not to notice Jorge's fall from grace. We smiled, fanned ourselves, and sang along.

The events of the day thus far had rendered me particularly vulnerable to the flirtations of Alemán, who suddenly struck me as the most charming man in creation. Also, I admit, the idea of having the penis of the president wriggling inside me and at my mercy for its pleasure, this was exciting to a beautiful, young, drunk, egotistical woman such as myself.

I left long before the end of the game (I was trying to entice Miguel by being elusive). It was lopsided in favor of the Cactus Fruit. If memory serves, it dropped the Veracruz Blues into last place.

In the next day's papers, Jorge Pasquel was criticized for making out a poor batting order, whatever that means. He did not call me, or call upon me, and I certainly did not call him. The day after, he resigned as manager, naming his friend Chile Gómez to succeed him. One newspaper showed my Jorge in the doorway of an airplane, shaking hands with Gómez and about to return to Veracruz to cast his vote for Miguel Alemán.

Years later, from Alfonso Pasquel, I heard a strange story. After arriving in Veracruz and casting their votes amid flashbulbs and newsreel-camera lights, Miguel Alemán and Jorge Pasquel spent the day together, hunting deer in the foothills near the city. They did not get off a shot all day. As the sun began to set, my Jorge heard a rustle from behind a thicket. He saw an animal's outline through the brush. Certain it was a deer, Jorge raised his rifle and took aim. Suddenly the creature bolted. It was a zebra, a descendant of those that had escaped from the petting zoo during the bombing of Veracruz. Jorge hesitated and, too late, fired. Then he heard a second shot. It was a kill for Alemán. Jorge claimed the first shot had killed the zebra, and Miguel diplomatically agreed. The hide of the zebra, Alfonso claimed, still hangs from a wall of the ancestral home of the Pasquels, where Ernestina and Jorge's grandchildren now live.

My father chose to campaign for Ezequiel Padilla, the opposition candidate. He even seduced himself into believing Padilla could win. The night of the election, both sides claimed victory, with the vote from the capital reported as a near tie [*Ed.: 28,370 for Alemán, 27,654 for Padilla*]. My father hoped Padilla's win would mean another diplomatic post. He spent the day leafing through a world atlas, lost in fantasy. All men are great big boys, no?

At the dawn of the next day, he ran to the smoke shop to buy a paper. The final count, he was shocked to see, was a landslide for Alemán [*Ed.: 1,110,760 to 124,331*]. We got drunk together that day, with him muttering over and over that the election has been stained by fraud. Six months later, his liver failed and he died. When I heard the news, I swore that I would quit drinking. I have remained sober every single one of the many thousands of days between then and now.

This talk of the Veracruzanos reminds me of a famous Mexican joke. A woman comes into a produce market and asks to buy half a melon. We don't sell them that way, says the clerk. You must buy the whole melon. I don't *want* the whole melon, the woman says. She gets more obstreperous about the matter and finally the clerk reluctantly agrees to go speak to the owner.

"Can you believe it?" he says to the owner in the back office. "A cheap hag bitch wants to buy half a melon." The clerk sees alarm in the owner's eyes and turns around. The woman is right behind him. "And *this* charming lady," he quickly says, "wishes to buy the other half."

The sale is consummated, the woman happily carts away her half melon, and the owner, impressed by the young clerk's quick mind, mentions that he is opening a new produce market in Veracruz. Someone so sharp-witted might be just the person to manage that market, no?

But the clerk is aghast. "Veracruz!" he says. "What a hellhole! There's nothing in Veracruz but whores and ballplayers."

The owner frowns; he is furious. "I'll have you know my dear wife comes from Veracruz."

"Is that so?" says the clerk, not missing a beat. "Does she bat right-handed or left?"

All you wish to know about Mexico, Frank, about our masks, our sense of humor, and the weaponry of our wits, about the way Mexican men see Mexican women, about the Mexican League and my poor dead Jorge, it is all contained in that joke.

10.

El Nudillero

[Further excerpts from my 1971 interview with Roberto Ortiz in his Miami, Florida, backyard. Interview conducted in Spanish; translation by the author.]

ROBERTO ORTIZ

I dissent. The second half of the season was no fiasco. It was glorious. It was not until the second half, for example, that all the ball clubs began to fly as a team from city to city. The first half was but a grand circus. The second half was about baseball. At last.

Understand, please, that I for one did not object when Baby Ruth was called upon to pinch-hit as a member of my team, the Mexico City Red Devils. It gave me a good story to tell the six strong, handsome children borne to me by the fair and statuesque Elena. But that was not baseball. It was theater.

Likewise I held no objection to the importing of Americans. As a Cuban, I was myself a foreigner. I valued the efforts of the Pasquels to create baseball for all races and nationalities. Latinos are more accepting of whites than

North Americans are of Latinos, Negroes, or Indians. Mexico City had many Japanese, who opened businesses and flourished while American Orientals were in concentration camps. But neither was this a baseball matter.

Further, I part company with those who feel that Mr. Jorge Pasquel violated the spirit of fair play. Each team was supplied with foreign stars. The teams in Mexico City had their share, true, but Mexico City attracted the most fans. They earned the right to good baseball (a right that my Reds granted but that Don Jorge's Veracruz Blues did not). This controversy concerned the jealousy the rest of Mexico harbors for Mexico City. Not baseball.

True, tempers fulgurated between the Negroes and the American whites. This happened on the field, but is it a baseball story? Does it differ from the racism you see in all the world?

About the politics, who knows? My baby brother Oliverio, the revolutionary, he paid heed to such things. To me, Batista, Castro, what's the difference? All políticos, all absurd. And that is *Cuban* politics. Mexican politics? Who knows? Sure, in this I was naive. My exile here in Florida and my estrangement from my brother, who remains in Cuba, these have taught me to heed the shifting sands of despotism and venality. But this, too—the crazy speeches by Mr. Jorge Pasquel, Mr. Alemán, and all the ambitious dandies—it had nothing to do with baseball.

Claims that money did not arrive as promised may be figments from the imaginations of Americans. Or perhaps the true amounts were lost in translation. Who knows? I did not play for money. I paid heed only to the next fat pitch I could smack, the next reckless runner I could gun down, the rank of my team in the standings, and the next night I could spend alone with the fair Elena. The second half of the Season of Gold held a bounty of such grand moments.

This was initiated by the All-Star game, held the day after the Mexican election. It was the last year the Stars of the North [*Monterrey, Nuevo Laredo, Tampico, and Torreón*] battled the Stars of the South [*Mexico City, Puebla, San Luis Potosí, and Veracruz*]. After that it became the Extranjeros against the Mexicanos. Don Jorge was a Mexican patriot, but when he ran the league, matters never became so—what is the word? Yes, xenophobic.

The day of the game dawned as one God created for baseball:

the sun shining, the breeze gentle, the sky blue and wide and cloudless. I rose, kissed the fair Elena, and said to her, "My darling, today I will hit a long home run just for you."

"I know you will," she said. Her skin shone in the morning light. It took all my strength not to make love to her, but that was for after the game. I had a ritual for game days, part of which was to resist the temptation of the fair Elena.

First I performed my ablutions. Then I came to breakfast, smelling of Skin Bracer and as nude as the palm of a hand. I ate huevos rancheros, a beefsteak, sweet rolls, coffee, and tomato juice. Always the same meal. As I ate I read the newspaper, looking first at the comics, so as to find levity in our crazy world. I then scanned the front page for news of Cuba, and then paged to sports. There I looked for news of Oliverio, lost in the minor leagues of the Senators of Washington. Only when I found no news of him did I glance at the standings of the Mexican League. The Red Devils of Mexico City had overcome a slow start and managed to achieve a first-place tie with pesky Tampico. That sunny morning, I ate my hearty meal confident that 1946 would be the year we would win the first championship in the history of the Mexico City team.

I dressed at home, putting my left leg through my jock, then my right, left arm through my undershirt, then my right, left sock, right, left stirrup, right, left pant leg, right, left shoe, right, right jersey sleeve, left. I inserted my cup, knelt, kissed the womanhood of the fair Elena, rose, donned my cap, grabbed my glove, and left for the park. I always arrived early.

Game time drew near with all the gay ceremony one expected of Delta Park, with a shocking exception: Mr. Jorge Pasquel was absent. His friend President Alemán used the game to make his first speech since his election. He spoke about the grand future of Mexico and denied any acquaintance with the men who had been arrested for electoral fraud. Finally he threw out the first ball and got his windy buttocks off our field. Still no Don Jorge. In his private box were Mr. Bernardo Pasquel and many military men. I expected Don Jorge to appear as one of the celebrity third-base coaches, a publicity stunt deployed in the first inning of many games. But no. For the Stars of the South, it was the hilarious comedian Cantinflas. For us, President Alemán and four bodyguards.

It was then I noticed an argument between Ernesto Carmona, manager of the Stars of the South, and Mickey Owen, catcher of the Blues, and for the South also. Owen refused to catch the warm-up pitches of Booker McDaniel, the "ace" of San Luis Potosí, an elegant Negro who threw so hard we called him "Balazos" [*gunshot*]. My English was not good enough then to understand when someone talked fast, as Americans do. Carmona's English was worse than mine. Finally he got Danny Gardella to translate.

"Mr. Owen must catch Balazos," Carmona said, "or be jailed for breach of contract."

Gardella translated, though I do not believe Carmona said anything that could be interpreted as "sister-loving cracker."

Burnis Wright and I had to separate the combatants.

The umpire shouted, "Play ball!"

"Go on the field, Mickey," said Carmona.

In the third-base coaching box, Cantinflas pretended to be sitting on an invisible throne.

Owen had daggers in his eyes, but he said nothing. He took his place, as did we all.

We were an explosive bunch, sure, but that extended to our bats. With all the hitting on those teams, plus the fact that the field was four kilometers above sea level, I expected much scoring. I was not surprised when Balazos gave up two runs in the top of the first, the key blow being a double off the Chiclets billboard by Lloyd Davenport, the burly little outfielder whom the other Negroes called "Bear Man."

In the bottom of the first, Babalú Pérez of the Cactus Fruit collected a leadoff single, Ray Dandridge of the Reds sacrifice-bunted expertly, and Luis Olmo—formerly a Red, now a Blue—flied out. I took my place at the plate. I am proud to say I singled to center, scoring speedy Babalú with our first run. The home fans gave me a standing ovation, and the game had to be stopped for me to remove my cap and acknowledge their fervent cheers.

Ay, did I love baseball! So enraptured was I that I paid little heed to my dugout, where the dispute among Carmona, McDaniel, and Owen was heating up further.

The next batter was my teammate Wright, who doubled. I was waved home by a político and four thugs in dark suits.

Next up was Danny Gardella, who dragged to the plate the same tremendous bat Baby Ruth used in that farcical exhibition.

On deck, Owen. When I asked Chile Gómez about the words that had been exchanged, he said, "McDaniel accused Owen of alerting the Stars of the North as to what pitch is coming, and where."

"I do not believe it," I said.

Gómez shrugged. "Owen denied it," he said. At the end of the bench, the Negroes huddled together. Anger exuded from them. I did not wish to become embroiled in this dispute, and I returned my attention to the man at the plate.

Gardella, what a harlequin! He stuck out his gut and mimed the waddling manner of Mr. Baby Ruth. He stepped to the plate and, still with that gargantuan bat, pointed to right field. The pitcher delivered; strike one. This provoked from the Federal District crowd a chorus of whistles—which grew louder when Gardella swung that log at the next pitch and missed badly.

Carmona had a fit. Gardella exchanged his stage prop for a regular bat. He ceased clowning and, after many fouls, ran the count full. Finally, in came ball four. However, Gardella prepared to swing, at a pitch near the top of his spikes!

In disgust, I screamed, "No!"

To my surprise, Gardella connected, sending a towering pop-up to center. It rose in the same lazy arc as a well-hit nine-iron. Burnis Wright, certain the ball was to be caught by the Bear Man in center, jogged toward third with his head down.

It was then that I saw Gardella sprinting around first.

The baseball kept rising, rising. The Bear Man drifted back toward the fence; he seemed confident he would catch the ball.

Gardella ran past second, still running, also head-down. The ball kept carrying, and, to my horror, I realized that it might clear the fence. But if he passed Burnis Wright, who did not see Gardella coming, Gardella would be called out, and the runs would not score. In the third-base coaching box, President Alemán had his back to the field, waving to the capacity crowd, in the prideful belief that all Mexican cheers were now rightfully his.

The baseball kept sailing.

Suddenly Burnis glanced up, saw the fast-closing Gardella, stood firm, and shoved him to the ground.

As Gardella's buttocks hit the dirt, the ball—still as high as the clouds—traveled over the Bear Man. Then, as if dropped from an American skyscraper, it plummeted to rest just a meter beyond the center-field fence. Home run, Gardella! Stars of the South 4, Stars of the North 2!

Owen singled, Gómez walked, and Balazos struck out to end the inning. President Alemán and his bodyguards took their seats. For the rest of the season, never did any but a baseball man set foot upon the sacrosanct diamonds of the Mexican League.

❧

I do not wish to slander the character of Mickey Owen. I do not know if he was tipping off the Stars of the North about the pitches of Balazos. After a bad first, Balazos emerged unscathed through the next two. It is remarkable that the best strikeout artist in Mexico recorded none, but maybe that was "just baseball." The outs he achieved came on balls hit with great force, but when your defense up the middle consists of Dandridge, Gómez, and Olmo, ferocious line drives can go down in the score book as outs.

Draw your own conclusions.

Tomás de la Cruz—late of the Reds of Cincinnati, now of the Red Devils of Mexico City—entered the game in the top of the fourth. As I said, Tommy had a Negro grandmother. I doubt Owen knew this. Anyone who knew that Tommy pitched in the Major Leagues would assume him to be Caucasian. Yet I overheard Gómez tell Carmona it would be sagacious to replace Owen with Sunset Colás of the Reds. Gómez was whispering, but I heard him say "abuela negra."

What smoke Tommy threw that day! Hard curves for strikes, fastballs that exploded at the plate—"the whole megillah." Next time up, we scored six, including Gardella's second home run. We led 10–2, and I retired to the bench. How grand to relax and watch those men ply their trade! I would have paid to watch Bonnie Serrell lay down a bunt, Ray Dandridge play the field, Daniel Ríos throw his befuddling knuckleball or Sal Maglie his amazing curve. What joy to sit back and soak up the smells, sounds, and sights of baseball, and to have the smells include piquant tacos, the sounds include the music of the Spanish tongue, the sights include brown men playing great ball for a fair wage before an adoring crowd!

As I mentioned, no lead is safe at such altitude. The Stars of the

North, down 11–3, staged a rally in the top of the ninth. The frightful lack of outs caused me to fear we might lose. A grand slam ignited my fears. The flames were fanned by a blast off the bat of the red-haired catcher from Torreón—Hayward? Felicitously, my countryman Tarzán Estalella achieved a great jump on the ball, and he made a diving catch to end the game. The rally by the Stars of the North allowed them a moral victory, but history's victors were the Stars of the South, 11–8.

My time alone that night with the fair Elena was sweetened by victory. She did not mind that I failed to hit her a home run. Such are the joys of married love.

The American All-Star game was played the same day. Vernon Stephens, the contract-breaking rat, who used the Mexican League like toilet paper, played shortstop and collected two hits. Had he stayed in Mexico, he would not have played. Stephens was no Ray Dandridge.

❖

Our first series after the All-Star break made things even more interesting. We flew to Monterrey for a four-game series in Cuauhtémoc Park against the third-place Sultans.

As is often the case in any baseball league, the men passed over for the teams of stars reacted colorfully. The hulking left fielder of the Sultans, Claro Duany, who led the league in hitting, was like a machine: hit, hit, hit, hit. On the other side were my tempestuous teammates Alejandro Carrasquel and Fireball Smith. They let their anger devour them.

In the first game, Fireball faced Nate Moreland, an American Negro. I found Moreland easy pickings [3–5, *with a homer and six RBIs*], as most Americans were, endeavoring to adjust to the heat, food, language, altitude, and travel. Yet we lost. The mercurial Smith tried to strike out everyone and did not last two innings. It is folly to throw fastball after fastball at men like Duany, Ed Stone, and Superman Pennington. If such hitters know what to expect, they will hit the ball no matter how hard it is thrown. I myself was such a hitter.

Game two was a pitchers' duel between Fred Martin, the big rustic from the Cardinals of St. Louis, and the player/manager of the Sultans, Lázaro Salazar. We loved Freddie. Not a bigoted bone in his body. Sadly, this was not his day. He could not retire the indefatigable Duany. Monterrey triumphed, 3–2.

How I remember game three! On the mound for Monterrey was Indian Torres. For us, de la Cruz. Tommy continued his excellence from the All-Star game, while we knocked that big Indian all around the park. I hit three home runs, one so long that only the immortal Negro Josh Gibson ever hit one farther! For two home runs, you were supposed to get a new pair of shoes. For three, what did I receive? Nothing. Such bonuses had been halted. All I have to show for my day is a framed page of newsprint—and the memory of a loss! It's true. We were up by ten runs, but Tommy grew weary, and his successor, Planchardón Quiñones, entered in the eighth. In two innings, he yielded twelve bases on balls, twelve runs, and we lost, 15–14.

That night I was so morose I nearly drank liquor. My team had sunk to second. My wife remained in Mexico City. My brother Oliverio was suffering racism and American food. And Ernesto Carmona told me I would get no free shoes. Fireball, Dandridge, Wild Bill, and Fred Martin, they dragged me from my hotel room and took me with them to a nightclub to cheer me. But the sight of dancing couples only made me miss Elena more. When my friends bought me a shot of whiskey, I stared at it for many minutes. Finally, I refused. "Take it, Fireball," I said.

He would not. That liquor remained untouched on our table until the club closed. The pretty women my friends brought to the table to meet me received no more of my attention than a flock of grandmothers. My resistance of temptation, *that* was what ultimately raised my spirits. That, and the prospect of another day, another chance to stroke long home runs into the bright blue sky.

Upon the wounds of merciful Jesus, do I miss this game of baseball! Looking through this cardboard box of memories is more sweet than I would have imagined. Look at these old gloves. Is it possible we might we take a break, Frank, and have a catch?

In memory, I went all of July without making an out. I was blessed with a streak where the ball seemed as fat as a casaba melon, its trajectory as straight as an arrow. That is, except for game four of the Monterrey series I was telling you about.

There was nothing straight about the trajectory of the offerings from Daniel "La Coyota" Ríos, that cunning little knuckleballer, from whom I could rarely coax even a single. Yet I was seeing the ball so well I felt invincible. Carmona threw us knuckleballs in practice, and I believed I had learned the supernatural vagaries of that pitch.

Before the game I went to the bullpen, where my friend Carrasquel was warming up, and told him he had nothing to fear. I felt capable of greatness. Alejandro, still bitter over the All-Star game, said he needed no great things from others. He himself intended to display greatness.

Ah, the arrogance of prideful young men.

Therefore, what Ríos did served justice. He produced from his bag of tricks *a sidearm release*! Under the dim lights of the Monterrey park, he threw his fluttering lobs sidearm! We flailed in vain. You should have seen big Burnis Wright swing from his heels. And as bad as Wright was, I was worse: a man trying to swat a sweat bee with an oar.

As for Alejandro, he was afflicted with the same condition that undid Fireball. (Like most people who hate each other, Alejandro and Fireball were more alike than different.) His third time through the order, he was bashed without mercy. We lost the game, many runs to zero, and sank to third. The quest to be the champions of the Season of Gold had evolved into a three-team race: Tampico, Monterrey, and Mexico City.

When we returned to the Federal District, the fans greeted us at the airport, cheering us on. That's Mexico. In another country we might have been chastised, the recipients of ugly threats. Not in Mexico. Mexicans are loyal to their heroes.

At my apartment there was a letter from Oliverio. He thanked me for my last letter and congratulated me for regaining the home-run lead. He did not share with me his statistics (if they were good, he would have filled a page with numbers). He then asked me for advice. His contract had been sold to a Class C team in Oil City, Pennsylvania. No one else on the team spoke Spanish. No one would room with him. He was restricted to Negro hotels. He celebrated his birthday in Youngstown, Ohio, by drinking martinis and committing what he described as "an immoral act."

His only comfort came each Sunday, listening to the familiar cadence of Latin Mass. I'll read you the end: "Brother, I beg you to
ask the Pasquels for a position for me. I will start or relieve. I will
join the worst team and accept work in lopsided games. You were
right to go to Mexico, brother, and I was wrong to remain in this
horrible place. I lay myself upon your mercy."

"You should refuse," said Elena. "You gave him advice this
spring that he was too arrogant to heed. He must learn he cannot
always run to his brother to rectify his mistakes."

At first I was shocked by her counsel. But Oliverio always was a
sore subject with Elena. She resented the money I "lent" him. She
resented when I accompanied him that spring to America. Years
later, I learned she also resented him for having once made to her
an indecorous proposal.

"How can I not intercede on my brother's behalf in this, his
time of trouble?" I said.

"It is always his time of trouble," said Elena.

"It involves no more than relaying his message to the Pasquels,"
I said. "How can I fail to do such a simple task?"

"If it is so simple, let Oliverio contact them himself."

And so it went, back and forth. The rare fights between myself
and the fair Elena also aroused great passions. We fought like lions, then reconciled like the god and goddess of love.

The next day I went to the Pasquels' offices. I was told that Don
Jorge was on safari in Africa and that Don Bernardo was busy or-
ganizing the Alemán government. A lackey said that they would
no longer have time to meet with the likes of ballplayers.

I held my ground, demanding to speak with one of the younger
Pasquels. Impossible, said the lackey. I'll wait, I said, and took a
seat, underneath a twelve-foot-high stuffed grizzly bear. On the
walls were mounted heads and photos of men in tuxedos, but no
baseball mementos.

After a long time, I got in to see Alfonso Pasquel, the young
baldy, who had been so long in American schools that he spoke
with an accent. He took me to his office and offered me a drink.

"I don't drink," I said. He looked at me funny. The castigation I
have received for not being a drinker! "I am here," I said, "to offer
you the services of a ballplayer with major-league experience."
Oliverio had pitched one game in 1944, when the shortage of
players was worst.

"We are signing no more foreigners," said Alfonso. His office lacked windows. Its walls were bare. "The season is half over. Crowds in most cities are smaller than we had hoped."

"The stands are always full, everywhere we go," I said.

"Your team is a good draw. Many others are not. Also, our parks are small. They don't seat enough."

"That you knew at the start of the season," I said. "Nothing has changed. Listen, I am offering to you a good player, who will come here for a reasonable price."

"I told you—"

"It's my brother Oliverio," I said. "Surely you, Alfonso, can comprehend the debts one brother owes another."

That little baldy laughed! "No more foreigners," he said. "I'm very sorry."

"When does Don Jorge return from Africa?"

"It is not known. But his return will make no difference in this matter. I am afraid my decision in this regard is final."

Soon, a rumor spread through the club that Don Jorge, now back from Africa, was weighing a trip to America to sign more players for his comical, underachieving Blues. Taking a chance, I rode a taxi out to Don Jorge's hacienda.

"He is not here," said the armed guard at the gate. Those Pasquels, they were surrounded by big men with big guns.

"When do you expect him to return?"

"He is not here."

In the distance, out beside the pool, I saw a man who looked like Jorge Pasquel. "Who is that?"

"It is not Don Jorge. He is not here."

"Do you know who I am?"

"He is not here."

"I am Roberto Ortiz," said I, standing tall. "Reigning homerun champion of La Liga Mexicana del Béisbol."

The puppet laughed. "Don Jorge is not here."

I returned to the taxi and told the driver to go around a bend in the road and let me out. I waited until the guards changed, then walked to the gate and asked the new man for Don Jorge.

"He is not here."

"Where is he?"

"Not here."

The man by the pool stood upon the diving board. I was certain it was Don Jorge, and so I shouted his name. "It is I, Roberto Ortiz!" The man looked over, then dove.

The soldier pointed his rifle at me, inches from my chest. "Flee," he said, "or you will die."

The man I thought was Don Jorge disappeared into the house.

"I need a taxi," I said. "Please, may I use the telephone?"

The man continued to hold the gun on me. "I will fire my weapon at you in one minute."

I turned and walked away. He would not dare shoot me in the back, I thought. But give an insignificant man a gun, and you never know what he might do.

A hundred meters from the gate, my luck changed. On the lawn of the hacienda, a car started. I glanced over my shoulder. A black Cadillac approached me. A chauffeur was driving. "Don Jorge extends his apologies," he said, "and his invitation."

I was ushered into the splendor of the hacienda. Statues, artwork, priceless furnishings. No one was there except servants and Don Jorge. He was in his game room, shooting billiards.

"Welcome," he said. He wore swim trunks and a terry-cloth top and he needed a shave. He looked tired. "Do you play?"

"A very little." In actuality, I was an excellent player.

"Whatever you came here for, Ortiz," he said, "I will give it to you if you can beat me in eight ball. Eh? Best of seven, as in the World Series."

"How do you know I have come here for anything?" I said.

"Do not insult me." He stroked the huge zebra hide on his wall, then shook his head with resignation. "I am not that stupid," he said. "Look, do you want to play or not?"

We played. He did not ask what I wanted, and I did not admit to wanting anything. We barely spoke. As for the billiards, I beat him four straight.

"You win, Ortiz. Now what do you want?"

I was surprised he was taking his defeat so casually. All that I knew of Don Jorge indicated that he was a poor loser.

"There is a rumor," I said, "that you intend to sign more foreign stars this season."

At this, he closed his eyes and said, "I wish that I could."

"Forgive me," I said, "if I ask why you cannot. You are commissioner of the league, no?"

"Things are complicated, Ortiz. Just tell me what Cuban friend of yours you wish me to sign and I'll look into it."

"No," I said. "I won. We had a deal."

"Bueno," he said. "It's your kid brother, right? The pitcher? How much does he want?"

I was shocked. "How did you know?"

"When it comes to brothers, and the favors and debts they expect, incur, receive, and renege upon, I am the world's expert."

"It is not just Oliverio." This was a lie; I felt so unnerved to have my mind read that I became a filthy liar. Having done so, I had to invent something plausible. "My teammates and I feel that in this, of all seasons, it is important the champion be from Mexico City. What a hero such a victory would make you in the eyes of the chilangos! What a legacy! What fun it would be to see your Blues surmount their bad luck and climb back into the pennant race."

Don Jorge frowned. "What concern is my legacy to you?"

None, of course. But one lie launches a thousand, no? "Having the champion be from the capital is good for the future of Mexican baseball," I said. "If the future of the league is sound, so is mine. I expect us to win, but if not, it should be your Blues."

"The future of Mexican baseball," he repeated, his voice in a whisper.

"Yes," I said.

He walked to the window and stared out toward his swimming pool. He remained quiet for so long I wondered if I was supposed to leave. A grandfather clock chimed. Don Jorge finally turned to me. "In truth, this is about your brother, right?"

"Yes," I said.

He laughed. "You are an honest giant, Ortiz, with a face evil men can read. Offer your brother five thousand dollars American. Tell him he can pitch relief for the Cactus Fruit. They need a lefty."

"You wish me to approach Oliverio myself?"

"It was your idea, no?"

"Yes," said I. "It was my idea."

◆

Life is like hitting. Education and technique are essential but only the foundation. You must learn when to swing and when to take. You must lay off the pitches you can't hit, no matter how much they make your mouth water. You must study each pitcher, learning from your mistakes and his, and adjust. Finally, you must learn to go with the pitch, to hit it where it's thrown.

The failure to accept this last tenet is the ruin of young hitters and all young men. It was why I was clay in the hands of Ríos, why Oliverio spent an unhappy year in the villages of America. And it was why Mr. Jorge Pasquel, who conducted his life and his business like an all-or-nothing slugger, failed in his attempt to make the Mexican League a true major league, and also failed to understand the magnitude of what he did do.

And it is the best way I have to explain what *I* did.

I left Don Jorge's hacienda that night having already decided not to relay the offer. I had already decided Oliverio needed to learn to adjust to the knuckleball, so to speak. I wrote him and told him Don Jorge's offer would not commence until the beginning of the 1947 season, then told Don Jorge that Oliverio had reconsidered. This was fine with Don Jorge, who by then was involved with larger matters than the services of a kid with nothing more to offer than a high opinion of himself and a curveball he could not throw for strikes.

For the rest of 1946, I put it out of my mind. For the rest of the season, I thought I had done the right thing.

Prideful me! How old and wise I imagined myself, at the age of thirty! I, too, had much to learn of life's knuckleballs.

11.

Bullinger *v.* Bullinger

I have known many poor bastards who quit jobs they needed and wives they had and saw their lives exposed as houses of cards, and had it happen in places like Cleveland and St. Louis, amid handsome dogs and neighbors in white frame homes. It's best to wreck your life abroad. Find a place where the weather's hot, the language is a breeze, liquor and hotels are cheap, and where most of the people around you can't afford ice or razor blades, and they look at their prospects and mutter, mañana, mañana, and no one ever says, hey, pal, mañana *what*? ¿Qué será diferente mañana? Such a place is Mexico. Careful with the pulque, sport.

One afternoon in July, I was at Delta Park in my office, a converted janitor's closet with damp wood walls, when there came a knock on my outflung door. Telegram. I took it from the kid. It was from a law firm in St. Louis. The loss of my job at the *Star-Times* and my wanton desertion of the plaintiff, Mrs. Harriet Lamartine Bullinger, for a foreign country, i.e., Mexico, had prompted the court to grant default judgment for failure to defend in re: Bullinger *v.* Bullinger. Custody of minor child Jerome Tristram Bullinger is granted exclusively to the mother. Alimony/support payments of $88 per month are due her and are to commence immediately.

The only unexpected thing was the $88. My Mexican paydays came in odd wads of cash and I doubted I would ever see anything near the six grand I'd been promised. I sat back down at my typing table and reread the telegram by the light of a banker's lamp. On shelves in the corner were leftover bottles of pine cleaner and two souvenirs I had bought from street vendors in the Zócalo: a plaster replica of the Aztec calendar stone and a Mason jar filled with formaldehyde and a human heart. No liquor. I tried not to drink at work.

I rose to tip the delivery boy, my eyes still on the telegram. I felt someone take the peso from my hand.

"¡Muchas gracias!" said Jorge Pasquel. "I will spend this vast sum wisely."

"It's you," I said. It was the first I had seen him since the election. Also the first time he had ever come to my office.

"Not bad news, I hope," he said.

"All news is bad news." He was there to fire me, I knew it.

Pasquel laughed. "You have the fatalism of a Mexican."

The only seat was my wooden folding chair. We stood on the threshold of the closet. "What can I do for you, Señor Pasquel?"

"Your directness pleases me." He stood with arms akimbo, suit coat pulled back to reveal those pearl-handled Colts. "I shall squander no more of your precious time. So let me ask you. How would you assess the state of the Mexican League?"

I tried to wipe his spit off my face without looking like I was wiping spit from my face. "The state of the league?"

"Be honest."

No one who says this means it. I wished he'd just fire me and be done with it. "The ball is close to big-league-caliber. The business and the political things, I don't know about."

"Ah," he said. "And what do you think about the Negroes?"

"Put all the Negroes in this league on one team and it'd hold its own with the Yankees or the Cardinals or anybody."

"¿Verdad?"

"Absolutely." How could he have been surprised?

"Well, that is not what I mean."

I knew what he meant. "The problem's not the Negroes."

"True. But I need the white players to give the league stature. Americans will never give credibility to a group of Mexicans, Cubans, and Negroes. We need to beat the whites."

"This is about Ramón Bragaña, isn't it?" In the six weeks since Bragaña had coldcocked Babe Ruth, the Blues had been through three more managers, lost two thirds of their games, and been purged of Negroes. If Bragaña rejoined the team, he'd be the Blues' only Negro.

"Bragaña is but part of this," said Pasquel. "Another question. How might it be perceived, both in Mexico and in the U.S., if I bolstered the Red Devils for a run at the pennant?"

"Bolstered?"

"More Americans."

"If you could get them to jump. With the ban—"

"I dislike that word, *jump*. Just answer my question."

"Well, the Reds lost Olmo. You could replace him with an outfielder and it'd only be fair, I guess."

"You wouldn't tell me, would you, Bullinger, if you thought my league was a laughingstock? If you thought it had embarrassed my family or my country?"

"Probably not," I said.

Pasquel took out a diamond-clad money clip. "If you tell me the truth, I will pay you a hundred dollars American."

"Keep your money," I said. It was enough that he wasn't going to fire me after all. "It's really not a laughingstock."

He forced the money into my palm. I took it.

"So what is it, if not a laughingstock?" He picked up my jar and was looking at the heart.

"A baseball league," I said. "A damn good one."

He smiled. "Were you told this jar contained a human heart?"

I shrugged. "Let me have my dreams, okay?"

"For luck in love, eh?" He set it down. He asked if I had anything to drink, and I said, truthfully, no. "Bueno." He seemed pleased. "Tell no one you saw me here. Bragaña and I are going to America. Tell no one that, either."

He asked about my job. My only official duty as press secretary was to help American reporters get their stories. This consisted of pointing out which players spoke English. Afterward, I would set the reporters up with hookers. These men (six, total) wrote nice things about the league. By July the story was cold. That was good. By July it would have taken more than a fast fuck to get them to write nice things. "The job's great," I said.

"How about your little redhead back at the Hotel Galveston?"

I said that all was well.

"And the wife and son in St. Louis? Are they well?"

My stomach lurched. How did he know that? "Yes," I said automatically. "They're well."

"Bueno," he said. And then, before I could think to fight back by asking him about *his* mistress, *his* wronged wife, and *his* neglected child, Jorge Pasquel was off to catch his plane.

I waited for his limo to pull away, and then I locked up my office. Delta Park was empty. No game that day. The city was returning to work from siesta. Down on the field, one of the Veracruz players was taking b.p. As I drew near, I saw that it was Mickey Owen. If anyone needed extra work, it was Owen. He was hitting .220 and dipping his right shoulder as he swung. I took a seat and reread my telegram and smelled the grass. Lou Klein, the Blues shortstop, was pitching. Owen kept hitting pop-ups and dribblers, and I tried hard to think of nothing at all.

"They got an unfayuh advantage," Klein said.

"How you figure?" said Owen.

"This climate. It's jungle-like." Both Klein and Owen were drenched with sweat. "Wuss than back home in Metairie."

Owen hit a Texas Leaguer. "That's true," he said.

"They'ah bred to wisstand jungle heat," Klein said. "Tha's why they adapted to the cotton fields, see."

Owen saw me sitting behind home, saw that it was only me, a white man. "I don't know about unfair advantage," he said to Klein. He swung and missed. "It's just not how it's supposed to be, is all."

Klein ran out of balls. "Frank! Hep us shag."

I put the telegram in my pocket and did as I was told.

"Way I see it," Klein said, "it's like playin any game against inferiah competition. Baseball, golf, cards, whatevah. Inferiah competition brings you down to their level."

"That's true," Owen said. "That happens." He paused. "Some of these guys, the Negroes, are pretty good ball players, Lou."

"Nothin against the niggers. It's not them who decided to mix up the races down heah. That got decided long ago."

"Huh," Owen said.

"This heah country is full of mulattoes. Why you think folks are so poor?"

I untucked my shirttail and held on to the end and carried the balls there. Klein kept going on, and Owen kept humoring him. They asked me what I thought. I said I didn't know. In my defense, I was just getting used to the idea that the Negro players were better than most of the men in the big leagues. Also, I had my mind on other things.

I dumped the balls into a wooden Peñafil crate beside the mound, waved goodbye, and decided to leave early, as if anyone cared. A job with nothing to do is hard work. I would write game stories, which I gave to English-language papers in Mexico City and Havana. I got a secondhand SuperGraphix and played at photography. I took speed-typing tests. I wrote letters to my other lover Frances and to my son Jerome. I began a series of features on Mexico in general and the league in particular, with no idea who might publish them. It was a thing to keep me away from the hotel, where Diana was writing poems about baseball, Mexico, making love, riding horses, and being high on grass as she watched her tobacco-farming father die of emphysema. Her poems were always about more things than my articles.

My walk home took me through neighborhoods of embassies and hospitals, then through the sunbaked edge of the Zona Rosa, the pink zone, full of tourist hotels and tourist bars.

I was free to marry Dr. Frances Kingston, professor of classics, and keep that baby she had decided not to get taken care of from being a bastard. She'd said she would not leave Ted and had gotten mad when I mentioned maybe marrying me. But that was back in Florida. Since then, she had returned to St. Louis and Ted had come home. According to her letters (posted to the Pasquels' offices), although Ted had taken the news of his cuckoldry "infuriatingly well," they had nevertheless separated. Frances had gone to her sister's cottage on the Lake of the Ozarks to have the baby. She was separated. I was divorced. That changed things.

At the corner of Insurgentes and Reforma I stepped off the curb and almost got flattened by a shiny new bus. It was the first new bus I had seen anywhere since before the war.

I was, of course, free to do the quixotic thing and marry Diana James. She was Catholic. It would be complicated. But I was free to do it. We had even talked about it, marriage.

At the corner of Insurgentes and San Cosme, in the newspaper district, I was beset by filthy children in Indian clothes, tugging at my pant legs, begging for centavos. I gave freely.

Freely. I was free to choose Frances, if she'd have me, or Diana, if she'd have me, or a lover-to-be-named-later. If she'd have me. In other words, I was cradled in Satan's left palm.

"So," said Diana, looking at the telegram from Harriet's lawyers. Men feel dread when a woman says *So* and then pauses. Women have a kind of a look when they do this. "How do you feel about it?"

"How do you think I feel?" If she'd had an answer, I'd have been grateful. She didn't. "I guess I don't feel like anything."

We were at the hotel bar, making ourselves late for dinner at the Gardellas'. The cook brought us free botanas—camarones pacíficos. He liked us. We spent a lot of money there.

"Don't expect me to like it if you're sad," Diana said. "Don't expect me to watch you get teary-eyed over your wife."

"Ex-wife."

She shrugged.

"Did you have a good day writing?" I said. "I did."

"Don't change the subject."

"Fine," I said. "I feel the way you do when a sick friend you can't bring yourself to go see anymore finally dies."

"It's a blessing, you mean."

"Yeah. A blessing."

Perhaps you know her poem "Blessed"? I am the *you* of the poem; I receive no royalties.

"No, I am *not* going to use it," she claimed. "Jesus, you flatter yourself. You think everything you do is a poem."

"Oh, right. That's what I think."

"It is what you think," she said.

"You're crazy," I said.

It was that linchpin part of an argument where you can escalate things or laugh. She sucked the shrimp and bacon whole off the toothpick. "Crazy for you," she said, and we laughed. The tension lifted, and we had two more ice-cold Bohemias. Then two more, two more, et cetera. We arrived at the Gardellas' late and drunk, which was no doubt the way they expected us.

"Bienvenidos a la casa de Daniel y Katerina!" said Danny. He had on a big smile and a suit. Chamber music wafted from the Victrola. Seated at the dinner table were Mr. and Mrs. Max

Lanier, in a suit and a cocktail dress, Mr. and Mrs. Harry Feldman, in a suit and a cocktail dress, Mr. Ace Adams, in a suit, and Kate Gardella, in a cocktail dress. There Diana and I were, sloppy drunk, her in pants, me with no tie. Also, we were empty-handed.

"Sorry we're late," I said.

"It's his fault," Diana said. "He got divorced today."

Everybody laughed. They thought it was a joke.

"We just started to eat," Danny said. "Wine okay or do you want the hard stuff?"

Everyone was finishing, but it was a gracious lie. Danny introduced us to people we already knew and smoothed over our rudeness as best one could. I kept expecting him to pull a stunt, but he was as proper a host as any of those Standard Oil muckamucks my parents hobnobbed with back in Cleveland Heights. Marriage had agreed with *him,* anyway.

Kate Gardella served us pork chops, mashed potatoes, applesauce, and cherry pie. The wine was Italian but there was also Coca-Cola. After dinner, we played bridge, and Danny put on some Bing Crosby 78s, and then Max Lanier took out his guitar and sang western songs about whippoorwills, ponies, lost love, and America. If I ever had a better time, I don't know when it was. At the stroke of midnight we all sang "The Star-Spangled Banner."

Diana and I let ourselves out onto the balcony, and I kissed her. A kiss for all time. The Mexican moon was yellow and full. The balcony overlooked a small, well-kept garden.

"I love you," she said. "I'm sorry if I was a cunt." This was her new word. She had exhausted *fuck* and was on to *cunt.*

"You weren't."

We kissed again. Better yet.

"Are you really okay? I didn't exactly give you much of a shoulder to lean on earlier."

"I'm afraid about Jerome," I blurted. I had been trying not to think about this. "I don't know when I'll see him. I don't know what she's telling Jerome about me."

"Jerome," she said. Her voice was flat.

"How do *you* feel about *that*?"

"About Jerome?"

"No. About Truman nationalizing the railroads."

She looked at me. She held that look. "I love the way your voice gets when you talk about Jerome, is how I feel."

"How does my voice get?"

We'd been involved a long time to hold a look so long. It is usually only in the first weeks that lovers look at each other like that and for so long.

"Marry me," she said.

"Excuse me?"

"You heard me."

"You're serious?"

She shrugged. The corners of her mouth twitched. She smiled. "Had you, there for a sec. Should have seen your face."

Danny shouted that the delivery from the bodega had come and now we had more bourbon. Kate called out hopefully about seconds of cherry pie. Bourbon and pie. We started in. Then Diana reached up, pulled my shoulder to her, kissed me, and whispered, "I'm serious."

We had reached that stage of things where a couple must get married or take up arms. "Yes," I said. Please don't shoot.

We went inside and announced our engagement. The rest of the night is sort of a blur.

The Mexico City Reds came home tied for second with Monterrey, three games back of Tampico. One article in my series was about how Monterrey and Mexico City were mostly Negroes, and Tampico was a mixed-race bunch of lesser-knowns. The second-division clubs were mostly white. The name players, in the eyes of American readers, were almost all on second-division clubs. I began to see that no one would ever publish this series. But I kept writing. I needed something to do to keep my hands and feet away from Diana. She planned our wedding and wrote poems bam-bam-bam and tried to pretend she was not anxious about her first book, which had been out for two weeks when she proposed and which we did not discuss.

It was not a big wedding. Her parents were dead, mine were dead to me. She wanted it small with a party afterward at the club where Hemingway had knocked me cold. It would have been a garden-variety city-hall wedding except for the Catholic thing.

She telegrammed her parish priest back in North Carolina, asking him to send to the Mexico City parish chancery a copy of her baptismal documents as well as a letter stating that she was a Catholic and had never been married.

"I can't get a letter like that," I told her. I was getting ready to leave for work. Well, for a game. Mexico City against Nuevo Laredo. "I'm not Catholic."

"All you need is a copy of your baptismal documents. You are baptized, right?"

"First Lutheran of Shaker Heights," I said. "That's not the letter I was talking about."

"Look. You have *not* been married before."

"Yes, I have."

She grabbed my head, like a dog's, and held it still and looked at me. "You haven't. Do you understand?"

I nodded, as best I could.

"You weren't married in the Catholic church. From where I stand you weren't married. Mention that improper marriage and you'll have to swim a sea of red tape to get an annulment which even if you do manage to get will take years." She let go of my head. It was in this way that Diana, after her early bout of la turista, came to be in harmony with Mexico. She, too, was defined by her contradictions: a dope-smoking, bohemian poet who remained devoutly Catholic; a devout Catholic who lied, committed superb adultery, and skirted church doctrine on the grounds of its bureaucracy.

Putting one over on Catholicism was nothing to me, of course. Committing a sin of omission and pretending that my first marriage had never happened? Didn't that mean that I was forsaking Jerome? Once that dawned on me, I realized I could also not forsake the baby Frances Kingston was going to have in a month. It was the first time I had thought of it as a baby. Up to then I had thought of it as a situation.

Did I mention any of this to Diana? I did not. I got dressed and took a cab to the ballpark and interviewed members of the Mexico City Red Devils for my series, and I wrote a few more pages of it and then it was game time.

Theolic Smith took the mound for the Reds. Although he had been mired in a terrible slump for weeks, both hitting and pitching, he had his best stuff that day: blazing fastball, knee-buckling curve, wicked slider. I was right down on the field with my camera, in a shady nook next to the Nuevo Laredo dugout. As Smith warmed up, the pop of the ball in the catcher's mitt echoed through Delta Park like gunshots. I told a reporter from *La Afición* that I wouldn't be surprised if Fireball pitched a no-hitter. Sometimes you just have that feeling about a guy.

The man shook his head. "Demasiado calor," he said. I thought he was talking about the weather, which *was* awfully hot.

Theolic's first pitch, right down the pipe, blew past the leadoff hitter, an aging speedster named Bejerano. Bejerano fouled off the next pitch, then Smith threw his curve, so far inside that Bejerano bailed out of the box, but the pitch broke sharply and caught the inside corner.

Ball one. Smith couldn't believe it. The crowd let loose with a whistle.

It was then I noticed that the umpire was Adolph Weimer, who had been in the big leagues for years before he changed his first name to Bud and started pronouncing his last name *Wee-mer*. He'd come out of semi-retirement in the Cotton States League when most of the younger umps were overseas. I had given him the Pasquels' card myself.

Theolic composed himself and threw an unhittable inside fastball. Clearly a strike.

Ball two. Bud Weimer smiled.

Without ever throwing a true ball, Theolic walked Bejerano, who promptly stole second. The next batter, Lloyd Davenport, with a strike zone the size of a playing card, benefited from a couple of piss-poor calls and also walked. Then he and Bejerano worked a double steal.

The whistling grew so loud I covered my ears. My lens was too weak to capture the anger on Smith's face.

On the first pitch to the next batter, Roy Zimmerman, who'd been with the New York Giants, Weimer called Smith for a balk and Bejerano scored. It was certainly not a balk. Zimmerman followed with a grounder to short, scoring Davenport.

Smith fell behind Roland Gladu 3–0 before getting him to strike out swinging. As Gladu headed back to the bench, Smith made his right hand into the shape of a gun, pointed it at

Weimer, and fired. Weimer stormed out from behind the plate, but Smith was cool enough to turn his back and act like nothing had happened. When play resumed, Jim Steiner, the Red Sox journeyman, grounded to first to end the inning.

As Nuevo Laredo took the field, I happened to look into the upper deck, where money changed hands on every batter, sometimes every pitch, and the shouts of the gamblers could be heard unabated from the first pitch to the last out. But not today. The upper deck sat still.

For Mexico City, Wright and Dandridge got on, Ortiz whacked a homer, and the Reds went up 3–2. But Weimer's umpiring seemed perfectly fine. Still no action in the upper deck.

The next batter was Theolic Smith. The first pitch was far outside. And Weimer called it a strike. The whistles resumed.

"We seein the same ball game, ump?" Smith said.

Weimer said nothing.

The next pitch was just as bad. Strike two.

Smith stepped out of the box. "Come Christmastime, I know what you can ask your grandkids for," he hissed. "Pair of specs."

I've seen players ejected for less. Weimer took off his mask. "Back in the box, nigger."

Smith's body went rigid and his eyes went cold and I snapped the picture. He took a step toward Weimer, thought better of it, stepped up to the plate, took a savage practice swing, dug in, and called out to the pitcher, "Bring the heat, chickenshit!"

Instead what he got was a brushback. The whistling was so loud that Theolic, in the dirt, didn't hear the call. He stood up, dusted himself off, and got back in the batter's box.

"Don't show me up, shine," Weimer roared. "Strike three, you're out!"

Theolic shook his head. Softly, he said, "Aw, shit."

Weimer ripped off his mask, jabbed Theolic in the breastbone, and pointed toward the sky. "You are out of here!" He drew his face inches from Theolic's. "Out of my sight, boy. Hit the shower. Go wash off your nigger stink."

Smith rocked back, planted his feet, and threw a punch. He connected with Weimer's jaw so hard one of Weimer's teeth shot out and pinged off my chest, twenty feet away. Only then did I think to hit the shutter. In the photo, Theolic Smith is standing over the crumpled form of Bud Weimer. Nearby, a few other players stand by, stunned. You can see three blurry members of Pasquel's militia in the very corner of the frame. One has a rifle drawn.

At first the crowd was silent. I don't remember hearing anyone say anything for what seemed like forever. The first sound I remember came from Theolic himself.

"Oh dear God," he said. "Please don't let him be dead."

Then things went wild in their predictable way: The crowd let out its held breath in a roar, the benches cleared, and the militia rode their steeds onto the field, et cetera.

Two things were new.

First, when play resumed, so did the gambling in the upper deck. The fix had been in: Weimer. Second was what happened to Theolic Smith. He got taken to the Federal District prison, booked for felonious assault, and thrown in a six-by-nine cell, still in his flannel uniform.

Danny Gardella stood in the front row of the balcony and sang the hell out of "Ave Maria." It was a Catholic wedding. Long. Everyone—as I remember it—was drunk or high on grass. For me it was the pulque. The line for the bathroom afterward was, despite the few people in attendance, long. People were still talking about Danny Gardella's "Ave Maria." He did such a good job that I invited him back for my third wedding. But that comes later.

On your wedding day, you believe in all sorts of things. One thing you believe in most is that your marriage won't fail, though if you had any sense you'd know it probably will. It's just a thing that happens to you—like a belly, or hair coming out of your ears, or becoming a reporter instead of a writer. The day of my second wedding, even I, Frank Bullinger, Jr., cynic and opportunist in matters of the heart, believed. I drank enough hallucinogenic liquor and distanced myself enough from the wrecked lives I'd led and left in America that I made and accepted toasts, laughed and danced and sang, kissed and kissed my petite genius bride, thanked everyone for their gifts and for coming, got into Jorge Pasquel's limo for the airport, got into one of Jorge's planes, flew to one of Jorge's houses—a small, elegant walled villa in Veracruz—and embarked on married life as if it would all be this way forever, until death parts us. True story.

The wedding vows, I have had occasion to notice, do not specify the death of whom. Or of what.

It was in that sunny villa—which Jorge Pasquel used as a library and a retreat, and where the book you are now reading was written—where, on day two of our married life, we came across the first review we'd seen of Diana James's first book of poems. There was a stack of magazines on the kitchen counter and in the newest of *The New Yorker*s, about two weeks old, there it was. It was written by Bunny Wilson, and though it was short it was a rave. Diana read it and fell apart.

"Do you know what this means?" She was naked and weeping and seemed altogether like an actress playing a mad scene.

"Hell, yes," I said. "It means you just got what lots of people— what *I*—would gladly cut off a useful body part for."

"That's what you think it means?" The look on her face turned hopeful.

"That's what I know it means. It's a really good review."

"I wish it were that simple," she said. She reread the review. "Maybe you're right," she said.

"Of course I'm right."

She looked me right in the eye and held that look for an awfully long time, in silence. "I don't want this." She thrust the magazine at me. "I don't want to be Edmund Wilson's new quote-unquote discovery."

I took it. "What *do* you want?" I said.

"Jesus, Frank, is there a bigger curse than early success?"

"Yes," I said. "The lack of it."

I slipped on some clothes and went out for sweet rolls, tequila, and orange juice. When I got back, Diana was locked in the library, writing. I made coffee. I read that whole stack of magazines. I smoked cigars. I tried not to think of Frances Kingston, and therefore couldn't think of anything else. Try it. Try not to think about what a shit I was to get divorced and, while another woman was pregnant with my baby, marry yet another other woman. I tried to think about worse things that people do. There are many. As you read this, someone you know is probably doing something much worse. Also, there's you, yourself. Think about the most ill-advised and evil thing *you've* ever done; be honest. I thought a lot, then, about the war, what people did to make it and about what it made people do. But it doesn't work, finally, thinking about other people's atrocities, scandals, and acts of cowardice. I walked the glistening black streets of Veracruz, past the Mexican Naval Academy, past the beachside construction sites where two new tourist hotels were going up, past old women cooking tortillas in tiny comida corrida stands, past hard-sell cabbies eager for an American fare, and no matter what I tried to think about, I kept thinking about me. It was a long day.

❧

In August, the day after we cut our honeymoon short, the Veracruz Blues came home for a series against the first-place Tampico Cottonpickers and the red-hot second-place Monterrey Sultans. The Mexico City papers, having said as much about election fraud as they were going to, covered the homestand as if it were Normandy, Louis/Schmeling II, and Fatty Arbuckle, all in one italicized, boldfaced, exclamatory package. Banner headlines touted the last, best chance for the rich, loutish Blues to salvage something from this wreckage of a season and show their true character to the upstart teams from the countryside.

Tampico took three of four games, losing only to stocky Max Lanier, who pitched a three-hitter, striking out fourteen and making the best team in Mexico look like a bunch of rank sandlotters. I'd seen Lanier pitch this well before (he was brilliant in the '42, '43, and '44 World Series), but not for so long. In '46 Max Lanier rode one of the great grooves of all time. When he jumped from the Cardinals, he was 6–0 and leading the league with a 1.93 ERA. After that first rocky relief appearance against Mexico City, Max reeled off win after win. He led the Mexican League in ERA, a full run better than the next guy. Overall, after waxing Tampico, he stood 12–0 with a 2.05 ERA.

The first three games against Monterrey were blowouts, 18–2, 7–1, and 5–0. Veracruz sank six games behind San Luis Potosí, dead last. The Blues played like goldbricking union-wage janitors. Danny Gardella cared more about being with his new wife. Ace Adams cared more about his next bottle of wine (I cast no stones). Luis Olmo cared more about his quest to sleep with every pretty girl in Mexico (again, no stones). Harry Feldman cared more about studying for his medical-school boards. Chile Gómez cared more about kissing up to the Pasquels. Mickey Owen cared more about his lawyer's efforts to get him reinstated by the Brooklyn Dodgers, who were in a pennant race and somehow imagined Owen could help.

At the same time, in Tampico, the Red Devils swept the Cotton-pickers, making the pennant race a three-team contest. There was one—*one!*—reporter at those games. Every paper in Mexico had, instead, sent men to Delta Park. By the last game of the home stand, reporters and photographers blanketed foul territory. Max Lanier's streak was only a small part of that. These men knew their readers. The story of the Veracruz Blues—young men with all the advantages, once heavily favored to win, now quite certain to lose, their year collapsing under the weight of pride, bigotry, violence, indolence, and ill-spent money—was the story of a florid, grandiose defeat. In Mexico, as in most of the non-American world, such a story has more hold on the common man than some bland tale of victory. Lanier's streak was but a compelling subplot, a narrative about the dogged emergence from ruin of sheer, point-less excellence.

When Lanier fell behind 2–0, a victim of a throwing error by Gardella and a dropped third strike by Owen, Delta Park grew quiet. Were they to root for Lanier, for a comeback victory? Were they to root for the Negroes and Latinos from Monterrey? Were they to deride the comical shortcomings of the fallen Blues? Delta Park was so quiet that, sitting in Jorge Pasquel's box with that kid from *El Norte* who had designs on my wife (despite myself, I liked the kid), I could hear the players' chatter. I could even hear the shouts of vendors in the outfield bleachers. When the Blues rallied in the sixth, scoring three runs and taking the lead, the crowd applauded no more than good manners minimally decreed. It was as if everyone had forgotten the object of the game.

In top of the eighth, Claro Duany, the hulking Cuban who was leading the league in hitting, slashed a liner down the first-base line, which Danny Gardella leapt for and would have caught except for the fact that he was the shortest first baseman this side of junior high school, and the ball rolled all the way into the corner, and Duany chugged around the bases for a triple.

Max Lanier's white flannels were drenched with sweat. He had nothing left. Ace Adams was up in the bullpen. But when Chile Gómez started to the mound from second, Max stared him down. Gómez retreated. On guile, will, veteran savvy, and spectacular luck with junk, Max struck out Superman Pennington and got Fantasma Heredia out on a hissing shot to short, which Lou Klein dove for and speared. Then, leaping to his feet, Klein showed the ball to the ump, flipped it to Lanier, and, laughing and pointing to Heredia, shouted, "Siddown, Cuban shineboy."

Ed Stone, a tall gray-haired Negro with a sweet left-handed stroke, came to the plate. Lanier, even with no gas left, was murder on lefties. But Stone was a professional hitter. Thirty years later, I saw him go four-for-four in an old-timers game in Chicago; there wasn't a kid on the White Six with a better swing.

Stone worked the count full, and it stayed full forever, foul after foul, and with each pitch the crowd came further alive, until, at last, they were on their feet, cheering neither for or against the Blues or the Sultans, but for the gutsy mano a mano between two men, each with one hand tied between his back—Lanier because he was exhausted, Stone because he was facing maybe the best left-handed pitcher alive. Time stopped. The reporters and photographers were all unabashedly cheering, and I said to the kid from *El Norte* that the ump ought to call it a draw and send everyone home with the image of that standoff in their minds.

The kid looked at me. "You are a sentimental man," he said.

Stone fouled off yet another pitch, but this one looked like it would stay in the park. Mickey Owen tore off his mask and camped under it. The ball drifted back, toward our box, and as Owen thrust his glove over the wall I leapt up to catch it, for myself. I dropped the ball. It slapped off my hands and landed a few rows behind me. Owen gave me a look. But he didn't say anything at all. He just stared me down, shook his head, spat, and returned to the plate.

"Damn," I said. "I really wanted that ball."

The kid smiled. If this scene sounds familiar, it's probably because he had a version of it in his first novel, which he later made into his fourth feature film, the one right before he won his Academy Award. Unlike in his magically real world, though, the standoff between the two foreigners, pitcher and hitter, did not last literally forever. Unlike in that lovely fictive dream, Ed Stone laced a single to left-center, where a weak-armed Canadian named Charlie Mead cut in front of Luis Olmo, fielded the ball cleanly, and threw it home. It was the throw of his life. He had Claro Duany dead to rights. Owen caught the ball, blocked the plate, and, when Duany lowered his shoulder and tried to score, hauled off and smashed him in the face with the tag.

What he said to Duany I could not hear. It is a safe bet it included the word *nigger*.

Fantasma Heredia leapt from the dugout and tackled the first Blue he found, mighty mite Danny Gardella. Both benches cleared. Although no one wound up in jail with Theolic Smith, this was the worst, lengthiest fight of the season, and, with Pasquel's militia curiously absent, the players just kept fighting. The newspapermen buzzed and swarmed about the periphery. And the Mexican crowd, mostly men in suits, stood and watched. They did not, as Americans might presume, riot. They did not cheer for either side. They just watched. Many, like me, had seen this movie already; many, like me, left long before the umpires and managers broke it up.

I wanted to go home. Not to the Hotel Galveston; *home* home.

If I'd only known where that was.

Instead, I bought a small bucket of Coronas, went up to my ammoniac office, slipped inside, and, while the tiresome battle raged outside, wrote a letter of resignation.

I kept writing. I wrote a letter to Danny Gardella, thanking him for everything and, as a token of my esteem, giving him that jarful of formaldehyde and human heart, for luck in love. I wrote a letter to Jerome. I wrote letters to Frances and to Diana, letters I realized were really written to myself, to sort things out.

The game was over now and the Blues had hung on to win, and I just kept writing. The beer grew warm. I chose not to drink it. I chose to keep writing. The door locked tight, I stayed there all night, finishing my series. Sometime the next morning there came an angry-sounding knock at the door. Diana. I nearly chose not to answer it, but I was done with the series and so proud of it—to this day, my greatest burst of inspiration and productivity—that I jumped up and pulled open the door.

It was Jorge Pasquel. He had on a tuxedo.

Behind him was Ramón Bragaña and a half-dozen other black

players, among whom I recognized the Negro League stars Buster Clarkson and Double Duty Radcliffe.

"What," said Pasquel, frowning, "is the meaning of this?"

I shook his hand. I was speechless. There was so much he could have meant by *this*.

The Witch's Double

THEOLIC "FIREBALL" SMITH

We had this coach everybody called El Brujo. The Witch. He was the guy gave the Red Devils our name. When I first joined up, the team was called just the Reds. Then one day we had a great comeback and he said, "Estos Rojos pelean como diablos." Meant it as a compliment. And the name took. The official name was just Reds but most folks called us Red Devils, a name the fans liked in spite of the fact of how Catholic those people are.

El Brujo said from the first day of spring training that 1946 was our year. I for one believed him. Why not? There are just some years where a certain team or certain guy is meant to win it all, and in 1946 the team was los Rojos de México and the guy was me. I honestly believe that.

It was in our control. It was in my control. Control. *Mercy.* I led the league in bases on balls that year. But, hell, I was never no control pitcher. I led lots of leagues in bases on balls. What it was in 1946 was something else.

The year they put Wild Bill Wright in the Mexican Baseball Hall of Fame, Dandy and me met up with him in Mexico City. Burnis come up from Zacatecas, where he's got a cantina called the Home Run Grille. Well, like everyplace, Mexico City's changed some since 1946 and we're these three old men, see, out on the town and such, and after finding our old haunts tore down or not where we remembered 'em, we admitted we was awful damn lost. Burnis is embarrassed, bein our host, but he's got bad arthritis and hadn't been in Mexico City himself for years. Finally, I get a idea. I hail a cab (they stop for black men there; why I left is a mystery to me now), and on account of my Spanish bein rusty I had Burnis tell the cabbie to take us to the city jail.

This cracks Burnis and Dandy up, see.

"Seriously, fellas," I says. "Get me to that fine Mexico City jail, I'll find anyplace from there."

Time I got tossed in jail for punching that Nazi umpire wasn't my first, wasn't my last. Don't look surprised. Black man my age, specially one with a taste for drink, we all seen the inside of a jail cell. In America, if I'd got arrested for knockin a white man cold, I'd've worried I might never see the light of day again, or that a lynch mob was out there makin plans. But in Mexico I knew my misdeeds was just gonna keep me locked up overnight or so. Plus, that Mexico City jail wasn't like other jails I spent nights in— St. Louis; Cleveland; Elkhart, Indiana; Pittsburgh, P-A; and some places down South I'd as soon not mention. That Mexico jail had good spicy food, firm mattresses, even a brand-new wing which was air-conditioned, which was where I got put. They treated me real nice in that jail. Yes, they did. *Specially* the time I got tossed in there for punchin that ump.

Turns out the head Mexican jailer is my biggest fan. True story. Remember me tellin about those eighty thousand Mexican workers who came to America in '43 so me and Quincy Trouppe could keep playin ball? Well, the jailer, Juan Madero, he had a job then that let him pick what eighty thousand got to go, and he gave jobs to all his wife's people, this big-ass family full of the worst freeloaders that ever drew breath. Or so Juan said. Every time Juan saw me he thought of how I got his mother-in-law shipped off to pick Texas tomatoes and his brother-in-law shipped off to work in an ammo plant in Birmingham, and his face lit up. Most nights I spent in jail I had supper in Juan's office, talkin baseball and listenin to jazz records on a basswood Victrola. Got to take visitors, too. Lady friends.

In fact, the time I was in for coldcockin the ump I'd just said goodbye to the Tall Inés and was waitin for Juan in his office listening to Lady Day and watchin our supper go cold, when who shows up—burstin in the office like he owned it, which maybe he did—but Jorge Pasquel. Behind him he's got four friendly faces, *black* faces: Felix McLaurin, Jesse Douglas, Joe Fillmore, and Earl Ashby. It was like some cowboy movie, when here comes the cavalry.

"Mr. Smith," says Pasquel, spittin his *s*'s, "allow me to introduce your new teammates."

"I know *these* rascals," says I, and everybody laughs. We shake hands and slap backs. Can't hardly believe the turn things all of a sudden took. Those four men could play *ball*, hear?

And then Jorge Pasquel bows real deep, like people with airs do, and he says, "I wish to personally apologize for the misunderstanding which resulted in your unfortunate imprisonment."

Don't get the idea I wasn't fit to be tied about bein thrown in there, mind. Lots of men got in fights. But as far as I know I was the only player who went to jail for it. It wasn't like I punched out Babe Ruth or something. So I just stand there, a long time, not acceptin the apology, not sayin nothin, in the hopes I can make Jorge Pasquel sweat.

He sizes me up.

Then he reaches in his pocket and produces a crisp American one-thousand-dollar bill. Picture of President Grover Cleveland on it.

"For your troubles," he said.

"Gracias," said I. What *could* I say? Everybody's got his price. That was big money. Mr. Cleveland could buy you a new automobile with enough left over for a night on the town. Jorge Pasquel was the world champ of knowin other men's prices.

Juan got back then, and he ordered up food and drink for everybody, and we all stayed and had us a time. All those fellas spent the night in jail with me. Pasquel was a puzzle to me to his dying day, but I spent time I coulda been figurin him out drinkin instead. That's a young man's sense of priority. What I remember from that night was, we left come morning with hangovers in our heads but joy in our hearts, sure that we be the capital city's first baseball champs.

"You men," said Jorge Pasquel, in his preacher voice, "will be heroes until the end of time."

"Sure," said I, "and so will you, right?" He was the kind of man who'd find a way to take credit for a sunny afternoon.

"Why not?" said Jorge. "Of course. I, too, will be a hero for all time. Me especially."

We all laughed, but none of us thought for one second, even half-drunk, that he was joking.

Give the devil his due, Jorge Pasquel knew what our club needed, talent-wise, to win his league. Ever since he robbed us of Lou Olmo we had a hole at center and leadoff. Felix McLaurin, a ball hawk who'd been with the Birmingham Black Barons, he filled that bill. All year we needed a second baseman and a two-hitter. Up and behold: Jesse Douglas of the Chicago American Giants, who'd been with Monterrey, and who could lay down a bunt on a buffalo nickel. Big Joe Fillmore, who'd have been a star except for losin his good years to the U.S. Army, he stepped in as our relief man. And Earl Ashby, a free-swingin Cuban I played with in Cleveland, old Earl gave us depth at catcher. Sunset Colás had caught every game that year and was more beat-up than Sugar Ray Robinson's sparring partner. Our first game after they joined and I rejoined the club, we had a showdown with the Monterrey Sultans, up at their place, last we'd played 'em all year. We took a brand-new charter airplane, with lovely Mexican stewardesses and steak dinners served, Kentucky bourbon flowin free. That was how it would be for the rest of the year, for us, all first-class.

Brother, did those Monterrey fans give us the business, Douglas in particular, though it wasn't nothin Jesse could have controlled, his changin teams. And to boot, the Sultans had already went into a tailspin. That game they lost to Veracruz, the one where Owen and Duany had that brawl and did not either one go to jail but only got a week's suspension, it started the Sultans off on a loss streak. No Duany, no Douglas, plus Art Pennington went in a slump, Ed Stone had a bum knee, and that fantastic knuckleball man, the Coyote, he missed some starts on account of a death in the family. It wasn't the same Monterrey club as early on.

We took the first three games of the series. Great pitching from that good-hearted Okie Fred Martin, Tommy de la Cruz, and, much as it pains me to admit, Alex Carrasquel. After a for-crap first half, that passin-for-white so-and-so showed up one day and was a new pitcher. That's baseball, ups and downs and maybe no reason why for either the up *or* the down. Or no reason you can see. Lookin back, Alex's turnabout probably had to do with a spitter El Brujo taught him.

Every day there for a while, I came to the park like a man reacquainted with Jesus, smilin, singin, born again. Sure, things went wrong—money hassles, gettin left off the All-Stars, fights, booze, jail—but a lot went right. We're all better at seein the wrong than the right. But then I *saw:* I played ball for a living, a good living, with great fellas like Dandy, Burnis, Freddie, and that moose Ortiz. I was balancin two great ladies, and I got to meet Mexican artists and big shots, which was an experience in itself. I'd had a great first half of the season, and I had six weeks to get back on track and finish strong. We had a great club, with a chance to be remembered. I never for a minute felt ashamed or humiliated on account of the color of my skin. These things was my focus, for a while.

I pitched game four of the Monterrey series. Hadn't had a drink since the flight up, hadn't pitched for two weeks. As I warmed up, my pitches hissed and broke and smacked into Earl Ashby's glove like firecrackers. Never had better stuff. Never felt stronger or better-lookin.

On the mound for the Sultans was Indian Torres, skinny Cuban kid who'd been in the league a while. Nothin great about him, just a guy who took the ball and ate innings. In the first, he shuts us down, but I don't think nothin of it. It's my day to shine. Struck out the side in inning one.

But that Indian hung tough. We hit him good but couldn't push nothin across. Been wars fought without as many dead as we had die at third that day.

Had me a no-hitter going for six and two thirds, which got broke up when their player/manager, Salazar, hit a bloop that Felix McLaurin raced in on and missed by a foot. I struck the next man's ass out, three pitches: See ya, see ya, wouldn't wanna be ya.

We wind up the ninth, and believe it or not, it's still no score. Tenth inning, out comes the Indian. Two outs, but then we get two men on and I'm up; lucky I was a good hitter, otherwise I'd have been lifted. I walk. Bases full. Up next came El Shorty Arroyo, who lines the first pitch right at Torres's head, which he saves his life by spearin for out number three.

I sail through the tenth, Torres struggles through the eleventh. Bottom of the eleventh, I walk the first man and Ernesto Carmona has Joe Fillmore warm up in the bullpen. I walk the next guy. Out trots Carmona. He asks what I got left and I say plenty, which is a lie but I got a shutout goin. He asks Earl in Spanish the same thing. Earl also says plenty. Good old Earl.

Well, I work my way out of that jam, out of jams in twelve and thirteen, too. Same for Torres! Unbelievable. I'm bushed, ready to let Carmona put Fillmore in to pitch. I wouldn't have said that, but it's a manager's job to do what's best for the team in spite of the prideful nature of the dumb-ass young men who play for him. Instead, Carmona sees Indian Torres take the mound, and he don't think about my arm, my career, or even the game, nothin but that macho shit, like somehow me outlastin Torres would add six inches to Carmona's dick.

McLaurin singles, Douglas bunts him over, and Dandy bunts him to third. Up comes Bob Ortiz. He takes the first three pitches for balls and then hauls off and smacks the next fat pitch high and down the line, headed for the mountains in the distance, sweet Jesus, let it stay fair.

It is! Just barely, but fair! We jump up and down and start celebratin.

Till we hear a roar go up from the crowd. Third-base ump signals—can you believe this?—foul ball. Carmona waddles out to argue, but the ump's from Monterrey and it's a hometown call, and that's just how it's sliced. Carmona got tossed from the game for callin the ump "a fucker of pigs."

Next pitch, Ortiz hits another blast, deep to center, way back, it could be, it might be . . . a-a-a-and, *no*. Superman Pennington grabs it at the fence, great catch.

Either of those balls leave the yard, I'm out of there, pitcher of record and Fillmore comin on to close up shop. But with my shutout still goin and the game still tied, I wanted to stay in.

El Brujo was acting manager. He didn't speak English and I pretended not to speak Spanish, which was ridiculous because we'd had whole *conversations* in Spanish before. "Escoger es ser," he said, which means "To choose is to be," whatever the hell that means.

"No comprende, boss," I said.

"Bien," he said, and a little sad smile appeared there on that old man's face. "En tal caso, hijo, escoja juiciosamente."

I shook his hand, laughed, and took the mound. I thought what he said was "in that case, son, choose juicily." That crazy witch.

And so I found my ass out there again, inning number fourteen, so exhausted that when I walk Pennington and Claro Duany smashes my second pitch into the Carta Blanca beer garden beyond center field and we lose 2–0—*I* lose 2–0—it takes me two full hours to react. When I did, back at the Hotel Colonial and ridiculous drunk, I trash my room and throw that little white benchwarmer Rizzuti off the balcony of Dandy's room, which luckily was just on the second floor.

Toughest loss of my or most any fella's career, that's how I saw it. Rest of the team, they saw it otherwise. We won three of four from the Sultans and more or less knocked them out of the pennant race. I pitched a great game they'd all remember for years to come, and they believed I ought to be damned proud for the moral victory of that. Moral victory? I couldn't see it like that.

At the time I blamed everyone else. My teammates for pickin the best game I pitched all year, maybe ever, as the day they couldn't score a single goddamn run. That damned ump, for cheating me. Carmona and El Brujo, for not taking me out. Bottle of tequila in me, I even blamed my daddy, for settin me up to live a life like his, out in the cold, bein this close to everything I wanted without gettin a damn bit of it.

Now I feel sick about blamin my daddy. But it's so much easier to blame than to understand.

Juiciosamente, by the by, means "judiciously." *Wisely.*

Back in Mexico City the big news was that Mickey Owen had snuck back to where he came from. Why this was front-page news, you'd need to be a white man or a Mexican to see. He was a so-called big-league catcher who couldn't have started for any Negro team except Bojangles Robinson's Black Yankees, *and* who pissed and moaned all year about how bush-league Mexico is but can't even hit .250 there, *and* who had a problem playin fair with the black man! Before Owen, Veracruz has got blacks, whites, Cubans, Mexicans, everything. Owen gets made manager, and all the brothers get sent packin. Then when Jorge Pasquel decides he's had enough of the Blues bein a well-fed dog for the rest of us to kick, he puts Ramón Bragaña back on the team and snags Double Duty Radcliffe and Buzz Clarkson from the Chicago American Giants. Before them three play a game for the Blues, poof, Mickey Owen's back in the U.S. of A., sayin he left Mexico 'cause he couldn't get a good beefsteak (ha!) and that his wife got hit on by Jorge Pasquel (line up Mrs. Mickey Owen next to Miss María Félix and make up your own mind about that whopper) and askin if he can be added to the Brooklyn Dodgers, who, unlike the club he deserted, are in a pennant race. Who needs him?

It was an off day, and me and the Short Inés went to her hometown, a village outside the city that her daddy was mayor of, to watch a tribe of workers move a sixty-foot-tall stone idol named Tlaloc. The workmen had two cranes going. Big-shots in suits and museum fellas in lab coats ran around bossin the workmen. Everyone was tense. Crowd was like twenty thousand, in a village the Short Inés said had five hundred people in it. And her daddy was *workin* that crowd. Light on his feet for a fat man. Though he was awful red-faced and sweatin from the heat. I confess that seein how fat he was made me size up the Short Inés, who wasn't fat but had a butt on her, and think of the shape of things to come.

"Mickey Owen," she said out of nowhere, "reveals to Mexicans the horrors of our history."

"How you figure?" I said, smilin, kind of like baitin her. She don't know much about baseball, so I know she's comin at this from her political angle. She was the political Inés.

"The United States was settled," she said. "It is a land of welcomed immigrants. Mexico and Latin America were conquered, exploited, reduced to grand, mineral-rich whores."

"Right," I said. Like my grandparents, all four born slaves. Welcomed immigrants my *ass.*

But the Short Inés was on a roll. "Mickey Owen is every Spaniard who came here for gold, silver, and the rape of the indigenous peoples," she said. "He is every nineteenth-century Frenchman and Englishman who got rich supporting repressive puppet governments. He is every American who ever came here hailed as a sign of the promise of a more prosperous tomorrow and then left under the cover of darkness and with his pockets stuffed with Mexican gold, a symbol of a failed today."

"All Mickey Owen is," I said, "is a Punch-and-Judy-hittin horse's ass."

She laughed, and I had to explain about Punch and Judy, which I couldn't. How them limey puppets got to mean a fella who can't hit nothin but singles and not too many of them, who knows?

Lots of the crowd were the mucky-mucks the Short and Tall Inés ran with. Diego Rivera was there and so was the Tall Inés, suspicious-close to Rivera. The new-guy president, Alemán, he's there, too, spreadin the news about a hotsy-totsy museum he wants to build, which was why they wanted mossy old six-story Tlaloc, with a face like a deformed cryin babe, complete with stone tears. And the Short Inés's daddy, he was the center of it all, second only to Tlaloc. Women and children grabbed him by the pant legs and kissed him.

"Aren't you going to introduce me," I said, "to your folks?"

The Short Inés shook her head. "I myself," she said, "am not speaking to my father."

"Why?" I said. "Them kind of grudges, you'll regret 'em when your folks pass. Believe me, I know."

" 'Pass'?" she said. "The same as *pasar*?"

"Pass on," I said. "Go to your heavenly reward. Die."

As the first strap was secured to Tlaloc's feet and crane one moved that statue just the least littlest bit, rain started to fall, although it wasn't called for. Not a cloud in the sky. Sunshine. Where the rain came from, you got me.

"My father is an opportunist," the Short Inés said. "A malinchist."

Now it was me who needed a definition. You know that word, *malinchist*? The Short Inés said it had to do with Cortés the Conquistador's Mexican woman. Something like how it was a filthy thing to copulate or cooperate with foreigners. The Short Inés's eyes were on fire as she explained this. Scared the hell out of me, bein a foreigner myself. I didn't ask for no clarification. I didn't see myself as no Cortés, but I didn't want to fight. I got the subject turned back to her daddy.

Mexican government, I guess, was after the village for years to get hold of Tlaloc, move it to the capital, put it in Chapultepec Park next to a museum about Mexican history and whatnot. Sounds like a good idea, I said, but the Short Inés says it's scandalous, moving a piece of Toltec or Olmec culture (whichever; I can't keep 'em straight) from where it had ought to be. Plus which, Tlaloc was some kind of water god, and water was always a problem. If Tlaloc's so great, said I, then how come there *is* a problem? Which the Short Inés said was not the point.

By this part of the story, Tlaloc was up in the air.

The villagers cheered, though there were whistles, too. The artists, they were too cool to cheer or whistle. They scowled, like a hungover pitcher who just found out the next batter's his wife's back-door man.

Underneath Tlaloc, the workmen backed up this huge red flatbed truck with rubber tires on its bed. And the rain! Lord, did it pour. Still, the sun kept shining, like it was ignorant. Gave me the shivers. We took shelter under the tin awning of a cantina, and I ordered us some beer.

"Your daddy's such a traitor," I said to the Short Inés, "how come these people treat him like he's Audie Murphy, the Pope, and Joe Louis all in one?"

After I explained who Joe Louis was, the Short Inés told me that in exchange for Tlaloc the government drilled a well, way down to some underground lake, then built 'em a school, too.

"And that's bad?"

"He sold our village's heritage—thousands of years old—for a schoolhouse and a well that will last a generation or two. No money for teachers, no money to get the water pumped anywhere. Just a well and a schoolhouse and glory for my father—all for the low, low price of my village's integrity."

She had a year of college in the U.S., and her time-to-time American sayings gave me a start.

The rain was biblical now. Across the zócalo, Tlaloc was gettin driven off, and we couldn't even see it, that's how thick the rain was. Still sunshiny. A rainbow spread out over the town and set foot in the mountains to the west.

"Maybe I don't understand all the significance of that Tlaloc thing," I said, "but it seems like with that new well he's still providin water to your village, better than ever before."

The Short Inés gave me a look.

All of a sudden the rain stopped, like someone threw a switch.

We stayed in that cantina and had more beer. We didn't talk much. And that, I knew, was the end of it with Short Inés. She had a red ribbon in her hair that day and she smelled like vanilla. Her makeup ran a little, and her blue dress was soaked so that you could just barely see her plain white cotton brassiere underneath. Breaks my heart to remember.

Punch line: The rain traveled west right along with Tlaloc, like he was that fella in *Li'l Abner*. And when it came to rest in Mexico City—*wham!*—the rain stopped. Right then, the Short Inés's daddy—who made the trip, too, soaking up all the rain and love a human being can on this earth—right as the rain quit, the Short Inés's daddy dropped dead of a heart attack.

It was in all the papers, coast to coast. Mexicans love a story like that. Like they say, Héroe hoy, trampe mañana. Hell, we all love that kind of story—until you the tramp. I've thought a lot about the Short Inés's daddy, a man I never met, and how he died, a thing I never saw. At the time, seemed like a bad way to go. But we all gotta die. Maybe it's good to die in a way that gets you remembered, specially if it don't do harm to no other person, nothin but a thousands-of-years-old statue of a space alien who crash-landed into Toltec Land and got named water god 'cause it happened to be the beginning of rainy season the day he crashed. (Read it in a book called *Chariots of the Gods*. You know that book?)

Is it bad to want to be remembered? Is it prideful? Sinful? Wrong? Do we all have these feelings? Tell me, Frank. I'm old. We both old. Congratulations: You've cornered the only man alive with nothin better to do than sit here, drink Maxwell House, and listen to what you got to say.

It was such a pleasure to pound the bejesus out of them Azules. August, homestretch, nut-cuttin time, we Red Devils pounded everybody. Went up to Torreón; they were hot, too, but we cooled 'em off. Even whipped Martín Dihigo, who always gave us fits. Went to Nuevo Laredo, that den of thieves, where they'd stooped so low as to sign this kid Hooper Triplett, who got banned from white baseball when, while he was leading a Triple A league in hitting, he bet against his team. We waxed 'em. Then we traveled up in the mountains to Puebla, where that cranky bastard Luque had his Parrots playin the best ball in Mexico. Nap Reyes and Bob Avila were both battin like .380, both white-hot. First game, I lost to that five-o'clock-shadowed Sal Maglie and his amazing curve—which he learned from Luque and Luque learned from Christy Mathewson and Christy Mathewson learned from Rube Foster, the greatest pitcher of all time and the founder of the Negro Leagues. Ain't no shame losin to Rube Foster. After that, we won the last three games of that series.

Still and all, there wasn't no better feeling than beatin the Azules. And not just beatin 'em. We wanted to show them, Jorge Pasquel, all Mexico, and all the world, that a team of black men could embarrass the cups and sannies off of the best-paid, mostly white talent money could buy. We didn't talk about it much. But everybody thought it.

Our last series against Veracruz we was flyin high, one behind Tampico, several games up on Puebla, Torreón, and Monterrey. This was our chance to go ahead and stay ahead.

First game, we had Tommy de la Cruz going against their best, Max Lanier, who hadn't lost a game all year. He was seven-and-oh for the Blues. Seven; lucky sign for them. But he'd been six-and-oh for St. Louis, which made him thirteen-and-oh overall. Thirteen; lucky for us.

We loaded the lineup with right-handed sticks and chased Max early, but the Blues chased Tommy the same inning. The lead see-sawed all game before we went ahead and won, with neither starter involved in the decision. Thing I remember most from that game, Frank, was you. Walkin into the bar at the Hotel Galveston and tellin us the news, Puebla had beat Tampico and that we were tied for first. I believe I kissed you, didn't I, Frank? Well, those was high-spirited days.

Game two of that series was the all-time greatest pounding of them Azules. Ramón Bragaña, tryin to play with our minds, started his relief man, Ace Adams. Top of the first, we batted around twice, scored like fifteen runs, with Ortiz crankin not one but two homers and Dandy gettin the other, and it was such a joyous slugfest that it took some sting out of me makin two of the three outs in the inning and out of Alex Carrasquel being the one who got staked to such a lead. Double Duty Radcliffe was the catcher for Veracruz, forty-some-year-old man behind the plate, and when I strike out and the inning's over, he laughs and says, "Boy, you *are* in a slump."

"Like to see you out there," I said. "I'd take you *deep*, old man."

But his double-duty days, when he'd catch half a doubleheader and pitch game two, they was over. By then he was just a catcher, a shell of what he was. I started to get in his face, but Double Duty shook his head and laughed. "This is a game," he said. "Okay? Have some fun, kid."

Then he walked away. The fights I could have avoided, on the field and off, if only every guy I got mad at had been Double Duty Radcliffe.

We waited in the hotel lobby for the news from Puebla. Tampico won. We still tied.

That game three! It was Freddie Martin for us against Harry Feldman for them, two former New York Giants. Carmona benched me, put Chorejas at first. I complained, but I'd have done the same. I was havin one of those stretches any ballplayer goes through, only mine was at a piss-poor time. I'm watchin the game with half a heart, wantin us to win, sure, but thinkin mostly about my pitching turn comin up the next day, my chance to get back on track.

Come the ninth inning we're down 3–2, but the mood on our bench is high. Feldman don't have a drop of gas left in his tank. Burnis comes up and says, "Be ready, Theo. Freddie's third up." I got the mixed feelings you get when you're in a slump. Why pinch-hit *me*, the way I'm goin? Same token, I *want* the bat in my hands with the game on the line. I'm a *ballplayer*.

Sunset Colás walks. The feeling in Delta Park is electric. I look down to Carmona, but he's watchin El Brujo in the coaching box at third. Like everyone in Mexico don't know El Shorty Arroyo's gonna bunt. Feldman tries to nibble, but, down in the count, he finally throws a strike. El Shorty hits a terrible bloop bunt, halfway to first. Dan Gardella races in, and Sunset freezes, sure it'll be caught. Gardella gets ready to dive, then hesitates—and it's over, Rover. Ball drops. Sunset speeds down to second, Feldman throws out Arroyo, and the crowd goes loony.

Ramón Bragaña walks to the mound, tappin his left arm. But there's no lefties in his pen. Suddenly, off the bench comes none other than Mr. Thirteen-and-Oh, Max Lanier.

Carmona calls Freddie Martin back from the on-deck circle.

I got a lump in my throat. But who better than me? Nobody. It's obvious. But Carmona walks out the dugout, puts his hands on his fat hips, and makes a show of lookin up and down the bench, sizin up his options—like he's really gonna put Frank Rizzuti in to hit in a game like this. Or one of the Mexican kids like Aldama or Mouse Vargas, who were only on the team for national-pride reasons and were also both lefties. No. Had to be me.

Finally, I can't take the suspense no longer and I stand up and go for a bat.

Carmona's hand shoots out. "Sit, Smeet!" Like I'm a dog.

"Fuck you, Skip."

That tore it. I did it to myself, though I didn't see it that way at the time.

Carmona turns around and waves at El Brujo. When I see Carmona means to have Grandpa grab a bat for the first time since Tlaloc was a gleam in the eye of a village sculptor, and send him in against the best pitcher in the league with a must-win game on the line, I lose it. Lucky for me, luckier for Carmona, Burnis and Dandy had had enough of me in jail. They held me back, bless 'em.

As Max Lanier is warming up, the umpires are called over to Jorge Pasquel's box. They give Lanier twice as many pitches as you're supposed to get. We shout about that, but nobody listens. Then the umps take their place, and before you know it, Max Lanier throws a fastball El Brujo probably never even saw and a curve nobody could've hit, and the count stands oh-two.

El Brujo, whose face was always a total blank, all of a sudden seems like a scared boy holdin a too-big bat. He steps out of the box to get his wits, and the crowd's on its feet, cheerin on this old-time legend—a guy who was a *pitcher*, not a hitter, in his playing days. In America, such a dumb-ass stunt would get a manager booed out of baseball. Nobody'd pull it, no crowd would cheer him for pullin it. Mexico's different. Those fans didn't think El Brujo was gonna win the game no more than I did. But Mexico, see, is a country built on grand gestures. Losin a ball game and maybe a pennant, hell, anyone can do that. But losin it in a noble but doomed way that'd leave people talkin about it for years to come, that's a feat, brother. That, ladies and gentlemen, *is* Mexico. That, ladies and gents, is what it means to have the Veracruz Blues.

El Brujo heaves the bat back up on his shoulder and steps back in the box.

Lanier checks the sign, nods, and wastes a pitch, way outside. El Brujo takes it.

I turn to Burnis. "We're dead," I said.

Burnis shrugs. "Stranger things have happened, Theo."

"Name one," says I.

Burnis thinks about this, then shrugs again.

Just then, while me and Burnis ain't lookin, there's a crack of the bat. We look up, and what do we see? El Brujo haulin ass down the line and the baseball sailin into the gap in left-center!

The left fielder, Superman Pennington, who Jorge Pasquel had took off the Monterrey team and who was playin his first game as a Blue, makes a diving catch.

End of game.

Or so I thought.

Pennington bounces up but instead of trottin in turns and runs to the fence. Ball got past him; how I don't know. Topspin? Backspin? Magic?

Sunset scores, and the Witch would've had a stand-up triple except for the fact that Tlaloc had more foot speed. Winds up slidin into second. Crowd loses *control.* This time I really thought they might topple that rickety grandstand. And for what? Not a big win or a home run. A freak pinch double that tied up a game. When Carmona sends Rizzuti in to pinch-run, fans from the on-field area run out and carry El Brujo off to glory on their shoulders, like an offering to heaven.

"Not that anybody seems to notice, fellas," I says to Burnis and Dandy—we'd walked out by home, clear of the stands in case they collapsed, and away from the mob—"but the score's only tied."

Burnis is laughin. "This damn place tickles me," he says.

Dandy nods toward Max Lanier, who's still out on the mound,

watchin the festivities, bug-eyed as a man who'd just seen Martians land. "Betcha this rattles him," says Dandy. "This is the kind of thing that breaks a streak." He smiles, sly-like. "Bet you boys a steak dinner we take him."

We didn't take the bet; we wanted to believe. But when Max finally got back on the rubber, pissed-off, he struck out McLaurin and Douglas—*bang-bang*—and I confess I had doubts.

Joe Fillmore came on in the bottom of the ninth and shut Veracruz down. In the tenth, Lanier struck out Dandy, Ortiz, and Burnis. Come the eleventh, I thought for sure when he loaded the bases that Bragaña would take him out, but no. And Max worked out of the jam.

"I figured out Max Lanier," says Burnis, as they gather up to take the field.

"Yeah?" says Dandy, who's scheduled to bat in the twelfth.

"Man ain't human."

"We all human," says Dandy.

"Up against old Max we are," says Burnis.

"Shut up." Dandy runs out to short. All inning it's eatin him, maybe Lanier's got his number. Top of the twelfth, Dandy sprints in, grabs a bat, and goes to the plate like a man with a mission.

Burnis elbows me. "Watch this." And just like that, Dandy lines Lanier's first pitch to left. Base hit. "Ought to make *me* the manager," says Burnis.

Next up is Roberto Ortiz. Lanier works the count full. Ortiz steps out, shakes his head like he's had enough of this nonsense, steps back in, and crunches the next pitch to deep center, over Luis Olmo's head, for a triple. Burnis sac-flies Ortiz home, and we go on to win 5–3.

Max Lanier dropped to 13–1. If I remember right, he didn't win another game all year.

El Brujo never played in another game the rest of his life.

Best news of the day: Puebla beat Tampico. For the first time all year, the Red Devils of Mexico were in first place, alone.

El Brujo was in the bar with us when we heard. He was sittin in a dark corner, couple of Pasquel's goons there to protect him from people who loved him maybe too much. When he caught wind of us talkin and carryin on about how it was our year, destiny and all that, he stood up, banged his shot glass on the table, and proclaimed, "Carácter es hado, y hado es carácter," which I believe means Character is fate, and fate is character—whatever *that's* supposed to mean.

Then he sat down.

We thought he was just drunk.

About the last game of the last Veracruz series, less said the better. I lost, okay? I lost. Bragaña won, and so did Tampico, both games of their doubleheader in Puebla. We were back in second place, half a game out. Half a game. As close to first as you can get without gettin it.

All the way in the plane ride to Tampico, I was moody and quiet, which scared my buddies, like I was the part of a cowboy movie where things are quiet, too quiet, and then Geronimo and a million braves ride over the crest of a hill. I just want to be alone, I said, with my thoughts. I didn't even drink, which probably also scared the fellas.

I never did explode, though. Thought about it. Never did. In fact, when we got to Tampico, and Alex Carrasquel pitched a shutout to put us back on top, I actually shook his hand and bought him dinner afterward. There at the table, he encouraged me. My worst enemy on the team looked me in the eye and told me he believed in me.

But when it came my turn to pitch, nothin changed. I walked their leadoff hitter. In the distance, I heard a train comin. The ump looked at me like Do you want to call time? But I was ticked about the base on balls, and I shook my head and went after their number two hitter, Bonnie Serrell. The train drew closer, and closer, and closer. Bonnie worked the count full. The ump started to signal to stop, but I got in one more pitch.

Bonnie stroked what looked like a clean single to center field.

Only, Felix McLaurin is back by the fence, waitin for this speeding train to pass, and as that silver train rocketed through the outfield, the baseball disappeared clean, through an open window of a passenger car.

The umpire, steamed I ignored him, ruled that the ball was a home run. I didn't so much as argue. I had to laugh, to be honest. But it wasn't no happy laugh. And by the time I gave up a couple more home runs, long and legitimate, and we fell too far behind to have any real shot at redemption, I had to face up to what I'd done. Other years, I'd carried worse teams than those 1946 Reds, much worse teams, right to the brink of victory. Now other men were carryin us. Carryin *me*.

Let me confess this, Frank, before I leave this earth. Been carryin it around too long. Been thinkin it but never said it to nobody, not my buddies or my women or, years later, to my lovely wife Betty, or to any of our kids like Octavia here. Not even out loud to myself in the mirror. So I'll say it for the record, for you to put in your book. I'll put it plain as I can: In my best-ever chance at bein remembered as a champion, I was why we lost.

13.

Los Niños Héroes

DANNY GARDELLA

I

If it looked good, it went bad. My ball club looked like the class of the league and spent all summer in last. The Mexican League looked like a good way to give the rat-bastard big-league owners some competition, but it turned out it was just a big show. My own season looked good up to where I made the All-Star game and hit two homers in it. Then I got mired in an awful slump. The broadening experience of playing ball with men of all races, that went bad because of that fight Mickey Owen started that I got caught in the middle of, where out of self-defense I beat Fantasma Heredia silly, after which the blacks grouped me with Owen, Klein, and the southerners, which was a lie, but I can see, looking back, how they came to that conclusion.

Another thing was when I made my professional singing debut at your wedding, Frank. Getting ten dollars to sing "Ave Maria," having everyone come up afterward with tears in their eyes and tell me how good I was, it made me think I could be an entertainer, a crazy dream that caused me a lot of pain over the years. Obviously, my singing wasn't no good-luck charm for you and Miss James. When your marriage busted up before the season ended, I guess that was a sign. I can see the signs in my rearview mirror, but as I pass by I'm as blind as George Shearing.

I did have my marriage. Kate and I were a hundred percent happy right till the end of our Mexican hayride. It was only after I thought I heard a call back to the path of my fate that I wondered if her and me might go the way of the dodo, too. But I'm getting ahead of myself.

Near the end of the season, Alfonso, Gerardo, and Mario Pasquel made the rounds, cutting all our salaries. I should have seen it coming, but I didn't. My 1947 salary, Alfonso said, was getting cut from ten grand to a lousy four, the same as I made my last year with the Giants!

I'd come too far to stand still. "Forget it," I said. We was at that famous pyramid. I was there with Kate, and also the guys. He could have taken me aside, huh? "Not a penny less than ten grand, take it or leave it."

"That's your prerogative, Señor Garday-a," Alfonso said.

"Gardella." A common mistake, down there. Drove me nuts.

"Of course." He shrugged. "If that is your choice, Señor Danny, my family chooses to leave it, or rather leave *you*. Not that this is our wish." He shrugged again. He was a shrugger, Alfonso. "My brothers and I would welcome you back."

Kate's eyebrows was raised. I couldn't tell who she was surprised by, me or Baldfonso.

"Right," I said. "We're free to go back to the States, only if we do, your stooges"—I pointed at Bob Janis, from Al Roon's, who was winning a bet he could lift a horse over his meaty head—"they'll stop our train and see we don't go nowhere. Not that we got anywhere to go."

I was ticked that Alfonso waited so long to tell us. To make it worse, we was at a team outing to the pyramids that he was escorting. I'd been there, but Kate hadn't. Kate and I wanted to see what sights we could before we went home. At the time we both meant to come back in '47, but underneath we must have known different.

As this embarrassing conversation with Alfonso continued, we went past a pit called a ball court. I never knew what kind of ball they played in there. Alfonso said the winners got sacrificed and became heroes. That's the sort of thing they tell gringos. Also I think he was making a point about athletes in the good old days versus mercenary jocks now, how we had it good compared to headless Mayan hero champs.

II

Sal Maglie was transformed from a journeyman with so-so stuff into an imposing figure with a curveball from the hand of God. We faced him and the Puebla Parrots on our next-to-last game of the year. *Penultimate,* the word is. We needed a win to escape last place, which the Mexican players was keen to do. Maglie was going for his twentieth win. When I went down to the pen to watch him warm up, I asked him straight out, "Where'd you get the yakker, Sal?"

"I had it."

"Had it, my hairy heinie. The curve you *had* I could hit. That one you just threw, Ted Williams couldn't have hit."

"Dolf Luque," Maglie said.

"He couldn't have hit it either," I said, but then I realized he meant he *learned* the pitch from Luque. Luque was with the Giants, too, remember. Another unappreciated man in their system.

"You get a pay cut for next year, Sal?" I asked.

"No." He was frowning, didn't want to talk to me.

"Really?"

"I got a raise."

"Did the other Americans on your club get pay cuts, Sal?"

"There aren't any," he said, which hadn't occurred to me but which was true.

"How about Zabala or Reyes?" They were Cubans who'd been with the Giants, too.

"Didn't ask."

"Anyone going back to the States to try to get reinstated?"

"No." He stopped pitching and turned to face me. "Go away."

Maybe it wasn't personal. A lot of pitchers are like that on their day to pitch.

So I went and found my old road-roomie Nap Reyes, that grand mambo-dancing Cuban who'd put up with a lot from me, including a faked suicide in St. Louis back when I first caught mental illness from Rocco . . . Oh. Right. Anyhow, Nap was in a pepper game with two other Cubans and, at bat, Bobby Avila, a Mexican teenager who later was a batting champ for the Cleveland Indians. I asked if I could play, too. Avila cussed at me in Spanish. Kids.

"You going back to the States, Nap, to try to get reinstated?" I said.

"¿Porqué?" Everyone all of a sudden didn't like me.

"To get back in the big leagues," I said. "This league's never gonna be the big leagues."

Avila smashed the next ball at my head. I ducked. "No offense, muchacho," I said.

"Chíngate, viejo."

I ignored that. "You coming back here next year, Nap?"

"¿Cómo no? ¿A qué otra liga?"

Which was a good point. Like me, Nap was banned from U.S. ball. Unlike me, when he played there, he had the race problems. Also, Nap was third in the batting race, behind Avila and Duany, up in the .380s; who'd leave after a year like that? He asked if I was coming back.

"Sure," I said. "Probably."

"Bien," he said. Then, in English, he said, "It is nice for our pitchers to have an easy out in the Veracruz lineup."

Everybody laughed, even me. Then I saw old Luque coming. I knew he wouldn't like it one bit to see his men fraternizing with the enemy, so I got out of there pronto.

That day, the Mexican Independence Day, should have been a pitchers' duel, Maglie versus Lanier, but when I got to our dugout I found out Max was gone. Mr. Pasquel shipped him to the Reds, playing up in Nuevo Laredo, tied with Tampico for first. Instead of Max, our pitcher was a guy named Francisco Mora, who was one of Mr. Pasquel's army men. The year before, he walked two hundred men and got saddled with the nickname "Free Pass." The next year he carried a gun instead of a glove. The Mexicans on our club, Chile Gómez and so forth, they was steamed. They wanted so bad to get out of last. The way I saw it, Max Lanier,

Maxene Andrews, Francisco Mora, Francisco Franco, when you're tied for last with a team called the Cactus Fruit, what's the diff? Last, next to last, what's it matter? One of our new guys, Double Duty Radcliffe, called it "another case of the golden rule. The guy with the gold rules."

"Amen, Brother Radcliffe," I said.

Double Duty stared at me. "What do you mean by that?"

"I mean 'Amen, brother,' is what I mean."

"You makin fun of the Negro church?" he said.

"I'm agreeing with you," I said. "As long as Mr. Pasquel's paying us and we're still drinking his whiskey—"

"I said, are you makin fun of the Negro church?"

"No," I said. "I'm all for Negro rights. When it comes to where I stand on the Negro question, you don't have to worry about where I stand."

He smiled. It wasn't a happy smile. "Some of your best friends are Negroes, right?"

What was that supposed to mean? "Right," I said. I thought I gave the right answer.

"That's what I thought," said Double Duty. He pulled on his mask, dropped to his knees, and did an impression of Jolson singing "Mammy" that was supposed to be a dig at me.

Radcliffe was a good man—okay?—a partyer and a clown, and if things had been different, even if we'd played together longer than one lousy, hot month, our misunderstandings could have been worked out, and him and me, we might have been friends.

Maglie's curve was his terrible swift sword, Excalibur drawn from out of that big rock Luque. It was nothing mortal man could hit. Free Pass Mora didn't pitch so bad, but not so good, either, plus which we made a million errors behind him, several thousand by yours truly. Sal got his twentieth win and we lost pretty bad.

If I can't remember the game so good, it's because it's overwhelmed in my head by all the crazy whatnot that happened after. I rushed to the apartment to shower and help Kate set up for our party that night, the one where you and Miss James had the . . . thing. But listen, Frank, you don't know the half of what all went wrong that night. Everything, is what. We went to a lot of trouble, too, hanging up lights and a piñata full of cigars, nylons, and lottery tickets, and hiring an expensive, hot-tempered Mexican chef, who Mr. Pasquel recommended himself. The works.

We got done setting up an hour before any guests arrived. We're not last-minute people. We would have helped the chef, too, but when we got near him he yelled at us, in Spanish so fast we had to guess that he meant scram, so we did.

"It does smell good," Kate said. We sat on our living-room couch, listening to a Mexican radio version of that show *Make-Believe Ballroom*. "I'll miss the food."

"Me, too," I said. "I'm used to it, finally."

We passed the time by reading poems to each other from that book of Miss James's you gave us, which I still have somewhere. Probably worth some money now. Finally, just before things got rolling, Kate smiled at me and said, "We've made a decision, haven't we?"

"To leave all this?" I was poking fun at our modest apartment, our station in life, and also the paintings we'd hung of saints and big-eyed children, but we was happy.

"The school year's already started," she said, "but I've put aside enough money that we could get by pretty well if I substituted and you caught on again at Mr. Roon's gym."

"I got another idea," I said. On the radio came Bing Crosby. I had a bigger voice than him. "Listen." I stood up and sang right over him. It was that "Glocca Morra" song. I sang it so good that when I finished, Kate gave me a standing ovation and that grumpy cook came in from the kitchen, removed his chef's hat, shook my hand, and returned to his work.

Kate frowned. "I'm confused. What's your idea, Ireland?"

"Ireland? No. Singing; a singing career."

"Singing?" she said. "How would you break into singing?"

"I know a lot of show"—I almost said *showgirls*—"show people, from Al Roon's. I could work there, make connections, take voice lessons . . . then, who knows, baby? Broadway bound."

"Broadway?"

"At least a good living up in the Catskills."

"You're serious, aren't you?"

I didn't know. "It's just a crazy dream I got," I said.

"How long have you had this dream?" she asked. "I'm your wife. I'm supposed to know about your crazy dreams. Right after you dream them, I'm supposed to hear about it."

Then I got saved by the doorbell. It was a bunch of the fellas. I slapped on some hot jazz sides and the party got off with a bang. Booze, laughs, finger food—it looked good, our party. People kept coming, Blues, Parrots, and wives. The blacks didn't come, but Alfonso and Gerardo Pasquel did, along with their dates, Bob Janis, and some other stray toadies.

Things was rolling when in walked you and that spitfire Miss James, drunk, carrying late editions of the afternoon papers. You and her grabbed drinks and headed to opposite corners of the room and, like they say in the land of tequila, the worm had turned. What you was fighting over, I don't know, and don't tell me. It's none of my business. My point is, you two brought a hush over things. Then you showed us the papers, like some kind of oracle, and the party went from uncomfortable to sort of bad.

Bad *how* depended on your perspective. The Mexican players, Gómez and them, got excited over the baseball results. Mexico City beat Nuevo Laredo and Tampico had beat San Luis Potosí, which meant that Tampico and Mexico City stayed tied for first and that San Luis and us stayed tied for last, which meant we still had a chance to finish next-to-last. Whoop-dee-doo, but, again, that meant the world to the Mexicans.

The games, though, wasn't the big news. From across the room I could see the headlines about the diabolical Max Lanier scandal. Tampico said they wouldn't play if Max pitched for the Red Devils. Thousands of fans all over Mexico signed a petition in protest. The papers accused the Pasquels of monopolistic practices contrary to the spirit of modern Mexico. Jorge Pasquel gave a press conference but wouldn't talk about Max. All he said was he planned to sue Mickey Owen in an American court, asking for the refund of Owen's $27,500 salary plus a hundred grand in damages. One paper—I got it here somewhere; here it is—had a quote from Owen: " 'They'll never get to first base on that lawsuit,' said the goat of the 1941 World Series. 'If organized baseball won't admit me, I'll just dedicate my life to working on my farm.' " You have to be around a lot of cattle to become that good of a bullshit artist.

But before I got a chance to read about the really big news, at least from where I stood, our surly cook called out that dinner was served, buffet-style. I put on more music and freshened everybody's drinks and the party got back in swing. I loaded up a plate and found your wife and mine on a love seat in the spare bedroom, talking about certain procedures in the Catholic church. When I tried to sit down next to them, on the arm of the love seat, it was clear I was butting in, so I made like a banana and split. I wanted to ask Diana questions about her poems, their themes and all that bit, but I never got a chance.

I ate on the balcony, next to Bob Janis, who had the biggest plate of food you ever saw. We talked about deltoids, pectorals, and all the good western movies we must have missed being down Mexico way. That exhausted everything Bob had to say. "You like your job?" I asked him.

Bob smiled real big. "Easy as pie," he said. "I show Mr. Pasquel how to touch his toes, give him his rubdowns, plus some protection work. And lemme tell you, Danny, the women . . ." He didn't finish, mostly, in my opinion, because he was lying. Bob never did well with the ladies.

I go inside for seconds and I see this tall Mexican girl, one of the Pasquel brothers' dates, standing at our mantel holding up the wedding candle I'd given Kate when I proposed.

"Hey," I said. "Careful with that."

"Where did you get it?" she asked me.

"Who are you?" I said. "Why do you want to know?"

"I am called Inés Castillo," she said. "I painted this."

I was thunderstruck. "I got it at the Zócalo," I said. "That man, he was your father?"

"The uncle of the cousin of my father," she said. "What did you pay for it?"

When I told her, she laughed. That was when I remembered that the man who'd lied and said he was her father had also said that his "daughter" was dying, when in fact here she was at my party, the picture of health. "Listen, that guy, when I bought the candle—"

"He said I was dying, yes?"

My heart fell. She wasn't dying?

"No," she said. "I am. It is the truth."

For a minute, I felt like I hadn't been had, but I had.

"You're a ballplayer, no?"

I told her who I was. I'd forgotten to introduce myself.

"I was briefly in love with one of the Red Devils of Mexico," she said, but she wouldn't tell me who. "He preferred my best friend. Now I have sworn off ballplayers."

I held up my left hand, waving my ring before her face. "It's nothing to me," I said.

Inés set the candle down. "I have painted thousands of those, every one sold to a tourist."

Why she felt the need to cheapen something with special meaning to me, who knows? "If I may be so bold," I said, "what are you dying of?"

"La vida." She laughed—*at* me, not *with* me. "It is killing us all, no?"

Before she could crush my heart any more, I again got saved by the doorbell. Who walks in, worse for the wear from his trip to Laredo, but Max Lanier! He had his guitar with him. "I've had a long day," he said. "I heard this might be a place to blow off steam."

What a fuss people made! Two days gone, and it was like he was being welcomed home from the Trojan Wars. The Mexicans caught on right away what it meant, too: For our last game, our shot at salvaging a sliver of honor from the season, we'd have the best pitcher in the league going for us. That Max hadn't pitched well for a month, that didn't occur to nobody at the time.

When Max finished eating, we switched off the Victrola and he accompanied me on guitar while I sang "Danny Boy." The party became a sing-along: western songs, Mexican songs, all kinds of songs. I thought I'd pee my pants from laughing, Frank, watching you croak "God Bless America" to Miss James like it was a love song. It wasn't till you finished that I noticed it made her mad. You two: screaming, cussing, throwing food—and over what? Who knows? The big fights, no one ever knows. Like how World War I supposedly started over the killing of Duke Ferdinand, only not. That's how it is with men and women. But when you told her she only married you so she could divorce you and write about it, that was a low blow for a newlywed. Forgive me, but it made me take her side.

Once she stormed out and you ran out behind her, there was a long silence. Kate, smoothing over things and being the good hostess, had a look on her face like We'll talk later. As it turned out, she and Diana had been talking about how your being married before was grounds enough for annulment and then some.

About then, as the party got back under way, Sal Maglie showed me the big news of the day. He pointed at an article. "If I translated it right," he said, "it just goes to show you."

"Show me what?"

"Read it," he said, and went to find his wife. Fights in public make men find their wives.

It was a wire story, dateline Chicago. The owners had bought off the players' union, for the price of a $5,000 minimum wage and a small pension fund. In exchange, the union more or less agreed to disband. I reread it, making sure I was translating okay. It was one of those times where you're alone despite the fact of being in the middle of a crowded room.

Criminy. It was *us* whose jumping to Mexico gave the players' union credibility, *us* who paid the price of losing our right to work in the U.S.A. so that other men who still had that right would get more—but still not enough—of what was rightfully theirs. It was *us*! Yet we got shut out. There wasn't no mention of the Mexican League in that story. Old news. No mention, either, of that cockamamie reserve clause or any of the other illegal things the owners got the players' union to stop challenging. Reporters are just freeloading shills for the status quo.

I looked up, but Sal was gone. I showed the article around, but nobody else got steamed. When I finally found Sal, in the kitchen with the other ex-Giants, he just shook his head. "What are you going to do, Danny? Take on major-league baseball all by yourself?"

"You don't get it," I said. "We'll all take 'em on, all *together*."

"Ballplayers are individualists," said Ace Adams. "They'll never go for a union. We'll never in a million years have as much power as the owners. That's how it is, Dan."

"It's not how it has to be."

Harry Feldman, a smart kid but usually real quiet, spoke up. "You think that if the Pasquels did get their league to be as good as the majors, do you really believe Jorge Pasquel would be one bit different than Horace Stoneham or the DeWitts?"

"Yes," I said. Though I wasn't sure. I was just mad.

"Wake up and smell the coffee," Sal said.

"I never touch the stuff," I said. "Makes me nervous."

"Do not make Danny nair-vous," said Nap Reyes. "Trust me."

"Laugh if you want," I said. I could swing a bat, but I wasn't God's gift to baseball. I knew, then, I had a different calling. "You'll see. I'll fight those rat bastards. I'll show you."

That brought more laughs. So what? Why are any of us alive but to change the world in one small way? If not *the* world, *a* world. If not *a* world, *our* world. Of course, Frank, we're both proof that it can be a long leap from clown to hero.

When I went to find Kate, she was in the bedroom, before the vanity, crying.

What next? Just as I made the mistake of thinking that, hollow thumping noises started coming from the living room.

Kate looked up. "Go see what it is," she said.

"Probably the piñata," I said. "Why are you crying, hon?"

"Go check for me, okay?" she said, "I'm fine."

But before I could, there came a gunshot, and then screams.

When I got to the living room, it was empty in the middle, like when someone's dancing and everyone's cheering. The air was filled with smoke, lottery tickets, and pieces of cigars. Nobody was hurt. The piñata was blown to smithereeens. Underneath what was left of it stood a man in an old-fashioned tuxedo. His back was to me. And then he turned around.

"Hello, Danny."

It was Rocco Coniglio. You could have knocked me over with a feather.

"Jorge Pasquel gave me directions." Rocco showed his gun to me. "And dumdum bullets. I thought that was the same as blanks." He smiled. "Guess not." He pointed at a hole in the ceiling, the size of a dinner plate. "How have you been, dear heart? I've missed you."

I took the gun away from him.

"You like the tux, I see," he said. "I got it off a dead nigger."

It was the only time all night I was glad none of the black guys showed.

Then, in the mouth of the hallway, Kate appeared. She saw Rocco. The look in her eyes wasn't quite angry, like a woman nowadays might be, and not quite surprised, like you'd think. It was the look of a woman who didn't know which way to turn. She'd stopped crying.

"Kate," I said. "Honey," I said. "It's not what you think."

Who knew what she thought, or what I thought she thought? I was only saying.

"Give me the gun," she said.

I wasn't about to do that, but she insisted. I took out the bullets and handed it over.

Then, in a real quiet and even voice, she said, "Get out."

At first I figured she meant me, but then I realized she meant Rocco. In the awkward aftermath of the gunshot, everyone at the party heard her and figured it meant them, or wanted to think that, and people got their things together to go.

I confess, again, I thought, *What next?* Can you believe it? The night got even stranger.

All of a sudden, without no warning, the church bells across the street started ringing and the whole city, including every single Mexican at my party, rose up as one and shouted, all at once, a terrible deafening roar: *¡Vivan los Mexicanos! ¡Viva México!*

It went on and on. It was like nothing in my life up to then. The Americans looked like we'd just seen the world go mad. The Cubans didn't look like it was nothing unusual. As for the Mexicans, they rushed out into the streets to join their voices to the choir of their people.

It's their shout of independence. *Viva!* Live long.

III

Bob Janis, Rocco, me, and Kate took a taxi to the Coyoacán to go see Mr. Pasquel, like we was off to see the wizard, in search of brains, heart, courage, and a way back home. Kate sat in front, quiet. As we drove through crowded streets, a river of fireworks-shooting Mexicans, Rocco explained about the shout, the grito. In the early 1800s, a musician/priest named Hidalgo, who once lost his college degree in a card game and somehow got real popular by planting mulberry trees, climbed in his pulpit, and, before a packed house at Mass, gave the shout. Somehow it was a declaration of independence from Spain and also Napoleon Bonaparte. It's complicated.

"Read a book, Danny," Rocco told me. "It won't hurt you."

"I do read," I said. "Kate's a teacher. We read things together."

"I am a professor," he said. "I *teach* teachers."

"You can say that again," Kate said.

"I *teach* teachers," Rocco said.

"Until you lost your job for being a lunatic."

"Meow," said Rocco.

Throughout all this, Bob Janis isn't saying nothing. He was good at taking orders, and when Kate had told him to help us take Rocco back where he came from, Bob slung Rocco over his shoulder and waited on the corner for us to lock up the apartment and for the next taxi to come. Rocco didn't even squirm; he just acted like a sack of flour until we got in the car.

"Will Mr. Pasquel be there?" I said. "Won't he be out celebrating Independence Day?"

"He'll be there," Rocco said. "God, I love fireworks."

My palms was sweaty and my chest was tight. I wanted to think it was nervousness about seeing Mr. Pasquel. But ten minutes with Rocco, already I got my bride mad at me and a hole in my ceiling to pay for. And inside my head, I was already starting to feel it, that manic depression Rocco was contagious with.

Rocco, before his brother Joey died in the war and he came undone, was a man who knew everybody. He said he knew Mr. Pasquel through María Félix, Mr. Pasquel's lady friend. He met her backstage after a performance in New York of one of the orchestras he played in, and for a while he gave her cello lessons. Mr. Pasquel paid for the lessons. Rocco kept Mr. Pasquel's card, called him up, and somehow convinced him to pay Rocco's plane fare to Mexico. When I tell Rocco stories, I keep using the word *somehow*.

When we got to Mr. Pasquel's city house, on a cobblestone street a few blocks from where Kate and I got married, the place was dark except for a flickering beam you could barely see from the front window. Bob had a key. "He's watching those movies." Bob led us through the front room, past gun racks full of rifles and baseball bats. "That's all he does, these days."

"What movies?"

"Miss Félix's films, of course," said Rocco. "Apparently, poor Jorge is paralyzed by the loss of his paramount paramour."

That came as a surprise. I had no idea Miss Félix and Mr. Pasquel had fallen out.

But Bob started laughing. "Wrong, egghead. He threw Miss Félix's movies out the day Alemán got elected president."

What the election had to do with it, I don't know. Probably another complicated story.

We turned a corner and there—in a room with nothing in it but two rows of red theater seats, a movie projector, a rack of movie cans, and, covering the whole far wall, a screen—was Jorge Pasquel, dressed in a Japanese silk bathrobe with a huge dragon on the back and watching movies of the 1920 World Series, Cleveland versus Brooklyn. I remember because it was the year I was born and also because of that famous triple play.

"I am watching my newsreels, in order." His hair was every which way and he needed a shave. The room smelled like cigars and, well, sex. I don't know who, or whatever. I'm just saying what I smelled. "Sit," he said. "You have missed the tainted 1919 win by my friend Adolfo Luque and his Cincinnati Reds. But this series, it is good. It is a rebirth for the game we love."

We? Who else *loved* baseball? Not me. But we humored him and took our seats.

"I see *The New York Times* found you." Mr. Pasquel nodded at Rocco. "I hope Danny said good things about me."

"Nothing but," Rocco said.

Kate frowned at me and whispered, "The *Times*?"

I had no idea.

"My cook is off," Mr. Pasquel said. "After this reel, I will enter the kitchen myself and prepare for you some food."

We assured him it wasn't necessary, that we'd eaten.

Nobody said nothing until Cleveland whipped Brooklyn. Then Mr. Pasquel got up and turned on the lights. "This is your first experience with our Independence Day, yes?"

It was, for all of us.

"Our holidays are more logical and democratic than yours," he said. "Did you know that?"

"I'll take you up on that offer for chow, Boss," Bob Janis said. "Got any flan?" He said it so it rhymed with "can."

"Flan," Mr. Pasquel corrected. "No. Be advised, Bob, I plan to exercise after the 1927 World Series."

"Whatever you say, boss."

"We're here to discuss next year, Mr. Pasquel," Rocco said. "Danny and I have spoken, and I am here as his agent."

"Agent?" Mr. Pasquel looked like Rocco had just explained how you make headcheese. It was thirty years before players had agents. Rocco was before his time. Who knows if by the standards of now he'd be crazy? "I sent a reporter from the *The New York Times* to your apartment to meet with my incompetent press secretary . . . and now this man is your agent?"

Kate looked at me. "That's *not* why we're here. That man was no one's agent, and he's no reporter. He's nuts."

"That doesn't disqualify one from being a reporter," said Rocco. "Quite the opposite."

"So you *are* a reporter for the *Times*?" I said.

Rocco smiled. "No."

"Wait," I said to Mr. Pasquel. "Didn't Rocco give your lady friend, Miss Félix, didn't he give her cello lessons?"

"Cello lessons?" Mr. Pasquel thought I was drunk.

"Danny!" It was the first time I saw Kate furious. Uh-oh, I thought, honeymoon's over.

"Look, Mr. Pasquel," I said. "Rocco's not who he says he is. He's not a reporter. He's just a guy from the neighborhood."

"Danny!" said Rocco, aghast. "You're siding with *her*?"

He said a filthy thing. Kate slapped him, and he laughed. Mr. Pasquel watched like it was a stage play, put on just for him.

I should have done more than just tell Rocco to keep his pie hole shut, but I was confused. I felt sorry for him, but also I admired him. Not the him who was there, but the him I knew he could be.

"Mr. Pasquel," Kate said. "Danny and I need to talk to you. Alone."

"Bring whiskey," Mr. Pasquel called out to Bob Janis. "And five glasses."

We all said we didn't want it, but Mr. Pasquel insisted, and Bob did what he was told.

Rocco asked where he could go to wash his hands. When he was gone, Kate elbowed me. "Okay," I said. "It's like this—"

Mr. Pasquel interrupted. "As I was saying, the American summer begins with Memorial Day. In July, you have your Independence Day. And the summer concludes with Labor Day. War dead, independence, work—in that order. You observe no deaths but soldiers' and Christ's."

Kate and I looked at each other.

Mr. Pasquel threaded the film into the projector, off in his own world. "In Mexico, summer begins with Labor Day. In summer, no holidays. Too hot. The fall begins with independence."

"How true," Rocco said. He was back, drying and drying his hands.

"Then," Mr. Pasquel continued, "only a few weeks into the fall comes the Day of the Dead. Not just martyred boys and Christ, but every departed soul."

Rocco cleared his throat. "My client," he said, "demands ten thousand dollars."

"Demand denied," Mr. Pasquel said. "Shut *up*." He said it vicious. It shut everyone up, not just Rocco. Mr. Pasquel had the 1921 World Series racked, Giants and Yankees. Bob Janis came back with a tray full of whiskies.

"So you see," Mr. Pasquel said, "Mexicans are more logical: work, endure the summer, affirm our independence, and finally death. An embracing of death. Everyone's. This is . . . egalitarian. You have that word in English, yes?"

"Yes," Rocco said.

Kate elbowed me again. So I answered, too. "Yes."

"That's not what I meant," Kate whispered.

"Oh." I stood up, took one of those whiskeys, and tossed it back. "Mr. Pasquel," I said. "The missus and I want to thank you for all you did and all you tried to do, but we got business to attend to back in the States and—"

That was as far as I got. Mr. Pasquel drained his glass and threw it hard against the wall. Shards flew everywhere.

"I, too, had immense plans!" Mr. Pasquel said.

This might have gotten to me, except for the spitting problem he had with *s*'s.

Then, in a murmur, he added, "I, too, was on the threshold of great things."

Rocco doubled over laughing. "Spare us," he said. I never found out what was so funny, or what he wanted Mr. Pasquel to spare us from, or, for that matter, who else had immense plans and was on the threshold of great things. Me?

"Go home, Gardella." Mr. Pasquel looked at Bob and Rocco. "Take your lovely wife and these two rude animals with you."

"But, boss," Bob said. "I live here." He had a bed and a chifforobe in the gym Mr. Pasquel had made out of the servants' quarters. "And what about your workout?"

"Go," he said. "Please, all of you, go."

He flicked on the projector and took a seat, trusting us to see ourselves out, the fool. In the end, Jorge Pasquel, for all his power and greatness and ambition and riches, was just another middle-aged guy in a bathrobe, sitting alone in a dark, smelly house, scratching his balls and wondering why he had a broken heart and why he had a tray full of good whiskey no one wanted to help him drink. Seen one, you seen 'em all.

Bob was mad he got cast out of there, and on our way out he opened up one of the gun cabinets, grabbed a big black baseball bat, and gave the bat to me. "Take this," he whispered.

Rocco Coniglio reached in and helped himself to two rifles.

"What is it?" I said.

Bob shushed me, and we was walking out toward a main drag to catch a cab before I stopped under a gaslight and saw what I was holding: Babe Ruth's souvenir bat, the one made in Cuba with all the carvings on it. The last bat the Babe ever swung. I'd copped it after the game and then used it myself in the Mexican League All-Star game. I got in dutch for that—using the bat—and it cost me the Chevrolet I was supposed to win for being the player of the game. I hadn't seen the bat since.

"Take it back," I said. "We can't keep this."

Rocco grabbed it from me. "Finders keepers," he said.

Kate waved at what I thought was a cab. It stopped. Out jumped two Mexican cops. In Spanish, she told them that Rocco had stolen the rifles and the baseball bat from the home of Jorge Pasquel. At the sound of Pasquel's name, the cops laughed.

"It is a lie," Rocco lied. He said it in Italian, though.

One cop pulled a pistol, then grabbed the rifles away from Rocco and threw them into their backseat. The other cop, un-armed, took the bat. "¿Qué es?"

"Un bat," I said. "Usado por el jonronero máximo, Babe Ruth."

"¿Béisbol?" he said. "No me gusta el béisbol. Es para los mari-cones. Me gusta el fútbol."

"A mi sobrinito loco," said the other cop, "le gusta."

So they took the bat, too, and then took off, laughing.

Finally, we got a cab. Over Kate's protests, I let Bob and Rocco sleep on couches at our place. They had nowhere else to go. Warts and all, they was friends. I didn't see what choice I had.

Looking back, I see I acted like hotels hadn't been invented, and I see why Kate got steamed.

I often picture the cop's nephew heaving the Babe's bat up on his little shoulders, never knowing where that bat had been, who swung it. Just playing with it.

IV

The last game of the season looked like it was going to get rained out. I hoped so. It had no bearing on nothing. The Cactus Fruit had lost the night before, so if we didn't play we escaped the cellar by half a game. Personally, I'd have greeted a rain-out as a bailout. Kate and me had our things packed, our passage booked, and our real work in front of us, cut out for us.

When I got to Delta Park, about an hour before game time, it was muddy and unplayable and the rain was pouring. And yet the place was packed. Even in the outfield bleachers, where there wasn't no overhang for shelter and where they didn't allow umbrellas on account of how the tips could be used if tempers flared, the fans was shoehorned in—cheek to cheek, as they say.

The players from both Veracruz and Puebla huddled together in that one tiny clubhouse, trying to keep dry.

Lou Klein was beside himself. "Can these people read a schedule? They must think it's the Red Devils playing for the title, instead of our raggedy asses playing for our last payday."

I gave him a half-smile—a wince, really. I didn't want to encourage him. I knew that getting out of last meant a lot to the Mexicans. But the thing is, they already *had* that. Call the game and everybody goes home happy.

Chile Gómez corrected me on that count. "We control our own destiny," he said. "Backing out of last place holds no meaning."

This makes sense, now. Then, no.

At noon on the dot, right when the game was supposed to start, the sun burst through a hole in the clouds and a rainbow sprouted from the right-field cemetery, stretching out in this big arc over the city. The crowd cheered like it was a grand slam. Then, like God heard the cheer—ba-*bing*, the rain just stopped. Up rose a bigger cheer.

The conditions, though, forget about it. There was a pond behind first and a lake in dead center. The mound looked like a Jersey swamp. But the managers, Bragaña and Luque, ordered us to limber up quick. The umpires came out and made a beeline to the owner's box, where Bernardo Pasquel sat with a bunch of dark suits, including President Alemán and, of all people, Miss Félix. Jorge Pasquel was nowhere to be seen. It was Bernardo who gave the umps the go-ahead, Bernardo who sat back in his seat like the cat who ate the canary.

Max Lanier, who hadn't had but maybe ten warm-up tosses when he was stopped to join in the singing of the Mexican national anthem, couldn't believe it. He'd had arm problems and always took forever to warm up, and was scared to take the mound before he was really ready.

"Ple-e-e-y bo-o-o-o-oll!" cried the ump.

Max tried talking to Ramón Bragaña, pitcher to pitcher. It was like talking to the dugout wall. Bragaña just pointed to the mound. Max went out there, mumbling and shaking his head.

Next thing you know, we're down, 4–0, with no outs.

Double Duty and the infield—me at first, Chile Gómez at second, Klein at short, Buster Clarkson at third—we all go to the mound. Two blacks, a patriotic Mexican, two southerners, and a gym rat from the Bronx. Recipe for the Tower of Babel. The question Double Duty got us all discussing, in our various tongues, was whether this one particular lady sitting behind the Blues dugout did or did not have a more spectacular bosom than Miss Félix. It was a polite, spirited debate, one with good points made on both sides, and the umpire had to break it up.

It worked. Max struck out the next guy.

The batter after that grounded to third, which Clarkson had to charge because of the wet grass. What a ballplayer. With two down, the next batter sent a humpbacked foul to the pond behind first. I dove, caught the ball, and came down with a big splash. The crowd loved it.

We came right back. Facing my old Giants teammate Adrían Zabala, Lou Olmo and Lou Klein hit back-to-back singles and Clarkson and Pennington hit back-to-back homers. The Mexican people—ye gods! We tie up a meaningless ball game in the first, but to listen to the roar you'd think we rallied in the bottom of the ninth to win game seven of the World Series. I killed the rally, though. I whiffed, which started a chain reaction by Bob Estalella and Double Duty and then also by all three Puebla guys in the top of the second. Still, the wet crowd was on fire.

Between innings, Bernardo Pasquel gave a sign, and the Mexican army—not the Pasquel militia, but real soldiers working as security for that last game—let the overflow crowd onto the field and roped them off. After that there was no foul territory whatsoever.

Then the rain started again. Soldiers suspended a tarp over the suits in Bernardo's box. We was playing this game rain or shine, and we'd seen all the shine we was going to.

The game stayed tied 4–4 until the top of the sixth. By then our flannels was so soaked they must have weighed fifty pounds. Skinny Zabala couldn't handle it; his pitches started coming in like beach balls. Pow, homer. Pow, triple. Pow, double. Pow, pow, single, single. Pow, another homer. I felt sorry for the guy. He was getting shelled, and yet Luque didn't have no one warming up. I wouldn't have minded making an out, just to move things along.

Zabala ran me to a full count. I would have been out three or four times on fouls, only without foul territory there's no foul pops to be had. Just souvenirs for the people.

Finally, fed up, I decided to swing from my heels no matter what Adrián served up. The pitch I got was outside, but I stepped out of the box and swung, tomahawking a rope right over Adrián's head. It stayed string-straight, barely clearing the glove of the Parrots' center fielder, too.

The ball, can you believe it, went right through the mouth of the smiling Negro on the Chiclets billboard.

Five hundred pesos for me!

First time in history it ever happened. I was the least likely guy to do it, too, the way I'd been hitting plus the way the conditions worked against me. But as I'm circling the bases and the crowd's singing my praises, all I can think is, *There's the do-re-mi you need to hire a Philadelphia lawyer and sue the nuts off those big-league owners.*

It was a sign. So it had a hole in it, so what?

Top of the seventh, up 11–4, Bragaña yanked Max and put himself in. Max didn't argue. He jumped at the chance to get into some dry threads. It was a popular move with the crowd, too. Max was a good pitcher, but old diamond-tooth was an adopted son. When Bragaña sailed through the inning, one routine inning, he came off the field to a standing ovation, like he'd pitched out of a jam. They stayed on their feet and the cheers grew louder. Even Bragaña himself didn't get it—until we looked out to the mound, where Dolf Luque had been waiting for a new pitcher to come in from the bullpen, and we realized he *was* the new pitcher. Dolf Luque, who'd pitched in a World Series a year before I was born, was taking himself out of retirement.

"That's it," Lou Klein said. "I seen everything."

I figured it was a stunt, something Bernardo Pasquel dreamed up to outshowboat his brother. But if it really had been a stunt, word of it would have been sent out to the newspapers, to create a bigger story. Second of all, Luque whipped our butts.

He didn't throw a single pitch hard enough to break glass, but he had the rain going for him, and for a throwback to the days when spitballs was legal, that was an edge. Luque stood out there in a rainstorm, a sixty-year-old man, staring in at his catcher like he meant it, getting down to business like this game itself, with its outcome already decided, still meant something.

Superman Pennington almost screwed himself into the ground trying to swing at that wild breaking stuff and got retired on a dribbler to first.

Bob Estalella actually swung at a blooper pitch and popped it to Nap Reyes at third.

Then it was up to me. I was never good against sneaky pitchers, plus I had a headache and a wet flannel uniform on, on top of which the game was already won and my mind was on my problems: Rocco, how to make up with Kate, how I was gonna earn a living . . . et cetera.

I kept getting wood on the ball and fouling it off. He couldn't throw the ball past me, and I couldn't hit one of those gyroscopes anywhere close to fair. Okay, so it was crazy, stepping across the plate to bat right-handed. I was waving a white flag, which seemed honorable enough. When Luque tossed away his glove and threw the next pitch left-handed instead of right, what was I supposed to do? I swung. It was the last out of the season for the Veracruz Blues.

Not one fan gave me the business for it. In fact, when Bragaña finished Puebla off and we won the game and the fans stormed the field, I was the first player who got hoisted up on their shoulders. Me. It was a peaceful, happy multitude. They stayed for what seemed like forever, and so did I. I wanted it to last forever, and—sloshing around in the mud, sharing beers and laughs with teammates and a few thousand cheering, adoring strangers—it felt like it *could*, like it *would*. I turned my face to the sky and let the rain beat down on me, and I paid attention. The smell of soaked flannel and summer mud. The feel of every tired muscle up and down my spine. The way they cheered me when I threw them my hat and my glove and then stripped off my jersey and spikes and gave 'em that, too. The strong fingers of every happy fan's hand that was lifting me up. I paid attention to all of it.

An hour later I was carted out of Bernardo Pasquel's office by two thugs who said Bernardo was too busy to see me but that my five hundred pesos would be wired to me tomorrow. Two hours later I was flying to New York, sitting next to Kate and hardly saying nothing. Twelve hours later I was home; flying was still a novelty, and getting so far so fast still felt like magic.

The next day I was back in the Bronx, eating dinner at Kate's pop's house, trying to explain about my shaky plans for a future with his daughter, and about Rocco, and wondering why my five hundred pesos never made it to Western Union. The day after that I got turned down for a job at Al Roon's. I wasn't a name no more, he said. A few days later, Rocco got me to make up a lie to Kate and sneak off with him to Staten Island for a meeting of the Communist party. Within just a couple of weeks of that, my mood swings got so bad Kate had me see a psychiatrist. He was the one who diagnosed me with folie à deux.

One lousy month after I came down off the shoulders of the Mexican people, my days was spent taking singing lessons from a drug-addicted Negro in Hoboken, meeting with a shrink, avoiding Rocco Coniglio, and waiting in the lobbies of lawyers who didn't want to take my case against Major League Baseball. I still hadn't seen my five hundred pesos. And Jorge Pasquel was dead.

He was flying his private airplane, coming home from an African safari, when something went wrong and he smashed head-on into the biggest mountain in Mexico. I don't know the details. Six months after he grabbed the headlines of every newspaper in New York, the same papers ran a story on his death that was so short it didn't even guess at the cause of the crash.

In spite of all that, Frank, here we sit in my kitchen, telling stories and digging through scrapbooks and shoe boxes, and I keep seeing Kate's pretty face looking in on us two old fools, and I hear my grandkids making mischief out in the family room of this house I bought with the bribe I broke down and accepted in exchange for dropping the lawsuit I'd fought so hard to bring, and I got news for you. When I rode on those shoulders, suspended over a sea of mud, a hero in a victory that was so small and surrounded by so much defeat that no one remembers it anymore—that, my friend, was a moment which lasted forever.

Epilogue

◈

Migratory Birds

The disgraced Jorge Pasquel will someday be convinced that these stars of the major leagues are a calamity. They are migratory birds who will never get acclimated to our customs. Each is a species of Mickey Owen. They come only to make money but never to feel any care for the Mexican land.
—*El Norte*, September 16, 1946

Danny Gardella remembered it wrong. Jorge Pasquel did not die in 1946. Yet while I have in this book endeavored to correct lapses of memory and errors of fact, I chose to let that one stand. In a sense, Jorge Pasquel did die in 1946. His dream of creating a third major league was dead. And he had disappeared from the public eye; that, for a man such as he, was also death.

That winter he stepped down as commissioner of the league (did he jump? was he pushed?) and devoted himself increasingly to business and politics, helping his brother Bernardo double the family fortune under the progressive but famously corrupt Alemán regime. After the 1948 season, the new commissioner put a quota on each team's number of foreign players, and all the Americans, black and white, returned home. Furious, Jorge sold the Veracruz Blues to his brother Alfonso for one peso. The next season, a new team sprung up in Veracruz: El Aguila, "the Eagle," the franchise's original name. For two years, both Veracruz teams were mediocre clubs. In 1951, Jorge Pasquel abruptly materialized at the helm of the Blues. He managed them to a 20–22 record and fired himself at the All-Star break. The new manager guided the Blues to a 29–13 second-half record and won the championship. At the award ceremony, Jorge Pasquel grabbed his penultimate banner headline by disbanding his baseball team.

In 1952, Alemán's bland successor, Cortines, was a one-issue president, and the issue was government reform. Jorge Pasquel was out in the cold. His wife wanted no part of him. His brother Bernardo was weary of cleaning up after him. His old mistress María Félix was sober and happily married, to the composer Augustín Lara, and had moved to Europe to make films with Luis Buñuel. Embittered, Jorge Pasquel became a charter member of the jet set—going on safari, gambling away millions in Havana and Monte Carlo, summering in Switzerland with store-bought Italian whores, et cetera. In 1955—finally, anticlimactically, and perhaps mercifully—the day came when, flying home, Jorge Pasquel smashed his plane into a mountain near San Luis Potosí. His four mourning brothers wore plain black ties every day for the rest of their lives.

A year later, the government razed Delta Park and erected upon the same ground a new ballpark. Alfonso Pasquel's request that it be named Jorge Pasquel Field was laughed out of hand. It was, instead, called Social Security Stadium. The Mexican League exists today as a loosely affiliated minor league, Double A caliber, stocked mostly with has-beens and never-weres. Every player you talk to has a story about how, except for a bad break here and there, he'd be in the big leagues.

This is the time my own life ceases to justify its telling. Curiously, without me doing much of anything right—or at least differently from how I was doing things before—things gelled. Frances Kingston got a quickie Maryland divorce, I had my Mexican caprice annulled, and Frances and I were married in a nononsense ceremony at the St. Louis city hall. At our reception, in an Italian restaurant on Highland Avenue, Danny Gardella, in town as a part of his Diogenesian quest for an honest labor lawyer, sang "Ave Maria." Our daughter, Elizabeth Kingston Bullinger, was born four days later. Frances had taken a year's leave from the university, and we all stayed home getting to know one another. This seems to be popular with today's young people, and I'm living proof it can build strong family ties. That year, Elizabeth even became a means for my parents and me to forge, if not a reconciliation, at least a truce. Frances and I had a long, improbably happy marriage. If such good fortune is even a story one can tell, it is a story for another book. Our Elizabeth is a four-term congresswoman, a Democratic incumbent in a Republican district. She is married to a wonderful fellow. They've given me three smart, well-adjusted grandchildren. Stop me before I tell you more and you hate me through and through.

I sold my series of articles about Mexico to *Liberty* magazine. They appeared in the fall of 1947, with the baseball sections excised. For no good reason I could see, they brought me a nomination (but, alas, not a victory) for the Pulitzer Prize. I parlayed that succès d'estime into a modest string of decent freelance jobs, and my name got around in certain circles, and it was a fine living. I was paid to take an interest in life. If you read magazines in the 1950s, you've read something by me other than this book. Don't feel bad about forgetting what it was; I couldn't recall a fraction of what all I wrote about.

You want conflict, thought, or unhappiness, I'll give it to you: Jerome. Harriet told him what you'd guess she might tell him, and my letters, which did, after all, get through, only made matters worse. One of his many therapists said I had hardened Jerome's heart with unvarnished candor, making him "a premature adult." A later therapist used the term "surrogate spouse." I paid for many of these sessions, mind you.

As Jerome was growing up, I saw him with embarrassing infrequency. And when I did see him, I was a parody of the divorced father: the zoo, the ballpark, the movies, the circus. As he got older, Jerome accused me of loving his half-sister more. I denied it.

When, in 1961, at a party in honor of his graduation from the University of Chicago (I footed the bill, for both the education and the party), Jerome stood up in a crowded downtown restaurant and proclaimed that he was a homosexual, I confess that I blamed myself. I confess that I told Jerome I blamed myself. I confess that I thought it was something for which someone deserved blame. It was the sort of thing you say that at the time seems fine—even sympathetic—but which you can spend the better part of a lifetime trying to get out from under.

❖

The 1946 home-run champion was supposed to win a free house. Roberto Ortiz never got his. The builder who'd sponsored the contest reneged on the deal, and according to Alfonso Pasquel, there was nothing anyone could do about it. Not only did Ortiz accept this, he returned the next year and won his third straight home-run crown. Still no house, of course.

Roberto and his brother Oliverio played together that year. But when Oliverio heard through the grapevine that the Pasquels had indeed been willing to sign him in 1946, the brothers had a terrible argument, which, according to Burnis Wright, went on day and night for a week. Dandridge told them to shut up. They wouldn't. The next day, Oliverio, 1–6 at the time, became a member of the Veracruz Blues.

In 1948, Oliverio left to play in Venezuela, and most of the other foreign-born players left, too. Roberto stayed (and won his fourth home-run title), but the competition was poor, too easy. When Danny Gardella dropped his suit and the runaway players were reinstated, Roberto returned to America for one last shot at the majors. He put in two years for the Senators, one for the Athletics, and made a name for himself as a nice guy, a good babysitter for the younger Latin players. He was a part-time coach in a couple of organizations, then had a failed comeback, in his forties with Dolf Luque's Yucatán Lions.

In 1959, as the door to Castro's Cuba was closing, Roberto Ortiz had returned to coaching. His old Red Devils teammate Freddie Martin, the White Sox pitching coach, helped Roberto get a minor-league job that rarely required him to leave Florida. Meanwhile, Oliverio had embraced the tenets of the revolution and become a popular speaker at Communist party rallies.

With the Sox in a pennant race that year, Roberto chose to stay in America (his visa called him "an alien of extraordinary ability"), working with the team's best Latin prospects. He promised his old friend Alejandro Carrasquel that if the Chicago went to the World Series, they would attend together, cheering on Carrasquel's speedy nephew, the Sox shortstop Luis Aparicio.

The White Sox won the pennant. Roberto kept his promise. By the time the Dodgers wrapped up the World Series, Roberto Ortiz was banned from returning home. "At the time," he told me, "I thought the differences between our countries would blow over in a few months. I thought my brother and I had a lifetime to work out our differences."

Oliverio and Roberto Ortiz never saw each other again.

In 1949, Mickey Owen and Roy Zimmerman, two of the twenty-seven ballplayers who'd jumped to Mexico and been banned from the big leagues ever since, showed up on the front porch of Danny Gardella's small rented house in Yonkers. Zimmerman, a hulk of a first baseman, wanted to beat Gardella up. Owen, who would later serve four terms as a county sheriff in southern Missouri, was to be the cooler-headed of the two.

"We came to ask you to drop the suit," Owen said. Gardella would not let them in; they were talking through the screen. "We're here to tell you, officially, that if you drop the suit, they'll reinstate the lot of us. You, too, Dan."

"Baloney." Gardella knew his services were in scant demand.

Zimmerman was turning red before Gardella's eyes. He started to say something but Owen shot him a look.

"Dan," Owen said. "Don't you miss it? Don't you miss playing ball?"

Gardella shook his head. "I miss the playing part, yes," he said. "So who sent you?"

"You son of a bitch," Zimmerman said. His hands were balled into fists. "I got a family to think of, but you, with your goddamned fancy lawyer—"

"Shut up, Roy," said Owen. "Sit down." He pointed to a porch swing, and Zimmerman obeyed. "Nobody sent us, Dan. Roy and I, we just—"

"Give me some credit for having half a brain."

Owen smiled. "That's all we ever gave you credit for, Dan."

Gardella laughed.

"You're gonna lose the suit, Dan. That's what everybody says.

Meanwhile, there's a couple dozen of us—just like you—shut out of ball. They're banning guys just for playing exhibitions against my barnstorming team, Dan."

Gardella nodded. "Same thing happened to me, playing for a sandlot team in Jersey."

"I'm thirty-three years old, Dan. Zim here, he's thirty-two. You're what, twenty-eight? You got time. But lots of us don't. Lou Klein, Moe Franklin, Ace Adams, Max Lanier. Not to mention the Cubans and the coloreds. You always got on with the coloreds, Dan. Can you sleep knowing you kept men like Ray Dandridge or Fireball Smith from getting their chance at the big leagues?"

"I'm not who's keeping those men out," Gardella said. "Then or now. It's those bloodsucking owners, Mick. They don't think they're accountable for obeying the laws that govern any other sort of business. *It's a game,* they say, *not a business.* But when it suits 'em . . . well, did you ever try to ask for a raise, Mick? Didn't they come back on you with just the opposite? *It's a business, Mickey. Just business. Sorry.*"

"Smart boy," mocked Zimmerman, getting up to leave.

"Think about it, Dan," said Owen. "We'd all be grateful." Gardella said nothing. Owen shrugged, then turned toward Zimmerman's Studebaker President, already idling.

"Hey, Mickey!" Gardella called. He stepped out onto the porch, hand extended. The two men shook hands, a long time, saying nothing until Zimmerman laid on the horn.

"Don't you see, Mick?" Gardella whispered. "We played this game for fun. We all did."

"Right," Owen said. "Fun. That explains why we went to Mexico. That explains why you're suing baseball for three hundred grand. For fun."

"In a way," said Gardella, "that does explain it."

A month later, Gardella accepted a $60,000 settlement on the condition that he did not disclose that he'd been paid off, "either the amount or the existence thereof." His attorney, who'd advised against settling, got half. Gardella surfaced in the big leagues in 1950 with, of all teams, the Cardinals, during my brief stint as a columnist at the *Post-Dispatch.* He batted once, pinch-hitting for, yes, Max Lanier, against—true!—Sal Maglie, the only reinstated player who was better than when he'd left. Curveball, fastball, curveball. That was it, Danny Gardella's last-ever at-bat. I tried to write a column about all the stories embedded in that one swift, uneventful at-bat, but my editor killed it. No one, he said, would care.

A quarter-century later, the Supreme Court finally struck down that preposterous reserve clause, which bound players like chattel to one team, with or without a contract. In the time of Gardella's suit, even the great, gray *New York Times* said that the removal of the reserve clause would mean the ruination of the game. Since then, the game has prospered as never before.

I would quote, here, from some of the poems "Diana James" wrote about me, Mexico, and our strange brief thrill of a marriage, but her pit-bull children would sue me. Just pick up any American literature anthology published after the dawn of feminism. There I am!

Her suicide came long after I was out of the picture, though I did have days when I blamed myself for that, too. But if I listened I could hear her voice, in the back of my head, telling me not to give myself that much credit.

Hemingway's suicide was the same year. Utter coincidence.

As it turned out, I lived too long, handled liquor too well, and was too egotistical for suicide, all of which seemed to disqualify me, in the end, from writing the books I set out to write. For which: Thank you, God.

Theolic Smith had the best year of his career in 1947, a year too late to win a championship, a year too soon to be noticed by big-league clubs looking for more where Jackie Robinson came from. He won twenty-two games, best in the league, with a 2.77 ERA, best of his career. The Red Devils were intact from the year before, when they'd finished only a game out of first. Ray Dandridge took over as manager. And it just didn't happen. The Monterrey Sultans got career years from all kinds of unlikely people and the Reds again finished second.

When the Americans came home in 1948, Theolic joined the Chicago American Giants. He was thirty-four. He went 4–5 with a 5.07 ERA; his season was cut short by arm problems.

He went down fighting. In the early fifties, when the Negro

Leagues died and fewer black men made a living playing baseball than at any time this century, the older players drifted back to Mexico for a few more paychecks. But Theolic Smith and his pal Ray Dandridge were among the few men their age stubborn enough to hang on playing Triple A ball, a notch away from the majors, waiting for a call that should have come fifteen years earlier.

Ray Dandridge went to the Minneapolis Millers, the New York Giants' affiliate. In 1952, Dandridge watched the Giants promote Monte Irvin, who helped the big club immediately. He watched them promote a skinny nineteen-year-old Dandridge had taken under his wing: a kid named Mays. Dandridge watched as the Giants' third baseman got hurt and—instead of replacing him with the best third baseman in baseball, who was hitting .350, still making plays you couldn't believe—they pressed outfielder Bobby Thomson into service at third. When that didn't work, they used a parade of sad-sack utility infielders. Sal Maglie begged the team to call up Dandridge. Monte Irvin begged. The kid begged. Even the manager, Leo Durocher, begged. But the Giants already had two Negroes, the unofficial quota. They lost the '52 pennant to Brooklyn (whose three blacks made them a quota scofflaw) by four games.

In what should have been one of many World Series years for Ray Dandridge, he was instead named MVP of a minor league.

Theolic Smith's story was sadder. He pitched four years, 1952–55, with the San Diego Padres, a club with no major-league affiliation, in the Pacific Coast League. He went 27–29. There is no record of any major-league team every inquiring with Padres management about Smith's asking price.

After the 1955 season, Dandridge got a phone call.

"Happy birthday, Dandy," Theolic said. "Old man."

"I'm old as you now," Dandridge said. They were forty-one.

"How'd you hit up in Bismarck?"

"About .350. How's the sea breeze treatin your arm?"

"Just fine," Theolic said. They asked about each other's wives (Dandridge had been best man in Theolic's wedding the year before) and kids, and talked about politics and jazz, this and that.

"Look, Dandy," Theolic blurted. "I'll say it if you will."

"Say what?"

But he knew. There was a long silence.

"It wasn't so awful," Dandridge said. "What we had."

"It wasn't so good."

"We didn't get what we wanted," Dandridge said, "but who the hell does?"

"Jackie."

"Enough about Jackie Robinson. Say the name Jackie Robinson once more, I'll hang up."

"Jackie Robinson."

There was another long silence.

"You still there, Theo?"

"Where would I go?"

"Look, what I'm tryin to say is, we didn't get all that we wanted, but what we got wasn't bad. In fact, it was terrific. We had fun. We played a great game and met nice people and saw the world and didn't get shot at. We managed to do things boys dream of."

"Like soakin their arms in a washtub full of ice."

"I'm serious. When's the last time you had to lift something heavy to make a dollar?"

"You mean, other than my sore arm?"

"We're old enough, Theo, to know getting what you want ain't necessarily no blessing."

There was another long pause. "I'll say it," said Theolic, "if you will."

"On the count of three," said Dandridge.

The men counted to three, then, in unison, shouted, "I quit!" Then they slammed down the receivers. Theolic stared at his black kitchen telephone for a long time. He whispered, "You said it first," then rose and went to the bedroom to wake his wife, kiss her pregnant belly, and tell her the news.

When I was a boy, I wanted to be a baseball player. When I was a young man, I wanted to be a writer, the voice of my generation. These are not dreams unique to me. Now, an old man, I think that anyone who accomplished all he set out to do needs to come back, live another life, and learn what living a life means. But when I had those boyish dreams, I believed in them, I wanted them, and I believed that they were special and that I was special: an American boy whose dreams had a divine right to come true. I did not fail at my dreams for lack of hard work, or nerve, or ambition. I practiced, ran, hit, threw, read, wrote—more of all of that than many people who had the same dreams I had but had theirs come true. I have known these people: Babe Ruth and Satchel Paige, Ernest Hemingway and "Diana James." Their stories you know. I wanted this story to be about people you have never heard of, who had the same exact dreams and got partway there. That's not nothing. It is, I now believe, everything.

When I interviewed Alfonso Pasquel for this book, he took grave issue with something I said. "My brother's legacy is not one of ambitious failure," he said. "It was a Mexican success."

At first I thought this was the fatalistic derision so many Mexicans hurl like sighs at their country. It was not. "Despite the time you have spent in our country," Alfonso said, "you don't understand it at all."

Maybe he's right. Mexico is so different from the United States, so near and yet so far, that Americans, or at least the ones I've known, never do quite manage to understand. But it's the mystery of the things you don't understand, finally, that makes life worth living. I love this place, and I keep working on it, in my dogged American way.

Elizabeth came to visit last fall. Her husband took care of the kids and she came alone, to recharge her batteries between sessions. We played cards and told stories and watched old Super 8's that Frances took of us on playgrounds and at Mount Rushmore and in three-legged races. On the more recent reels, Jerome began to peek into the frame here and there, an ever-shifting embodiment of the hairstyles and obsolete clothing of the time. "There's not much of Mom here, is there?" Elizabeth said.

"It was her camera. She didn't like other people using it."

It's a crime, I thought, whose lives get recorded, and the arbitrary reasons why.

"It's just as well," Elizabeth said. "All these movies look false, in a way. Us, but not us. Flat. Stark. Too real. They don't fit with the pictures I have in my head. But Mom, I don't know. Somehow I can see her better than anyone. My memories of her are truer than all this."

The night before Elizabeth left was the Day of the Dead. It was a part of Mexico I'd avoided, until then. Even with the passing years, my grief for Frances was nothing I could make light of. My grief for Jerome was even more complicated. His diagnosis shocked us both into action and was, in a horrible way, a stroke of luck. We came to know and accept each other. I gave him my house. He did not refuse it. Those feelings, too, seemed like nothing I wanted to observe by eating candies in the shape of skulls, breads in the shape of bones, and by laughing. But Elizabeth wanted to get out of the house, to go see what it was all about. And so we went.

The old city cemetery, a few blocks from the zócalo, was filled with people and good cheer, lit with the flickering light of ten thousand long candles, heavy with the smells of a million flowers and the gunpowder of spent firecrackers. Everywhere there was music, song, dance. Tossed hats sailed through the air. Children in bright clothes held hands and brayed at the moon. Here and there, skeletons were strung with strands of Christmas lights, or cast ablaze with popping ladyfingers. Elizabeth and I milled among these happy people, who believed that on this, of all days, the dead were granted appetites and the power to hear. Plates of food, destined to go uneaten, were spread out on every tomb. Long-faced men and round-faced women held merry conversations with the unseen.

From a distance, I saw the Pasquel family plot. I recognized Alfonso and Mario, the two surviving brothers. The rest of the people in their midst were old ladies and children: strangers. Draped over the pink granite statue of the Virgin of Guadalupe was the faded gray flannel road jersey of the Veracruz Blues.